TIME OF CONTEMPT

Also by Andrzej Sapkowski

from Gollancz:

The Last Wish
Blood of Elves
Time of Contempt
Baptism of Fire (forthcoming)

TIME OF
CONTEMPT

ANDRZEJ SAPKOWSKI

Translated by David French

GOLLANCZ

LONDON

Original text Copyright © Andrzej Sapkowski 1995
English translation Copyright © David French 2013

The right of Andrzej Sapkowski and David French to be identified as the author
and translator of this work has been asserted by them in accordance with the
Copyright, Designs and Patents Act 1988.

First published in Great Britain in 2013 by
Gollancz
An imprint of the Orion Publishing Group
Orion House, 5 Upper St Martin's Lane, London WC2H 9EA
An Hachette UK Company

Published by arrangement with Literary Agency 'Agence de l'Est'

A CIP catalogue record for this book is available
from the British Library

ISBN (Cased) 978 0 575 08495 7
ISBN (Trade Paperback) 978 0 575 08508 4

1 3 5 7 9 10 8 6 4 2

Typeset by Input Data Services Ltd, Bridgwater, Somerset

Printed and bound by CPI Group (UK) Ltd, Croydon, CR0 4YY

The Orion Publishing Group's policy is to use papers that
are natural, renewable and recyclable products and made from
wood grown in sustainable forests. The logging and manufacturing
processes are expected to conform to the environmental
regulations of the country of origin.

www.andrzejsapkowski.pl
www.orionbooks.co.uk
www.gollancz.co.uk

Blood on your hands, Falka,
Blood on your dress.
Burn, burn, Falka, and die,
Die in agony for your crimes!

Vedymins, *called witchers among the Nordlings (q.v.), a mysterious and elite caste of warrior-priests, probably an offshoot of the druids (q.v.). In the folk consciousness, they are endowed with magical powers and superhuman abilities; **v.** were said to fight evil spirits, monsters and all manner of dark forces. In reality, since they were unparalleled in their ability to wield weapons, **v.** were used by the rulers of the north in the tribal fighting they waged with each other. In combat **v.** fell into a trance, brought on, it is believed, by autohypnosis or intoxicating substances, and fought with pure energy, being utterly invulnerable to pain or even grave wounds, which reinforced the superstitions about their superhuman powers. The theory, according to which **v.** were said to have been the products of mutation or genetic engineering, has not found confirmation. **V.** are the heroes of numerous Nordling tales (cf. F. Delannoy,* Myths and Legends of the Nordlings*).*

Effenberg and Talbot
Encyclopaedia Maxima Mundi, Vol. XV

CHAPTER ONE

When talking to youngsters entering the service, Aplegatt usually told them that in order to make their living as mounted messengers two things would be necessary: a head of gold and an arse of iron.

A head of gold is essential, Aplegatt instructed the young messengers, since in the flat leather pouch strapped to his chest beneath his clothing the messenger only carries news of less vital importance, which could without fear be entrusted to treacherous paper or manuscript. The really important, secret tidings – those on which a great deal depended – must be committed to memory by the messenger and only repeated to the intended recipient. Word for word; and at times those words are far from simple. Difficult to pronounce, let alone remember. In order to memorise them and not make a mistake when they are recounted, one has to have a truly golden head.

And the benefits of an arse of iron, oh, every messenger will swiftly learn those for himself. When the moment comes for him to spend three days and nights in the saddle, riding a hundred or even two hundred miles along roads or sometimes, when necessary, trackless terrain, then it is needed. No, of course you don't sit in the saddle without respite; sometimes you dismount and rest. For a man can bear a great deal, but a horse less. However, when it's time to get back in the saddle after resting, it's as though your arse were shouting, 'Help! Murder!'

'But who needs mounted messengers now, Master Aplegatt?' young people would occasionally ask in astonishment. 'Take Vengerberg to Vizima; no one could knock that off in less than four – or even five – days, even on the swiftest steed. But how long does a sorcerer from Vengerberg need to send news to a sorcerer from Vizima? Half an hour, or not even that. A messenger's horse may go lame, but a sorcerer's message always arrives. It never loses its way.

It never arrives late or gets lost. What's the point of messengers, if there are sorcerers everywhere, at every kingly court? Messengers are no longer necessary, Master Aplegatt.'

For some time Aplegatt had also been thinking he was no longer of any use to anyone. He was thirty-six and small but strong and wiry, wasn't afraid of hard work and had – naturally – a head of gold. He could have found other work to support himself and his wife, to put a bit of money by for the dowries of his two as yet unmarried daughters and to continue helping the married one whose husband, the sad loser, was always unlucky in his business ventures. But Aplegatt couldn't and didn't want to imagine any other job. He was a royal mounted messenger and that was that.

And then suddenly, after a long period of being forgotten and humiliatingly idle, Aplegatt was once again needed. And the highways and forest tracks once again echoed to the sound of hooves. Just like the old days, messengers began to travel the land bearing news from town to town.

Aplegatt knew why. He saw a lot and heard even more. It was expected that he would immediately erase each message from his memory once it had been given, that he would forget it so as to be unable to recall it even under torture. But Aplegatt remembered. He knew why kings had suddenly stopped communicating with the help of magic and sorcerers. The news that the messengers were carrying was meant to remain a secret from them. Kings had suddenly stopped trusting sorcerers; stopped confiding their secrets in them.

Aplegatt didn't know what had caused this sudden cooling off in the friendship between kings and sorcerers and wasn't overly concerned about it. He regarded both kings and magic-users as incomprehensible creatures, unpredictable in their deeds – particularly when times were becoming hard. And the fact that times were now hard could not be ignored, not if one travelled across the land from castle to castle, from town to town, from kingdom to kingdom.

There were plenty of troops on the roads. With every step one came across an infantry or cavalry column, and every commander you met was edgy, nervous, curt and as self-important as if the fate of the entire world rested on him alone. The cities and castles were also full of armed men, and a feverish bustle went on there, day and night. The usually invisible burgraves and castellans now ceaselessly rushed along walls and through courtyards, angry as wasps before a storm, yelling, swearing and issuing orders and kicks. Day and night, lumbering columns of laden wagons rolled towards strongholds and garrisons, passing carts on their way back, moving quickly, unburdened and empty. Herds of frisky three-year-old mounts taken straight out of stables kicked dust up on the roads. Ponies not accustomed to bits nor armed riders cheerfully enjoyed their last days of freedom, giving stable boys plenty of extra work and other road users no small trouble.

To put it briefly, war hung in the hot, still air.

Aplegatt stood up in his stirrups and looked around. Down at the foot of the hill a river sparkled, meandering sharply among meadows and clusters of trees. Forests stretched out beyond it, to the south. The messenger urged his horse on. Time was running out.

He'd been on the road for two days. The royal order and mail had caught up with him in Hagge, where he was resting after returning from Tretogor. He had left the stronghold by night, galloping along the highway following the left bank of the Pontar, crossed the border with Temeria before dawn, and now, at noon of the following day, was already at the bank of the Ismena. Had King Foltest been in Vizima, Aplegatt would have delivered him the message that night. Unfortunately, the king was not in the capital; he was residing in the south of the country, in Maribor, almost two hundred miles from Vizima. Aplegatt knew this, so in the region of the White Bridge he left the westward-leading road and rode through woodland towards Ellander. He was taking a risk. The Scoia'tael* continued to roam the forests, and woe betide anyone who fell into their hands or came within arrowshot. But a royal messenger had to take risks. Such was his duty.

He crossed the river without difficulty – it hadn't rained since

---

* The Scoia'tael – commonly known as the Squirrels – are non-human guerrillas. Predominantly elves, their ranks also include halflings and dwarves, and they are so named due to their habit of attaching squirrel tails to their caps or clothing. Allied with Nilfgaard, motivated by the racism of men, they fight all humans in the Northern Kingdoms.

June and the Ismena's waters had fallen considerably. Keeping to the edge of the forest, he reached the track leading south-east from Vizima, towards the dwarven foundries, forges and settlements in the Mahakam Mountains. There were plenty of carts along the track, often being overtaken by small mounted units. Aplegatt sighed in relief. Where there were lots of humans, there weren't any Scoia'tael. The campaign against the guerrilla elves had endured in Temeria for a year and, being harried in the forests, the Scoia'tael commandos had divided up into smaller groups. These smaller groups kept well away from well-used roads and didn't set ambushes on them.

Before nightfall he was already on the western border of the duchy of Ellander, at a crossroads near the village of Zavada. From here he had a straight and safe road to Maribor: forty-two miles of hard, well-frequented forest track, and there was an inn at the crossroads. He decided to rest his horse and himself there. Were he to set off at daybreak he knew that, even without pushing his mount too hard, he would see the silver and black pennants on the red roofs of Maribor Castle's towers before sundown.

He unsaddled his mare and groomed her himself, sending the stable boy away. He was a royal messenger, and a royal messenger never permits anyone to touch his horse. He ate a goodly portion of scrambled eggs with sausage and a quarter of a loaf of rye bread, washed down with a quart of ale. He listened to the gossip. Of various kinds. Travellers from every corner of the world were dining at the inn.

Aplegatt learned there'd been more trouble in Dol Angra; a troop of Lyrian cavalry had once again clashed with a mounted Nilfgaardian unit. Meve, the queen of Lyria, had loudly accused Nilfgaard of provocation – again – and called for help from King Demavend of Aedirn. Tretogor had seen the public execution of a Redanian baron who had secretly allied himself with emissaries of the Nilfgaardian emperor, Emhyr. In Kaedwen, Scoia'tael commandos, amassed into a large unit, had orchestrated a massacre in Fort Leyda. To avenge the massacre, the people of Ard Carraigh had organised a pogrom, murdering almost four hundred non-humans residing in the capital.

Meanwhile the merchants travelling from the south described

6

the grief and mourning among the Cintran emigrants gathered in Temeria, under the standard of Marshal Vissegerd. The dreadful news of the death of Princess Cirilla, the Lion Cub, the last of the bloodline of Queen Calanthe, had been confirmed.

Some even darker, more foreboding gossip was told. That in several villages in the region of Aldersberg cows had suddenly begun to squirt blood from their udders while being milked, and at dawn the Virgin Bane, harbinger of terrible destruction, had been seen in the fog. The Wild Hunt, a spectral army galloping across the firmament, had appeared in Brugge, in the region of Brokilon Forest, the forbidden kingdom of the forest dryads; and the Wild Hunt, as is generally known, always heralds war. And a spectral ship had been spotted off Cape Bremervoord with a ghoul on board: a black knight in a helmet adorned with the wings of a bird of prey ...

The messenger stopped listening; he was too tired. He went to the common sleeping chamber, dropped onto his pallet and fell fast asleep.

He arose at daybreak and was a little surprised as he entered the courtyard – he was not the first person preparing to leave, which was unusual. A black gelding stood saddled by the well, while nearby a woman in male clothing was washing her hands in the trough. Hearing Aplegatt's footsteps she turned, gathered her luxuriant black hair in her wet hands, and tossed it back. The messenger bowed. The woman gave a faint nod.

As he entered the stable he almost ran into another early riser, a girl in a velvet beret who was just leading a dapple grey mare out into the courtyard. The girl rubbed her face and yawned, leaning against her horse's withers.

'Oh my,' she murmured, passing the messenger, 'I'll probably fall asleep on my horse ... I'll just flake out ... Auuh ...'

'The cold'll wake you up when you give your mare free rein,' said Aplegatt courteously, pulling his saddle off the rack. 'Godspeed, miss.'

The girl turned and looked at him, as though she had only then noticed him. Her eyes were large and as green as emeralds. Aplegatt threw the saddlecloth over his horse.

'I wished you a safe journey,' he said. He wasn't usually talkative or effusive but now he felt the need to talk to someone, even if this someone was just a sleepy teenager. Perhaps it was those long days of solitude on the road, or possibly that the girl reminded him a little of his middle daughter.

'May the gods protect you,' he added, 'from accidents and foul weather. There are but two of you, and womenfolk at that ... And times are ill at present. Danger lurks everywhere on the highways.'

The girl opened her green eyes wider. The messenger felt his spine go cold, and a shudder passed through him.

'Danger ...' the girl said suddenly, in a strange, altered voice. 'Danger comes silently. You will not hear it when it swoops down on grey feathers. I had a dream. The sand ... The sand was hot from the sun.'

'What?' Aplegatt froze with the saddle pressed against his belly. 'What say you, miss? What sand?'

The girl shuddered violently and rubbed her face. The dapple grey mare shook its head.

'Ciri!' shouted the black-haired woman sharply from the court-yard, adjusting the girth on her black stallion. 'Hurry up!'

The girl yawned, looked at Aplegatt and blinked, appearing sur-prised by his presence in the stable. The messenger said nothing.

'Ciri,' repeated the woman, 'have you fallen asleep in there?'

'I'm coming, Madam Yennefer.'

By the time Aplegatt had finally saddled his horse and led it out into the courtyard there was no sign of either woman or girl. A cock crowed long and hoarsely, a dog barked, and a cuckoo called from among the trees. The messenger leapt into the saddle. He suddenly recalled the sleepy girl's green eyes and her strange words. *Danger comes silently? Grey feathers? Hot sand? The maid was probably not right in the head*, he thought. *You come across a lot like that these days; deranged girls spoiled by vagabonds or other ne'er-do-wells in these times of war ... Yes, definitely deranged. Or possibly only sleepy, torn from her slumbers, not yet fully awake. It's amazing the poppycock people come out with when they're roaming around at dawn, still caught between sleep and wakefulness ...*

A second shudder passed through him, and he felt a pain between his shoulder blades. He massaged his back with a fist.

Weak at the knees, he spurred his horse on as soon as he was back on the Maribor road, and rode away at a gallop. Time was running out.

The messenger did not rest for long in Maribor – not a day had passed before the wind was whistling in his ears again. His new horse, a roan gelding from the Maribor stable, ran hard, head forward and its tail flowing behind. Roadside willows flashed past. The satchel with the diplomatic mail pressed against Aplegatt's chest. His arse ached.

'Oi! I hope you break your neck, you blasted gadabout!' yelled a carter in his wake, pulling in the halter of his team, startled by the galloping roan flashing by. 'See how he runs, like devils were licking his heels! Ride on, giddy-head, ride; you won't outrun Death himself!'

Aplegatt wiped an eye, which was watering from the speed.

The day before he had given King Foltest a letter, and then recited King Demavend's secret message.

'Demavend to Foltest. All is prepared in Dol Angra. The disguised forces await the order. Estimated date: the second night after the July new moon. The boats are to beach on the far shore two days later.'

Flocks of crows flew over the highway, cawing loudly. They flew east, towards Mahakam and Dol Angra, towards Vengerberg. As he rode, the messenger silently repeated the confidential message the king of Temeria had entrusted to him for the king of Aedirn.

'Foltest to Demavend. Firstly: let us call off the campaign. The windbags have called a council. They are going to meet and debate on the Isle of Thanedd. This council may change much. Secondly: the search for the Lion Cub can be called off. It is confirmed. The Lion Cub is dead.'

Aplegatt spurred on his horse. Time was running out.

The narrow forest track was blocked with wagons. Aplegatt slowed down and trotted unhurriedly up to the last wagon in the long column. He saw he could not force his way through the obstruction, but nor could he think about heading back; too much time would be lost. Venturing into the boggy thicket and riding around the obstruction was not an attractive alternative either, particularly since darkness was falling.

'What's going on?' he asked the drivers of the last wagon in the column. They were two old men, one of whom seemed to be dozing and the other showing no signs of life. 'An attack? Scoia'tael? Speak up! I'm in a hurry ...'

Before either of the two old men had a chance to answer, screams could be heard from the head of the column, hidden amongst the trees. Drivers leapt onto their wagons, lashing their horses and oxen to the accompaniment of choice oaths. The column moved off ponderously. The dozing old man awoke, moved his chin, clucked at his mules and flicked the reins across their rumps. The moribund old man came to life too, drew his straw hat back from his eyes and looked at Aplegatt.

'Mark him,' he said. 'A hasty one. Well, laddie, your luck's in. You've joined the company right on time.'

'Aye,' said the other old man, motioning with his chin and urging the mules forward. 'You are timely. Had you come at noon, you'd have come to a stop like us and waited for a clear passage. We're all in a hurry, but we had to wait. How can you ride on, when the way is closed?'

'The way closed? Why so?'

'There's a cruel man-eater in these parts, laddie. He fell on a knight riding along the road with nowt but a boy for company. They say the monster rent the knight's head right off – helmet and all – and spilt his horse's gizzards. The boy made good his escape and said it was a fell beast, that the road was crimson with gore—'

'What kind of monster is it?' asked Aplegatt, reining in his horse in order to continue talking to the wagoners as they drove on. 'A dragon?'

'Nay, it's no dragon,' said the one in the straw hat. ''Tis said to be a manticore, or some such. The boy said 'tis a flying beast, awful huge. And vicious! We reckoned he would devour the knight and fly away, but no! They say he settled on the road, the whoreson, and was sat there, hissing and baring its fangs ... Yea, and the road all stopped up like a corked-up flagon, for whoever drove up first and saw the fiend left his wagon and hastened away. Now the wagons are backed up for a third of a league, and all around, as you see, laddie, thicket and bog. There's no riding around or turning back. So here we stood ...'

'Such a host!' snorted the horseman. 'And they were standing by like dolts when they ought to've seized axe and spear to drive the beast from the road, or slaughter it.'

'Aye, a few tried,' said the old wagoner, driving on his mules, for the column was now moving more quickly. 'Three dwarves from the merchants' guard and, with them, four recruits who were heading to the stronghold in Carreras to join the army. The monster carved up the dwarves horribly, and the recruits –'

'– bolted,' finished the other old man, after which he spat rapturously. The gob flew a long way ahead of him, expertly falling into the space between the mules' rumps. 'Bolted, after barely setting their eyes on the manticore. One of them shat his britches, I hear. Oh, look, look, laddie. That's him! Yonder!'

'What are you blathering on about?' asked Aplegatt, somewhat annoyed. 'You're pointing out that shitty arse? I'm not interested—'

'Nay! The monster! The monster's corpse! They're lifting it onto a wagon! D'you see?'

Aplegatt stood in his stirrups. In spite of the gathering darkness and the crowd of onlookers he saw the great tawny body being lifted up by soldiers. The monster's bat-like wings and scorpion tail dragged inertly along the ground. Cheering, the soldiers lifted the corpse higher and heaved it onto a wagon. The horses harnessed to it, clearly disturbed by the stench of the carcass and the blood, neighed and tugged at the shaft.

'Move along!' the sergeant shouted at the old men. 'Keep moving! Don't block the road!'

The greybeard drove his mules on, the wagon bouncing over the rutted road. Aplegatt, urging on his horse with his heel, drew alongside.

11

'Looks like the soldiers have put paid to the beast.'

'Not a bit of it,' rejoined the old man. 'When the soldiers arrived, all they did was yell and order people around. "Stand still! Move on!" and all the rest of it. They were in no haste to deal with the monster. They sent for a witcher.'

'A witcher?'

'Aye,' confirmed the second old man. 'Someone recalled he'd seen a witcher in the village, and they sent for him. A while later he rode past us. His hair was white, his countenance fearful to behold, and he bore a cruel blade. Not an hour had passed than someone called from the front that the road would soon be clear, for the witcher had dispatched the beast. So at last we set off; which was just about when you turned up, laddie.'

'Ah,' said Aplegatt absentmindedly. 'All these years I've been scouring these roads and never met a witcher. Did anyone see him defeat the monster?'

'I saw it!' called a boy with a shock of tousled hair, trotting up on the other side of the wagon. He was riding bareback, steering a skinny, dapple grey nag using a halter. 'I saw it all! I was with the soldiers, right at the front!'

'Look at him, snot-nosed kid,' said the old man driving the wagon. 'Milk not dried on his face, and see how he mouths off. Looking for a slap?'

'Leave him, father,' interrupted Aplegatt. 'We'll reach the crossroads soon and I'm riding to Carreras, so first I'd like to know how the witcher got on. Talk, boy.'

'It was like this,' he began quickly, still trotting alongside the wagon. 'That witcher comes up to the officer. He says his name's Geralt. The officer says it's all the same to him, and it'd be better if he made a start. Shows him where the monster is. The witcher moves closer and looks on. The monster's about five furlongs or more away, but he just glances at it and says at once it's an uncommon great manticore and he'll kill it if they give him two hundred crowns.'

'Two hundred crowns?' choked the other old man. 'Had he gone cuckoo?'

'The officer says the same, only his words were riper. So the witcher says that's how much it will cost and it's all the same to him; the monster can stay on the road till Judgement Day. The officer says he won't pay that much and he'll wait till the beast flies off by itself. The witcher says it won't because it's hungry and pissed off. And if it flies off, it'll be back soon because that's its hunting terri–terri– territor—'

'You whippersnapper, don't talk nonsense!' said the old man driving the cart, losing his temper, unsuccessfully trying to clear his nose into the fingers he was holding the reins with. 'Just tell us what happened!'

'I *am* telling you! The witcher goes, "The monster won't fly away, he'll spend the entire night eating the dead knight, nice and slow, because the knight's in armour and it's hard to pick out the meat." So some merchants step up and try making a deal with the witcher, by hook or by crook, that they'll organise a whip-round and give him five score crowns. The witcher says that beast's a manticore and is very dangerous, and they can shove their hundred crowns up their arses, he won't risk his neck for it. So the officer gets pissed off and says tough luck, it's a witcher's fate to risk his neck, and that a witcher is perfectly suited to it, like an arse is perfectly suited to shitting. But I can see the merchants get afeared the witcher would get angry and head off, because they say they'll pay seven score and ten. So then the witcher gets his sword out and heads off down the road towards where the beast's sitting. And the officer makes a mark behind him to drive away magic, spits on the ground and says he doesn't know why the earth bears such hellish abominations. One of the merchants says that if the army drove away monsters from roads instead of chasing elves through forests, witchers wouldn't be needed and that—'

'Don't drivel,' interrupted the old man. 'Just say what you saw.'

'I saw,' boasted the boy, 'the witcher's horse, a chestnut mare with a white blaze.'

'Blow the mare! Did you see the witcher kill the monster?'

'Err ...' stammered the boy. 'No I didn't ... I got pushed to the back. Everybody was shouting and the horses were startled, when—'

'Just what I said,' declared the old man contemptuously. 'He didn't see shite, snotty-nosed kid.'

'But I saw the witcher coming back!' said the boy, indignantly. 'And the officer, who saw it all, he was as pale as a ghost and said quietly to his men it was magic spells or elven tricks and that a normal man couldn't wield a sword that quickly ... While the witcher ups and takes the money from the merchants, mounts his mare and rides off.'

'Hmm,' murmured Aplegatt. 'Which way was he headed? Along the road to Carreras? If so, I might catch him up, just to have a look at him ...'

'No,' said the boy. 'He took the road to Dorian from the cross-roads. He was in a hurry.'

The Witcher seldom dreamed at all, and he never remembered those rare dreams on waking. Not even when they were nightmares – and they were usually nightmares.

This time it was also a nightmare, but at least the Witcher remembered some of it. A distinct, clear image had suddenly emerged from a swirling vortex of unclear but disturbing shapes, of strange but foreboding scenes and incomprehensible but sinister words and sounds. It was Ciri, but not as he remembered her from Kaer Morhen. Her flaxen hair, flowing behind her as she galloped, was longer – as it had been when they first met, in Brokilon. When she rode by he wanted to shout but no words came. He wanted to run after her, but it was as if he were stuck in setting pitch to half-way up his thighs. And Ciri seemed not to see him and galloped on, into the night, between misshapen alders and willows waving their boughs as if they were alive. He saw she was being pursued. That a black horse was galloping in her tracks, and on it a rider in black armour, wearing a helmet decorated with the wings of a bird of prey.

He couldn't move, he couldn't shout. He could only watch as the winged knight chased Ciri, caught her hair, pulled her from the saddle and galloped on, dragging her behind him. He could only watch Ciri's face contort with pain, watch her mouth twist into a soundless cry. *Awake!* he ordered himself, unable to bear the night-mare. *Awake! Awake at once!*

He awoke.

He lay motionless for a long while, recalling the dream. Then he rose. He drew a pouch from beneath his pillow and quickly counted out some ten-crown coins. One hundred and fifty for yesterday's manticore. Fifty for the fogler he had been commissioned to kill by the headman of a village near Carreras. And fifty for the werewolf some settlers from Burdorff had driven out of hiding for him.

Fifty for a werewolf. That was plenty, for the work had been easy. The werewolf hadn't even fought back. Driven into a cave from which there was no escape, it had knelt down and waited for the sword to fall. The Witcher had felt sorry for it.

But he needed the money.

Before an hour had passed he was ambling down the streets of the town of Dorian, looking for a familiar lane and sign.

The wording on the sign read: 'Codringher and Fenn, legal consul-tation and services'. But Geralt knew only too well that Codringher and Fenn's trade had little in common with the law, while the part-ners themselves had a host of reasons to avoid any kind of contact either with the law or its enforcers. He also seriously doubted if any of the clients who showed up in their chambers knew what the word 'consultation' meant.

There was no entrance on the ground floor of the small building; there was only a securely bolted door, probably leading to a coach house or a stable. In order to reach the door one had to venture around the back of the building, enter a muddy courtyard full of ducks and chickens and, from there, walk up some steps before pro-ceeding down a narrow gallery and along a cramped, dark corridor. Only then did one find oneself before a solid, studded mahogany door, equipped with a large brass knocker in the form of a lion's head.

Geralt knocked, and then quickly withdrew. He knew the mech-anism mounted in the door could shoot twenty-inch iron spikes through holes hidden among the studs. In theory the spikes were only released if someone tried to tamper with the lock, or if Codringher or Fenn pressed the trigger mechanism, but Geralt had discovered, many times, that all mechanisms are unreliable. They only worked when they ought not to work, and vice versa.

There was sure to be a device in the door – probably magic – for identifying guests. Having knocked, as today, no voice from within ever plied him with questions or demanded that he speak. The door opened and Codringher was standing there. Always Codringher, never Fenn.

'Welcome, Geralt,' said Codringher. 'Enter. You don't need to flatten yourself against the doorframe, I've dismantled the security device. Some part of it broke a few days ago. It went off quite out of the blue and drilled a few holes in a hawker. Come right in. Do you have a case for me?'

'No,' said the Witcher, entering the large, gloomy anteroom which, as usual, smelled faintly of cat. 'Not for you. For Fenn.'

Codringher cackled loudly, confirming the Witcher's suspicions that Fenn was an utterly mythical figure who served to pull the wool over the eyes of provosts, bailiffs, tax collectors and any other individuals Codringher detested.

They entered the office, where it was lighter because it was the topmost room and the solidly barred windows enjoyed the sun for most of the day. Geralt sat in the chair reserved for clients. Opposite, in an upholstered armchair behind an oaken desk, lounged Codringher; a man who introduced himself as a 'lawyer', a man for whom nothing was impossible. If anyone had difficulties, troubles, problems, they went to Codringher. And would quickly be handed proof of his business partner's dishonesty and malpractice. Or he would receive credit without securities or guarantees. Or find himself the only one, from a long list of creditors, to exact payment from a business which had declared itself bankrupt. He would receive his inheritance even though his rich uncle had threatened he wouldn't leave them a farthing. He would win an inheritance case when even the most determined relatives unexpectedly withdrew their claims. His son would leave the dungeon, cleared even of charges based on irrefutable evidence, or would be released due to the sudden absence of any such proof. For, when Codringher and Fenn were involved, if there had been proof it would mysteriously disappear, or the witnesses would vie to retract their earlier testimonies. A dowry hunter courting their daughter would suddenly direct his affections towards another. A wife's lover or daughter's seducer would suffer a complicated fracture of three members – including at least one upper one – in an unfortunate accident. Or a fervent enemy or other extremely inconvenient individual would stop doing him harm; as a rule they were never seen or heard of again. Yes, if someone had a problem they could always ride to Dorian, run swiftly to Codringher and Fenn and knock at the mahogany door. Codringher, the 'lawyer', would be standing in the doorway, short, spare and grizzled, with the unhealthy pallor of a person who seldom spent time in the fresh air. Codringher would lead them into his office, sit down in his armchair, lift his large black and white tomcat onto his lap and stroke it. The two of them – Codringher and the tomcat – would measure up the client with identical, unpleasant, unsettling expressions in their yellowish-green eyes.

'I received your letter,' said Codringher, while he and the tomcat weighed the Witcher up with their yellowish-green gaze. 'Dandelion also visited. He passed through Dorian a few weeks ago and told me a little about your concerns. But he said very little. Really too little.'

'Indeed? You astonish me. That's the first time I've heard that Dandelion didn't say too much.'

'Dandelion,' said Codringher unsmilingly, 'said very little because he knew very little. He said even less than he knew because you'd forbidden him to speak about certain issues. Where does your lack of trust come from? Especially towards a professional colleague?'

This visibly annoyed Geralt. Codringher would probably have pretended not to notice, but he couldn't because of the cat. It opened its eyes wide, bared its white fangs and hissed almost silently.

'Don't annoy my cat,' said the lawyer, stroking the animal to calm it. 'Did it bother you to be called a colleague? But it's true. I'm also a witcher. I also save people from monsters and from monstrous difficulties. And I also do it for money.'

17

'There are certain differences,' muttered Geralt, still under the tomcat's unpleasant gaze.

'There are,' agreed Codringher. 'You are an anachronistic witcher, and I'm a modern witcher, moving with the spirit of the times. Which is why you'll soon be out of work and I'll be doing well. Soon there won't be any strigas, wyverns, endriagas or werewolves left in the world. But there'll always be whoresons.'

'But it's mainly the whoresons you get out of difficulties, Codringher. Paupers with difficulties can't afford your services.'

'Paupers can't afford your services either. Paupers can never afford anything, which is precisely why they're called paupers.'

'Astonishingly logical of you. And so original it takes the breath away.'

'The truth always has that effect. And it's the truth that being a bastard is the basis and mainstay of our professions. Except your business is almost a relic and mine is genuine and growing in strength.'

'All right, all right. Let's get down to our business.'

'About time,' said Codringher, nodding his head and stroking his cat, which had arched its back and was now purring loudly, sinking its claws into his knee. 'And we'll sort these things out in order of importance. The first issue: the fee, my friend, is two hundred and fifty Novigrad crowns. Do you have that kind of money? Or perhaps you number yourself among the paupers with difficulties?'

'First let's establish whether you've done enough to deserve a sum like that.'

'Decide for yourself,' said the lawyer coldly, 'and be quick about it. Once you feel convinced, lay the money on the table. Then we'll move on to other, less important matters.'

Geralt unfastened a purse from his belt and threw it, with poor grace and a clink of coins, onto the desk. The tomcat jumped off Codringher's lap with a bound and ran away. The lawyer dropped the purse in a drawer without checking the contents.

'You alarmed my cat,' he said with undisguised reproach.

'I do beg your pardon. I thought the clink of money was the last thing that could scare it. Tell me what you uncovered.'

'That Rience,' began Codringher, 'who interests you so much, is quite a mysterious character. I've been able to ascertain that he was a student at the school for sorcerers in Ban Ard for two years. They threw him out after catching him thieving. Recruiting officers from the Kaedwen secret service were waiting outside the school, as usual, and Rience allowed himself to be recruited. I was unable to determine what he did for the Kaedwen secret service, but sorcerers' rejects are usually trained as killers. Does that fit?'

'Like a glove. Go on.'

'My next information comes from Cintra. Rience served time in the dungeons there, during Queen Calanthe's reign.'

'What for?'

'For debts, would you believe? He didn't stay long though, because someone bought him out after paying off the debts along with the interest. The transaction took place through a bank, with the anonymity of the benefactor preserved. I tried to uncover the identity of this benefactor but admitted defeat after checking four banks in turn. Whoever bought Rience out was a pro. And cared a great deal about preserving their anonymity.'

Codringher fell silent and then coughed loudly, pressing a hand-kerchief to his mouth.

'And suddenly, as soon as the war was over, Mr Rience showed up in Sodden, Angren and Brugge,' he continued after a moment, wiping his lips and looking down at the handkerchief. 'Changed beyond recognition, at least as regards his behaviour and the quantities of cash he had to throw around. Because, as far as his identity went, the brazen son of a bitch didn't bother with secrecy: he continued to use the name "Rience". And as Rience he began to search intensively for a certain party; to be precise a young, female party. He visited the druids from the Angren Circle, the ones who looked after war orphans. One druid's body was found some time later in a nearby forest, mutilated, bearing the marks of torture. Rience showed up afterwards in Riverdell—'

'I know,' interrupted Geralt. 'I know what he did to the Riverdell peasant family. And I was expecting more for my two hundred and fifty crowns. Up to now, your only fresh information has been about the sorcerers' school and the Kaedwen secret service. I know the rest. I know Rience is a ruthless killer. I know he's an arrogant rogue who doesn't even bother to use aliases. I know he's working for somebody. But for whom, Codringher?'

'For some sorcerer or other. It was a sorcerer who bought him out of that dungeon. You told me yourself – and Dandelion confirmed it – that Rience uses magic. Real magic, not the tricks that some expellee from the academy might know. So someone's backing him, they're equipping him with amulets and probably secretly training him. Some officially practising sorcerers have secret pupils and factotums like him for doing illegal or dirty business. In sorcerers' slang it's described as "having someone on a leash".'

'Were he on a magician's leash Rience would be using camouflaging magic. But he doesn't change his name or face. He hasn't even got rid of the scar from the burn Yennefer gave him.'

'That confirms precisely that he's on a leash,' said Codringher, coughing and wiping his lips again with his handkerchief, 'because magical camouflage isn't camouflage at all; only dilettantes use stuff like that. Were Rience hiding under a magical shield or illusory mask, it would immediately set off every magical alarm, and there are currently alarms like that at practically every city gate. Sorcerers never fail to detect illusory masks. Even in the biggest gathering of people, in the biggest throng, Rience would attract all of their attention, as if flames were shooting out of his ears and clouds of smoke out of his arse. So I repeat: Rience is in the service of a sorcerer and is operating so as not to draw the attention of other sorcerers to himself.'

'Some say he's a Nilfgaardian spy.'

'I know. For example, Dijkstra, the head of the Redania secret service, thinks that. Dijkstra is seldom wrong, so one can only assume he's right this time, too. But having one role doesn't rule out the other. A sorcerer's factotum may be a Nilfgaardian spy at the same time.'

'You're saying that a sanctioned sorcerer is spying for Nilfgaard through Rience?'

'Nonsense,' coughed Codringher, looking intently into his

handkerchief. 'A sorcerer spying for Nilfgaard? Why? For money? Risible. Counting on serious power under the rule of the victorious Emperor Emhyr? Even more ludicrous. It's no secret that Emhyr var Emreis keeps his sorcerers on a short leash. Sorcerers in Nilfgaard are treated about the same as, let's say, stablemen. And they have no more power than stablemen either. Would any of our headstrong mages choose to fight for an emperor who would treat them as a stable boy? Filippa Eilhart, who dictates addresses and edicts to Vizimir of Redania? Sabrina Glevissig, who interrupts the speeches of Henselt of Kaedwen, banging her fist on the table and ordering the king to be silent and listen? Vilgefortz of Roggeveen, who recently told Demavend of Aedirn that, for the moment, he has no time for him?'

'Get to the point, Codringher. What does any of that have to do with Rience?'

'It's simple. The Nilfgaardian secret service is trying to get to a sorcerer by getting their factotum to work for them. From what I know, Rience wouldn't spurn the Nilfgaardian florin and would probably betray his master without a second thought.'

'Now *you're* talking nonsense. Even our headstrong mages know when they're being betrayed and Rience, were he exposed, would dangle from a gibbet. If he was lucky.'

'You're acting like a child, Geralt. You don't hang exposed spies – you make use of them. You stuff them with disinformation and try to make double agents out of them—'

'Don't bore this child, Codringher. Neither the arcana of intelligence work nor politics interest me. Rience is breathing down my neck, and I want to know why and on whose orders. On the orders of some sorcerer, it would appear. So who is it?'

'I don't know yet. But I soon will.'

'Soon,' muttered the Witcher, 'is too late for me.'

'I in no way rule that out,' said Codringher gravely. 'You've landed in a dreadful pickle, Geralt. It's good you came to me; I know how to get people out of them. I already have, essentially.'

'Indeed?'

'Indeed,' said the lawyer, putting his handkerchief to his lips and

21

coughing. 'For you see, my friend, in addition to the sorcerer, and possibly also Nilfgaard, there is a third party in the game. I was visited, and mark this well, by agents from King Foltest's secret service. They had a problem: the king had ordered them to search for a certain missing princess. When finding her turned out not to be quite so simple, those agents decided to enlist a specialist in such thorny problems. While elucidating the case to the specialist, they hinted that a certain witcher might know a good deal about the missing princess. That he might even know where she was.'

'And what did the specialist do?'

'At first he expressed astonishment. It particularly astonished him that the aforementioned witcher had not been deposited in a dungeon in order to find out – in the traditional manner – everything he knew, and even plenty of what he didn't know but might invent in order to satisfy his questioners. The agents replied that they had been forbidden to do that. Witchers, they explained, have such a sensitive nervous system that they immediately die under torture when, as they described quite vividly, a vein bursts in their brains. Because of that, they had been ordered to hunt the witcher. This task had also turned out to be taxing. The specialist praised the agents' good sense and instructed them to report back in two weeks.'

'And did they?'

'I'll say they did. This specialist, who already regarded you as a client, presented the agents with hard evidence that Geralt the Witcher has never had and could never have anything in common with the missing princess. For the specialist had found witnesses to the death of Princess Cirilla; granddaughter of Calanthe, daughter of Queen Pavetta. Cirilla died three years ago in a refugee camp in Angren. Of diphtheria. The child suffered terribly before her death. You won't believe it, but the Temerian agents had tears in their eyes as they listened to my witnesses' accounts.'

'I have tears in my eyes too. I presume these Temerian agents could not – or would not – offer you more than two hundred and fifty crowns?'

'Your sarcasm pains my heart, Witcher. I've got you out of a pickle, and you, rather than thank me, wound my heart.'

'I thank you and I beg your pardon. Why did King Foltest order his agents to search for Ciri, Codringher? What were they ordered to do, should they have found her?'

'Oh, but you are slow-witted. Kill her, of course. She is considered a pretender to the throne of Cintra, for which there are other plans.'

'It doesn't add up, Codringher. The Cintran throne was burnt to the ground along with the royal palace, the city and the rest of the country. Nilfgaard rules there now. Foltest is well aware of that; and other kings too. How, exactly, can Ciri pretend to a throne that doesn't exist?'

'Come,' said Codringher, getting up, 'let us try to find an answer to that question together. In the meanwhile, I shall give you proof of my trust ... What is it about that portrait that interests you so much?'

'That it's riddled with holes, as though a woodpecker had been pecking at it for a few seasons,' said Geralt, looking at a painting in a gilt frame hanging on the wall opposite the lawyer's desk, 'and that it portrays a rare idiot.'

'It's my late father,' said Codringher, grimacing a little. 'A rare idiot indeed. I hung his portrait there so as to always have him before my eyes. As a warning. Come, Witcher.'

They went out into the corridor. The tomcat, which had been lying in the middle of the carpet, enthusiastically licking a rear paw extended at a strange angle, vanished into the darkness of the corridor at the sight of the witcher.

'Why don't cats like you, Geralt? Does it have something to do with the—'

'Yes,' he interrupted, 'it does.'

One of the mahogany panels slid open noiselessly, revealing a secret passage. Codringher went first. The panel, no doubt set in motion by magic, closed behind them but did not plunge them into darkness. Light reached them from the far end of the secret passage.

It was cold and dry in the room at the end of the corridor, and the oppressive, stifling smell of dust and candles hung in the air.

'You can meet my partner, Geralt.'

'Fenn?' smiled the Witcher. 'You jest.'

'Oh, but I don't. Admit it, you suspected Fenn didn't exist!'

'Not at all.'

A creaking could be heard from between the rows of bookcases and bookshelves that reached up to the low vaulted ceiling, and a moment later a curious vehicle emerged. It was a high-backed chair on wheels. On the chair sat a midget with a huge head, set directly on disproportionately narrow shoulders. The midget had no legs.

'I'd like to introduce Jacob Fenn,' said Codringher, 'a learned legist, my partner and valued co-worker. And this is our guest and client –'

'– the Witcher, Geralt of Rivia,' finished the cripple with a smile. 'I guessed without too much difficulty. I've been working on the case for several months. Follow me, gentlemen.'

They set off behind the creaking chair into the labyrinth of book-cases, which groaned beneath a weight of printed works that even the university library of Oxenfurt would have been proud to have in its collection. The incunabula, judged Geralt, must have been collected by several generations of Codringhers and Fenns. He was pleased by the obvious show of trust, and happy to finally have the chance to meet Fenn. He did not doubt, however, that the figure of Fenn, though utterly genuine, was also partially fictitious. The ficti-tious Fenn, Codringher's infallible alter ego, was supposedly often seen abroad, while the chair-bound, learned legist probably never left the building.

The centre of the room was particularly well lit, and there stood a low pulpit, accessible from the chair on wheels and piled high with books, rolls of parchment and vellum, great sheets of paper, bottles of ink, bunches of quills and innumerable mysterious utensils. Not all of them were mystifying. Geralt recognised moulds for forging seals and a diamond grater for removing the text from official docu-ments. In the centre of the pulpit lay a small ball-firing repeating arbalest, and next to it huge magnifying glasses made of polished rock crystal peeped out from under a velvet cloth. Magnifying glasses of that kind were rare and cost a fortune.

'Found anything new, Fenn?'

'Not really,' said the cripple, smiling. His smile was pleasant and very endearing. 'I've reduced the list of Rience's potential paymasters to twenty-eight sorcerers ...'

'Let's leave that for the moment,' Codringher interrupted quickly. 'Right now something else is of interest to us. Enlighten Geralt as to the reasons why the missing princess of Cintra is the object of extensive search operations by the agents of the Four Kingdoms.'

'The girl has the blood of Queen Calanthe flowing in her veins,' said Fenn, seeming astonished to be asked to explain such obvious matters. 'She is the last of the royal line. Cintra has considerable strategic and political importance. A vanished pretendress to the crown remaining beyond the sphere of influence is inconvenient, and may be dangerous were she to fall under the wrong influence. For example, that of Nilfgaard.'

'As far as I recall,' said Geralt, 'Cintran law bars women from succession.'

'That is true,' agreed Fenn and smiled once more. 'But a woman may always become someone's wife and the mother of a male heir. The Four Kingdoms' intelligence services learned of Rience's feverish search for the princess and were convinced that's what it's all about. It was thus decided to prevent the princess from becoming a wife or a mother. Using simple but effective means.'

'But the princess is dead,' said Codringher, seeing the change the smiling midget's words had evoked on Geralt's face. 'The agents learned of it and have called off their hunt.'

'Only for now,' said the Witcher, working hard to remain calm and sound unemotional. 'The thing about falsehoods is that they usually come to light. What's more, the royal agents are only one of the parties participating in this game. The agents – you said yourselves – were tracking Ciri in order to confound the other hunters' plans. Those others may be less susceptible to disinformation. I hired you to find a way of guaranteeing the child's safety. So what do you propose?'

'We have a certain notion,' said Fenn, glancing at his partner but seeing no instructions to remain silent in his expression. 'We want to circulate the news – discretely but widely – that neither Princess

Cirilla nor any of her male heirs will have any right to the throne of Cintra.'

'In Cintra, the distaff side does not inherit,' explained Codringher, fighting another coughing fit. 'Only the spear side does.'

'Precisely,' confirmed the learned legist. 'Geralt said so himself a moment ago. It's an ancient law, which even that she-devil Calanthe was unable to revoke – though not for want of trying.'

'She tried to nullify the law using intrigue,' said Codringher with conviction, wiping his lips with a handkerchief. 'Illegal intrigue. Explain, Fenn.'

'Calanthe was the only daughter of King Dagorad and Queen Adalia. After her parents' death she opposed the aristocracy, who only saw her as the wife of the new king.

'She wanted to reign supreme. At most, for the sake of formality and to uphold the dynasty, she agreed to the institution of a prince consort who would reign with her, but have as much importance as a straw doll. The old houses defied this. Calanthe had three choices: a civil war; abdication in favour of another line; or marriage to Roegner, Prince of Ebbing. She chose the third option and she ruled the country ... but at Roegner's side. Naturally, she didn't allow herself to be subjugated or bundled off to join the womenfolk. She was the Lioness of Cintra. But it was Roegner who was the formal ruler – though none ever called him "the Lion".'

'So Calanthe,' Codringher took up, 'tried very hard to fall pregnant and produce a son. Nothing came of it. She bore a daughter, Pavetta, and miscarried twice after which it became clear she would have no more children. All her plans had fallen through. There you have a woman's fate. A ravaged womb scuppers her lofty ambitions.'

Geralt scowled.

'You are execrably crude, Codringher.'

'I know. The truth was also crude. For Roegner began looking around for a young princess with suitably wide hips, preferably from a family of fertility proven back to her great-great-grandmother. And Calanthe found herself on shaky ground. Every meal, every glass of wine could contain death, every hunt might end with an unfortunate accident. There is much to suggest that at the moment the Lioness of Cintra took the initiative, Roegner died. The pox was raging across the country, and the king's death surprised no one.'

'I begin to understand,' said the Witcher, seemingly dispassionately, 'what news you plan to circulate discreetly but widely. Ciri will be named the granddaughter of a poisoner and husband-killer?'

'Don't get ahead of yourself, Geralt. Go on, Fenn.'

'Calanthe had saved her own life,' said the cripple, smiling, 'but the crown was further away than ever. When, after Roegner's death, the Lioness tried to seize absolute power, the aristocracy once again strongly opposed this violation of the law and tradition. A king was meant to sit on Cintra's throne, not a queen. The solution was eventually made clear: as soon as young Pavetta began to resemble a woman in any way, she should be married off to someone suitable to become the new king. A second marriage for the barren queen wasn't an option. The most the Lioness of Cintra could hope for was the role of queen mother. To cap it all, Pavetta's husband could turn out to be someone who might totally remove his mother-in-law from power.'

'I'm going to be crude again,' warned Codringher. 'Calanthe delayed marrying off Pavetta. She wrecked the first marital project when the girl was ten and the second when she was thirteen. The aristocracy demanded that Pavetta's fifteenth birthday would be her last as a maiden. Calanthe had to agree; but first she achieved what she had been counting on. Pavetta had remained a maiden too long. She'd finally got the itch, and so badly that she was knocked up by the first stray to come along; and he was an enchanted monster to boot. There were some kind of supernatural circumstances too, some prophecies, sorcery, promises . . . Some kind of Law of Surprise? Am I right, Geralt? What happened next you probably recall. Calanthe brought a witcher to Cintra, and the witcher stirred up trouble. Not knowing he was being manipulated, he removed the curse from the monstrous Urcheon, enabling his marriage to Pavetta. In so doing, the witcher also made it possible for Calanthe to retain the throne. Pavetta's marriage to a monster – even a now unenchanted one – was such a great shock to the noblemen that they could suddenly accept the marriage of the Lioness to Eist Tuirseach. For the jarl of the Isles of Skellige seemed better than the stray Urcheon. Thus, Calanthe continued to rule the country. Eist, like all islanders, gave the Lioness of Cintra too much respect to oppose her in anything, and kingly duties simply bored him. He handed over his rule whole-sale to her. And Calanthe, stuffing herself with medicaments and elixirs, dragged her husband into bed day and night. She wanted to reign until the end of her days. And, if not as queen mother, then as the mother of her own son. As I've already said, great ambitions, but—'

'You've already said it. Don't repeat yourself.'

'It was too late. Queen Pavetta, wife of the weird Urcheon, was wearing a suspiciously loose-fitting dress even during the marriage ceremony. Calanthe, resigned, changed her plans; if it she couldn't rule through her son, let it be Pavetta's son. But she gave birth to a daughter. A curse, or what? Queen Pavetta could still have had a child though. I mean would have been able to. For a mysterious accident occurred. Pavetta and the weird Urcheon perished in an unexplained maritime disaster.'

'Aren't you implying too much, Codringher?'

'I'm trying to explain the situation, nothing more. Calanthe was devastated after Pavetta's death, but not for long. Her granddaugh-ter was her final hope. Pavetta's daughter, Cirilla. Ciri; a little devil incarnate, roaring around the royal palace. She was the apple of some people's eyes, particularly the older folk because she was so like Calanthe had been as a child. To others ... she was a changeling, the daughter of the monstrous Urcheon, the girl to whom some witcher or other was also claiming rights. And now we're getting to the nub of the matter: Calanthe's little darling, clearly being groomed as her successor, treated almost as a second incarnation, the Lion Cub of the Lioness's blood, was already viewed by some as bereft of any right to the throne. Cirilla was ill-born. Pavetta's marriage had been a misalliance. She had mixed royal blood with the inferior blood of a stray of unknown origin.'

'Crafty, Codringher. But it wasn't like that. Ciri's father wasn't inferior in any way. He was a prince.'

'What are you saying? I didn't know that. From which kingdom?'

28

'One of the southern ones ... From Maecht ... ? Yes, indeed, from Maecht.'

'Interesting,' mumbled Codringher. 'Maecht has been a Nilfgaardian march for a long time. It's part of the Province of Metinna.'

'But it's a kingdom,' interrupted Fenn. 'A king reigns there.'

'Emhyr var Emreis rules there,' Codringher cut him off. 'Whoever sits on that throne does so by the grace and will of Emhyr. But while we're on the subject, find out who Emhyr made king. I can't recall.'

'Right away,' said the cripple, pushing the wheels of his chair and creaking off in the direction of a bookcase. He took down a thick roll of scrolls and began looking at them, discarding them on the floor after checking them. 'Hmm ... Here it is. The Kingdom of Maecht. Its coat of arms presents quarterly, azure and gules, one and four two fishes argent, two and three a crown of the same—'

'To hell with heraldry, Fenn. The king, who is the king?'

'Hoët the Just. Chosen by means of election ...'

'By Emhyr of Nilfgaard,' postulated Codringher coldly.

'... nine years ago.'

'Not that one,' said the lawyer, counting quickly. 'He doesn't concern us. Who was before him?'

'Just a moment. Here it is. Akerspaark. Died—'

'Died of acute pneumonia, his lungs having been pierced by the dagger of Emhyr's hit men or Hoët the Just,' said Codringher, once again displaying his perspicacity. 'Geralt, does Akerspaark ring any bells for you? Could he be Urcheon's father?'

'Yes,' said the Witcher after a moment's thought. 'Akerspaark. I recall that's what Duny called his father.'

'Duny?'

'That was his name. He was a prince, the son of that Akerspaark—'

'No,' interrupted Fenn, staring at the scrolls. 'They are all mentioned here. Legitimate sons: Orm, Gorm, Torm, Horm and Gonzalez. Legitimate daughters: Alia, Valia, Nina, Paulina, Malvina and Argentina ...'

'I take back the slander spread about Nilfgaard and Hoët the Just,' announced Codringher gravely. 'Akerspaark wasn't murdered, he bonked himself to death. I presume he had bastards too, Fenn?'

'Indeed. Aplenty. But I see no Duny here.'

'I didn't expect you to see him. Geralt, your Urcheon was no prince. Even if that boor Akerspaark really did sire him on the side, he was separated from the rights to such a title by – aside from Nilfgaard – a bloody long queue of legitimate Orms, Gorms and other Gonzalezes and their own, probably abundant, offspring. From a technical point of view Pavetta committed a misalliance.'

'And Ciri, being the child of a misalliance, has no rights to the throne?'

'Bullseye.'

Fenn creaked up to the pulpit, pushing the wheels of his chair.

'That is an argument,' he said, raising his huge head. 'Purely an argument. Don't forget, Geralt, we are neither fighting to gain the crown for Princess Cirilla, nor to deprive her of it. The rumour we're spreading is meant to show that the girl can't be used to seize Cintra. That if anyone makes an attempt of that kind, it will be easy to challenge, to question. The girl will cease to be a major piece in this political game; she'll be an insignificant pawn. And then . . .'

'They'll let her live,' completed Codringher unemotionally.

'How strong is your argument,' asked Geralt, 'from the formal point of view?'

Fenn looked at Codringher and then at the Witcher.

'Not that strong,' he admitted. 'Cirilla is still Calanthe, albeit somewhat diluted. In normal countries she might have been removed from the throne, but these circumstances aren't normal. The Lioness's blood has political significance . . .'

'Blood . . .' said Geralt, wiping his forehead. 'What does "Child of the Elder Blood" mean, Codringher?'

'I don't understand. Has anyone used such a term with reference to Cirilla?'

'Yes.'

'Who?'

'Never mind who. What does it mean?'

'Luned aep Hen Ichaer,' said Fenn suddenly, pushing off from the pulpit. 'It would literally be not *Child*, but *Daughter* of the Elder

30

Blood. Hmm ... Elder Blood ... I've come across that expression. I don't remember exactly ... I think it concerns some sort of elven prophecy. In some versions of Itlina's prophecy, the older ones, it seems to me there are mentions of the Elder Blood of the Elves, or Aen Hen Ichaer. But we don't have the complete text of that prophecy. We would have to ask the elves—'

'Enough,' interrupted Codringher coldly. 'Not too many of these matters at one time, Fenn, not too many irons in the fire, not too many prophecies or mysteries. That's all for now, thank you. Farewell, and fruitful work. Geralt, if you would, let's go back to the office.'

'Too little, right?' the Witcher asked to be sure, when they had returned and sat down in their chairs, the lawyer behind his desk, and he facing him. 'Too low a fee, right?'

Codringher lifted a metal star-shaped object from the desk and turned it over in his fingers several times.

'That's right, Geralt. Rootling around in elven prophecies is an infernal encumbrance for me; a waste of time and resources. The need to search out contacts amongst the elves, since no one aside from them is capable of understanding their writings. Elven manuscripts, in most cases, mean tortuous symbolism, acrostics, occasionally even codes. The Elder Speech is always, to put it mildly, ambiguous and, when written down, may have as many as ten meanings. The elves were never inclined to help humans who wanted to fathom their prophecies. And in today's times, when a bloody war against the Squirrels is raging in the forests, when pogroms are taking place, it's dangerous to approach them. Doubly dangerous. Elves may take you for a provocateur, while humans may accuse you of treachery ...'

'How much, Codringher?'

The lawyer was silent for a moment, still playing with the metal star.

'Ten per cent,' he said finally.

'Ten per cent of what?'

'Don't mock me, Witcher. The matter is becoming serious. It's becoming ever less clear what this is all about, and when no one

31

knows what something's about it's sure to be all about money. In which case a percentage is more agreeable to me than an ordinary fee. Give me ten per cent of what you'll make on this, minus the sum already paid. Shall we draw up a contract?'

'No. I don't want you to lose out. Ten per cent of nothing gives nothing, Codringher. My dear friend, I won't be making anything out of this.'

'I repeat, don't mock me. I don't believe you aren't acting for profit. I don't believe that, behind this, there isn't some ...'

'I'm not particularly bothered what you believe. There won't be any contract. Or any percentages. Name your fee for gathering the information.'

'Anyone else I would throw out of here,' said Codringher, coughing, 'certain they were trying to pull the wool over my eyes. But noble and naive disinterestedness, my anachronistic Witcher, strangely suits you. It's your style, it's so wonderfully and pathetically outmoded to let yourself be killed for nothing ...'

'Let's not waste time. How much, Codringher?'

'The same again. Five hundred in total.'

'I'm sorry,' said Geralt, shaking his head, 'I can't afford a sum like that. Not right now at least.'

'I repeat the proposition I laid before you at the beginning of our acquaintance,' said the lawyer slowly, still playing with the star. 'Come and work for me and you will. You will be able to afford information and other luxuries besides.'

'No, Codringher.'

'Why not?'

'You wouldn't understand.'

'This time you're wounding not my heart, but my professional pride. For I flatter myself, believing that I generally understand everything. Being a downright bastard is the basis of our professions, but you insist on favouring the anachronistic version over the modern one.'

The Witcher smiled.

'Bullseye.'

Codringher coughed violently once again, wiped his lips, looked down at his handkerchief, and then raised his yellow-green eyes.

'You took a good look at the list of sorcerers and sorceresses lying on the pulpit? At the list of Rience's potential paymasters?'

'Indeed.'

'I won't give you that list until I've checked it thoroughly. Don't be influenced by what you saw there. Dandelion told me Filippa Eilhart probably knows who's running Rience, but she didn't let you in on it. Filippa wouldn't protect any old sucker. It's an important character running that bastard.'

The Witcher said nothing.

'Beware, Geralt. You're in grave danger. Someone's playing a game with you. Someone is accurately predicting your movements, if not actually controlling them. Don't give in to arrogance and self-righteousness. Whoever's playing with you is no striga or werewolf. It's not the brothers Michelet. It's not even Rience. The Child of the Elder Blood, damn it. As if the throne of Cintra, sorcerers, kings and Nilfgaard weren't enough, now there are elves. Stop playing this game, Witcher. Get yourself out of it. Confound their plans by doing what no one expects. Break off that crazy bond; don't allow yourself to be linked to Cirilla. Leave her to Yennefer; go back to Kaer Morhen and keep your head down. Hole yourself up in the mountains, and I'll root around in elven manuscripts, calmly, unhurriedly and thoroughly. And when I have some information about the Child of the Elder Blood, when I have the name of the sorcerer who's involved in it, you'll get the money together and we'll do a swap.'

'I can't wait. The girl's in danger.'

'That's true. But I know you're considered an obstacle on the way to her. An obstacle to be ruthlessly removed. Thus, you are in danger too. They'll set about getting the girl once they've finished you off.'

'Or when I leave the game, withdraw and hole up in Kaer Morhen. I've paid you too much, Codringher, for you to be giving me advice like that.'

The lawyer turned the steel star over in his fingers.

'I've been busily working for some time, for the sum you paid me today, Witcher,' he said, suppressing a cough. 'The advice I'm giving you has been thoroughly considered. Hide in Kaer Morhen; disappear. And then the people who are looking for Cirilla will get her.'

Geralt squinted and smiled. Codringher didn't blench. 'I know what I'm talking about,' he said, impervious to the look and the smile. 'Your Ciri's tormentors will find her and do with her what they will. And meanwhile, both she and you will be safe.'

'Explain, please. And make it quick.'

'I've found a certain girl. She's from the Cintra nobility, a war orphan. She's been through refugee camps, and is currently measuring cloth in ells and cutting it out, having been taken in by a Brugge draper. There is nothing remarkable about her, aside from one thing. She is quite similar in likeness to a certain miniature of the Lion Cub of Cintra ... Fancy a look?'

'No, Codringher. No, I don't. And I can't permit a solution like that.'

'Geralt,' said the lawyer, closing his eyes. 'What drives you? If you want to save Ciri ... I wouldn't have thought you could afford the luxury of contempt. No, that was badly expressed. You can't afford the luxury of spurning contempt. A time of contempt is approaching, Witcher, my friend, a time of great and utter contempt. You have to adapt. What I'm proposing is a simple solution. Someone will die, so someone else can live. Someone you love will survive. A girl you don't know, and whom you've never seen, will die—'

'And who am I free to despise?' interrupted the Witcher. 'Am I to pay for what I love with contempt for myself? No, Codringher. Leave the girl in peace; may she continue to measure cloth. Destroy her portrait. Burn it. And give me something else for the two hundred and fifty hard-earned crowns which you threw into a drawer. I need information. Yennefer and Ciri have left Ellander. I'm certain you know that. I'm certain you know where they are headed. And I'm certain you know who's chasing them.'

Codringher drummed his fingers on the table and coughed.

'The wolf, heedless of warnings, wants to carry on hunting,' he said. 'He doesn't see he's being hunted, and he's heading straight for some tasty kippers hung up as bait by a real hunter.'

'Don't be trite. Get to the point.'

'If you wish. It's not difficult to guess that Yennefer is riding to the Conclave of Mages, called at the beginning of July in Garstang on the Isle of Thanedd. She is cleverly staying on the move and not using magic, so it's hard to locate her. A week ago she was still in Ellander, and I calculate that in three or four days she will reach the city of Gors Velen; from there Thanedd is a stone's throw. On the way to Gors Velen she has to ride through the hamlet of Anchor. Were you to set off immediately you would have a chance of catching those who are pursuing her. Because someone is pursuing her.'

'They wouldn't, by any chance,' said Geralt, smiling hideously, 'be royal agents?'

'No,' said the lawyer, looking at the metal star he was playing with. 'They aren't agents. Neither is it Rience, who's cleverer than you, because after the ruckus with the Michelets he's crawled into a hole somewhere and he's keeping his head down. Three hired thugs are after Yennefer.'

'I presume you know them?'

'I know them all. Which is why I suggest something to you: leave them alone. Don't ride to Anchor. And I'll use all the contacts and connections I possess. I'll try to bribe the thugs and reword the contract. In other words, I'll set them on Rience. If I succeed ...'

He broke off suddenly and swung an arm powerfully. The steel star whirred through the air and slammed with a thud into the portrait, right into the forehead of Codringher senior, cutting a hole in the canvas and embedding itself almost halfway into the wall.

'Not bad, eh?' grinned the lawyer. 'It's called an orion. A foreign invention. I've been practising for a month; I never miss now. It might come in useful. This little star is unerring and lethal at thirty feet, and it can be hidden in a sleeve or stuck behind a hatband. Orions have been part of the Nilfgaardian secret service equipment for a year now. Ha, ha, if Rience is spying for Nilfgaard, it would be amusing if they found him with an orion in his temple ... What do you say to that?'

35

'Nothing. That's your business. Two hundred and fifty crowns are lying in your drawer.'

'Sure,' said Codringher, nodding. 'I treat your words to mean you're giving me a free hand. Let's be silent for a moment, Geralt. Let's honour Rience's imminent death with a minute's silence. Why the hell are you frowning? Have you no respect for the majesty of death?'

'I do. Too great a respect to listen to idiots mocking it. Have you ever thought about your own death, Codringher?'

The lawyer coughed heavily and looked for a long time at the handkerchief in front of his mouth. Then he raised his eyes.

'Of course,' he said quietly. 'I have. Intensively, at that. But my thoughts are nothing to do with you, Witcher. Will you ride to Anchor?'

'I will.'

'Ralf Blunden, a.k.a. the Professor. Heimo Kantor. Little Yaxa. Do those names mean anything to you?'

'No.'

'All three are pretty handy with a sword. Better than the Michelets. So I would suggest a more reliable, long-range weapon. These Nilfgaardian throwing stars, for example. I'll sell you a few if you like. I've plenty of them.'

'No thanks. They're impractical. Noisy in flight.'

'The whistling has a psychological element. They're capable of paralysing their victim with fear.'

'Perhaps. But they can also warn them. I'd have time to dodge it.'

'If you saw it being thrown at you, you could. I know you can dodge an arrow or a quarrel ... But from behind—'

'From behind as well.'

'Bullshit.'

'Let's try a wager,' said Geralt coldly. 'I'll turn my face to the portrait of your dullard of a father, and you throw an orion at me. Should you hit me, you win. Should you not, you lose. Should you lose, you'll decipher those elven manuscripts. You'll get hold of information about the Child of the Elder Blood. Urgently. And on credit.'

'And if I win?'

'You'll still get that information but you'll pass it on to Yennefer. She'll pay. You won't be left out of pocket.'

Codringher opened the drawer and took out another orion.

'You don't expect me to accept the wager.' It was a statement, not a question.

'No,' smiled the Witcher. 'I'm sure you'll accept it.'

'A daredevil, I see. Have you forgotten? I don't have any scruples.'

'I haven't forgotten. After all, the time of contempt is approaching, and you keep up with progress and the zeitgeist. But I took your accusations of anachronistic naivety to heart, and this time I'll take a risk, though not without hope of profit. What's it to be then? Is the bet on?'

'Yes.' Codringher took hold of the steel star by one of its arms and stood up. 'Curiosity always won out over good sense in me, not to mention unfounded mercy. Turn around.'

The Witcher turned around. He glanced at the face on the portrait riddled with holes and with the orion sticking into it. And then he closed his eyes.

The star whistled and thudded into the wall four inches from the frame of the portrait.

'Damn and blast!' roared Codringher. 'You didn't even flinch, you whoreson!'

Geralt turned back and smiled. Quite hideously.

'Why should I have flinched? I could hear you aiming to miss.'

The inn was empty. A young woman with dark rings under her eyes sat on a bench in the corner. Bashfully turned away to one side, she was breastfeeding a child. A broad-shouldered fellow, perhaps her husband, dozed alongside, his back resting against the wall. Someone else, whose features Aplegatt couldn't make out in the gloom of the inn, sat in the shadows behind the stove.

The innkeeper looked up, saw Aplegatt, noticed his attire and the badge with the arms of Aedirn on his chest, and his face immediately darkened. Aplegatt was accustomed to welcomes like that. As a royal messenger he was absolute entitled to a mount. The royal decrees were explicit – a messenger had the right to demand a fresh horse in every town, village, inn or farmyard – and woe betide anyone who refused. Naturally, the messenger left his own horse, and signed a receipt for the new one; the owner could appeal to the magistrate and receive compensation. But you never knew. Thus a messenger was always looked upon with dislike and anxiety; would he demand a horse or not? Would he take our Golda, never to be seen again? Or our Beauty, reared from a foal? Our pampered Ebony? Aplegatt had seen sobbing children clinging to their beloved playmate as it was being led out of the stable, saddled, and more than once had looked into the faces of adults, pale with the sense of injustice and helplessness.

'I don't need a fresh horse,' he said brusquely. It seemed to him the innkeeper sighed with relief.

'I'll only have a bite to eat; the road's given me an appetite,' added the messenger. 'Anything in the pot?'

'There's some gruel left over. I'll serve you d'reckly. Sit you down. Needing a bed? Night's falling.'

Aplegatt thought it over. He had met Hansom two days before. He knew the messenger and they had exchanged messages as ordered. Hansom took the letters and the message for King Demavend and galloped off through Temeria and Mahakam to Vengerberg. Aplegatt, meanwhile, having received the messages for King Vizimir of Redania, rode towards Oxenfurt and Tretogor. He had over three hundred miles to cover.

'I'll eat and be on my way,' he declared. 'The moon is full and the road is level.'

'As you will.'

The gruel he was served was thin and tasteless, but the messenger paid no attention to such trifles. At home, he enjoyed his wife's cooking, but on the road he made do with whatever came his way. He slowly slurped it, clumsily gripping the spoon in fingers made numb from holding the reins.

A cat that had been snoozing on the stove bench suddenly lifted its head and hissed.

'A royal messenger?'

Aplegatt shuddered. The question had been asked by the man sitting in the shadows, who now emerged to stand beside him. His hair was as white as milk. He had a leather band stretched across his forehead and was wearing a silver-studded leather jacket and high boots. The pommel of the sword slung across his back glistened over his right shoulder.

'Where does the road take you?'

'Wherever the royal will sends me,' answered Aplegatt coldly. He never answered any other way to questions of that nature.

The white-haired man was silent for some time, looking searchingly at the messenger. He had an unnaturally pale face and strange, dark eyes.

'I imagine,' he finally said, in an unpleasant, somewhat husky voice, 'the royal will orders you to make haste? Probably in a hurry to get off, are you?'

'What business is it of yours? Who are you to hasten me?'

'I'm no one,' said the white-haired man, smiling hideously, 'and I'm not hurrying you. But if I were you I'd leave here as quickly as possible. I wouldn't want anything ill to befall you.'

Aplegatt also had a tried and tested answer to comments like that. Short and blunt. Not aggressive, calm; but emphatically reminding the listener who the royal messenger served and what was risked by anyone who dared touch him. But there was something in the white-haired man's voice that stopped Aplegatt from giving his usual answer.

'I must let my horse rest, sir. An hour, maybe two.'

'Indeed,' nodded the white-haired man, upon which he lifted his head, seeming to listen to the sounds which reached him from outside. Aplegatt also pricked up his ears but heard only crickets.

'Then rest,' said the white-haired man, straightening the sword belt which passed diagonally across his chest. 'But don't go out into the courtyard. Whatever happens, don't go out.'

Aplegatt refrained from further questions. He felt instinctively it would be better not to. He bent over his bowl and resumed fishing out the few bits of pork floating in the gruel. When he looked up the white-haired one was no longer in the room.

A moment later a horse neighed and hooves clattered in the courtyard.

Three men entered the inn. On seeing them the innkeeper began wiping the beer mug he was holding more quickly. The woman with the baby moved closer to her slumbering husband and woke him with a poke. Aplegatt grabbed the stool where he had laid his belt and short sword and pulled it a little closer.

The men went over to the bar, casting keen glances at the guests and sizing them up. They walked slowly, their spurs and weapons jangling.

'Welcome, good sirs,' said the innkeeper, clearing his throat. 'How may I serve you?'

'With vodka,' said one of them, short and stocky with long arms like an ape's, furnished with two Zerrikan sabres hanging crossed on his back. 'Fancy a drop, Professor?'

'With the utmost pleasure,' responded the other man, straightening a pair of gold-framed glasses made of bluish-coloured crystal, which were perched on his hooked nose. 'As long as the liquor hasn't been adulterated with any additives.'

The innkeeper poured. Aplegatt noticed that his hands were trembling slightly. The men leaned back against the bar and unhurriedly drank from the earthenware cups.

'My dear innkeeper,' began the one in the glasses suddenly. 'I conjecture that two ladies rode through here not long ago, speeding their way towards Gors Velen?'

'All sorts ride through here,' mumbled the innkeeper.

'You could not have missed the aforementioned ladies,' said the bespectacled one slowly. 'One is black-haired and exceedingly fair. She rides a black gelding. The other is younger, fair-haired and green-eyed and journeys on a dappled grey mare. Have they been here?'

'No,' interrupted Aplegatt, suddenly going cold, 'they haven't.'

Grey-feathered danger. Hot sand . . .

'A messenger?'

Aplegatt nodded.

'Travelling from where to where?'

40

'From where and to where the royal fortune sends me.'

'Have your travels adventitiously crossed the path of the women on the road about whom I enquired?'

'No.'

'Your denial is too swift,' barked the third man, as tall and thin as a beanpole. His hair was black and glistened as if covered in grease. 'And it seems to me you weren't trying especially hard to remember.'

'Let it drop, Heimo,' said the bespectacled man, waving his hand. 'He's a messenger. Don't vex yourself. What is this station's name, innkeeper?'

'Anchor.'

'What is the proximity of Gors Velen?'

'Beg pardon?'

'How many miles?'

'Can't say I've ever measured it. But it'll be a three-day journey . . .'

'On horseback?'

'By cart.'

'Hey,' called the stocky one suddenly in a hushed voice, straightening up and looking out onto the courtyard through the wide-open door. 'Have a butchers, Professor. Who would that be? Isn't it that . . . ?'

The man in glasses also looked out at the courtyard, and his face suddenly tightened.

'Yes,' he hissed. 'It's indisputably him. It appears fortune smiles on us.'

'Will we wait till he comes in?'

'He won't. He saw our horses.'

'He knows we're—'

'Silence, Yaxa. He's saying something.'

'You have a choice,' a slightly gruff but powerful voice resounded from the courtyard, a voice which Aplegatt recognised at once. 'One of you will come out and tell me who hired you. Then you may ride away without any trouble. Or all three of you may come out. I'm waiting.'

'Whoreson ...' growled the black-haired man. 'He knows. What do we do?'

The bespectacled man put his mug down on the bar with a slow movement.

'We do what we're paid to do.'

He spat on his palm, flexed his fingers and drew his sword. At the sight of it the two other men also bared their blades. The innkeeper opened his mouth to shout but quickly shut it on seeing the cold eyes peering above the blue glasses.

'Nobody moves,' hissed the bespectacled man. 'And keep schtum. Heimo, when it all kicks off, endeavour to get behind him. Very well, boys, good luck. Out we go.'

It began at once. Groans, the stamping of feet, the crash of blades. And then a scream of the kind that makes one's hair stand on end.

The innkeeper blanched, the woman with the dark rings under her eyes screamed too, clutching her suckling to her breast. The cat behind the stove leapt to its feet and arched its back, its tail fluffing up like a brush. Aplegatt slid into the corner on his stool. He had his short sword in his lap but didn't draw it.

Once again the thudding of feet across boards and the whistle and clang of blades came from the courtyard.

'You ...' shouted someone wildly, but even though it ended with a vile insult, there was more despair in it than fury. 'You ...'

The whistle of a blade. And immediately after it a high, penetrating scream shredded the air. A thud as if a heavy sack of grain had hit the ground. The clatter of hooves from the hitching post and the neighing of terrified horses.

A thud on the boards once more and the quick, heavy steps of a man running. The woman with the baby clung to her husband, and the innkeeper pressed his back against the wall. Aplegatt drew his short sword, still hiding the weapon beneath the table. The running man was heading straight for the inn, and it was clear he would soon appear in the doorway. But before he did, a blade hissed.

The man screamed and lurched inside. It seemed as though he would fall across the threshold, but he didn't. He took several staggering, laboured steps forward and only then did he topple, falling heavily into the middle of the chamber, throwing up the dust gathered between the floorboards. He fell on his face, inertly, pinning his arms underneath him, his legs bent at the knee. The crystal glasses fell to the floorboards with a clatter and shattered into tiny blue pieces. A dark, gleaming puddle began to spread from beneath the body.

No one moved. Or cried out.

The white-haired man entered the inn.

He deftly sheathed the sword he was holding into the scabbard on his back. He approached the bar, not even gracing the body lying on the floor with a glance. The innkeeper cringed.

'Those evil men ...' said the white-haired one huskily, 'those evil men are dead. When the bailiff arrives, it may turn out there was a bounty on their heads. He should do with it as he sees fit.'

The innkeeper nodded eagerly.

'It may turn out,' said the white-haired man a moment later, 'that their comrades or cronies may ask what befell these evil men. Tell them the Wolf bit them. The White Wolf. And add that they should keep glancing over their shoulders. One day they'll look back and see the Wolf.'

When, after three days, Aplegatt reached the gates of Tretogor, it was well after midnight. He was furious because he'd wasted time at the moat and shouted himself hoarse – the guards were sleeping sinfully and had been reluctant to open the gate. He got it all off his chest and cursed them painstakingly and comprehensively back to the third generation. He then overheard with pleasure as the commander of the watch – now awake – added totally new details to the charges he had levelled against the soldiers' mothers, grandmothers and great-grandmothers. Of course, gaining access to King Vizimir was out of the question. That actually suited him, as he was counting on sleeping until matins and the morning bell. He was wrong. Instead of being shown to his billet he was rushed to the guardhouse. Waiting for him there was not the king but the other one, immense and fat. Aplegatt knew him; it was Dijkstra, confidant of the King of Redania. Dijkstra – the messenger knew – was authorised to receive

43

messages meant exclusively for the king's ears. Aplegatt handed him the letters.

'Do you have a spoken message?'

'Yes, sire.'

'Speak.'

'Demavend to Vizimir,' recited Aplegatt, closing his eyes. 'Firstly: the disguised troops are ready for the second night after the July new moon. Take care that Foltest does not let us down. Secondly: I will not grace the conclave of the devious old windbags in Thanedd with my presence, and I advise you to do the same. Thirdly: the Lion Cub is dead.'

Dijkstra grimaced and drummed his fingers on the table.

'Here are letters for King Demavend. And a spoken message ... Prick up your ears and pay attention. Repeat this to your king, word for word. Only to him, to no one else. No one, do you understand?'

'I do, sire.'

'The message runs thus: Vizimir to Demavend. You must hold back the disguised troops. There has been a betrayal. The Flame has mustered an army in Dol Angra and is only waiting for an excuse. Now repeat.'

Aplegatt repeated it.

'Good,' Dijkstra nodded. 'You will leave at sunup.'

'I've been on the road for five days, Your Excellency,' said the messenger, rubbing his rump. 'Might I but sleep to the morning ... Will you permit it?'

'Does now your king, Demavend, sleep at night? Do I sleep? You deserve a punch in the face for the question alone, laddie. You will be given vittles, then stretch out a while on the hay. But you ride at dawn. I've ordered a pure-bred young stallion for you. It'll bear you like the wind. And don't make faces. Take this purse with an extra gratuity, so as not to call Vizimir a skinflint.'

'Thank you, sire.'

'Be careful in the forests by the Pontar. Squirrels have been seen there. But there's no shortage of ordinary brigands in those parts anyway.'

'Oh, I know, sire. Oh, what I did see three days past ...'

44

'What did you see?'

Aplegatt quickly reported the events in Anchor. Dijkstra listened, his powerful forearms lying crossed on his chest.

'The Professor ...' he said lost in thought. 'Heimo Kantor and Little Yaxa. Dispatched by a witcher. In Anchor, on the road to Gors Velen; in other words the road to Thanedd and Garstang ... And the Lion Cub is dead?'

'What's that, sire?'

'It's of no concern.' Dijkstra raised his head. 'At least not to you. Rest. And at dawn you ride.'

Aplegatt ate what he was brought, lay for a while without sleeping a wink, and was outside the gate by daybreak. The stallion was indeed swift, but skittish. Aplegatt didn't like horses like that.

Something itched unbearably on his back, between his left shoulder blade and his spine. A flea must have bitten him when he was resting in the stable. But there was no way to scratch it.

The stallion danced and neighed. The messenger spurred him and he galloped away. Time was short.

'Gar'ean,' Cairbre hissed, peering from behind a branch, from where he was observing the road. 'En Dh'oine aen evall a strsede!'

Toruviel leapt to her feet, seizing and belting on her sword, and poked Yaevinn in the thigh with the toe of her boot. He had been dozing, leaning against the wall of a hollow, and when he sprang up he scorched his hand as he pushed off from the hot sand.

'Que suecc's?'

'A rider on the road.'

'One?' said Yaevinn, lifting his bow and quiver. 'Cairbre? Only one?'

'Only one. He's getting closer.'

'Let's fix him then. It'll be one less Dh'oine.'

'Forget it,' said Toruviel, grabbing him by the sleeve. 'Why bother? We were supposed to carry out reconnaissance and then join the commando. Are we to murder civilians on the road? Is that what fighting for freedom is about?'

'Precisely. Stand aside.'

'If a body's left on the road, every passing patrol will raise the alarm. The army will set out after us. They'll stake out the fords, and we might have difficulty crossing the river!'

'Few people ride along this road. We'll be far away before anyone finds the body.'

'That rider's already far away,' said Cairbre from the tree. 'You should have shot instead of yapping. You won't hit him now. He's a good two hundred paces away.'

'With my sixty-pounder?' Yaevinn stroked his bow. 'And a thirty-inch arrow? And anyway, that's never two hundred paces. It's hundred and fifty, tops. Mire, que spar aen'le.'

'Yaevinn, forget it ...'

'Thaess aep, Toruviel.'

The elf turned his hat around so the squirrel's tail pinned to it wouldn't get in the way, quickly and powerfully drew back his bowstring, right to his ear, and then aimed carefully and shot.

Aplegatt did not hear the arrow. It was a 'silent' arrow, specially fledged with long, narrow grey feathers, its shaft fluted for increased stiffness and weight reduction. The three-edged, razor-sharp arrow hit the messenger in the back with great force, between his left shoulder blade and his spine. The blades were positioned at an angle – and as they entered his body, the arrow rotated and bored in like a screw, mutilating the tissue, cutting through blood vessels and shattering bone. Aplegatt lurched forward onto his horse's neck and slid to the ground, limp as a sack of wool.

The sand on the road was hot, heated up so much by the sun that it was painful to the touch. The messenger didn't feel it. He died at once.

To say I knew her would be an exaggeration. I think that, apart from the Witcher and the enchantress, no one really knew her. When I saw her for the first time she did not make a great impression on me at all, even in spite of the quite extraordinary accompanying circumstances. I have known people who said that, right away, from the very first encounter, they sensed the foretaste of death striding behind the girl. To me she seemed utterly ordinary, though I knew that ordinary she was not; for which reason I tried to discern, discover – sense – the singularity in her. But I noticed nothing and sensed nothing. Nothing that could have been a signal, a presentiment or a harbinger of those subsequent, tragic events. Events caused by her very existence. And those she caused by her actions.

Dandelion, *Half a Century of Poetry*

CHAPTER TWO

Right by the crossroads, where the forest ended, nine posts were driven into the ground. Each was crowned by a cartwheel, mounted flat. Above the wheels teemed crows and ravens, pecking and tearing at the corpses bound to the rims and hubs. Owing to the height of the posts and the great number of birds, one could only imagine what the unidentifiable remains lying on top of the wheels might be. But they were bodies. They couldn't have been anything else.

Ciri turned her head away and wrinkled her nose in disgust. The wind blew from the posts and the sickening stench of rotting corpses drifted above the crossroads.

'Wonderful scenery,' said Yennefer, leaning out of the saddle and spitting on the ground, forgetting that a short time earlier she had fiercely scolded Ciri for doing the same thing. 'Picturesque and fragrant. But why do this here, at the edge of the wilderness? They usually set things like that up right outside the city walls. Am I right, good people?'

'They're Squirrels, noble lady,' came the hurried explanation from one of the wandering traders they had caught up with at the crossroads. He was guiding the piebald horse harnessed to his fully laden cart. 'Elves. There, on those posts. And that's why the posts are by the forest. As a warning to other Squirrels.'

'Does that mean,' said the enchantress, looking at him, 'that captured Scoia'tael are brought here alive ... ?'

'Elves, m'lady, seldom let themselves be taken alive,' interrupted the trader. 'And even if the soldiers catch one they take them to the city, because civilised non-humans dwell there. When they've watched Squirrels being tortured in the town square, they quickly lose interest in joining them. But if any elves are killed in combat, their bodies are taken to a crossroads and hung on posts like this. Sometimes they're brought from far away and by the time they get here they reek—'

'To think,' snapped Yennefer, 'we have been forbidden from necromantic practices out of respect for the dignity of death and mortal remains; on the grounds that they deserve reverence, peace, and a ritual and ceremonial burial ...'

'What are you saying, m'lady?'

'Nothing. We're leaving, Ciri, let's get away from this place. Ugh, I feel as though the stench were sticking to me.'

'Yuck. Me too,' said Ciri, trotting around the trader's cart. 'Let's gallop, yes?'

'Very well ... Ciri! Gallop, but don't break your neck!'

They soon saw the city; surrounded by walls, bristling with towers with glistening, pointed roofs. And beyond the city was the sea; grey-green, sparkling in the morning sun, flecked here and there with the white dots of sails. Ciri reined in her horse at the edge of a sandy drop, stood up in her stirrups and greedily breathed in the wind and the scent.

'Gors Velen,' said Yennefer, riding up and stopping at her side. 'We finally made it. Let's get back on the road.'

They rode off down the road at a canter, leaving several ox carts and people walking, laden down with faggots, behind them.

Once they had overtaken them all and were alone, though, the enchantress slowed and gestured for Ciri to stop.

'Come closer,' she said. 'Closer still. Take the reins and lead my horse. I need both hands.'

'What for?'

'I said take the reins, Ciri.'

Yennefer took a small, silver looking glass from her saddlebags, wiped it and then whispered a spell. The looking glass floated out of her hand, rose up and remained suspended above her horse's neck, right before the enchantress's face.

Ciri let out a sigh of awe and licked her lips.

The enchantress removed a comb from her saddlebags, took off her beret and combed her hair vigorously for the next few minutes. Ciri remained silent. She knew she was forbidden to disturb or distract Yennefer while she combed her hair. The arresting and apparently careless disarray of her wavy, luxuriant locks was the result of long, hard work and demanded no little effort.

The enchantress reached into her saddlebags once more. She attached some diamond earrings to her ears and fastened bracelets on both wrists. She took off her shawl and undid a few buttons on her blouse, revealing her neck and a black velvet ribbon decorated with an obsidian star.

'Ha!' said Ciri at last, unable to hold back. 'I know why you're doing that! You want to look nice because we're going to the city! Am I right?'

'Yes, you are.'

'What about me?'

'What *about* you?'

'I want to look nice, too! I'll do my hair—'

'Put your beret on,' said Yennefer sharply, eyes still fixed on the looking glass floating above the horse's ears, 'right where it was before. And tuck your hair underneath it.'

Ciri snorted angrily but obeyed at once. She had long ago learned to distinguish the timbre and shades of the enchantress's voice. She had learned when she could get into a discussion and when it was wiser not to.

Yennefer, having at last arranged the locks over her forehead, took a small, green, glass jar out of her saddlebags.

'Ciri,' she said more gently. 'We're travelling in secret. And the journey's not over yet. Which is why you have to hide your hair under your beret. There are people at every gate who are paid for their accurate and reliable observation of travellers. Do you understand?'

'No!' retorted Ciri impudently, reining back the enchantress's black stallion. 'You've made yourself beautiful to make those gate watchmen's eyes pop out! Very secretive, I must say!'

'The city to whose gates we are heading,' smiled Yennefer, 'is Gors Velen. I don't have to disguise myself in Gors Velen; quite

51

the contrary, I'd say. With you it's different. You ought not to be remembered by anyone.'

'The people who'll be staring at you will see me too!'

The enchantress uncorked the jar, which gave off the scent of lilac and gooseberries. She stuck her index finger in and rubbed a little of it under her eyes.

'I doubt,' she said, still smiling mysteriously, 'whether anyone will notice you.'

A long column of riders and wagons stood before the bridge, and travellers crowded around the gatehouse, waiting for their turn to be searched. Ciri fumed and growled, angry at the prospect of a long wait. Yennefer, however, sat up straight in the saddle and rode at a trot, looking high over the heads of the travellers – they parted swiftly for her and made room, bowing in respect. The guards in hauberks also noticed the enchantress at once and gave her free passage, liberally handing out blows with their spear shafts to the stubborn or the overly slow.

'This way, this way, noble lady,' called one of the guards, staring at Yennefer and flushing. 'Come through here, I entreat you. Make way, make way, you churls!'

The hastily summoned officer of the watch emerged from the guardhouse sullen and angry, but at the sight of Yennefer he blushed, opened his eyes and his mouth wide and made a low bow.

'I humbly welcome you to Gors Velen, Your Ladyship,' he mumbled, straightening up and staring. 'I am at your command . . . May I be of any service to you? Perhaps an escort? A guide? Should I summon anyone?'

'That will not be necessary,' replied Yennefer, straightening up in her saddle and looking down at him. 'My stay in the city shall be brief. I am riding to Thanedd.'

'Of course, ma'am,' said the soldier, shifting from foot to foot and unable to tear his eyes from the enchantress's face. The other guards also stared. Ciri proudly pulled her shoulders back and raised her head, only to realise no one was looking at her. It was as if she didn't exist.

'Yes, ma'am,' repeated the officer of the guard. 'To Thanedd, yes

... For the conclave. I understand, very well. Then I wish you—'

'Thank you,' said the enchantress, spurring her horse, clearly uninterested in whatever the officer wanted to wish her. Ciri followed her. The guardsmen bowed to Yennefer as she rode by, but none of them paid Ciri so much as a glance.

'They didn't even ask your name,' she muttered, catching up with Yennefer and carefully guiding her horse between the ruts worn into the muddy road. 'Did you put a spell on them?'

'Not on them. On myself.'

The enchantress turned back and Ciri sighed. Yennefer's eyes burnt with a violet light and her face radiated with beauty. Dazzling beauty. Provocative. Dangerous. And unnatural.

'The little green jar,' Ciri realised. 'What was in it?'

'Glamarye. An elixir. Or rather a cream for special occasions. Ciri, must you ride into every puddle in the road?'

'I'm trying to clean my horse's fetlocks.'

'It hasn't rained for a month. That's slops and horse piss, not water.'

'Aha ... Tell me, why did you use that elixir? Did it matter so much to you to—'

'This is Gors Velen,' interrupted Yennefer. 'A city that owes much of its prosperity to sorcerers and enchantresses. Actually, if I'm honest, chiefly to enchantresses. You saw for yourself how enchantresses are treated here. And I had no desire to introduce myself or prove who I am. I preferred to make it obvious at first glance. We turn left after that red house. We'll walk, Ciri. Slow your horse down or you'll trample a child.'

'But why did we come *here* then?'

'I just told you.'

Ciri snorted, thinking hard, then pursed her lips and dug her heels hard into her horse. Her mare skittered, almost colliding with a passing horse and cart. The carter got up from his seat, ready to unleash a stream of professional abuse at her, but on seeing Yennefer sat down quickly and began a thorough analysis of the state of his clogs.

'Try to bolt like that once more,' enunciated Yennefer, 'and we'll get cross. You're behaving like an adolescent goat. You're embarrassing me.'

'I figured it out. You want to put me in some school or orphanage, don't you? I don't want to go!'

'Be quiet. People are staring.'

'They're staring at you, not at me! I don't want to go to school! You promised me you'd always be with me, and now you're planning to leave me all by myself! I don't want to be alone!'

'You won't be alone. There are plenty of girls your age at the school. You'll have lots of friends.'

'I don't want any friends. I want to be with you and ... I thought we'd—'

Yennefer suddenly turned to face her.

'What did you think?'

'I thought we were going to see Geralt,' said Ciri, tossing her head provocatively. 'I know perfectly well what you've been thinking about the entire journey. And why you were sighing at night—'

'Enough,' hissed the enchantress, and the sight of her glaring eyes made Ciri bury her face in her horse's mane. 'You've overstepped the mark. May I remind you that the moment when you could defy me has passed for ever? You only have yourself to blame and now you have to be obedient. You'll do as I say. Understood?'

Ciri nodded.

'Whatever I say will be the best for you. Always. Which is why you will obey me and carry out my instructions. Is that clear? Rein in your horse. We're here.'

'That's the school?' grunted Ciri, looking up at the magnificent facade of a building. 'Is that—?'

'Not another word. Dismount. And mind your manners. This isn't the school. It's in Aretuza, not in Gors Velen. This is a bank.'

'Why do we need a bank?'

'Think about it. And dismount, as I said. Not in a puddle! Leave your horse; that's the servant's job. Take off your gloves. You don't go into a bank wearing riding gloves. Look at me, Ciri. Straighten your beret. And your collar. Stand up straight. And if you don't know what to do with your hands then don't do anything with them!'

Ciri sighed.

The servants who poured out of the entrance and assisted them – falling over each other as they bowed – were dwarves. Ciri looked at them with interest. Although they were all short, sturdy and bearded, in no way did they resemble her companion Yarpen Zigrin or his 'lads'. These servants looked grey: identically uniformed and unremarkable. They were subservient, too, which could never be said about Yarpen and his lads.

They went inside. The magic elixir was still working, so Yennefer's appearance immediately caused a great commotion. More dwarves bustled and bowed, and there were further obsequious welcomes and declarations of readiness to serve, which only subsided on the appearance of a fat, opulently attired and white-bearded dwarf.

'My dear Yennefer!' boomed the dwarf, jingling a golden chain which dangled from a powerful neck and fell to considerably below his white beard. 'What a surprise! And what an honour! Please, please come to my office. And you lot; don't stand there staring. To work, to your abacuses. Wilfli, bring a bottle of Castel de Neuf to my office. Which vintage … ? You know what vintage. Be quick, jump to it! This way, this way, Yennefer. It's an unalloyed joy to see you. You look … Oh, dammit, you look drop-dead gorgeous!'

'As do you,' the enchantress smiled. 'You're keeping well, Giancardi.'

'Naturally. Please, come through to my office. But no, no, you go first. You know the way after all, Yennefer.'

It was a little dark but pleasantly cool in the office, and the air held a scent Ciri remembered from Jarre the scribe's tower: the smell of ink and parchment and dust covering the oak furniture, tapestries and old books.

'Sit down, please,' said the banker, pulling a heavy armchair away from the table for Yennefer, and throwing Ciri a curious glance. 'Hmm …'

'Give her a book, Molnar,' said the enchantress carelessly, noticing his look. 'She adores books. She'll sit at the end of the table and won't disturb us. Will you, Ciri?'

Ciri did not deign to reply.

'A book, hmm, hmm,' said the dwarf solicitously, going over to a chest of drawers. 'What have we here? Oh, a ledger ... No, not that. Duties and port charges ... Not that either. Credit and reimbursement? No. Oh, how did that get here? God only knows ... But this will probably be just the thing. There you go, miss.'

The book bore the title *Physiologus* and was very old and very tattered. Ciri carefully opened the cover and turned several pages. The book immediately caught her interest, since it concerned mysterious monsters and beasts and was full of illustrations. For the next few moments, she tried to divide her interest between the book and the conversation between the enchantress and the dwarf.

'Do you have any letters for me, Molnar?'

'No,' said the banker, pouring wine for Yennefer and himself. 'No new ones have arrived. I delivered the last ones a month ago, using our usual method.'

'I received them, thank you. Did anyone show interest in those letters, by any chance?'

'No one here,' smiled Molnar Giancardi. 'But your suspicions are not unwarranted, my dear. The Vivaldi Bank informed me, confidentially, that several attempts were made to track the letters. Their branch in Vengerberg also uncovered an attempt to track all transactions of your private account. A member of the staff proved to be disloyal.'

The dwarf broke off and looked at the enchantress from beneath his bushy eyebrows. Ciri listened intently. Yennefer said nothing and toyed with her obsidian star.

'Vivaldi,' said the banker, lowering his voice, 'couldn't or didn't want to conduct an investigation into the case. The corrupt, disloyal clerk fell, drunk, into a ditch and drowned. An unfortunate accident. Pity. Too quick, too hasty ...'

'No use crying over spilt milk,' the enchantress pouted. 'I know who was interested in my letters and account; the investigation at Vivaldi's wouldn't have produced any revelations.'

'If you say so ...' Giancardi ruffled his beard. 'Are you going to Thanedd, Yennefer? To the General Mages' Conclave?'

'Indeed.'

'To determine the fate of the world?'

'Let's not exaggerate.'

'Various rumours are doing the rounds,' said the dwarf coldly. 'And various things are happening.'

'What might they be, if it's not a secret?'

'Since last year,' said Giancardi, stroking his beard, 'strange fluctuations in taxation policy have been observed ... I know it doesn't interest you ...'

'Go on.'

'Poll tax and winter billeting tax, both of which are levied directly by the military authorities, have been doubled. Every merchant and entrepreneur also has to pay their "tenth groat" into the royal treasury. This is an entirely new tax: one groat on every noble of turnover. In addition, dwarves, gnomes, elves and halflings are paying increased poll and chimney tax. If they engage in trade or manufacturing they are also charged with a compulsory "non-human" donation of ten per hundred groats. In this way, I hand over sixty per cent of my income to the treasury. My bank, including all its branches, gives the Four Kingdoms six hundred marks a year. For your information, that's almost three times as much as a wealthy duke or earl pays in levy on an extensive estate.'

'Are humans not also charged with making the donation for the army?'

'No. Only the winter billeting tax and poll tax.'

'That means,' the enchantress nodded, 'that the dwarves and other non-humans are financing the campaign being waged against the Scoia'tael in the forests. I expected something like that. But what do taxes have to do with the conclave on Thanedd?'

'Something always happens after your conclaves,' muttered the banker. 'Something *always* happens. This time, I hope it will finally be the opposite. I'm counting on your conclave *stopping* things from happening. I'd be very happy, for example, if these strange price rises were to stop.'

'Be precise.'

The dwarf leaned back in his chair and linked his fingers across his beard-covered belly.

'I've worked for a good many years in this profession,' he said. 'Sufficiently long to be able to connect certain price fluctuations with certain facts. And recently the prices of precious stones have risen sharply. Because there's a demand for them.'

'Isn't cash usually exchanged for gemstones to avoid losses based on fluctuations in exchange rates and parities of coinage?'

'That too. But gemstones have one other considerable virtue. A pouch of diamonds weighing a few ounces, which can fit inside a pocket, corresponds in value to some fifty marks. The same sum in coins weighs twenty-five pounds and would fill a fair-sized sack. It is considerably quicker and easier to run away with a pouch in one's pocket than with a sack over one's shoulder. And one has one's hands free, which is of no small import. One can hold onto one's wife with one hand and, if needs must, punch someone with the other.'

Ciri snorted quietly, but Yennefer immediately quietened her with a fierce look.

'Which means' – she looked up – 'that some people are preparing, well in advance, to run away. But where to, I wonder?'

'The far north tops the list. Hengfors, Kovir and Poviss. Firstly because it is indeed far away, and secondly because those countries are neutral and are on good terms with Nilfgaard.'

'I see,' said the enchantress, a nasty smile on her lips. 'So it's dia-monds into your pocket, grab the wife and head for the north … Not too premature? Oh, never mind. So tell me: what else is getting dearer?'

'Boats.'

'What?'

'Boats,' repeated the dwarf, grinning. 'All the boat builders from the coast are building boats, their orders placed by quartermasters from King Foltest's army. The quartermasters pay well and keep placing new orders. Invest in boats, Yennefer, if you have any spare capital. It's a gold mine. You can build a boat from bark and reeds, make out a bill for a barque made of first-rate pine and split the profit with the quartermaster …'

'Don't joke, Giancardi. Tell me what it's about.'

'Those boats,' said the banker casually, looking at the ceiling, 'are transported south. To Sodden and Brugge, to the River Jaruga. But from what I hear they aren't used for catching fish on the river. They're being hidden in the forest, on the east bank. It's said the army are spending hours on embarkation and disembarkation drills. But it's not for real yet.'

'Aha,' said Yennefer, biting her lip. 'And why are some people in such a rush to lend a hand? Jaruga is in the south.'

'There's some understandable anxiety,' muttered the dwarf, glancing over at Ciri, 'that Emperor Emhyr var Emreis will not be overjoyed when he hears that the aforementioned boats have been launched. Some people think it is sure to infuriate him, and then it'll be better to be as far as possible from the Nilfgaardian border ... Hell, at least until the harvest. Once the harvest's in I'll sigh with relief. If something's going to happen, it'll happen before the harvest.'

'Before the crops are in the granaries,' said Yennefer slowly.

'That's right. It's hard to graze horses on stubble, and strongholds with full granaries can endure long sieges. The weather is favourable for farmers and the harvest looks promising ... yes, the weather is exceptionally beautiful. The sun's hot, so cats and dogs alike are hoping it'll soon rain cats and dogs ... And the Jaruga in Dol Angra is very shallow. It's easy to ford it. In both directions.'

'Why Dol Angra?'

'I hope,' said the banker, stroking his beard and fixing the sorceress with a penetrating glance, 'I can trust you.'

'You've always been able to, Giancardi. Nothing has changed.'

'Dol Angra,' said the dwarf slowly, 'means Lyria and Aedirn, who have a military alliance with Temeria. You surely don't think that Foltest, who's buying the boats, intends to use them for his own ends, do you?'

'No,' said the enchantress slowly. 'I don't. Thank you for the information, Molnar. Who knows, perhaps you're right. Perhaps at the conclave we'll somehow manage to influence the fate of the world and the people living in it.'

'Don't forget about the dwarves,' snorted Giancardi. 'Or their banks.'

'We'll try not to. Since we're on the subject …'

'I'm all ears.'

'I have some expenses, Molnar. And should I take something from my account at the Vivaldi Bank, someone is bound to drown again, so …'

'Yennefer,' interrupted the dwarf. 'You have unlimited credit with me. The pogrom in Vengerberg took place long ago. Perhaps you have forgotten, but I never will. None of the Giancardi family will forget. How much do you need?'

'One thousand five hundred Temerian orens, transferred to the branch of the Cianfanelli Bank in Ellander, in favour of the Temple of Melitele.'

'Consider it done. A nice transfer; donations to temples aren't taxed. What else?'

'What are the annual fees for the school at Aretuza?'

Ciri listened carefully.

'One thousand two hundred Novigrad crowns,' said Giancardi. 'And then you have to add the matriculation fee; around two hundred for a new novice.'

'It's bloody gone up.'

'Everything has. They don't skimp on novices though; they live like queens at Aretuza. And half the city lives off them: tailors, shoemakers, confectioners, suppliers—'

'I know. Pay two thousand into the school's account. Anonymously. With a note that it's the registration fee and payment of the annual fees for one novice.'

The dwarf put down his quill, looked at Ciri and smiled in understanding. Ciri, pretending to leaf through the book, listened intently.

'Will that be all, Yennefer?'

'And three hundred Novigrad crowns for me, in cash. I'll need at least three dresses for the conclave on Thanedd.'

'Why cash? I'll give you a banker's draft for five hundred. The prices of imported fabric have risen damnably, and you don't dress in wool or linen, after all. And should you need anything – for yourself or for the future pupil at Aretuza – my shops and storehouses are at your disposal.'

'Thank you. What interest rate shall we say?'

'Interest?' said the dwarf, looking up. 'You paid the Giancardi family in advance, Yennefer. In Vengerberg. Let's talk no more about it.'

'I don't like debts of this kind, Molnar.'

'Neither do I. But I'm a merchant, a business-dwarf. I know what an obligation is. I know its value. So I repeat, let's speak no more about it. You may consider the favours you've asked of me sorted. And the favour you didn't ask about, too.'

Yennefer raised an eyebrow.

'A certain witcher I consider family,' chuckled Giancardi, 'visited the city of Dorian recently. I was informed he ran up a debt of a hundred crowns with a moneylender there. The said moneylender works for me. I'll cancel the debt, Yennefer.'

The enchantress glanced at Ciri and made a sour grimace.

'Molnar,' she said coldly, 'don't stick your fingers in a door with broken hinges. I doubt he still holds me dear, and if he learns about any debts being cancelled he'll hate my guts. You know him, don't you? Honour is an obsession with him. Was he in Dorian a long time ago?'

'Some ten days ago. Then he was seen in Little Marsh. I'm informed he went from there to Hirundum, since he had a commission from the farmers there. Some kind of monster to kill, as usual ...'

'And, as usual, they'll be paying him peanuts for killing it.' Yennefer's voice changed a little. 'Which, as usual, will barely cover the cost of medical treatment should he be mauled by the monster. Business as usual. If you really want to do something for me, Molnar, get involved. Contact the farmers from Hirundum and raise the bounty. Give him enough to live on.'

'Business as usual,' snorted Giancardi. 'And if he eventually finds out about it?'

Yennefer fixed her eyes on Ciri, who was watching and listening now, not even attempting to feign interest in *Physiologus*.

'And from whom,' she muttered, 'might he find out?'

Ciri lowered her gaze. The dwarf smiled meaningfully and stroked his beard.

'Will you be heading towards Hirundum before setting off for Thanedd? Just by chance, of course?'

'No,' said the enchantress, turning away. 'I won't. Change the subject, Molnar.'

Giancardi stroked his beard again and looked at Ciri. She lowered her head, cleared her throat and fidgeted in her chair.

'Quite,' he said. 'Time to change the subject. But your charge is clearly bored by that book, and by our conversation. And my next topic will bore her even more, I suspect; the fate of the world; the fate of the dwarves of this world; the fate of their banks. What a boring subject for girls, for future graduates of Aretuza ... Let her spread her wings a little, Yennefer. Let her take a walk around the city—'

'Oh, yes!' cried Ciri.

The enchantress looked annoyed and was opening her mouth to protest, but suddenly changed tack. Ciri wasn't certain, but she suspected the faint wink that accompanied the banker's suggestion influenced her decision.

'Let the girl have a look at the wonders of the ancient city of Gors Velen,' added Giancardi, smiling broadly. 'She deserves a little free-dom before Aretuza. And we'll chat about certain issues of a ... hmm ... personal nature. No, I'm not suggesting the girl goes alone, even though it's a safe city. I'll assign her a companion and guard-ian. One of my younger clerks ...'

'Forgive me, Molnar,' said Yennefer, ignoring the smile, 'but I'm not convinced that, in the present times and even in a safe city, the presence of a dwarf ...'

'It didn't even occur to me,' said Giancardi indignantly, 'to send her with a dwarf. The clerk I have in mind is the son of a respected merchant, every inch a human, if you'll excuse the expression. Did you think I only employ dwarves? Hey, Wifli! Summon Fabio, and look lively!'

'Ciri.' The enchantress walked over to her, bending forward slightly. 'Make sure there's no funny business, nothing I'll have to be ashamed of. And keep schtum, got it? Promise me you'll watch your words and deeds. Don't just nod. Promises are made aloud.'

'I promise, Yennefer.'

'And glance at the sun from time to time. You're to be back at noon. Punctually. And should ... no, I don't imagine anyone will recognise you. But should you notice someone observing you too intently ...'

The enchantress put her hand in her pocket and pulled out a small piece of chrysoprase marked with runes, ground and polished into the shape of an hourglass.

'Put that in your pouch and don't lose it. In case of emergencies ... do you recall the spell? Just use it discreetly; activation emits a powerful echo, and the amulet transmits waves when it's in use. Should there be someone nearby who's sensitive to magic, you'll reveal yourself to them rather than remain hidden. Ah, and take this ... should you wish to buy something.'

'Thank you, madam.' Ciri put the amulet and coins into her pouch and looked with interest at the boy who had rushed into the office. He was freckled, and his wavy, chestnut hair fell onto the high collar of his grey clerk's uniform.

'Fabio Sachs,' said Giancardi by way of introduction. The boy bowed courteously.

'Fabio, this is Madam Yennefer, our honoured guest and respected client. And this young lady, her ward, wishes to visit our city. You shall be accompanying her and acting as her guide and guardian.'

The boy bowed once more, this time towards Ciri.

'Ciri,' said Yennefer coldly. 'Please stand up.'

She stood up, slightly taken aback, for she knew the custom well enough to know it wasn't expected of her. And she understood at once what Yennefer had seen. The clerk might look the same age as Ciri, but he was a head shorter.

'Molnar,' said the enchantress. 'Who is taking care of whom? Couldn't you assign someone of slightly more substantial dimensions to this task?'

The boy blushed and looked at his superior questioningly. Giancardi nodded his head in assent. The clerk bowed a third time.

'Your Highness,' he began, fluently and confidently. 'I may not be tall, but you can rely on me. I know the city, the suburbs and the surroundings very well. I shall look after this young lady to the best of my ability. And if I, Fabio Sachs the Younger, son of Fabio Sachs, do something to the best of my ability, then ... many an older boy would not better it.'

Yennefer looked at him for a while and then turned towards the banker.

'Congratulations, Molnar,' she said. 'You know how to choose your staff. You will have cause to be grateful to your young clerk in the future. It's true: the purest gold rings truest when you strike it. Ciri, I entrust you into the care of Fabio, son of Fabio, in absolute confidence, since he is a serious, trustworthy man.'

The boy blushed to the roots of his chestnut hair. Ciri felt herself blushing, too.

'Fabio,' said the dwarf, opening a small chest and rummaging around in its clinking contents, 'here's half a noble and three – two – five-groat pieces, in the event the young lady requests anything. Should she not, you shall return it. Very well, you may go.'

'By noon, Ciri,' reminded Yennefer. 'And not a moment later.'

'I remember, I remember.'

'My name is Fabio,' said the boy, as soon as they'd run down the stairs and out into the busy street. 'And you're Ciri, right?'

'Yes.'

'What would you like to see in Gors Velen, Ciri? The main street? Goldsmiths' alley? The seaport? Or maybe the market square and the market?'

'Everything.'

'Hmm ...' mused the boy seriously. 'We've only got till noon ... It would be best to go to the market square. It's market day today; you can see heaps of amazing things! But first we'll go up onto the wall, where there's a view of the entire bay and the famous Isle of Thanedd. How does that sound?'

'Let's go.'

Carts rumbled past, horses and oxen plodded, coopers rolled barrels along the noisy street, and everyone was in a hurry. Ciri was a little bewildered by the bustle and commotion; she clumsily stepped off the wooden footpath and ended up ankle-deep in mud and muck.

Fabio tried to take her arm, but she pulled away.

'I don't need any help to walk!'

'Hmm ... of course not. Let's go then. We're in the main street here. It's called Kardo Street and connects the two gates: the main gate and the sea gate. You get to the town hall that way. Do you see the tower with the gold weathervane? That's the town hall. And there, where that colourful sign's hanging, that's a tavern called The Unlaced Corset. But we won't, ah ... won't be going there. We're going over there. We'll take a short cut through the fish market in Winding Street.'

They turned into a narrow street and came out into a small square squeezed between some buildings. It was full of stalls, barrels and vats, all strongly smelling of fish. The market was full of bustle and noise, with the stallholders and customers alike trying to outshout the seagulls circling above. There were cats sitting at the foot of the wall, pretending that the fish didn't interest them in the least.

'Your mistress,' said Fabio suddenly, weaving his way between the stalls, 'is very strict.'

'I know.'

'She isn't a close relative, is she? It's obvious right away.'

'Is it? How can you tell?'

'She's very beautiful,' said Fabio, with the cruel, casual frankness of a young person. Ciri turned away abruptly. But before she could treat Fabio to a stinging comment about his freckles or his height, the boy was pulling her between handcarts, barrels and stalls, explaining all the time that the bastion towering above the square was called the Thief's Bastion, that the stones used for its construction came from the seabed and that the trees growing at its foot were called plantains.

'You're very quiet, Ciri,' he suddenly said.

'Me?' Ciri pretended to be astonished. 'Not at all! I'm just listening carefully to what you're saying. It's all really interesting, you know? And I just wanted to ask you ...'

'Fire away.'

'Is it far to ... to the city of Aretuza?'

'It isn't far at all. Aretuza isn't even a city. We'll go up on the wall and I'll show you. Look, the steps are over there.'

The wall was high and the steps steep. Fabio was sweating and panting, and no small wonder, because he never stopped talking while they climbed. Ciri learned that the wall surrounding the city of Gors Velen was a recent construction, much more recent than the city itself, which had been built long before by the elves. She also found out it was thirty-five feet high and that it was a so-called casemate wall, made of hewn stones and unfired brick, because that type of construction was the most resistant to blows from battering rams.

At the top they were greeted and fanned by a fresh sea wind. Ciri breathed it in joyfully after the heavy, stagnant stuffiness of the city. She rested her elbows on the top of the wall, looking down over the harbour dotted with colourful sails.

'What's that, Fabio? That mountain?'

'That's the Isle of Thanedd.'

The island seemed very close, and it didn't resemble an island. It looked like the base of a gigantic stone column stuck into the seabed, a huge ziggurat encircled by a spirally twisting road and zigzagging steps and terraces. The terraces were green with groves and gardens, and protruding from the greenery – which clung to the rocks like swallows' nests – rose soaring white towers and the ornate domes of groups of buildings framed by cloisters. The buildings gave no clue at all that they had been constructed from stone. They seemed to have been carved directly from the mountain's rocky slopes.

'All of this was built by elves,' explained Fabio. 'It's said they did it with the help of magic. However, for as long as anyone can remember, Thanedd has belonged to sorcerers. Near the summit, where you can see those gleaming domes, is Garstang Palace. The great Conclave of Mages will begin there in a few days. And there, look, on the very top. That solitary tower with battlements is Tor Lara, the Tower of Gulls ...'

'Can you get there overland? I can see it's very close.'

'Yes, you can. There's a bridge connecting the bay to the island. We can't see it because the trees are in the way. Do you see those red roofs at the foot of the mountain? That's Loxia Palace. The bridge

66

ends there. You have to pass through Loxia to reach the road to the upper terraces . . .'

'And those lovely cloisters and little bridges? And those gardens? How do they stay on the rock without falling off . . . ? What is that palace?'

'That's Aretuza, the place you were asking about. The famous school for young enchantresses is there.'

'Oh,' said Ciri, moistening her lips, 'it's there . . . Fabio?'

'Yes.'

'Do you ever see the young enchantresses who attend the school? The school at Aretuza?'

The boy looked at her, clearly astonished.

'No, never! No one sees them! They aren't allowed to leave the island or visit the city. And no one has access to the school. Even the burgrave and the bailiff can only travel as far as Loxia if they have business for the enchantresses. It's on the lowest level.'

'That's what I thought.' Ciri nodded, staring at Aretuza's shimmering roofs. 'It's not a school. It's a prison. On an island, on a rock, above a cliff. Quite simply: a prison.'

'I suppose it is,' admitted Fabio after a moment's thought. 'It's pretty difficult to get out of there . . . But no, it's not like being in prison. The novices are girls, after all. They need protecting—'

'From what?'

'Er . . .' the boy stammered. 'I mean, you know what . . .'

'No, I don't.'

'Oh . . . I think . . . Look, Ciri, no one locks them up in the school by force. They must want to be there . . .'

'Of course,' smiled Ciri mischievously. 'If they want to, they can stay in that prison. If they didn't, they wouldn't allow themselves to be locked up there. There's nothing to it. You'd just have to choose the right moment to make a break for it. But you'd have to do it before you end up there, because once you went in it would be too late . . .'

'What? Run away? Where would they run to—?'

'They,' she interrupted, 'probably wouldn't have anywhere to go, the poor things. Fabio? Where's that town . . . Hirundum?'

The boy looked at her in surprise.

'Hirundum's not a city,' he said. 'It's a huge farm. There are orchards and gardens there which supply vegetables and fruit to all the towns and cities in the area. There are also fishponds where they breed carp and other fish.'

'How far is it from here to Hirundum? Which way is it? Show me.'

'Why do you want to know?'

'Just show me, will you?'

'Do you see that road leading westwards? Where those wagons are? That's the road to Hirundum. It's about fifteen miles away, through forests all the way.'

'Fifteen miles,' repeated Ciri. 'Not far, if you've got a good horse ... Thank you, Fabio.'

'What are you thanking me for?'

'Never mind. Now take me to the town square. You promised.'

'Let's go.'

Ciri had never before seen such a crush and hubbub as there was in the market square in Gors Velen. The noisy fish market they'd walked through a little earlier seemed like a quiet temple compared to this place. It was absolutely huge, but still so crowded that Ciri assumed they would only be able to look at it from a distance. There would be no chance of actually getting into it. Fabio, however, bravely forced his way into the seething crowd, pulling her along by the hand. Ciri felt dizzy at once.

The market traders bellowed, the customers bellowed even louder, and children lost in the crowd howled and wailed. Cattle lowed, sheep bleated, and poultry clucked and quacked. Dwarven crafts-men doggedly banged their hammers onto sheets of metal, cursing foully whenever they interrupted their hammering to take a drink. Pipes, fiddles and dulcimers could be heard from various parts of the square; apparently some minstrels and musicians were performing. To cap it all, someone hidden in the crowd was blowing a brass trumpet incessantly. That someone was clearly not a musician.

Dodging a pig that trotted past with a piercing squeal, Ciri fell against a cage of chickens. A moment later, she was jostled by a passer-by and trod on something soft that meowed. She jumped back and barely avoided being trampled on by a huge, smelly, revolting, fearsome-looking beast, shoving people aside with its shaggy flanks.

'What was that?' she groaned, trying to regain her balance. 'Fabio?'

'A camel. Don't be afraid.'

'I'm not afraid! The thought of it!'

Ciri looked around curiously. She watched halflings at work creating ornate wineskins from goat's hide in full view of the public, and she was delighted by the beautiful dolls on display at a stall run by a pair of half-elves. She looked at wares made of malachite and jasper, which a gruff, gloomy gnome was offering for sale. She inspected the swords in a swordsmith's workshop with interest and the eye of an expert. She watched girls weaving wicker baskets and concluded that there was nothing worse than work.

The horn blower stopped blowing. Someone had probably killed him.

'What smells so delicious round here?'

'Doughnuts,' said Fabio, feeling the pouch. 'Do you wish to eat one?'

'I wish to eat two.'

The vendor handed them three doughnuts, took the five-groat piece and gave them four coppers in change, one of which he broke in half. Ciri, slowly regaining her poise, watched the operation of the coin being broken while voraciously devouring the first doughnut.

'Is that,' she asked, getting started on the second, 'where the expression "not worth a broken groat" comes from?'

'That's right,' said Fabio, swallowing his doughnut. 'There aren't any smaller coins than groats. Don't people use half-groats where you come from?'

'No.' Ciri licked her fingers. 'Where I come from we used gold ducats. And anyway all that breaking business was stupid and pointless.'

'Why?'

'Because I wish to eat a third doughnut.'

The plum-jam-filled doughnuts acted like the most miraculous elixir. Ciri was now in a good mood, and the teeming square had stopped terrifying her and had even begun to please her. Now she didn't let Fabio drag her behind him, but pulled him into the biggest crowd herself, towards a place where someone on a make-shift rostrum built of barrels was addressing the crowd. The speaker was fat and a bit past it. Ciri recognised him as a wandering priest by his shaved head and greyish-brown robes. She had seen his kind before, as they would occasionally visit the Temple of Melitele in Ellander. Mother Nenneke never referred to them as anything other than 'fanatical chumps'.

'There is but one law in the world!' roared the podgy priest. 'Divine law! The whole of nature is subject to that law, the whole of earth and everything that lives on the earth! And spells and magic are contrary to that law! Thus are sorcerers damned, and close is the day of wrath when fire will pour from the heavens and destroy their vile island! Then down will come the walls of Loxia, Aretuza and Garstang, where those pagans are gathering to hatch their intrigues! Those walls will tumble down ...'

'And we'll have to build the sodding things again,' muttered a journeyman bricklayer in a lime-spattered smock standing next to Ciri.

'I admonish you all, good and pious people,' yelled the priest. 'Don't believe the sorcerers, don't turn to them for advice or aid! Be beguiled neither by their beautiful looks nor their clever speech, for verily I do say to you that those magicians are like whitened graves, beautiful on the outside but full of putrefaction and rotten bones on the inside!'

'See what a powerful gob 'e 'as on 'im?' remarked a young woman with a basket full of carrots. 'E's 'aving a go at the magicians, coz 'e's jealous of 'em and that's that.'

'Course he is,' said the bricklayer. 'Look at his noggin, he's bald as an egg, and that belly hangs down to his knees. On the other hand, sorcerers are handsome; they don't get fat or bald ... And sorceresses, well, they're just gorgeous ...'

'Only because they've sold their souls to the devil for their beauty!' yelled a short individual with a shoemaker's hammer stuck into his belt.

70

'Fool of a cobbler! Were it not for the ladies of Aretuza, you'd long since have gone begging! Thanks to them you've got food in your belly!'

Fabio pulled Ciri by the sleeve, and they plunged once more into the crowd, which carried them towards the middle of the square. They heard the pounding of a drum and loud shouting, calling for silence. The crowd had no intention of being quiet, but it didn't bother the town crier on the wooden platform in the least. He had a powerful, trained voice and knew how to use it.

'Let it be known,' he bellowed, unfurling a roll of parchment, 'that Hugo Ansbach of halfling stock is outlawed, for he gave lodgings and victuals to those villainous elves called Squirrels. The same applies to Justin Ingvar, a blacksmith of dwarven stock, who forged arrowheads for those wrongdoers. Thus does the burgrave announce that both are wanted and orders them to be hunted down. Whosoever seizes them will earn a reward of fifty crowns. Any who gives them victuals or shelter shall be considered an accomplice to their crime and shall suffer the same punishment. And should they be apprehended in a village or hamlet, the entire village or hamlet will pay a fine—'

'But who,' shouted someone in the crowd, 'would give a halfling shelter? They should be hunted on their farms, and when they're found, all those non-humans should be slung into the dungeons!'

'To the gallows, not the dungeons!'

The town crier began to read further announcements issued by the burgrave and town council, and Ciri lost interest. She was just about to extricate herself from the crowd when she suddenly felt a hand on her bottom. A totally non-accidental, brazen and extremely skilled hand.

The crush ought to have prevented her from turning around to look, but in Kaer Morhen Ciri had learned how to manoeuvre in places that were difficult to move around in. She turned around, causing something of a disturbance. The young priest with the shaved head standing right behind her smiled an arrogant, rehearsed smile. 'Right, then,' said that smile, 'what are we going to do now? You'll blush sweetly and that'll be the end of it, won't it?'

71

It was clear the priest had never had to deal with one of Yennefer's pupils.

'Keep your hands to yourself, baldy!' yelled Ciri, white with rage. 'Grab your own arse, you ... You whitewashed tomb!'

Taking advantage of the fact that the priest was pinned in by the crowd and couldn't move, she intended to kick him, but Fabio prevented that, hurriedly pulling her well away from the priest and the site of the incident. Seeing that she was trembling with rage, he treated her to a few fritters dusted with caster sugar, at the sight of which Ciri immediately calmed down and forgot about the incident. From where they were standing by the stall they had a view of a scaffold with a pillory, but with no criminal in it. The scaffold itself was decorated with garlands of flowers and was being used by a group of wandering minstrels, dressed up like parrots, sawing away vigorously at violins and playing flutes and bagpipes. A young black-haired woman in a sequined waistcoat sang and danced, shaking a tambourine and merrily stamping tiny slippers.

To bite a witch beside a path,
Some vipers did contrive.
The snakes all perished one by one,
The witch is still alive.

The crowd gathered around the scaffold laughed heartily and clapped along. The fritter seller threw another batch into the hot oil. Fabio licked his fingers and tugged Ciri away by the sleeve.

There were innumerable stalls and delicious foods were being offered everywhere. They each ate a cream bun, then shared a smoked eel, which they followed with something very strange, which had been fried and impaled on a skewer. After that, they stopped by some barrels of sauerkraut and pretended to be tasting it, as if intending to buy a large quantity. When they had eaten their fill but then didn't buy anything the stallholder called them 'a pair of little shits'.

They walked on. Fabio bought a small basket of bergamot pears with the rest of the money. Ciri looked up at the sky but decided it still wasn't noon.

'Fabio? What are those tents and booths over there, by the wall?'

'Sideshows. Want to see?'

'Yes.'

There was a crowd of men in front of the first tent, shuffling about excitedly. The sounds of a flute floated out from inside.

'The black-skinned Leila ...' read Ciri, struggling to decipher the lopsided, crooked writing on the flap, 'reveals all the secrets of her body in the dance ... What nonsense! What kind of secrets ... ?'

'Come on, let's go,' said Fabio, urging her on and blushing slightly. 'Oh, look, this is more interesting. There's a clairvoyant here who'll tell your fortune. I've still got two groats. That should be enough—'

'Waste of money,' snorted Ciri. 'Some prophecy it'll be, for two groats! To predict the future you have to be a prophetess. Divination is a great gift. Even among enchantresses, no more than one in a hundred has that kind of ability—'

'A fortune-teller predicted,' interrupted the boy, 'that my eldest sister would get married and it came true. Don't make faces, Ciri. Come on, let's have our fortunes told ...'

'I don't want to get married. I don't want my fortune told. It's hot and that tent stinks of incense. I'm not going in. Go in yourself, if you want, and I'll wait. I just don't understand why you want a prophecy. What would you like to know?'

'Well ...' stammered Fabio. 'Mostly, it's ... it's if I'm going to travel. I'd like to travel. And see the whole world ...'

He will, thought Ciri suddenly, feeling dizzy. *He'll sail on great white sailing ships ... He'll sail to countries no one has seen before him ... Fabio Sachs, explorer. He'll give his name to a cape, to the very furthest point of an as-yet unnamed continent. When he's fifty-four, married with a son and three daughters, he'll die far from his home and his loved ones ... of an as-yet unnamed disease ...*

'Ciri! What's the matter with you?'

She rubbed her face. She felt as though she were coming up through water, rising to the surface from the bottom of a deep, ice-cold lake.

'It's nothing ...' she mumbled, looking around and coming back

73

to herself. 'I felt dizzy ... It's because of this heat. And because of that incense from the tent ...'

'Because of that cabbage, more like,' said Fabio seriously. 'We oughtn't to have eaten so much. My belly's gurgling too.'

'There's nothing wrong with me!' snapped Ciri, lifting her head briskly and actually feeling better. The thoughts that had flown through her mind like a whirlwind dissipated and were lost in oblivion. 'Come on, Fabio. Let's go.'

'Do you want a pear?'

'Course I do.'

A group of teenage boys were playing spinning tops for money. The top, carefully wound up with string, had to be set spinning with a deft tug, like cracking a whip, to make it follow a circular path around a course drawn with chalk. Ciri had beaten most of the boys in Skellige and all the novices at the Temple of Melitele at spinning tops. So she was toying with the thought of joining the game and relieving the urchins not only of their coppers, but also of their patched britches, when her attention was suddenly caught by some loud cheering.

At the very end of a row of tents and booths stood a curious semi-circular enclosure squeezed between the foot of the wall and some stone steps. It was formed from sheets of canvas stretched over six-foot poles. There was an entrance between two of the poles, blocked by a tall, pockmarked man wearing a jerkin and striped trousers tucked into sailor's boots. A small group of people milled around in front of him, and folk would throw a few coppers into the pock-marked man's hand and then disappear behind the canvas. The pockmarked man was dropping the money into a large sack, which he jingled as he shouted hoarsely.

'Roll up, roll up! Over here! You will see, with your own eyes, the most frightful creature the gods ever created! Horror of horrors! A live basilisk, the venomous terror of the Zerrikan deserts, the devil incarnate, an insatiable man-eater! You've never seen such a monster, folks. Freshly caught, brought from beyond the seas in a coracle. Come and see this vicious, live basilisk with your own eyes, because you'll never see one again. Not never, not nowhere! Last chance! Here, behind me, for a mere fifteen groats. Just ten groats for women with children!'

'Ha,' said Ciri, shooing wasps away from the pears. 'A basilisk? A live one? This I must see. I've only seen them in books. Come on, Fabio.'

'I haven't got any more money ...'

'But I have. I'll pay for you. Come on, in we go.'

'That'll be six,' said the pockmarked man, looking down at the four coppers in his palm. '*Three* five-groat pieces each. Only women with children get in cheap.'

'He,' replied Ciri, pointing at Fabio with a pear, 'is a child. And I'm a woman.'

'Only women carrying children,' growled the pockmarked man. 'Go on, chuck in two more five-groat pieces, clever little miss, or scram and let other people through. Make haste, folks! Only three more empty spaces!'

Inside the canvas enclosure townspeople were milling around, forming a solid ring around a stage constructed of wooden planks. On the stage stood a wooden cage covered with a carpet. Having let in the final spectators, the pockmarked man jumped onto the stage, seized a long pole and used it to pull the carpet away. The air filled with the smell of offal mixed with an unpleasant reptilian stench. The spectators rumbled and stepped back a little.

'You are being sensible, good people,' said the pockmarked man. 'Not too close, for it may be perilous!'

Inside the cage, which was far too cramped for it, lay a lizard. It was covered in dark, strangely shaped scales and curled up into a ball. When the pockmarked man knocked the cage with his pole, the reptile writhed, grated its scales against the bars, extended its long neck and let out a piercing hiss, revealing sharp, white fangs, which contrasted vividly with the almost black scales around its maw. The spectators exhaled audibly. A shaggy little dog in the arms of a woman who looked like a stallholder yapped shrilly.

'Look carefully, good people,' called the pockmarked man. 'And be glad that beasts like this don't live near our city! This monstrous basilisk is from distant Zerrikania! Don't come any closer because,

75

though it's secure in a cage, its breath alone could poison you!'

Ciri and Fabio finally pushed their way through the ring of spectators.

'The basilisk,' continued the pockmarked man on stage, resting on the pole like a guard leaning on his halberd, 'is the most venomous beast in the world! For the basilisk is the king of all the serpents! Were there more basilisks, this world would disappear without a trace! Fortunately, it is a most rare monster; it only ever hatches from an egg laid by a cockerel. And you know yourselves that not every cockerel can lay an egg, but only a knavish one who presents his rump to another cockerel in the manner of a mother hen.'

The spectators reacted with general laughter to this superior – or possibly posterior – joke. The only person not laughing was Ciri. She didn't take her eyes off the creature, which, disturbed by the noise, was writhing and banging against the bars of the cage, biting them and vainly trying to spread its wings in the cramped space.

'An egg laid by a cockerel like that,' continued the pockmarked man, 'must be brooded by a hundred and one venomous snakes! And when the basilisk hatches from the egg –'

'That isn't a basilisk,' said Ciri, chewing a bergamot pear. The pockmarked man looked at her, askance.

'– when the basilisk hatches, I was saying,' he continued, 'then it devours all the snakes in the nest, imbibing their venom without suffering any harm from it. It becomes so swollen with venom itself that it is able to kill not only with its teeth, not only with its touch, but with its breath alone! And when a mounted knight ups and stabs a basilisk with his spear, the poison runs up the shaft, killing both rider and horse outright!'

'That's the falsest lie,' said Ciri aloud, spitting out a pip.

'It's the truest truth!' protested the pockmarked man. 'He kills them; he kills the horse and its rider!'

'Yeah, right!'

'Be quiet, miss!' shouted the market trader with the dog. 'Don't interfere! We want to marvel and listen!'

'Ciri, stop it,' whispered Fabio, nudging her in the ribs. Ciri snorted at him, reaching into the basket for another pear.

76

'Every animal,' said the pockmarked man, raising his voice against the murmur which was intensifying among the spectators, 'flees the basilisk as soon as it hears its hiss. Every animal, even a dragon – what am I saying? – even a cockrodile, and a cockrodile is awfully dreadful, as anyone who's seen one knows. The one and only animal that doesn't fear the basilisk is the marten. The marten, when it sees the monster in the wilderness, runs as fast as it can into the forest, looks for certain herbs known only to it and eats them. Then the basilisk's venom is harmless, and the marten can bite it to death ...'

Ciri snorted with laughter and made a long-drawn-out, extremely rude noise with her lips.

'Hey, little know-it-all!' burst out the pockmarked man. 'If it's not to your liking, you know where the door is! No one's forcing you to listen or look at the basilisk!'

'That's no basilisk!'

'Oh, yeah? So what is it, Miss Know-It-All?'

'It's a wyvern,' said Ciri, throwing away the pear stalk and licking her fingers. 'It's a common wyvern. Young, small, starving and dirty. But a wyvern, that's all. Vyverne, in the Elder Speech.'

'Oh, look at this!' shouted the pockmarked man. 'What a clever clogs! Shut your trap, because when I—'

'I say,' spoke up a fair-haired young man in a velvet beret and a squire's doublet without a coat of arms. He had a delicate, pale girl in an apricot dress on his arm. 'Not so fast, my good animal catcher! Do not threaten the noble lady, for I will readily tan your hide with my sword. And furthermore, something smacks of trickery here!'

'What trickery, young sir knight?' choked the pockmarked man. 'She's lying, the horri— I meant to say, the high-born young lady is in error. It *is* a basilisk!'

'It's a wyvern,' repeated Ciri.

'What do you mean, a Vernon! It's a basilisk! Just look how menacing it is, how it hisses, how it bites at its cage! Look at those teeth! It's got teeth, I tell you, like—'

'Like a wyvern,' scowled Ciri.

'If you've taken leave of your senses,' said the pockmarked man, fixing her with a gaze that a real basilisk would have been proud of, 'then come closer! Step up, and let it breathe on you! You laughed at its venom. Now let's see you croak! Come along, step up!'

'Not a problem,' said Ciri, pulling her arm out of Fabio's grasp and taking a step forward.

'I shan't allow it!' cried the fair-haired squire, dropping his apricot companion's arm and blocking Ciri's way. 'It cannot be! You are risking too much, fair lady.'

Ciri, who had never been addressed like that before, blushed a little, looked at the young man and fluttered her eyelids in a way she had tried out numerous times on the scribe Jarre.

'There's no risk whatsoever, noble knight,' she smiled seductively, in spite of all Yennefer's warnings, and reminders about the fable of the simpleton gazing foolishly at the cheese. 'Nothing will happen to me. That so-called poisonous breath is claptrap.'

'I would, however, like to stand beside you,' said the youth, putting his hand on the hilt of his sword. 'To protect and defend ... Will you allow me?'

'I will,' said Ciri, not knowing why the expression of rage on the apricot maiden's face was causing her such pleasure.

'It is I who shall protect and defend her!' said Fabio, sticking his chest out and looking at the squire defiantly. 'And I shall stand with her too!'

'Gentlemen.' Ciri puffed herself up with pride and stuck her nose in the air. 'A little more dignity. Don't shove. There'll be room enough for everyone.'

The ring of spectators swayed and murmured as she bravely approached the cage, followed so closely by the boys that she could almost feel their breath on her neck. The wyvern hissed furiously and struggled, its reptilian stench assaulting their noses. Fabio gasped loudly, but Ciri didn't withdraw. She drew even closer and held out a hand, almost touching the cage. The monster hurled itself at the bars, raking them with its teeth. The crowd swayed once more and someone cried out.

'Well?' Ciri turned around, hands proudly on her hips. 'Did I die? Has that so-called venomous monster poisoned me? He's no more a basilisk than I'm a—'

She broke off, seeing the sudden paleness on the faces of Fabio and the squire. She turned around quickly and saw two bars of the cage parting under the force of the enraged lizard, tearing rusty nails out of the frame.

'Run!' she shouted at the top of her voice. 'The cage is breaking!'

The crowd rushed, screaming, for the door. Several of them tried to tear their way through the canvas sheeting, but they only managed to entangle themselves and others in it, eventually collapsing into a struggling, yelling mass of humanity. Just as Ciri was trying to jump out of the way the squire seized her arm, and the two of them staggered, tripped and fell to the ground, taking Fabio down with them. Anxious yaps came from the stallholder's shaggy little dog, colourful swearwords from the pockmarked man and piercing shrieks from the disorientated apricot maiden.

The bars of the cage broke with a crack and the wyvern struggled free. The pockmarked man jumped down from the stage and tried to restrain it with his pole, but the writhing monster knocked it out of his hand with one blow of its claws and lashed him with its spiny tail, transforming his pockmarked cheek into a bloody pulp. Hissing and spreading its tattered wings, the wyvern flew down from the stage; its sights were set on Ciri, Fabio and the squire, who were trying to get to their feet. The apricot maiden fainted and fell flat on her back. Ciri tensed, preparing to jump, but realised she wouldn't make it.

They were saved by the shaggy little dog who, still yapping shrilly, broke free from its owner's arms – she had fallen and become entangled in her own six skirts – and lunged at the monster. The wyvern hissed, rose up, pinned the cur down with its talons, twisted its body with a swift, serpentine movement and sank its teeth into the dog's neck. The dog howled wildly.

The squire struggled to his knees and reached down to his side, but didn't find his hilt. Ciri had been too quick for him. She had drawn his sword from its scabbard in a lightning-fast movement and leapt into a half-turn. The wyvern rose, the dog's severed head hanging in its sharp-toothed jaws.

It seemed to Ciri that all the movements she had learned in Kaer Morhen were performing themselves, almost without her conscious will or participation. She slashed the astonished wyvern in the belly and immediately spun away to avoid it. The lunging lizard fell to the sand spurting blood. Ciri jumped over it, skilfully avoiding its swishing tail. Then, with a sure, accurate and powerful blow, she hacked into the monster's neck, jumped back, and made an instinctive – but now unnecessary – evasive manoeuvre, and then struck again at once, this time chopping through its backbone. The wyvern writhed briefly in pain and then stopped moving; only its serpentine tail continued to thrash and slap the ground, raining sand all around.

Ciri quickly shoved the bloodied sword into the squire's hand.

'Danger over!' she shouted to the fleeing crowd and the spectators still trying to extricate themselves from the canvas sheeting. 'The monster's dead! This brave knight has killed him dead ...'

She suddenly felt a tightening in her throat and a whirling in her stomach; everything went black. Something hit her in the bottom with tremendous force, making her teeth snap together. She looked around blankly. The thing that had struck her was the ground.

'Ciri ...' whispered Fabio, kneeling beside her. 'What's the matter? By the gods, you're as white as a sheet ...'

'It's a pity,' she muttered, 'you can't see yourself.'

People crowded around. Several of them prodded the wyvern's body with sticks and pokers. A few of them began dressing the pock-marked man's wounds. The rest cheered the heroic squire: the fearless dragon killer, the only person to keep a cool head, and prevent a massacre. The squire revived the apricot maiden, still staring somewhat dumbstruck at the blade of his sword which was covered with smeared streaks of drying blood.

'My hero ...' said the apricot maiden, coming to and throwing her arms around the squire's neck. 'My saviour! My darling!'

'Fabio,' said Ciri weakly, seeing the city constables pushing through the crowd. 'Help me get up and get us out of here. Quickly.'

'Poor children ...' said a fat townswoman in a cap as she watched them sneak away from the crowd. 'Oh, you were lucky. Were it not for this valiant young knight, your mothers would be sorely grieving!'

'Find out who that young squire serves!' shouted a craftsman in a leather apron. 'That deed deserves a knightly belt and spurs!'

'And to the pillory with the animal catcher! He deserves a thrashing! Bringing a monster like that into the city, among people ...'

'Water, and quickly! The maiden's fainted again!'

'My darling Foo-Foo!' the stallholder suddenly howled, as she leaned over what was left of the shaggy little dog. 'My poor little sweetheart! Someone, please! Catch that wench, that rascal who infuriated the dragon! Where is she? Someone grab her! It wasn't the animal catcher; she's to blame for all this!'

The city constables, helped by numerous volunteers, began to shove their way through the crowd and look around. Ciri had overcome her dizziness.

'Fabio,' she whispered. 'Let's split up. We'll meet up in a bit in that alleyway we came along. Go. And if anyone stops you to ask, you don't know me or anything about me.'

'But ... Ciri—'

'Go!'

She squeezed Yennefer's amulet in her fist and murmured the activation spell. It started working in an instant, and there was no time to lose. The constables, who had been forcing their way through the crowd towards her, stopped, confused.

'What the bloody hell?' said one of them in astonishment, looking, it would have seemed, straight at Ciri. 'Where is she? I just saw her ...'

'There, over there!' yelled another, pointing the wrong way.

Ciri turned around and walked away, still a little dazed and weakened by the rush of adrenaline and the activation of the amulet. The amulet was working perfectly; no one could see her and no one was paying any attention to her. Absolutely no one. As a consequence she was jostled, stamped on and kicked innumerable times before she finally extricated herself from the crowd. By some miracle she escaped being crushed by a chest thrown from a cart. She almost had an eye poked out by a pitchfork. Spells, it turned out, had their good and bad sides, and as many advantages as disadvantages.

The amulet's effects did not last long. Ciri was not powerful enough to control it or extend the time the spell was active. Fortunately, the spell wore off at the right moment, just as she left the crowd and saw Fabio waiting for her in the alley.

'Oh my,' said the boy. 'Oh my goodness, Ciri. You're here. I was worried ...'

'You needn't have been. Come on, quickly. Noon has passed. I've got to get back.'

'You were pretty handy with that monster.' The boy looked at her in admiration. 'You moved like lightning! Where did you learn to do that?'

'What? The squire killed the wyvern.'

'That's not true. I saw—'

'You didn't see anything! Please, Fabio, not a word to anyone. Anyone. And particularly not to Madam Yennefer. Oh, I'd be in for it if she found out ...'

She fell silent.

'Those people were right.' She pointed behind her, towards the market square. 'I provoked the wyvern ... It was all my fault ...'

'No, it wasn't,' retorted Fabio firmly. 'That cage was rotten and bodged together. It could have broken any second: in an hour, tomorrow, the next day ... It's better that it happened now, because you saved—'

'The squire did!' yelled Ciri. 'The squire! Will you finally get that into your head? I'm telling you, if you grass me up, I'll turn you into a ... a ... well something horrible! I know spells! I'll turn you into—'

'Stop,' someone called out behind them. 'That's quite enough of that!'

One of the women walking behind them had dark, smoothly combed hair, shining eyes and thin lips. She had a short mauve camaka cape trimmed with dormouse fur thrown over her shoulders.

'Why aren't you in school, novice?' she asked in a cold, resonant voice, eyeing Ciri with a penetrating gaze.

'Wait, Tissaia,' said the other woman, who was younger, tall and fair-haired, and wore a green dress with a plunging neckline. 'I don't know her. I don't think she's—'

'Yes, she is,' interrupted the dark-haired woman. 'I'm certain she's one of your girls, Rita. You can't know them all. She's one of the ones who sneaked out of Loxia during the confusion when we were moving dormitories. And she'll admit as much in a moment. Well, novice, I'm waiting.'

'What?' frowned Ciri.

The woman pursed her thin lips and straightened her cuffs.

'Who did you steal that amulet of concealment from? Or did someone give it to you?'

'What?'

'Don't test my patience. Name, class, and the name of your preceptress. Quickly!'

'What?'

'Are you acting dumb, novice? Your name! What is your name?'

Ciri clenched her teeth together and her eyes flared with a green glow.

'Anna Ingeborga Klopstock,' she muttered brazenly.

The woman raised a hand and Ciri immediately realised the full extent of her error. Only once had Yennefer, wearied by Ciri's endless complaining, showed her how a paralysing spell worked. The sensation had been extremely unpleasant. It was the same this time, too.

Fabio yelled weakly and lunged towards her, but the fair-haired woman seized him by the collar and held him fast. The boy struggled but the woman's grip was like iron. Ciri couldn't budge an inch either. She felt as though she were slowly becoming rooted to the spot. The dark-haired woman leaned over her and fixed her with her shining eyes.

'I do not approve of corporal punishment,' she said icily, straightening her cuffs once more. 'But I'll do my best to have you flogged, novice. Not for disobedience, nor for theft, nor for truancy. Not because you are wearing non-regulation clothing. Not for being in the company of a boy and not even for talking to him about matters you are forbidden to speak of. You will be flogged for not recognising an arch-mistress.'

'No!' shrieked Fabio. 'Don't harm her, noble lady! I'm a clerk in Mr Molnar Giancardi's bank, and this young lady is—'

'Shut up!' yelled Ciri. 'Shut—' The gagging spell was cast quickly and brutally. She tasted blood in her mouth.

'Well?' the fair-haired woman urged Fabio, releasing the boy and tenderly smoothing his ruffled collar. 'Speak. Who is this haughty young maid?'

Margarita Laux-Antille emerged from the pool with a splash, spraying water everywhere. Ciri couldn't stop herself looking. She had seen Yennefer naked on several occasions and hadn't imagined anyone could have a more shapely figure. She was wrong. Even marble statues of goddesses and nymphs would have blushed at the sight of Margarita Laux-Antille undressed.

The enchantress took a pail of cold water and poured it over her breasts, swearing lewdly and then shaking herself off.

'You, girl.' She beckoned to Ciri. 'Be so good as to hand me a towel. And please stop being angry with me.'

Ciri snorted quietly, still piqued. When Fabio had revealed who she was, the enchantresses had dragged her half the length of the city, making a laughing stock of her. Naturally, the matter was cleared up instantly in Giancardi's bank. The enchantresses apologised to Yennefer, asking for their behaviour to be excused. They explained that the Aretuza novices had been temporarily moved to Loxia because the school's rooms had been turned into accommodation for the participants of the mages' conclave. Taking advantage of the confusion around the move, several novices had slipped out of Thanedd and played truant in the city. Margarita Laux-Antille and Tissaia de Vries, alarmed by the activation of Ciri's amulet, had mistaken her for one of their truants.

The enchantresses apologised to Yennefer, but none of them thought of apologising to Ciri. Yennefer, listening to the apologies, simply looked at her and Ciri could feel her ears burning with shame. But it was worse for Fabio; Molnar Giancardi admonished him so severely the boy had tears in his eyes. Ciri felt sorry for him but was also proud of him; Fabio kept his promise and didn't breathe a word about the wyvern.

Yennefer, it turned out, knew Tissaia and Margarita very well.

The enchantresses invited her to the Silver Heron, the best and most expensive inn in Gors Velen, where Tissaia de Vries was staying, delaying her trip to the island for reasons known only to herself. Margarita Laux-Antille, who, it turned out, was the rectoress of Aretuza, had accepted the older enchantress's invitation and was temporarily sharing the apartment with her. The inn was truly luxurious; it had its own bathhouse in the cellars, which Margarita and Tissaia had hired for their exclusive use, paying extortionate sums of money for it. Yennefer and Ciri, of course, were encouraged to use the bathhouse too. As a result, all of them had been soaking in the pool and perspiring in the steam by turns for several hours, gossiping the entire time.

Ciri gave the enchantress a towel. Margarita pinched her gently on the cheek. Ciri snorted again and dived with a splash into the rosemary-perfumed water of the pool.

'She swims like a young seal,' laughed Margarita, stretching out beside Yennefer on a wooden lounger, 'and is as shapely as a naiad. Will you give her to me, Yenna?'

'That's why I brought her here.'

'Which class shall I put her in? Does she know the basics?'

'She does, but she can start at the beginning like everyone else. It won't do her any harm.'

'That would be wise,' said Tissaia de Vries, busily correcting the arrangement of cups on the marble tabletop, which was covered in a thin layer of condensation. 'That would be wise indeed, Yennefer. The girl will find it easier if she begins with the other novices.'

Ciri hauled herself out of the pool and sat on the edge, wringing her hair out and splashing her feet in the water. Yennefer and Margarita gossiped lazily, wiping their faces from time to time with cloths soaked in cold water. Tissaia, modestly swathed in a sheet, didn't join in the conversation, and gave the impression of being utterly absorbed in tidying the objects on the table.

'My humble apologies, noble ladies,' called the innkeeper suddenly, unseen, from above. 'Please forgive my daring to disturb, but ... an officer wishes to talk to Madam de Vries urgently. Apparently the matter will brook no delay!'

Margarita Laux-Antille giggled and winked at Yennefer, upon which they pulled the towels from their hips and assumed exotic and extremely provocative poses.

'Let the officer enter,' shouted Margarita, trying not to laugh. 'Welcome. We're ready.'

'Children,' sighed Tissaia de Vries, shaking her head. 'Cover yourself, Ciri.'

The officer came in, but the enchantresses' prank misfired. The officer wasn't embarrassed at the sight of them, and didn't blush, gape or goggle, because the officer was a woman. A tall, slender woman with a thick, black plait and a sword at her side.

'Madam,' said the woman stiffly, her hauberk clanking as she gave Tissaia de Vries a slight bow, 'I report the execution of your instructions. I would like to ask for permission to return to the garrison.'

'You may,' replied Tissaia curtly. 'Thank you for the escort and your help. Have a safe journey.'

Yennefer sat up on her lounger, looking at the black, gold and red rosette on the soldier's shoulder.

'Do I know you?'

The warrior bowed stiffly and wiped her sweat-covered face. It was hot in the bathhouse, and she was wearing a hauberk and leather tunic.

'I often used to visit Vengerberg, Madam Yennefer,' she said. 'My name is Rayla.'

'Judging by the rosette, you serve in King Demavend's special units.'

'Yes, madam.'

'Your rank?'

'Captain.'

'Very good.' Margarita Laux-Antille laughed. 'I note with pleasure that Demavend's army has finally begun to award commissions to soldiers with balls.'

'May I withdraw?' said the soldier, standing up straight and resting her hand on the hilt of her sword.

'You may.'

'I sensed hostility in your voice, Yenna,' said Margarita a moment

86

later. 'What do you have against the captain?'

Yennefer stood up and took two goblets from the table.

'Did you see the posts by the crossroads?' she asked. 'You must have seen them, must have smelled the stench of rotting corpses. Those posts are their idea and their work. She and her subordinates from the special units. They're a gang of sadists!'

'There's a war on, Yennefer. Rayla must have seen her comrades-in-arms falling, alive, into the Squirrels' clutches many times. Then hung by their arms from trees as target practice. Blinded, castrated, with their feet burnt in campfires. Falka herself wouldn't have been ashamed of the atrocities committed by the Scoia'tael.'

'The methods of the special units are remarkably similar to those of Falka. But that's not the point, Rita. I'm not getting sentimental about the fate of elves and I know what war is. I know how wars are won, too. They're won by soldiers who fight for their countries and homes with conviction and sacrifice. Not by soldiers like her, by mercenaries fighting for money who are unable and unwilling to sacrifice themselves. They don't even know what sacrifice is. And if they do, they despise it.'

'To hell with her, her dedication and her contempt. What does it matter to us? Ciri, throw something decent on, pop upstairs and fetch us another carafe. I feel like getting drunk today.'

Tissaia de Vries sighed, shaking her head. It didn't escape Margarita's attention.

'Fortunately,' she giggled, 'we aren't at school any longer, mistress dear. We can do what we want now.'

'Even in the presence of a future novice?' asked Tissaia scathingly. 'When I was rectoress at Aretuza—'

'We remember, we remember,' interrupted Yennefer with a smile, 'and even if we'd prefer to forget, we never will. Go and fetch that carafe, Ciri.'

Upstairs, waiting for the carafe, Ciri witnessed the officer depart with her squad of four soldiers. She watched their posture, expressions, clothing and arms in fascination and admiration. Right then Rayla, the captain with the black plait, was arguing with the innkeeper.

'I'm not going to wait until daybreak! And I couldn't give a damn if the gates are locked. I want to leave immediately. I know the inn has its own postern in the stables. I order it to be opened!'

'But the regulations—'

'I don't give a damn about the regulations! I'm carrying out the orders of Arch-Mistress de Vries!'

'All right, all right, captain. Don't shout. I'll open up ...'

The postern, it turned out, was in a narrow, securely gated passageway, leading straight beyond the city walls. Before Ciri took the carafe from the servant's hands, she saw the postern being opened and Rayla and her unit riding out, into the night.

Ciri was deep in thought.

'Oh, at last,' said Margarita cheerfully, though it was unclear whether she was referring to the sight of Ciri or the carafe she was carrying. Ciri put the carafe on the table – very clearly wrongly, because Tissaia de Vries repositioned it at once. When Yennefer poured, she spoiled the entire arrangement too, and Tissaia had to put it right again. Imagining Tissaia as a teacher filled Ciri with dread.

Yennefer and Margarita returned to their interrupted conversation, not sparing the contents of the carafe. Ciri realised it wouldn't be long before she would have to go and get a fresh one. She pondered, listening to the enchantresses' discussion.

'No, Yenna.' Margarita shook her head. 'You aren't up to speed, I see. I've dumped Lars. That's history. Elaine deireadh, as the elves would say.'

'And that's why you want to get drunk?'

'That's one of the reasons,' confirmed Margarita Laux-Antille. 'I'm sad. I can't hide it. I was with him for four years, after all. But I had to dump him. It was hopeless ...'

'Particularly,' snorted Tissaia de Vries, staring at the golden wine as she swilled it around her cup, 'since Lars was married.'

'I consider that of no importance,' said the enchantress, shrugging. 'All the attractive men of a certain age and who interest me are married. I can't help that. Lars loved me and, I would add, loved me for quite some time ... Ah, what can I say? He wanted too much. He jeopardised my freedom, and the thought of monogamy makes me sick. And after all, I was only following your example, Yenna. Do you remember that conversation in Vengerberg? When you decided to break up with that witcher of yours? I advised you then to think twice. I told you, you can't find love in the street. But you were right. Love is love, and life is life. Love passes ...'

'Don't listen to her, Yennefer,' said Tissaia coldly. 'She's bitter and full of regrets. Do you know why she's not going to the banquet at Aretuza? Because she's ashamed to show up alone, without the man she's been involved with for four years. The man people envied her for. Who she lost because she was unable to value his love.'

'Perhaps we could talk about something else,' suggested Yennefer in an apparently carefree but slightly altered voice. 'Ciri, pour us some wine. Oh hell, that carafe's small. Be so kind as to bring us another.'

'Bring two,' laughed Margarita, 'and as a reward you'll get a sip and be able to sit with us; you won't have to strain your ears from a distance. Your education can begin here, right now, before you join me at Aretuza.'

'Education!' Tissaia raised her eyes to the ceiling. 'By the gods!'

'Oh, do be quiet, beloved mistress,' said Margarita, slapping a hand against her wet thigh, pretending to be angry. 'I'm the rectoress of the school now! You didn't manage to flunk me during the final exams!'

'I regret that.'

'I do, too! Just imagine, I'd have a private practice now, like Yenna. I wouldn't have to sweat with novices. I wouldn't have to wipe the noses of the blubbering ones or lock horns with the cheeky ones. Ciri, listen to me and learn. An enchantress always takes action. Wrongly or rightly; that is revealed later. But you should act, be brave, seize life by the scruff of the neck. Believe me, little one, you should only regret inactivity, indecisiveness, hesitation. You shouldn't regret actions or decisions, even if they occasionally end in sadness and regret. Look at that serious lady sitting there pulling faces and pedantically correcting everything in sight. That's Tissaia de Vries, arch-mistress, who has educated dozens of enchantresses. Teaching them how to act. Teaching them that indecision—'

'Enough, Rita.'

'Tissaia's right,' said Yennefer, still staring into the corner of the bathhouse. 'Stop. I know you're feeling low because of Lars, but don't moralise. The girl still has time for that kind of learning. And she won't receive it in school. Ciri, go and get another carafe.'

Ciri stood up. She was completely dressed.

And her mind was utterly made up.

'What?' Yennefer shrieked. 'What do you mean she's gone?'

'She ordered me ...' mumbled the innkeeper, pale, with his back pressed against the wall. 'She ordered me to saddle a horse ...'

'And you obeyed her? Rather than ask us?'

'Madam! How was I to know? I was sure she was leaving on your orders ... It never once occurred to me—'

'You damned fool!'

'Take it easy, Yennefer,' said Tissaia, pressing a hand against her forehead. 'Don't succumb to your emotions. It's night. They won't let her through the gate.'

'She ordered the postern opened ...' whispered the innkeeper.

'And was it?'

'Because of the conclave, madam,' said the innkeeper, lowering his eyes, 'the city is full of sorcerers ... People are afraid. No one dares to get in their way ... How could I refuse her? She spoke just like you do, madam, in exactly the same tone, and she looked the same way ... No one even dared to look her in the eye, never mind ask a question ... She was like you ... The spitting image ... She even ordered a quill and ink and wrote a letter.'

'Hand it over!'

Tissaia de Vries was quicker, and read aloud:

Madam Yennefer,

   Forgive me. I'm riding to Hirundum because I want to see Geralt. I want to see him before I start school. Forgive my disobedience, but I must. I know you'll punish me, but I don't want to regret my indecision and hesitation. If I'm to have regrets, let them be for deeds and actions. I'm an enchantress. I seize life by the scruff of the neck. I'll return when I can.

Ciri

'Is that all?'
'There's also a postscript.'

Tell Madam Rita she won't have to wipe my nose at school.

Margarita Laux-Antille shook her head in disbelief as Yennefer cursed. The innkeeper flushed and opened his mouth. He'd heard many curses in his life, but never that one.

The wind blew from the land towards the sea. Waves of cloud drifted over the moon, suspended over the forest. The road to Hirundum was plunged into darkness making galloping too dangerous. Ciri slowed to a trot, but she didn't consider slowing to a walk. She was in a hurry.

The growling of an approaching storm could be heard in the distance, and from time to time the horizon was lit up by a flash of lightning, revealing the toothed saw of treetops against the dusk.

She reined in her horse. She was at a junction; the road forked and both forks looked identical.

Why hadn't Fabio said anything about a fork in the road? *And anyway, I never get lost. After all, I always know which way to walk or ride ...*

So why don't I know which road to take now?

A huge shape glided silently past her head and Ciri felt her heart in her throat. The horse neighed, kicked and galloped off, choosing the right-hand fork. After a moment, she reined it in.

'It was just an owl,' she panted, trying to calm herself and the horse. 'Just an ordinary bird ... There's nothing to be afraid of ...'

The wind grew stronger, and the dark clouds completely covered the moon. But before her, in the vista of the road, in the hole gaping among the trees, it was light. She rode faster, the sand flying up from the horse's hooves.

A little later she had to stop. In front of her was a cliff and the sea, from which the familiar black cone of the island rose up. The lights of Garstang, Loxia and Aretuza could not be seen from where she was. She could only see the soaring, solitary tower which crowned Thanedd.

Tor Lara.

A blinding bolt of lightning connected the overcast sky to the pinnacle of the tower, and a moment later it thundered. Tor Lara glowered at her, its windows become red eyes. For a second it seemed a fire was burning inside the tower.

Tor Lara ... The Tower of Gulls ... *Why does its name fill me with such dread?*

The gale tossed the trees around. The branches whispered. Ciri screwed up her eyes, and dust and leaves struck her cheek. She turned the snorting, skittering horse back, having regained her orientation. The Isle of Thanedd faced north, so she must have ridden westwards. The sandy road lay in the dusk like a bright, white ribbon. She set off again at a gallop.

Ciri suddenly saw some riders in a flash of lightning. Dark, vague, moving shapes on both sides of the road. It thundered once more and she heard a cry.

'Gar'ean!'

Without thinking, she spurred her horse, reined it back, turned around and galloped away. Behind her there were shouts, whistles, neighing and the thudding of hooves.

'Gar'ean! Dh'oine!'

Galloping, the thud of hooves, the rush of the wind. Darkness, with the white trunks of roadside birches flashing by. Lightning. A thunderclap. And, in its light, two riders trying to block her way. One reached out, trying to grab her reins. He had a squirrel's tail attached to his hat. Ciri kicked her horse with her heels, clinging to its neck, the speed pulling her over to one side. Lightning. Behind her rose shouting, whistling and a clap of thunder.

'Spar'le, Yaevinn!'

92

Gallop, gallop! Quicker, horse! Lightning. Thunder. A fork in the road. *To the left! I never lose my way!* Another fork. *To the right! Gallop, horse! Faster, faster!*

The road went uphill, sand under the horse's hooves. The horse, even though it was being spurred on, slowed ...

She looked around at the top of the hill. Another lightning flash lit up the road. It was totally empty. She listened hard but only heard the wind whistling in the leaves. It thundered again.

There's no one here. Squirrels ... it's just a memory from Kaedwen. The Rose of Shaerrawedd ... I imagined it. There isn't a living soul here. No one's chasing me ...

The wind struck her. *The wind's blowing from the land*, she thought, *and I can feel it on my right cheek ...*

I'm lost.

Lightning. It lit up the surface of the sea against the black cone of the Isle of Thanedd. And Tor Lara. The Tower of Gulls. The tower that was drawing Ciri like a magnet ... *But I don't want to go to that tower. I'm riding to Hirundum. I must see Geralt.*

Lightning flashed again.

A black horse stood between her and the cliff. And on it sat a knight in a helmet adorned with the wings of a bird of prey. Its wings suddenly flapped, the bird took flight ...

Cintra!

Paralysing fear. Her hands gripping the reins tightly. Lightning. The black knight spurred his horse. He had a ghastly mask instead of a face. The wings flapped ...

The horse set off at a gallop without needing to be urged. Darkness illuminated by lightning. The forest was coming to an end. The splash and squelch of swamp under the horse's hooves. Behind her the swish of a raptor's wings. Closer and closer ... Closer ...

A furious gallop, her eyes watering from their speed. Lightning sliced the sky, and in its flash Ciri saw alders and willows on either side of the road. But they weren't trees. They were the servants of the Alder King. Servants of the black knight, who was galloping after her, with raptor's wings swishing on his helmet. Misshapen monsters on both sides of the road stretched their gnarled arms towards her; they laughed insanely, the black jaws of their hollows opening wide. Ciri flattened herself against the horse's neck. Branches whistled, lashed her and tore at her clothes. The distorted trunks creaked and the hollow jaws snapped, howling with scornful laughter ...

The Lion Cub of Cintra! Child of the Elder Blood!

The black knight was right behind her; Ciri felt his hand trying to seize her long hair. The horse, urged on by her cries, leapt forward, cleared an unseen obstacle with a powerful bound, crashed through reeds, stumbled ...

She reined it in, leaning back in the saddle, and turned the snorting horse back. She screamed wildly, furiously. She yanked her sword from its scabbard and whirled it above her head. *This is Cintra no longer! I'm no longer a child! I'm no longer helpless! I won't allow it ...*

'I forbid it! You will not touch me again! You will never touch me!'

Her horse landed in the water with a splash and a squelch, belly-deep. Ciri leaned forward, cried out, urged her mount on with her heels and struggled back onto the causeway again. *Ponds*, she thought. *Fabio talked about fishponds. It's Hirundum. I've made it. I never lose my way ...*

Lightning. Behind her the causeway, ahead of her a black wall of forest cutting into the sky like a saw blade. And no one there. Silence broken only by the howling of the gale. Somewhere on the marsh she could hear a frightened duck quacking.

Nobody. There is no one on the causeway. No one's following me. It was a phantom, a nightmare. Memories from Cintra. I only imagined it.

A small light in the distance. A lighthouse. Or a fire. *It's a farm. Hirundum. It's close now. Only one more effort ...*

Flashes of lightning. One. Another. Yet another. Each without a thunderclap. The wind suddenly dropped. The horse neighs, tosses its head and rears up.

Against the black sky appears a milky, quickly brightening ribbon, writhing like a serpent. The wind hits the willows once more, throwing up clouds of leaves and dry grass.

The distant lights vanish. They disappear and blur in the deluge of the million blue sparks which suddenly light up the entire swamp.

The horse snorts, whinnies and charges frantically across the causeway. Ciri struggles to remain in the saddle.

The vague, ghastly shapes of riders become visible in the ribbon sliding across the sky. As they come closer and closer, they can be seen ever more clearly. Buffalo horns and ragged crests sway on their helmets, and cadaverous masks show white beneath them. The riders sit on horses' skeletons, cloaked in ragged caparisons. A fierce gale howls among the willows, blades of lightning slash the black sky. The wind moans louder and louder. No, it's not the wind. It's ghostly singing.

The ghastly cavalcade turns and hurtles straight at her. The hooves of the spectral horses stir up the glow of the will o' the wisps suspended above the swamps. At the head of the cavalcade gallops the King of the Wild Hunt. A rusty helmet sways above his skull-like face, its gaping eye sockets burning with a livid flame. A ragged cloak flutters. A necklace, as empty as an old peapod, rattles against the rusty cuirass, a necklace which, it is said, once contained precious stones, which fell out during the frenzied chase across the heavens. And became stars ...

It isn't true! It doesn't exist! It's a nightmare, a phantom, an illusion! I'm only imagining this!

The King of the Wild Hunt spurs on his skeleton steed and erupts in wild, horrifying laughter.

O, Child of the Elder Blood! You belong to us! You are ours! Join our procession, join our hunt! We will race, race unto the very end, unto eternity, unto the very end of existence! You are ours, starry-eyed daughter of chaos! Join us; learn the joy of the hunt! You are ours. You are one of us! Your place is among us!

'No!' she cries. 'Be gone! You are corpses!'

The King of the Wild Hunt laughs, the rotten teeth snapping above his rusted gorget. The skull's eye sockets glitter lividly.

Yes, we are corpses. But you are death.

Ciri clung to the horse's neck. She didn't have to urge her horse on. Sensing the pursuing apparitions behind her, the steed thundered across the causeway at a breakneck gallop.

*

The halfling Bernie Hofmeier, a Hirundum farmer, lifted his shock of curly locks, listening to the sound of the distant thunder.

'It's a dangerous thing,' he said, 'a storm like this without any rain. Lightning will strike somewhere and then you've got a fire on your hands ...'

'A little rain would come in handy,' sighed Dandelion, tightening up the pegs of his lute, 'because you could cut the air with a knife ... My shirt's stuck to my back and the mosquitoes are biting ... But I reckon it'll blow over. The storm has been circling, circling, but for a while there's been lightning somewhere in the north. Over the sea, I think.'

'It's hitting Thanedd,' confirmed the halfling, 'the highest point in the area. That tower on the island, Tor Lara, attracts lightning like nobody's business. It looks like it's on fire during a decent storm. It's a wonder it doesn't fall apart ...'

'It's magic,' said the troubadour with conviction. 'Everything on Thanedd is magic, even the rock itself. And sorcerers aren't afraid of thunderbolts. What am I saying? Did you know, Bernie, that they can even catch thunderbolts?'

'Get away! You're lying, Dandelion.'

'May the lightning strike me—' the poet broke off, anxiously looking up at the sky. 'May a goose nip me if I'm lying. I'm telling you, Hofmeier, sorcerers catch thunderbolts. I've seen it with my own eyes. Old Gorazd, the one who was killed on Sodden Hill, once caught a thunderbolt in front of my very eyes. He took a long, thin piece of metal, he hooked one end of it onto the top of his tower, and the other—'

'You should put the other end in a bottle,' suddenly squeaked Hofmeier's son, who was hanging around on the veranda. He was a tiny little halfling with a thick mop of hair as curly as a ram's fleece. 'In a glass demijohn, like the ones Daddy makes wine in. The lightning whizzes down the wire into the demijohn—'

'Get inside, Franklin!' yelled the farmer. 'Time for bed, this minute! It'll be midnight soon and there's work to be done tomorrow! And just you wait till I catch you, spouting off about demijohns and wires. The strap'll be out for you! You won't be able to sit down for the next two Sundays! Petunia, get him out of here! And bring us more beer!'

'You've had quite enough,' said Petunia Hofmeier angrily, gathering up her son from the veranda. 'You've already put away a skinful.'

'Stop nagging. Just look out for the Witcher's coming. A guest ought to be offered hospitality.'

'When the Witcher arrives I'll bring some. For him.'

'Stingy cow,' muttered Hofmeier so that his wife didn't hear. 'All her kin, the Biberveldts from Knotweed Meadow, every last one of them is a tight-fisted, stingy, skinflint ... But the Witcher's taking his time. He went over to the ponds and disappeared. 'E's a strange one. Did you see how he looked at the girls, at Cinia and Tangerine, when they were playing in the yard of an evening? He had a strange look about him. And now ... I can't help feeling he went away to be by himself. And he took shelter with me because my farm's out of the way, far from the others. You know him best, Dandelion, you say ...'

'Do I know him?' said the poet, swatting a mosquito on his neck, plucking his lute and staring at the black outlines of willows by the pond. 'No, Bernie. I don't know him. I don't think anyone knows him. But something's happening to him, I can see it. Why did he come here, to Hirundum? To be nearer the Isle of Thanedd? And yesterday, when I suggested we both ride to Gors Velen, from where you can see Thanedd, he refused without a second thought. What's keeping him here? Did you give him some well-paid contracts?'

'Not a chance,' muttered the halfling. 'To be honest, I don't believe there was ever a monster here at all. That kid who drowned in the pond might have got cramp. But everyone started yelling that it was a drowner or a kikimora and we ought to call a witcher ... And they promised him such a paltry purse it's shameful. And what does he do? He's been roaming around the causeway for three nights; he sleeps during the day or sits saying nothing, like a straw man, watching the children and the house ... Strange. Peculiar, I'd say.'

'And you'd be right.'

Lightning flashed, lighting up the farmyard and the farm buildings. For a moment, the ruins of the elven palace at the end of the causeway flashed white. A few seconds later, a clap of thunder rolled over the ponds. A sudden wind got up, and the trees and reeds by the pond whispered and bent. The surface of the water rippled, went dull and then ruffled up the leaves of the water lilies.

'The storm seems to be coming towards us,' said the farmer, looking up at the sky. 'Perhaps the sorcerers used magic to drive it from the island. They say at least two hundred of them have turned up on Thanedd ... What do you think, Dandelion, what will they be debating on that island of theirs? Will any good come of it?'

'For us? I doubt it,' said the troubadour, strumming the lute strings with his thumb. 'Those conclaves usually mean a fashion show, lots of gossiping, and a good chance for backbiting and infighting. Arguments about whether to make magic more universal, or make it more elite. Quarrels between those who serve kings and those who prefer to bring pressure to bear on kings from afar ...'

'Ha,' said Bernie Hofmeier. 'Seems to me that during the conclave there'll be as much thunder and lightning on Thanedd as there is during a storm.'

'Perhaps. But of what interest is it to us?'

'To you, none,' said the halfling gloomily. 'Because all you do is pluck away at your lute and screech. You look at the world around and see only rhymes and notes. But just last Sunday some horsemen trampled my cabbages and turnips. Twice. The army are chasing the Squirrels, the Squirrels are evading the army and running from them, and they both use the same road through my cabbage patch ...'

'Do not grieve for the cabbage when the forest is burning,' recited the poet.

'You, Dandelion,' said Bernie Hofmeier, frowning at him. 'When you come out with stuff like that I don't know whether to cry, laugh or kick your arse. I kid you not! And I'm telling you, a wretched time has come. There are stakes and gibbets by the highways, corpses in the fields and by forest tracks. Gorblimey, the country must have looked like this in Falka's times. And how can anyone live here? During the day, the king's men come and threaten to put us in the stocks for helping the Squirrels; at night the elves show up, and just try turning them down! They poetically promise that we'll see the night sky glow red. They're so poetic you could throw up. But anyhow, with them both we're caught between two fires ...'

'And are you counting on the mages' conclave changing anything?'

'That I am. You said yourself that two factions are battling it out among the mages. It was sometimes thus, that the sorcerers held the kings back and put an end to wars and disturbances. After all, it was the sorcerers who made peace with Nilfgaard three years since. Mebbe this time too ...'

Bernie Hofmeier fell silent and listened carefully. Dandelion silenced the resonating strings with his hand.

The Witcher emerged from the gloom on the causeway. He walked slowly towards the house. Lightning flashed once more. By the time it thundered, the Witcher was already with them on the veranda.

'Well, Geralt?' asked Dandelion, by way of ending the awkward silence. 'Did you track the fiend down?'

'No. It isn't a night for tracking. It's a turbulent night. Uneasy ... I'm tired, Dandelion.'

'Well, sit down, relax.'

'You misunderstood me.'

'Indeed,' muttered the halfling, looking at the sky and listening. 'A turbulent night, something ill is hanging in the air ... The animals are restless in the barn ... And screams can be heard in that wind ...'

'The Wild Hunt,' said the Witcher softly. 'Close the shutters securely, Mr Hofmeier.'

'The Wild Hunt?' said Bernie, terrified. 'Spectres?'

'Never fear. It'll pass by high up. It always passes by high during the summer. But the children may wake, for the Hunt brings nightmares. Better close the shutters.'

'The Wild Hunt,' said Dandelion, glancing anxiously upwards, 'heralds war.'

'Poppycock. Superstitions.'

'Wait! A short time before the Nilfgaardian attack on Cintra—'

'Silence!' the Witcher gestured him to be quiet and sat up straight with a jerk, staring into the darkness.

'What the ... ?'

'Horsemen.'

'Hell,' hissed Hofmeier, springing up from the bench. 'At night it can only be Scoia'tael ...'

'A single horse,' the Witcher interrupted, picking his sword up from the bench. 'A single, real horse. The rest are the spectres of the Hunt ... Damn, it can't be ... in the summer?'

Dandelion had also leapt to his feet but was too ashamed to run away, because neither Geralt nor Bernie was preparing to flee. The Witcher drew his sword and ran towards the causeway, and the half-ling rushed after him without a second thought, armed with a pitch-fork. Lightning flashed once more, and a galloping horse came into view on the causeway. Behind the horse came something vague, an irregular cloud, a whirl, a phantom, woven from the gloom and glow. Something that caused panicky fear and a revolting, gut-wrenching dread.

The Witcher yelled, lifting his sword. The rider saw him, spurred the horse on and looked back. The Witcher yelled again. The thunder boomed.

There was a flash, but it wasn't lightning this time. Dandelion crouched by the bench and would have crawled under it had it not been too low. Bernie dropped the pitchfork. Petunia Hofmeier, who had run out of the house, shrieked.

A blinding flash materialised into a transparent sphere, and inside it loomed a shape, assuming contours and shapes at frightening speed. Dandelion recognised it at once. He knew those wild, black curls and the obsidian star on a velvet ribbon. What he didn't know and had never seen before was the face. It was a face of rage and fury, the face of the goddess of vengeance, destruction and death.

Yennefer raised a hand and screamed a spell. Spirals shot from her hands with a hiss, showering sparks, cutting the night sky and reflect-ing thousands of sparkles on the surface of the ponds. The spirals penetrated the cloud that was chasing the lone rider like lances. The cloud seethed, and it seemed to Dandelion that he could hear ghastly cries, that he could see the vague, nightmarish silhouettes of spectral horses. He only saw it for a split second, because the cloud suddenly contracted, clustered up into a ball and shot upwards into the sky, lengthening and dragging a tail behind it like a comet's as it sped away. Darkness fell, only lit by the quivering glare of the lamp being held by Petunia Hofmeier.

The rider came to a halt in the yard in front of the house, slithered down from the saddle, and took some staggering steps. Dandelion realised who it was immediately. He had never seen the slim, flaxen-haired girl before. But he knew her at once.

'Geralt . . .' said the girl softly. 'Madam Yennefer . . . I'm sorry . . . I had to. You know, I mean . . .'

'Ciri,' said the Witcher. Yennefer took a step towards the girl, but then stopped. She said nothing.

Who will the girl choose? wondered Dandelion. *Neither of them – the Witcher nor the enchantress – will take a step nor make a gesture. Which will she approach first? Him? Or her?*

Ciri did not walk to either of them. She was unable to decide. Instead of moving, she fainted.

The house was empty. The halfling and his entire family had left for work at daybreak. Ciri pretended to be asleep but she heard Geralt and Yennefer go out. She slipped out from the sheets, dressed quickly and stole silently out of the room, following them to the orchard.

Geralt and Yennefer turned to face the causeway between the ponds, which were white and yellow with water lilies. Ciri hid behind a ruined wall and watched them through a crack. She had imagined that Dandelion, the famous poet whose work she had read count-less times, was still asleep. But she was wrong. The poet Dandelion wasn't asleep. And he caught her in the act.

'Hey,' he said, coming up unexpectedly and chuckling. 'Is it polite to eavesdrop and spy on people? More discretion, little one. Let them be together for a while.'

Ciri blushed, but then immediately narrowed her lips.

'First of all, I'm not your little one,' she hissed haughtily. 'And second of all, I'm not really disturbing them, am I?'

Dandelion grew a little serious.

101

'I suppose not,' he said. 'It seems to me you might even be help-ing them.'

'How? In what way?'

'Don't kid me. That was very cunning yesterday, but you didn't fool me. You pretended to faint, didn't you?

'Yes, I did,' she muttered, turning her face away. 'Madam Yennefer realised but Geralt didn't . . .'

'They carried you into the house together. Their hands were touching. They sat by your bed almost until morning but they didn't say a word to each other. They've only decided to talk now. There, on the causeway, by the pond. And you've decided to eavesdrop on what they're saying . . . And watch them through a hole in the wall. Are you so desperate to know what they're doing there?'

'They aren't doing anything there,' said Ciri, blushing slightly. 'They're talking a little, that's all.'

'And you,' said Dandelion, sitting down on the grass under an apple tree and leaning back against the trunk, having first checked whether there were any ants or caterpillars on it. 'You'd like to know what they're talking about, wouldn't you?'

'Yes . . . No! And anyway . . . Anyway, I can't hear anything. They're too far away.'

'I'll tell you,' laughed the bard. 'If you want.'

'And how are you supposed to know?'

'Ha, ha. I, my dear Ciri, am a poet. Poets know everything about things like this. I'll tell you something else; poets know more about this sort of thing than the people involved do.'

'Of course you do!'

'I give you my word. The word of a poet.'

'Really? Well then . . . Tell me what they're talking about? Tell me what it all means!'

'Look through that hole again and tell me what they're doing.'

'Hmm . . .' Ciri bit her lower lip, then leaned over and put her eye closer to the hole. 'Madam Yennefer is standing by a willow . . . She's plucking leaves and playing with her star. She isn't saying anything and isn't even looking at Geralt . . . And Geralt's standing beside her. He's looking down and he's saying something. No, he isn't. Oh, he's pulling a face ... What a strange expression ...'

'Childishly simple,' said Dandelion, finding an apple in the grass, wiping it on his trousers and examining it critically. 'He's asking her to forgive him for his various foolish words and deeds. He's apologising to her for his impatience, for his lack of faith and hope, for his obstinacy, doggedness. For his sulking and posing; which are unworthy of a man. He's apologising to her for things he didn't understand and for things he hadn't wanted to understand—'

'That's the falsest lie!' said Ciri, straightening up and tossing the fringe away from her forehead with a sudden movement. 'You're making it all up!'

'He's apologising for things he's only now understood,' said Dandelion, staring at the sky, and he began to speak with the rhythm of a balladeer. 'For what he'd like to understand, but is afraid he won't have time for ... And for what he will never understand. He's apologising and asking for forgiveness ... Hmm, hmm ... Meaning, conscience, destiny? Everything's so bloody banal ...'

'That's not true!' Ciri stamped. 'Geralt isn't saying anything like that! He's not even speaking. I saw for myself. He's standing with her and saying nothing ...'

'That's the role of poetry, Ciri. To say what others cannot utter.'

'It's a stupid role. And you're making everything up!'

'That is also the role of poetry. Hey, I hear some raised voices coming from the pond. Have a quick look, and see what's happening there.'

'Geralt,' said Ciri, putting her eye once more to the hole in the wall, 'is standing with his head bowed. And Yennefer's yelling at him. She's screaming and waving her arms. Oh dear ... What can it mean?'

'It's childishly simple.' Dandelion stared at the clouds scudding across the sky. 'Now she's saying sorry to him.'

Thus do I take you, to have and to hold, for the most wondrous and terrible of times, for the best and the worst of times, by day and by night, in sickness and in health. For I love you with all my heart and swear to love you eternally, until death do us part.

Traditional marriage vows

We know little about love. Love is like a pear. A pear is sweet and has a distinct shape. Try to define the shape of a pear.

Dandelion, *Half a Century of Poetry*

CHAPTER THREE

Geralt had reason to suspect – and had long suspected – that sorcerers' banquets differed from the feasts of ordinary mortals. He never suspected, however, that the differences could be so great or so fundamental.

The offer of accompanying Yennefer to the banquet preceding the sorcerers' conclave surprised but did not dumbfound him, since it was not the first such proposal. Previously, when they lived together and things were good between them, Yennefer had wanted to attend assemblies and conclaves with him at her side. At that time, he steadfastly refused. He was convinced he would be treated by the sorcerers at best as a freak and a spectacle, and at worst as an intruder and a pariah. Yennefer scoffed at his fears, but had never insisted. Since in other situations she was capable of insisting until the house shook and windows shattered, that had confirmed Geralt's belief that his decision had been right.

This time he agreed. Without a second thought. The offer came after a long, frank and emotional conversation. After a conversation which had brought them closer again, consigned the old conflicts to the shadows and to oblivion, and melted the ice of resentment, pride and stubbornness. After their conversation on the causeway in Hirundum, Geralt would have agreed to any – absolutely any – proposition of Yennefer's. He would not even have declined had she suggested they walked into hell to drink a cup of boiling tar with some fiery demons.

And on top of it there was Ciri, without whom neither that conversation nor that meeting could have happened. Ciri, in whom – according to Codringher – some unknown sorcerer had taken an interest. Geralt expected his presence at the convocation to provoke that sorcerer and force his hand. But he didn't tell Yennefer a single word about it.

They rode straight from Hirundum to Thanedd: Geralt, Yennefer, Ciri and Dandelion. First they stopped at the immense palace complex of Loxia, at the south-eastern foot of the mountain. The palace was already teeming with delegates to the conclave and their companions but accommodation was immediately found for Yennefer. They spent the entire day in Loxia. Geralt whiled away the day talking to Ciri. Dandelion ran around collecting and spreading gossip, and the enchantress measured and chose clothes. When evening finally came, the Witcher and Yennefer joined the colourful procession heading towards Aretuza and the palace, where the banquet was due to take place. And now, in Aretuza, Geralt knew surprise and astonishment, even though he'd vowed to himself he wouldn't be surprised by anything and nothing would astonish him.

The palace's huge central hall had been constructed in the shape of a letter 'T'. The long side had narrow and extremely tall windows, reaching almost to the tops of the columns that supported the ceiling. The ceiling was so high it was difficult to make out the details of the frescoes decorating it, in particular the gender of the naked figures, which were their most common motif. The windows were of stained glass, which must have cost an absolute fortune, but in spite of that a draught could be felt distinctly in the hall. Geralt was initially surprised the candles didn't go out, but on closer inspection he understood why. The candelabras were magical, and possibly even illusory. In any case, they gave plenty of light, incomparably more than candles would have.

When they entered, a good hundred people were already there. The hall, the Witcher estimated, could have held at least three times as many, even if the tables had been arranged in a semicircle in the centre, as was customary. But there was no traditional semicircle. It appeared they would be banqueting standing up, doggedly wandering along walls adorned with tapestries, garlands and pennants, all waving in the draught. Rows of long tables had been arranged under the tapestries and garlands, and the tables were piled high with elaborate dishes served on even more elaborate table settings, among elaborate flower arrangements and extraordinary ice carvings. On closer examination, Geralt noted there was considerably more elaboration than food.

'There's no fare,' he stated in a glum voice, smoothing down the short, black, silver-braided, narrow-waisted tunic Yennefer had dressed him in. Tunics like that – the latest fashion – were called doublets. The Witcher had no idea where the name came from. And no desire to find out.

Yennefer didn't react. Geralt wasn't expecting her to, knowing well that the enchantress was not generally inclined to react to statements of that kind. But he didn't give up. He continued to complain. He simply felt like moaning.

'There's no music. It's draughty as hell. There's nowhere to sit down. Are we going to eat and drink standing up?'

The enchantress gave him a meaningful, violet glance.

'Indeed,' she said, surprisingly calmly. 'We shall be eating standing up. You should also know that stopping too long by the food table is considered an indiscretion.'

'I shall try to behave,' he muttered. 'Particularly since I observe there isn't much to stop by.'

'Drinking in an unrestrained way is also considered a breach of etiquette,' said Yennefer, continuing her instructions and paying absolutely no attention to his grizzling. 'Avoiding conversations is considered an inexcusable indiscretion—'

'And if that beanpole in those ridiculous pantaloons points me out to his two girlfriends,' he interrupted, 'is that considered a faux pas?'

'Yes. But a minor one.'

'What are we going to be doing, Yen?'

'Circulating around the hall, greeting people, paying them compliments, engaging in conversation … Stop tugging your doublet and flattening your hair.'

'You wouldn't let me wear a headband …'

'Your headband's pretentious. Well then, take my arm and let's go. Standing near the entrance is considered a faux pas.'

They wandered through the hall, which was gradually filling up with guests. Geralt was ravenously hungry but quickly realised Yennefer hadn't been joking. It became clear that the etiquette observed by mages did indeed demand that one eat and drink very little, and do it with a nonchalant air. To cap it all, every stop at the food table carried with it social obligations. Someone would notice you, express their joy

109

at the fact and then approach and offer their greetings, which were as effusive as they were disingenuous. After the compulsory air kisses or unpleasantly weak handshakes, after the insincere smiles and even less sincere, although well-concocted, compliments, followed a brief and tediously banal conversation about nothing.

The Witcher looked around eagerly, searching for familiar faces, mainly in the hope he wasn't the only person present who didn't belong to this magical fraternity. Yennefer had assured him he wouldn't be, but in spite of that he couldn't see anyone who wasn't a member of the Brotherhood, or at least he was unable to recognise anyone.

Pageboys carrying trays weaved among the guests, serving wine. Yennefer didn't drink at all. The Witcher wanted to get tight, but couldn't. Instead, he found his doublet was. Under the arms.

Skilfully steering Geralt with her arm, the enchantress pulled him away from the table and led him into the middle of the hall, to the very centre of general interest. His resistance counted for nothing. He realised what this was all about. It was quite simply a display.

Geralt knew what to expect, so with stoical calm he endured the glances of the enchantresses, brimming with insalubrious curiosity, and the enigmatic smirks of the sorcerers. Although Yennefer assured him that propriety and tact forbade the use of magic at this kind of event, he didn't believe the mages were capable of restraining themselves, particularly since Yennefer was provocatively thrusting him into the limelight. And he was right not to believe. He felt his medallion vibrating several times, and the pricking of magical impulses. Some sorcerers, or more precisely some enchantresses, brazenly tried to read his thoughts. He was prepared for that, knew what was happening, and knew how to respond. He looked at Yennefer walking alongside him, at white-and-black-and-diamond Yennefer, with her raven hair and violet eyes, and the sorcerers trying to sound him out became unsettled and disorientated; confronted with his blissful satisfaction, they were clearly losing their composure and poise. *Yes*, he answered in his thoughts, *you're not mistaken. There is only she, Yennefer, at my side, here and now, and only she matters. Here and now. And what she was long ago, where she was long ago and who she was with long ago doesn't have any, doesn't have the slightest, importance. Now she's with me, here, among you all. With me, with no one else. That's what I'm thinking right now, thinking only about her, thinking endlessly about her, smelling the scent of her perfume and the warmth of her body. And you can all choke on your envy.*

The enchantress squeezed his forearm firmly and moved closer to his side.

'Thank you,' she murmured, guiding him towards the tables once again. 'But without such excessive ostentation, if you don't mind.'

'Do you mages always take sincerity for ostentation? Is that why you don't believe in sincerity, even when you read it in someone's mind?'

'Yes. That *is* why.'

'But you still thank me?'

'Because I believe you,' she said, squeezing his arm even tighter and picking up a plate. 'Give me a little salmon, Witcher. And some crab.'

'These crabs are from Poviss. They were probably caught a month ago; and it's really hot right now. Aren't you worried ... ?'

'These crabs,' she interrupted, 'were still creeping along the seabed this morning. Teleportation is a wonderful invention.'

'Indeed,' he concurred. 'It ought to be made more widely available, don't you think?'

'We're working on it. Come on, give me some. I'm hungry.'

'I love you, Yen.'

'I said drop the ostentation ...' she broke off, tossed her head, drew some black curls away from her cheek and opened her violet eyes wide. 'Geralt! It's the first time you've ever said that!'

'It can't be. You're making fun of me.'

'No, no I'm not. You used only to think it, but today you said it.'

'Is there such a difference?'

'A huge one.'

'Yen ...'

'Don't talk with your mouth full. I love you too. Haven't I ever told you? Heavens, you'll choke! Lift your arms up and I'll thump you in the back. Take some deep breaths.'

'Yen ...'

'Keep breathing, it'll soon pass.'

'Yen!'

'Yes. I'm repaying sincerity with sincerity.'

'Are you feeling all right?'

'I was waiting,' she said, squeezing lemon on the salmon. 'It wouldn't have been proper to react to a declaration made as a thought. I was waiting for the words. I was able to reply, so I replied. I feel wonderful.'

'What's up?'

'I'll tell you later. Eat. This salmon is delicious, I swear on the Power, absolutely delicious.'

'May I kiss you? Right now, here, in front of everyone?'

'No.'

'Yennefer!' A dark-haired sorceress passing alongside freed her arm from the crook of her companion's elbow and came closer. 'So you made it? Oh, how divine! I haven't seen you for ages!'

'Sabrina!' said Yennefer, displaying such genuine joy that anyone apart from Geralt might have been deceived. 'Darling! How wonderful!'

The enchantresses embraced gingerly and kissed each other beside their ears and their diamond and onyx earrings. The two enchantresses' earrings, resembling miniature bunches of grapes, were identical; but the whiff of fierce hostility immediately floated in the air.

'Geralt, if I may. This is a school friend of mine, Sabrina Glevissig of Ard Carraigh.'

The Witcher bowed and kissed the raised hand. He had already observed that all enchantresses expected to be greeted by being kissed on the hand, a gesture which awarded them the same status as princesses, to put it mildly. Sabrina Glevissig raised her head, her earrings shaking and jingling. Gently, but ostentatiously and impudently.

'I've been so looking forward to meeting you, Geralt,' she said with a smile. Like all enchantresses, she didn't recognise any 'sirs', 'Your Excellencies' or other forms of address used among the nobility. 'You can't believe how delighted I am. You've finally stopped

112

hiding him from us, Yenna. Speaking frankly, I'm amazed you put it off for so long. You have absolutely nothing to be ashamed of.'

'I agree,' replied Yennefer nonchalantly, narrowing her eyes a little and ostentatiously tossing her hair back from her own earrings. 'Gorgeous blouse, Sabrina. Simply stunning. Isn't it, Geralt?'

The Witcher nodded and swallowed. Sabrina Glevissig's blouse, made of black chiffon, revealed absolutely everything there was to reveal, and there was plenty of it. Her crimson skirt, gathered in by a silver belt with a large rose-shaped buckle, was split up the side, in keeping with the latest fashion. Fashion demanded it be split half-way up the thigh, but Sabrina wore hers split to halfway up her hip. And a very nice hip at that.

'What's new in Kaedwen?' asked Yennefer, pretending not to see what Geralt was looking at. 'Is your King Henselt still wasting energy and resources chasing the Squirrels through the forests? Is he still thinking about a punitive expedition against the elves from Dol Blathann?'

'Let's give politics a rest,' smiled Sabrina. Her slightly too-long nose and predatory eyes made her resemble the classic image of a witch. 'Tomorrow, at the Council, we'll be politicking until it comes out of our ears. And we'll hear plenty of moralising, too. About the need for peaceful coexistence ... About friendship ... About the necessity to adopt a loyal position regarding the plans and ambitions of our kings ... What else shall we hear, Yennefer? What else are the Chapter and Vilgefortz preparing for us?'

'Let's give politics a rest.'

Sabrina Glevissig gave a silvery laugh, echoed by the gentle jingling of her earrings.

'Indeed. Let's wait until tomorrow. Tomorrow ... Everything will become clear tomorrow. Oh, politics, and those endless debates, what an awful effect they have on the complexion. Fortunately, I have an excellent cream. Believe me, darling, wrinkles disappear like morning mist ... Shall I give you the formula?'

'Thank you, darling, but I don't need it. Truly.'

'Oh, I know. I always envied your complexion at school. How many years is it now, by the gods?'

Yennefer pretended she was returning a greeting to someone passing alongside, while Sabrina smiled at the Witcher and joyously thrust out everything the black chiffon wasn't hiding. Geralt swallowed again, trying not to look too blatantly at her pink nipples, only too visible beneath the transparent material. He glanced timidly at Yennefer. The enchantress smiled, but he knew her too well. She was incandescent.

'Oh, forgive me,' said Yennefer suddenly. 'I can see Philippa over there; I just have to talk to her. Come with me, Geralt. Bye-bye, Sabrina.'

'Bye, Yenna,' said Sabrina Glevissig, looking the Witcher in the eyes. 'Congratulations again on your ... taste.'

'Thank you,' said Yennefer, her voice suspiciously cold. 'Thank you, darling.'

Philippa Eilhart was accompanied by Dijkstra. Geralt, who'd once had a fleeting contact with the Redanian spy, ought in principle to have been pleased; he had finally met someone he knew, who – like he – didn't belong to the fraternity. Yet he wasn't glad at all.

'How lovely to see you, Yenna,' said Philippa, giving Yennefer an air kiss. 'Greetings, Geralt. You both know Count Dijkstra, don't you?'

'Who doesn't?' said Yennefer, bowing her head and proffering her hand to Dijkstra. The spy kissed it with reverence. 'I'm delighted to see you again, Your Excellency.'

'It's a joy for me to see you again, Yennefer,' replied the chief of King Vizimir's secret service. 'Particularly in such agreeable company. Geralt, my respects come from the bottom of my heart ...'

Geralt, refraining from telling Dijkstra *his* respect came from the heart of his bottom, shook the proffered hand – or rather tried to. Its dimensions exceeded the norm which made made shaking it practically impossible.

The gigantic spy was dressed in a light beige doublet, unbuttoned informally. He clearly felt at ease in it.

'I noticed,' said Philippa, 'you talking to Sabrina.'

'That's right,' snorted Yennefer. 'Have you seen what she's wearing? You'd either have to have no taste or no shame to ... She's

114

bloody older than me by at least— Never mind. And as if she still had anything to show! The revolting cow!'

'Did she try to question you? Everyone knows she spies for Henselt of Kaedwen.'

'You don't say?' said Yennefer, faking astonishment, which was rightly considered an excellent joke.

'And you, Your Excellency, are you enjoying our celebration?' asked Yennefer, after Philippa and Dijkstra had stopped laughing.

'Extraordinarily,' said King Vizimir's spy, giving a courtly bow.

'If we presume,' said Philippa, smiling, 'that the Count is here on business, such an assurance is extremely complimentary. And, like every similar compliment, not very sincere. Only a moment ago, he confessed he'd prefer a nice, murky atmosphere, the stink of flaming brands and scorched meat on a spit. He also misses a traditional table swimming in spilt sauce and beer, which he could bang with his beer mug to the rhythm of a few filthy, drunken songs, and which he could gracefully slide under in the early hours, to fall asleep among hounds gnawing bones. And, just imagine, he remains deaf to my arguments extolling the superiority of our way of banqueting.'

'Indeed?' said the Witcher, looking at the spy more benignly. 'And what were those arguments, if I might ask?'

This time his question was clearly treated as an excellent joke, because both enchantresses began laughing at the same time.

'Oh, you men,' said Philippa. 'You don't understand anything. How can you show off your dress or your figure if you're hiding behind a table in the gloom and smoke?'

Geralt, unable to find the words, merely bowed. Yennefer squeezed his arm gently.

'Oh,' she said. 'I see Triss Merigold over there. I just have to exchange a few words with her ... Excuse me for abandoning you. Take care, Philippa. We will certainly find an opportunity for a chat today. Won't we, Your Excellency?'

'Undoubtedly,' said Dijkstra, smiling and bowing low. 'At your service, Yennefer. Your wish is my command.'

They went over to Triss, who was shimmering in shades of blue and pale green. On seeing them, Triss broke off her conversation

115

with two sorcerers, smiled radiantly and hugged Yennefer; the ritual of kissing the air near each other's ears was repeated. Geralt took the proffered hand, but decided to act contrary to the rules of etiquette; he embraced the chestnut-haired enchantress and kissed her on her soft cheek, as downy as a peach. Triss blushed faintly.

The sorcerers introduced themselves. One of them was Drithelm of Pont Vanis, the other his brother, Detmold. They were both in the service of King Esterad of Kovir. Both proved to be taciturn and both moved away at the first opportunity that presented itself.

'You were talking to Philippa and Dijkstra of Tretogor,' observed Triss, playing with a lapis-lazuli heart set in silver and diamonds, which hung around from her neck. 'You know who Dijkstra is, of course?'

'Yes, we do,' said Yennefer. 'Did he talk to you? Did he try to get anything out of you?'

'He tried,' said the enchantress, smiling knowingly and giggling. 'Quite subtly. But Philippa was doing a good job throwing him off his stride. And I thought they were on better terms.'

'They're on excellent terms,' Yennefer warned her gravely. 'Be careful, Triss. Don't breathe a word to him about – about you know who.'

'I know. I'll be careful. And by the way ...' Triss lowered her voice. 'How's she doing? Will I be able to see her?'

'If you finally decide to run classes at Aretuza,' smiled Yennefer, 'you'll be able to see her very often.'

'Ah,' said Triss, opening her eyes widely. 'I see. Is Ciri ... ?'

'Be quiet, Triss. We'll talk about it later. Tomorrow. After the Council.'

'Tomorrow?' said Triss, smiling strangely. Yennefer frowned, but before she had time to ask a question, a slight commotion suddenly broke out in the hall.

'They're here,' said Triss, clearing her throat. 'They've finally arrived.'

'Yes,' confirmed Yennefer, tearing her gaze from her friend's eyes. 'They're here. Geralt, at last you'll have a chance to meet the members of the Chapter and the High Council. If the opportunity presents itself I'll introduce you, but it won't hurt if you know who's who beforehand.'

The assembled sorcerers parted, bowing with respect at the personages entering the hall. The first was a middle-aged but vigorous man in extremely modest woollen clothing. At his side strode a tall, sharp-featured woman with dark, smoothly combed hair.

'That is Gerhart of Aelle, also known as Hen Gedymdeith, the oldest living sorcerer,' Yennefer informed Geralt in hushed tones. 'The woman walking beside him is Tissaia de Vries. She isn't much younger than Hen, but is not afraid of using elixirs to hide it.'

Behind the couple walked an attractive woman with very long, dark golden hair, and a grey-green dress decorated with lace, which rustled as she moved.

'Francesca Findabair, also called Enid an Gleanna, the Daisy of the Valleys. Don't goggle, Witcher. She is widely considered to be the most beautiful woman in the world.'

'Is she a member of the Chapter?' he whispered in astonishment. 'She looks very young. Is that also thanks to magical elixirs?'

'Not in her case. Francesca is a pure-blooded elf. Observe the man escorting her. He's Vilgefortz of Roggeveen and he really is young. But incredibly talented.'

In the case of sorcerers, as Geralt knew, the term 'young' covered any age up to and including a hundred years. Vilgefortz looked thirty-five. He was tall and well-built, wore a short jerkin of a knightly cut – but without a coat of arms, naturally. He was also fiendishly handsome. It made a great impression, even considering that Francesca Findabair was flowing gracefully along at his side, with her huge, doe eyes and breathless beauty.

'That short man walking alongside Vilgefortz is Artaud Terranova,' explained Triss Merigold. 'Those five constitute the Chapter—'

'And that girl with a strange face, walking behind Vilgefortz?'

'That's his assistant, Lydia van Bredevoort,' said Yennefer coldly. 'A meaningless individual, but looking her directly in the face is considered a serious faux pas. Take note of those three men bringing up the rear; they're all members of the Council. Fercart of Cidaris, Radcliffe of Oxenfurt and Carduin of Lan Exeter.'

117

'Is that the whole Council? In its entirety? I thought there were more of them.'

'The Chapter numbers five, and there are another five in the Council. Philippa Eilhart is another Council member.'

'The numbers still don't add up,' he said, shaking his head. Triss giggled.

'Haven't you told him? Do you really not know, Geralt?'

'Know what, exactly?'

'That Yennefer's also a member of the Council. Ever since the Battle of Sodden. Haven't you boasted about it to him yet, darling?'

'No, darling,' said the enchantress, looking her friend straight in the eyes. 'For one thing, I don't like to boast. For another, there's been no time. I haven't seen Geralt for ages, and we have a lot of catching up to do. There's already a long list. We're going through it point by point.'

'I see,' said Triss hesitantly. 'Hmm ... After such a long time I understand. You must have lots to talk about ...'

'Talking,' smiled Yennefer suggestively, giving the Witcher another smouldering glance, 'is way down the list. Right at the very bottom, Triss.'

The chestnut-haired enchantress was clearly discomfited and blushed faintly.

'I see,' she said, playing in embarrassment with her lapis-lazuli heart.

'I'm so glad you do. Geralt, bring us some wine. No, not from that page. From that one, over there.'

He complied, sensing at once a note of compulsion in her voice. As he took the goblets from the tray the page was carrying, he discreetly observed the two enchantresses. Yennefer was speaking quickly and quietly, while Triss Merigold was listening intently, with her head down. When he returned, Triss had gone. Yennefer didn't show any interest in the wine, so he placed the two unwanted goblets on a table.

'Sure you didn't go a bit too far?' he asked coldly. Yennefer's eyes flared violet.

'Don't try to make a fool out of me. Did you think I don't know about you and her?'

'If that's what you—'

'That's precisely what,' she said, cutting him off. 'Don't make stupid faces, and refrain from comments. And above all, don't try to lie to me. I've known Triss longer than I've known you. We like each other. We understand each other wonderfully and will always do so, irrespective of various minor ... incidents. Just then it seemed to me she had some doubts. So I put her right, and that's that. Let's not discuss it any further.'

He didn't intend to. Yennefer pulled her curls back from her cheek.

'Now I shall leave you for a moment; I must talk to Tissaia and Francesca. Have some more food, because your stomach's rumbling. And be vigilant. Several people are sure to accost you. Don't let them walk all over you and don't tarnish my reputation.'

'You can be sure of that.'

'Geralt?'

'Yes.'

'A short while ago you expressed a desire to kiss me here, in front of everyone. Do you still hold to that?'

'I do.'

'Just try not to smudge my lipstick.'

He glanced at the assembly out of the corner of his eye. They were watching the kiss, but not intrusively. Philippa Eilhart, standing nearby, with a group of young sorcerers, winked at him and feigned applause.

Yennefer pulled her mouth away from his and heaved a deep sigh.

'A trifling thing, but pleasing,' she purred. 'All right, I'm going. I'll be right back. And later, after the banquet ... Hmm ...'

'I beg your pardon?'

'Please don't eat anything containing garlic.'

After she had gone the Witcher abandoned convention, unfastened his doublet, drank both goblets of wine and tried to get down to some serious eating. Nothing came of it.

'Geralt.'

'Your Excellency.'

'Lay off the titles,' frowned Dijkstra. 'I'm no count. Vizimir ordered

119

me to introduce myself like that, so as not affront courtiers or sorcerers with my peasant origins. So, how's it going impressing people with your outfit and your figure? And pretending to have fun?'

'I don't have to pretend. I'm not here in a professional capacity.'

'That's interesting,' smiled the spy, 'but confirms the general opinion, that says you're special; one of a kind. Because everyone else is here in a professional capacity.'

'That's what I was afraid of,' said Geralt, also deeming it appropriate to smile. 'I guessed I'd be one of a kind. Meaning out of place.'

The spy inspected the nearby dishes and then picked up and devoured the large, green pod of a vegetable unfamiliar to Geralt.

'By the way,' he said, 'thank you for the Michelet brothers. Plenty of people in Redania sighed with relief when you hacked the four of them to death in the port in Oxenfurt. I laughed out loud when the university physician who was summoned to the investigation concluded – after examining the wounds – that someone had used a scythe blade mounted upright.'

Geralt didn't comment. Dijkstra put another pod into his mouth.

'It's a pity,' he continued, chewing, 'that after dispatching them you didn't report to the mayor. There was a bounty on them, dead or alive. A considerable one.'

'Too many problems with my tax return already,' said the Witcher, also deciding to sample a green pod, which turned out to taste like soapy celery. 'Besides, I had to get away quickly, because ... But I'm probably boring you, Dijkstra. You know everything, after all.'

'Not a bit of it,' smiled the spy. 'I really don't. Where would I learn such things from, anyway?'

'From the reports of, oh, I don't know, Philippa Eilhart.'

'Reports, tales, rumours. I have to listen to them; it's my job. But at the same time, my job forces me to sift every detail through a very fine sieve. Recently, just imagine, I heard that someone hacked the infamous Professor and his two comrades to death. It happened outside an inn in Anchor. The person who did it was also in too much of a hurry to collect the bounty.'

Geralt shrugged.

'Rumours. Sift them through a fine sieve and you'll see what remains.'

'I don't have to. I know what will remain. Most often, it's a deliberate attempt at disinformation. Ah, and while we're on the subject of disinformation, how is little Cirilla doing? Poor, sickly little girl, so prone to diphtheria? She's healthy, I trust?'

'Drop it, Dijkstra,' replied the Witcher coldly, looking the spy straight in the eye. 'I know you're here in a professional capacity, but don't be overzealous.'

The spy chortled and two passing sorceresses looked at him in astonishment. And with interest.

'King Vizimir,' said Dijkstra, his chuckle over, 'pays me an extra bonus for every mystery I solve. My zealousness guarantees me a decent living. You can laugh, but I have a wife and children.'

'I don't see anything funny about it. Work to support your wife and children, but not at my expense, if you don't mind. It seems to me there's no shortage of mysteries and riddles in this hall.'

'Quite. The whole of Aretuza is one great riddle. You must have noticed. Something's in the air, Geralt. And, for the sake of clarity, I don't mean the candelabras.'

'I don't get it.'

'I believe you. Because I don't get it either. And I'd like very much to. Wouldn't you? Oh, I beg your pardon. Because you're sure to know it all too. From the reports of, oh, I don't know, the enchanting Yennefer of Vengerberg. But just think, there were times when I would pick up scraps of information from the enchanting Yennefer too. Ah, where are the snows of yesteryear?'

'I really don't know what you mean, Dijkstra. Could you express your thoughts more lucidly? Do your best. On condition you're not doing it out of professional considerations. Forgive me, but I have no intention of earning you an extra bonus.'

'Think I'm trying to trick you dishonourably?' scowled the spy. 'To get information out of you using deceit? You're being unfair, Geralt. It simply interests me whether you see the same patterns in this hall that are so obvious to me.'

'So what's so obvious to you?'

121

'Doesn't the total absence of crowned heads – which is blatantly apparent at this gathering – surprise you?'

'It doesn't surprise me in the least,' said Geralt, finally managing to stab a marinated olive with a toothpick. 'I'm sure kings prefer traditional banquets, seated at a table, which one can gracefully slide beneath in the early hours. And what's more . . .'

'What is more?' asked Dijkstra, putting four olives – which he had unceremoniously extracted from the bowl with his fingers – into his mouth.

'What is more,' said the Witcher, looking at the small crowd passing through the hall, 'the kings didn't bother to make the effort. They sent an army of spies in their stead. Both members of the fraternity and not. Probably in order to find out what's really in the air here.'

Dijkstra spat the olive stones out onto the table, took a long fork from the silver tray and used it to rummage around in a deep, crystal bowl.

'And Vilgefortz,' he said, continuing to rummage, 'made sure no spy was absent. He has all the royal spies in one pot. Why would Vilgefortz want all the royal spies in one pot, Witcher?'

'I have no idea. And it interests me little. I told you I'm here as a private individual. I'm – how shall I put it? – outside the pot.'

King Vizimir's spy fished a small octopus out of the bowl and examined it in disgust.

'People eat these?' he said, shaking his head in fake sympathy, and then turning towards Geralt.

'Listen to me carefully, Witcher,' he said quietly. 'Your convictions about privacy, your certainty that you don't care about anything and that you couldn't possibly care about anything . . . they perturb me and that inclines me to take a gamble. Do you like a flutter?'

'Be precise, please.'

'I suggest a wager,' said Dijkstra, raising the fork with the octopus impaled on it. 'I venture that in the course of the next hour, Vilgefortz will ask you to join him in a long conversation. I venture that during this conversation he will prove to you that you aren't here as a private individual and you *are* in his pot. Should I be wrong, I'll eat this shit in front of you, tentacles and all. Do you accept the wager?'

'What will I have to eat, should I lose?'

'Nothing,' said Dijkstra and quickly looked around. 'But should you lose, you'll report the entire content of your conversation with Vilgefortz to me.'

The Witcher was silent for a while, and looked calmly at the spy.

'Farewell, Your Excellency,' he said at last. 'Thank you for the chat. It was educational.'

Dijkstra was somewhat annoyed.

'Would you say so—?'

'Yes, I would,' interrupted Geralt. 'Farewell.'

The spy shrugged his shoulders, threw the octopus and fork into the bowl, turned on his heel and walked away. Geralt didn't watch him go. He slowly moved to the next table, led by the desire to get his hands on some of the huge pink and white prawns piled up on a silver platter among lettuce leaves and quarters of lime. He had an appetite for them but, still feeling curious eyes on him, wanted to consume the crustaceans in a dignified manner, without losing face. He approached extravagantly slowly, picking at delicacies from the other dishes cautiously and with dignity.

Sabrina Glevissig stood at the next table, deep in conversation with a flame-haired enchantress he didn't know. The redhead wore a white skirt and a blouse of white georgette. The blouse, like that of Sabrina's, was totally transparent, but had several strategically placed appliqués and embroideries. The appliqués – noticed Geralt – had an interesting quality: they became opaque and then transparent by turns.

The enchantresses were talking, sustaining themselves with slices of langouste. They were conversing quietly in the Elder Speech. And although they weren't looking at him, they were clearly talking about him. He discreetly focused his sensitive witcher hearing, pretending to be utterly absorbed by the prawns.

'... with Yennefer?' enquired the redhead, playing with a pearl necklace, coiled around her neck like a dog's collar. 'Are you serious, Sabrina?'

'Absolutely,' answered Sabrina Glevissig. 'You won't believe it, but it's been going on for several years. And I'm surprised indeed he can stand that vile toad.'

'Why be surprised? She's put a spell on him. She has him under a charm. Think I've never done that?'

'But he's a witcher! They can't be bewitched. Not for so long, at any rate.'

'It must be love then,' sighed the redhead. 'And love is blind.'

'He's blind, more like,' said Sabrina, grimacing. 'Would you believe, Marti, that she dared to introduce me to him as an old school friend? Bloody hell, she's older than me by ... Oh, never mind. I tell you, she's hellishly jealous about that Witcher. Little Merigold only smiled at him and that hag bawled her out and sent her packing in no uncertain terms. And right now ... Take a look. She's standing there, talking to Francesca, without ever taking her eyes off her Witcher.'

'She's afraid,' giggled the redhead, 'that we'll have our way with him, even if only for tonight. Are you up for it, Sabrina? Shall we try? He's a fit lad, not like those conceited weaklings of ours with all their complexes and pretensions ...'

'Don't talk so loud, Marti,' hissed Sabrina. 'Don't look at him and don't grin. Yennefer's watching us too. And stay classy. Do you really want to seduce him? That would be in bad taste.'

'Hmm, you're right,' agreed Marti after a moment's thought. 'But what if he suddenly came over and suggested it himself?'

'In that case,' said Sabrina Glevissig, glancing at the Witcher with a predatory, coal-black eye. 'I'd give it to him without a second thought, even lying on a rock.'

'I'd even do it lying on a hedgehog,' sniggered Marti.

The Witcher, staring at the tablecloth, hid his foolish expression behind a prawn and a lettuce leaf, extremely pleased to have the mutation of his blood vessels which prevented him from blushing.

'Witcher Geralt?'

He swallowed the prawn and turned around. A sorcerer who looked familiar smiled faintly, touching the embroidered facings of his purple doublet.

'Dorregaray of Vole. But we are acquainted. We met ...'

'I remember. Excuse me; I didn't recognise you right away. Glad to ...'

The sorcerer smiled a little more broadly, taking two goblets from a tray being carried by a pageboy.

'I've been watching you for some time,' he said, handing one of the glasses to Geralt. 'You've told everyone Yennefer has introduced you to that you're enjoying yourself. Is that duplicity or a lack of criticism?'

'Courtesy.'

'Towards them?' said Dorregaray, indicating the banqueters with a sweeping gesture. 'Believe me, it's not worth the effort. They're a vain, envious and mendacious bunch; they don't appreciate your courtesy. Why, they treat it as sarcasm. With them, Witcher, you have to use their own methods. Be obsessive, arrogant and rude, and then at least you'll impress them. Will you drink a glass of wine with me?'

'The gnat's piss they serve here?' smiled Geralt pleasantly. 'With the greatest revulsion. Well, but if you like it ... then I'll force myself.'

Sabrina and Marti, listening intently from their table, snorted noisily. Dorregaray sized them both up with a contemptuous glance, turned, clinked his goblet against the Witcher's and smiled, this time genuinely.

'A point to you,' he admitted freely. 'You learn quickly. Where the hell did you acquire that wit, Witcher? On the road you insist on roaming around, hunting endangered species? Your good health. You may laugh, but you're one of the few people in this hall I feel like proposing such a toast to.'

'Indeed?' said Geralt, delicately slurping the wine and savouring the taste. 'In spite of the fact I make my living slaughtering endangered species?'

'Don't try to trip me up,' said the sorcerer, slapping him on the back. 'The banquet has only just begun. A few more people are sure to accost you, so ration out your scathing ripostes more sparingly. But as far as your profession is concerned ... You, Geralt, at least have enough dignity not to deck yourself out with trophies. But take a good look around. Go on, forget convention for a moment; they like people to stare at them.'

The Witcher obediently fixed his gaze on Sabrina Glevissig's breasts.

'Look,' said Dorregaray, seizing him by the sleeve and pointing at a sorceress walking past, tulle fluttering. 'Slippers made from the skin of the horned agama. Had you noticed?'

He nodded, ingenuously, since he'd only noticed what her transparent tulle blouse *wasn't* covering.

'Oh, if you please, rock cobra,' said the sorcerer, unerringly spotting another pair of slippers being paraded around the hall. The fashion, which had shortened hemlines to a span above the ankle, made his task easier. 'And over there . . . White iguana. Salamander. Wyvern. Spectacled caiman. Basilisk . . . Every one of those reptiles is an endangered species. Can't people bloody wear shoes of calfskin or pigskin?'

'Going on about leather, as usual, Dorregaray?' asked Philippa Eilhart, stopping beside them. 'And tanning and shoemaking? What vulgar, tasteless subjects.'

'People find a variety of things tasteless,' said the sorcerer grimacing contemptuously. 'Your dress has a beautiful trim, Philippa. Diamond ermine, if I'm not mistaken? Very tasteful. I'm sure you're aware this species was exterminated twenty years ago owing to its beautiful pelt?'

'Thirty,' corrected Philippa, stuffing the last of the prawns – which Geralt hadn't been quick enough to eat – into her mouth one after the other. 'I know, I know, the species would surely have come back to life, had I instructed my dressmaker to trim my dress with bunches of raw flax. I considered it. But the colours wouldn't have matched.'

'Let's go to that table over there,' suggested the Witcher easily. 'I saw a large bowl of black caviar there. And, since the shovelnose sturgeon has almost totally died out, we ought to hurry.'

'Eating caviar in your company? I've dreamed about that,' said Philippa, fluttering her eyelashes and smelling enticingly of cinnamon and muskroot as she slipped her arm into his. 'Let's not hang around. Will you join us, Dorregaray? You won't? Well, see you later and enjoy yourself.'

The sorcerer snapped his fingers and turned away. Sabrina Glevissig and her redheaded friend watched them walk away with looks more venomous than the endangered rock cobra's.

'Dorregaray,' murmured Philippa, unashamedly snuggling up to Geralt, 'spies for King Ethain of Cidaris. Be on your guard. That reptiles and skin talk of his is the prelude to being interrogated. And Sabrina Glevissig was listening closely –'

'– because she spies for Henselt of Kaedwen,' he finished. 'I know; you mentioned it. And that redhead, her friend—'

'She's no redhead – it's dyed. Haven't you got eyes? That's Marti Södergren.'

'Who does she spy for?'

'Marti?' Philippa laughed, her teeth flashing behind her vividly painted lips. 'Not for anyone. Marti isn't interested in politics.'

'Outrageous! I thought everyone here was a spy.'

'Many of them are,' said the enchantress, narrowing her eyes. 'But not everyone. Not Marti Södergren. Marti is a healer. And a nymphomaniac. Oh, damn, look! They've scoffed all the caviar! Down to the last egg; they've licked the plate clean! What are we going to do now?'

'Now,' smiled Geralt innocently, 'you'll announce that something's in the air. You'll say I have to reject neutrality and make a choice. You'll suggest a wager. I daren't even imagine what the prize might be. But I know I'll have to do something for you should I lose.'

Philippa Eilhart was quiet for a long time, her eyes fixed on his.

'I should have guessed,' she said quietly. 'Dijkstra couldn't restrain himself, could he? He made you an offer. And I warned him you detest spies.'

'I don't detest spies. I detest spying. And I detest contempt. Don't propose any wagers to me, Philippa. Of course I can sense something in the air. And it can hang there, for all I care. It doesn't affect or interest me.'

'You already told me that. In Oxenfurt.'

'I'm glad you haven't forgotten. You also recall the circumstances, I trust?'

'Very clearly. Back then I didn't reveal to you who Rience – or whatever his name is – was working for. I let him get away. Oh, you were so angry with me ...'

'To put it mildly.'

'Then the time has come for me to be exonerated. I'll give you Rience tomorrow. Don't interrupt and don't make faces. This isn't a wager à la Dijkstra. It's a promise, and I keep my promises. No, no questions, please. Wait until tomorrow. Now let's concentrate on caviar and trivial gossip.'

'There's no caviar.'

'One moment.'

She looked around quickly, waved a hand and mumbled a spell. The silver dish in the shape of a leaping fish immediately filled with the roe of the endangered shovelnose sturgeon. The Witcher smiled.

'Can one eat one's fill of an illusion?'

'No. But snobbish tastes can be pleasantly titillated by it. Have a try.'

'Hmm ... Indeed ... I'd say it's tastier than the real thing ...'

'And it's not at all fattening,' said the enchantress proudly, squeezing lemon juice over a heaped teaspoon of caviar. 'May I have another goblet of white wine?'

'At your service. Philippa?'

'Yes.'

'I'm told etiquette precludes the use of spells here. Wouldn't it be safer, then, to conjure up the illusion of the taste of caviar alone, without the caviar? Just the sensation? You'd surely be able to ...'

'Of course I would,' said Philippa Eilhart, looking at him through her crystal goblet. 'The construction of such a spell is easy as pie. But were you only to have the sensation of taste, you'd lose the pleasure the activity offers. The process, the accompanying ritual movements, the gestures, the conversation and eye contact which accompanies the process ... I'll entertain you with a witty comparison. Would you like that?'

'Please do. I'm looking forward to it.'

'I'd also be capable of conjuring the sensation of an orgasm.'

Before the Witcher had regained the power of speech, a short, slim sorceress with long, straight, straw-coloured hair came over to him. He recognised her at once – she was the one in the horned agama skin slippers and the green tulle top, which didn't even cover a minor detail like the small mole above her left breast.

'I'm sorry,' she said, 'but I have to interrupt your little flirting session, Philippa. Radcliffe and Detmold would like to talk to you for a moment. It's urgent.'

'Well, if it's like that, I'm coming. Bye, Geralt. We'll continue our flirting later!'

'Ah,' said the blonde, sizing him up. 'Geralt. The Witcher, the man Yennefer lost her head over? I've been watching you and wondering who you might be. It was tormenting me terribly.'

'I know that kind of torment,' he replied, smiling politely. 'I'm experiencing it right now.'

'Do excuse the gaffe. I'm Keira Metz. Oh, caviar!'

'Be careful. It's an illusion.'

'Bloody hell, you're right!' said the sorceress, dropping the spoon as though it was the tail of a black scorpion. 'Who was so bare-faced ... You? Can you create fourth-level illusions?'

'I,' he lied, continuing to smile, 'am a master of magic. I'm pretending to be a witcher to remain incognito. Do you think Yennefer would bother with an ordinary witcher?'

Keira Metz looked him straight in the eyes and scowled. She was wearing a medallion in the form of an ankh cross; silver and set with zircon.

'A drop of wine?' he suggested, trying to break the awkward silence. He was afraid his joke hadn't been well received.

'No thank you ... O fellow master,' said Keira icily. 'I don't drink. I can't. I plan to get pregnant tonight.'

'By whom?' asked the fake-redheaded friend of Sabrina Glevissig, who was dressed in a transparent, white, georgette blouse, decorated with cleverly positioned details, walking over to them. 'By whom?' she repeated, innocently fluttering her long eyelashes.

Keira turned and gave her an up-and-down glare, from her white iguana slippers to her pearl-encrusted tiara.

'What business is it of yours?'

'It isn't. Professional curiosity. Won't you introduce me to your companion, the famous Geralt of Rivia?'

'With great reluctance. But I know I won't be able to fob you off. Geralt, this is Marti Södergren, seductress. Her speciality is aphrodisiacs.'

'Must we talk shop? Oh, have you left me a little caviar? How kind of you.'

'Careful,' chorused Keira and the Witcher. 'It's an illusion.'

'So it is!' said Marti Södergren, leaning over and wrinkling her nose, after which she picked up a goblet and looked at the traces of crimson lipstick on it. 'Ah, Philippa Eilhart. I should have known. Who else would have dared to do something so brazen? That revolting snake. Did you know she spies for Vizimir of Redania?'

'And is a nymphomaniac?' risked the Witcher. Marti and Keira snorted in unison.

'Is that what you were counting on, fawning over her and flirting with her?' asked the seductress. 'If so, you ought to know someone's played a mean trick on you. Philippa lost her taste for men some time ago.'

'But perhaps you're really a woman?' asked Keira Metz, pouting her glistening lips. 'Perhaps you're only pretending to be a man, my fellow master of magic? To remain incognito? Do you know, Marti, he confessed a moment ago that he likes to pretend.'

'He likes to and knows how to,' smiled Marti spitefully. 'Right, Geralt? A while back I saw you pretending to be hard of hearing and unable to understand the Elder Speech.'

'He has endless vices,' said Yennefer coldly, walking over and imperiously linking arms with the Witcher. 'He has practically nothing but vices. You're wasting your time, ladies.'

'So it would seem,' agreed Marti Södergren, still smiling spitefully. 'Here's hoping you enjoy the party, then. Come on, Keira, let's have a goblet of something ... alcohol-free. Perhaps I'll also decide to have a try tonight.'

'Phew,' he exclaimed, once they'd gone. 'Right on time, Yen. Thank you.'

'You're thanking me? Not sincerely, I should imagine. There are precisely eleven women in this hall flashing their tits through transparent blouses. I leave you for just half an hour, and I catch you talking to two of them –'

Yennefer broke off and looked at the fish-shaped dish.

'– and eating illusions,' she finished. 'Oh, Geralt, Geralt. Come with me. I can introduce you to several people who are worth knowing.'

'Would one of them be Vilgefortz?'

'Interesting,' said the enchantress, squinting, 'that you should ask about him. Yes, Vilgefortz would like to meet you and talk to you. I warn you that the conversation may appear banal and frivolous, but don't let that deceive you. Vilgefortz is an expert, exceptionally intelligent old hand. I don't know what he wants from you, but stay vigilant.'

'I will,' he sighed. 'But I can't imagine your wily old fox is capable of surprising me. Not after what I've been through here. I've been mauled by spies and jumped by endangered reptiles and ermines. I've been fed non-existent caviar. Nymphomaniacs with no interest in men have questioned my manhood. I've been threatened with rape on a hedgehog, menaced by the prospect of pregnancy, and even of an orgasm, but one without any of the ritual movements. Ugh ...'

'Have you been drinking?'

'A little white wine from Cidaris. But there was probably an aphrodisiac in it ... Yen? Are we going back to Loxia after the conversation with Vilgefortz?'

'No, we aren't.'

'I beg your pardon?'

'I want to spend the night in Aretuza. With you. An aphrodisiac, you say? In the wine? How fascinating ...'

'Oh heavens, oh heavens,' sighed Yennefer, stretching and throwing a thigh over the Witcher's. 'Oh heavens, oh heavens. I haven't made love for so long ... For so very long.'

Geralt disentangled his fingers from her curls without responding. Firstly, her statement might have been a trap; he was afraid there might be a hook hidden in the bait. Secondly, he didn't want to wipe away with words the taste of her delight, which was still on his lips.

'I haven't made love to a man who declared his love to me and to whom I declared my love for a very long time,' she murmured a moment later, when it was clear the Witcher wasn't taking the bait. 'I forgot how wonderful it can be. Oh heavens, oh heavens.'

She stretched even more vigorously, reaching out with her arms and seizing the corners of the pillow in both hands, so that her breasts, now flooded in moonlight, took on curves that made themselves felt as a shudder in the Witcher's lower back. He hugged her, and they both lay still, spent, their ardour cooled.

Outside their chamber cicadas chirped and from far off quiet voices and laughter could also be heard, testimony that the banquet still wasn't over, in spite of the late hour.

'Geralt?'

'Yes, Yen?'

'Tell me.'

'About the conversation with Vilgefortz? Now? I'll tell you in the morning.'

'Right now, if you please.'

He looked at the writing desk in the corner of the chamber. On it were various books and other objects which the novice who had been temporarily rehoused to accommodate Yennefer in Loxia had been unable to take with her. A plump ragdoll in a ruffled dress, lovingly placed to lean up against the books and crumpled from frequent cuddling, was also there. She didn't take the doll, he thought, to avoid exposing herself to her friends' teasing in a Loxia dormitory. She didn't take her doll with her. And she probably couldn't fall asleep without it tonight.

The doll stared at him with button eyes. He looked away.

When Yennefer had introduced him to the Chapter, he'd observed the sorcerers' elite intently. Hen Gedymdeith only gave him a tired glance; it was apparent the banquet had already exhausted the old man. Artaud Terranova bowed with an ambiguous grimace, shifting his eyes from him to Yennefer, but immediately became serious when he realised others were watching him. The blue, elven eyes of Francesca Findabair were as inscrutable and hard as glass. The Daisy of the Valleys smiled when he was introduced to her. That smile, although incredibly beautiful, filled the Witcher with dread. During the introductions Tissaia de Vries, although apparently preoccupied with her sleeves and jewellery, which seemed to required endless straightening, smiled at him considerably less beautifully but with considerably more sincerity. And it was Tissaia who immediately struck up a conversation with him, referring to one of his noble witcher deeds which he, incidentally, could not recall and suspected she had invented.

And then Vilgefortz joined the conversation. Vilgefortz of Roggeveen, a sorcerer of imposing stature, with noble and beautiful features and a sincere and honest voice. Geralt knew he could expect anything from people who looked like that.

They spoke briefly, sensing plenty of anxious eyes on them. Yennefer looked at the Witcher. A young sorceress with friendly eyes, constantly trying to hide the bottom of her face behind a fan, was looking at Vilgefortz. They exchanged several conventional comments, after which Vilgefortz suggested they continue their conversation in private. It seemed to Geralt that Tissaia de Vries was the only person surprised by this proposition.

'Have you fallen asleep, Geralt?' muttered Yennefer, shaking him out of his musings. 'You're meant to be telling me about your conversation.'

The doll looked at him from the writing desk with its button gaze. He looked away again.

'As soon as we entered the cloister,' he began a moment later, 'that girl with the strange face ...'

'Lydia van Bredevoort. Vilgefortz's assistant.'

'Yes, that's right, you said. Just a meaningless person. So, when we entered the cloister that meaningless person stopped, looked at him and asked him something. Telepathically.'

'It wasn't an indiscretion. Lydia can't use her voice.'

'I guessed as much. Because Vilgefortz didn't answer her using telepathy. He replied ...'

'Yes, Lydia, that's a good idea,' answered Vilgefortz. 'Let's take a walk through the Gallery of Glory. You'll have the opportunity to take a look at the history of magic, Geralt of Rivia. I have no doubt you're familiar with it, but now you'll have the chance to become acquainted with its visual history, too. If you're a connoisseur of painting, please don't be horrified. Most of them are the work of the enthusiastic students of Aretuza. Lydia, be so good as to lighten the gloom around here a little.'

Lydia van Bredevoort passed her hand through the air, and it immediately became lighter in the corridor.

The first painting showed an ancient sailing craft being hurled around by whirlpools among reefs protruding from the surf. A man in white robes stood on the prow of the ship, his head encircled by a bright halo.

'The first landing,' guessed the Witcher.

'Indeed,' Vilgefortz confirmed. 'The Ship of Outcasts. Jan Bekker is bending the Power to his will. He calms the waves, proving that magic need not be evil or destructive but may save lives.'

'Did that event really take place?'

'I doubt it,' smiled the sorcerer. 'It's more likely that, during the first journey and landing, Bekker and the others were hanging over the side, vomiting bile. After the landing which, by a strange twist of fate, was successful, he was able to overcome the Power. Let's go on. Here we see Jan Bekker once more, forcing water to gush from the rock, in the very spot where the first settlement was established. And here, if you please, Bekker – surrounded by settlers – drives away the clouds and holds back a tempest to save the harvest.'

'And here? What event is shown in this painting?'

'The identification of the Chosen Ones. Bekker and Giambattista put the children of the settlers through a magical test as they arrived, in order to reveal Sources. The selected children were taken from their parents and brought to Mirthe, the first seat of the mages. Right now, you are looking at a historical moment. As you can see, all the children are terrified, and only that determined brown-haired girl is holding a hand out to Giambattista with a completely trusting smile. She became the famous Agnes of Glanville, the first woman to become an enchantress. The woman behind her is her mother. You can see sadness in her expression.'

'And this crowd scene?'

'The Novigradian Union. Bekker, Giambattista and Monck are

concluding a pact with rulers, priests and druids. A pact of non-aggression codifying the separation of magic and state. Dreadful kitsch. Let's go on. Here we see Geoffrey Monck setting off up the Pontar, which at that time was still called Aevon y Pont ar Gwennelen, the River of Alabaster Bridges. Monck sailed to Loc Muinne, to persuade the elves there to adopt a group of Source children, who were to be taught by elven sorcerers. It may interest you to know that among those children was a little boy, who came to be known as Gerhart of Aelle. You met him a moment ago. That little boy is now called Hen Gedymdeith.'

'This,' said the Witcher, looking at the sorcerer, 'is just calling out for a battle scene. After all, several years after Monck's successful expedition, the forces of Marshal Raupenneck of Tretogor carried out a pogrom in Loc Muinne and Est Haemlet, killing all of the elves, regardless of age or sex. And a war began, ending with the massacre at Shaerrawedd.'

'And your impressive knowledge of history,' Vilgefortz smiled once again, 'will remind you, however, that no sorcerer of any note took part in those wars. For which reason the subject did not inspire any of the novices to paint a work to commemorate it. Let's move on.'

'Very well. What event is shown in this canvas? Oh, I know. It's Raffard the White reconciling the feuding kings and putting an end to the Six Years' War. And here we have Raffard refusing to accept the crown. A beautiful, noble gesture.'

'Do you think so?' said Vilgefortz, tilting his head. 'Well, in any case, it was a gesture with the weight of precedent behind it. Raffard did, however, accept the position of first adviser so became the de facto ruler, since the king was an imbecile.'

'The Gallery of Glory ...' muttered the Witcher, walking up to the next painting. 'And what do we have here?'

'The historical moment when the first Chapter was installed and the Law enacted. From the left you see seated: Herbert Stammelford, Aurora Henson, Ivo Richert, Agnes of Glanville, Geoffrey Monck and Radmir of Tor Carnedd. This, if I'm to be honest, also cries out for a battle scene to complete it. For soon after, those who refused to acknowledge the Chapter and submit to the Law were wiped out in a brutal war. Raffard the White died, among others. But historical treatises remain silent about it, so as not to spoil a beautiful legend.'

'And here ... Hmm ... Yes, a novice probably painted this. And a very young one, at that ...'

'Undoubtedly. It's an allegory, after all. I'd call it an allegory of triumphant womanliness. Air, water, earth and fire. And four famous enchantresses, all masters at wielding the forces of those elements. Agnes of Glanville, Aurora Henson, Nina Fioravanti and Klara Larissa de Winter. Look at the next – and more effective – painting. Here you also see Klara Larissa opening the academy for girls here, in the building where we now stand. And those are por- traits of renowned Aretuza graduates. This shows a long history of triumphant womanhood and the growing feminisation of the pro- fession: Yanna of Murivel, Nora Wagner, her sister Augusta, Jada Glevissig, Leticia Charbonneau, Ilona Laux-Antille, Carla Demetia Crest, Yiolenta Suarez, April Wenhaver ... And the only surviving one: Tissaia de Vries ...'

They continued. The silk of Lydia van Bredevoort's dress whis- pered softly, and the whisper contained a menacing secret.

'And that?' Geralt stopped. 'What is this dreadful scene?'

'The martyrdom of the sorcerer Radmir, flayed alive during the Falka rebellion. In the background burns the town of Mirthe, which Falka had ordered to be consumed by flame.'

'For which act Falka herself was soon consumed by flame. At the stake.'

'That is a widely known fact; Temerian and Redanian children still play at burning Falka on Saovine's Eve. Let's go back, so that you may see the other side of the gallery ... Ah, I see you have a question.'

'I'm wondering about the chronology. I know, naturally, how elixirs of youth work, but the simultaneous appearance of living people and long dead ones in these paintings ...'

'You mean: you are astonished that you met Hen Gedymdeith and Tissaia de Vries at the banquet, but Bekker, Agnes of Glanville, Stammelford or Nina Fioravanti are not with us?'

'No. I know you're not immortal—'

'What is death?' interrupted Vilgefortz. 'To you?'

'The end.'

'The end of what?'

'Existence. It seems to me we've moved from art history to philosophy.'

'Nature doesn't know the concept of philosophy, Geralt of Rivia. The pathetic – ridiculous – attempts which people undertake to try to understand nature are typically termed philosophy. The results of such attempts are also considered philosophy. It's as though a cabbage tried to investigate the causes and effects of its existence, called the result of these reflections "an eternal and mysterious conflict between head and root", and considered rain an unfathomable causative power. We, sorcerers, don't waste time puzzling out what nature is. We know what it is; for we are nature ourselves. Do you understand?'

'I'm trying to, but please talk more slowly. Don't forget you're talking to a cabbage.'

'Have you ever wondered what happened when Bekker forced the water to gush from the rock? It's generally put very simply: Bekker tamed the Power. He forced the element to be obedient. He subdued nature; controlled it ... What is your relationship to women, Geralt?'

'I beg your pardon?'

Lydia van Bredevoort turned with a whisper of silk and froze in anticipation. Geralt saw she was holding a wrapped-up painting under one arm. He had no idea where the picture had come from, since Lydia had been empty-handed a moment before. The amulet around his neck vibrated faintly.

Vilgefortz smiled.

'I enquired,' he repeated, 'as to your views concerning the relationship between men and women.'

'Regarding what respect of that relationship?'

'Can obedience, in your opinion, be forced upon women? I'm talking about real women, of course, not just the female of the species. Can a real woman be controlled? Overcome? Made to surrender to your will? And if so, how? Answer me.'

*

137

The ragdoll didn't take her eyes off them. Yennefer looked away.

'Did you answer?'

'Yes, I did.'

With her left hand, the enchantress squeezed his elbow, and with her right squeezed his fingers, which were touching her breasts.

'How?'

'You surely know.'

'You've understood,' said Vilgefortz a moment later. 'And you've probably always understood. And thus you will also understand that if the concept of will and submission, of commands and obedience, and of male ruler and servant woman will perish and disappear, then unity will be achieved. A community merging into a single entity will be achieved. All will be as one. And if something like that were to occur, death would lose its meaning. Jan Bekker, who was water gushing from the rock, is present there in the banqueting hall. To say that Bekker died is like saying that water has died. Look at that painting.'

Geralt looked.

'It's unusually beautiful,' he said after a moment. At once he felt a slight vibration of his witcher's medallion.

'Lydia,' smiled Vilgefortz, 'thanks for your acknowledgement. And I congratulate you on your taste. The landscape depicts the meeting between Cregennan of Lod and Lara Dorren aep Shiadhal, the legendary lovers, torn apart and destroyed by the time of contempt. He was a sorcerer and she was an elf, one of the elite of Aen Saevherne, or the Knowing Ones. What might have been the beginning of reconciliation was transformed into tragedy.'

'I know that story. I always treated it as a fairytale. What really happened?'

'That,' said the sorcerer, becoming serious, 'nobody knows. I mean almost nobody. Lydia, hang up your picture over here. Geralt, have a look at another of Lydia's impressive works. It's a portrait of Lara Dorren aep Shiadhal taken from an ancient miniature.'

'Congratulations,' said the Witcher, bowing to Lydia van Bredevoort, finding it hard to keep his voice from quavering. 'It's a true masterpiece.'

138

His tone didn't quaver, even though Lara Dorren aep Shiadhal looked at him from the portrait with Ciri's eyes.

'What happened after that?'

'Lydia remained in the gallery. The two of us went out onto the terrace. And he enjoyed himself at my expense.'

'This way, Geralt, if you would. Step only on the dark slabs, please.'

The sea roared below, and the Isle of Thanedd stood in the white foam of the breakers. The waves broke against the walls of Loxia, directly beneath them. Loxia sparkled with lights, as did Aretuza. The stone block of Garstang towering above them was black and lifeless, however.

'Tomorrow,' said the sorcerer, following the Witcher's gaze, 'the members of the Chapter and the Council will don their traditional robes: the flowing black cloaks and pointed hats known to you from ancient prints. We will also arm ourselves with long wands and staffs, thus resembling the wizards and witches parents frighten children with. That is the tradition. We will go up to Garstang in the company of several other delegates. And there, in a specially prepared chamber, we will debate. The other delegates will await our return and our decisions in Aretuza.'

'Are the smaller meetings in Garstang, behind closed doors, also traditional?'

'But of course. It's a long tradition and one which has come about through practical considerations. Gatherings of mages are known to be tempestuous and have led to very frank exchanges of views. During one of them, ball lightning damaged Nina Fioravanti's coiffure and dress. Nina reinforced the walls of Garstang with an incredibly powerful aura and an anti-magic blockade, which took her a year to prepare. From that day on, no spells have worked in Garstang and the discussions have proceeded altogether more peacefully. Particularly when it is remembered to remove all bladed weapons from the delegates.'

'I see. And that solitary tower on the very summit above Garstang. What is it? Some kind of important building?'

139

'It is Tor Lara, the Tower of Gulls. A ruin. Is it important? It probably is.'

'Probably?'

The sorcerer leaned on the banisters.

'According to elvish tradition, Tor Lara is connected by a portal to the mysterious, still undiscovered Tor Zireael, the Tower of Swallows.'

'According to tradition? You haven't managed to find the portal? I don't believe you.'

'You are right not to. We discovered the portal, but it was necessary to block it. There were protests. Everyone was itching to conduct experiments; everyone wanted the fame of being the first to discover Tor Zireael, the mythical seat of elven mages and sages. But the portal is irreversibly warped and transports people chaotically. There were casualties, so it was blocked up. Let's go, Geralt, it's getting cold. Carefully. Only walk on the dark slabs.'

'Why only the dark ones?'

'These buildings are in ruins. Damp, erosion, strong winds, the salt air; they all have a disastrous effect on the walls. Repairs would cost too much, so we make use of illusion instead of workmen. Prestige, you understand.'

'It doesn't apply to everything.'

The sorcerer waved a hand and the terrace vanished. They were standing over a precipice, over an abyss bristling far below with the teeth of rocks jutting from the foam. They were standing on a narrow belt of dark slabs, stretched like a tightrope between the rocky ledge of Aretuza and the pillar holding up the terrace.

Geralt had difficulty keeping his balance. Had he been a man and not a witcher, he would have failed. But even he was rattled. His sudden movement could not have escaped the attention of the sorcerer, and his reaction must also have been visible. The wind rocked him on the narrow footbridge, and the abyss called to him with a sinister roaring of the waves.

'You're afraid of death,' noted Vilgefortz with a smile. 'You are afraid, after all.'

*

140

The ragdoll looked at them with button eyes.

'He tricked you,' murmured Yennefer, cuddling up to the Witcher. 'There was no danger. He's sure to have protected you and himself with a levitational field. He wouldn't have taken the risk ... What happened then?'

'We went to another wing of Aretuza. He led me to a large chamber, which was probably the office of one of the teachers, or even the rectoress. We sat by a table with an hourglass on it. The sand was trickling through it. I could smell the fragrance of Lydia's perfume and knew she had been in the chamber before us ...'

'And Vilgefortz?'

'He asked me a question.'

'Why didn't you become a sorcerer, Geralt? Weren't you ever attracted by the Art? Be honest.'

'I will. I was.'

'Why, then, didn't you follow the voice of that attraction?'

'I decided it would be wiser to follow the voice of good sense.'

'Meaning?'

'Years of practice in the witcher's trade have taught me not to bite off more than I can chew. Do you know, Vilgefortz, I once knew a dwarf who, as a child, dreamed of being an elf. What do you think; would he have become one had he followed the voice of attraction?'

'Is that supposed to be a comparison? A parallel? If so, it's utterly ill-judged. A dwarf could not become an elf. Not without having an elf for its mother.'

Geralt remained silent for a long time.

'I get it,' he finally said. 'I should have guessed. You've been having a root around in my life history. To what purpose, if you don't mind?'

'Perhaps,' smiled the sorcerer faintly. 'I'm dreaming of a painting in the Gallery of Glory. The two of us seated at a table and on a brass plaque the title: *Vilgefortz of Roggeveen entering into a pact with Geralt of Rivia.*'

'That would be an allegory,' said the Witcher, 'with the title: *Knowledge Triumphing Over Ignorance.* I'd prefer a more realistic painting, entitled: *In Which Vilgefortz Explains To Geralt What This Is All About.*'

Vilgefortz brought the tips of his fingers together in front of his mouth.

'Isn't it obvious?'

'No.'

'Have you forgotten? The painting I'm dreaming about hangs in the Gallery of Glory, where future generations, who know perfectly well what it's all about, what event is depicted in the picture, can look at it. On the canvas, Vilgefortz and Geralt are negotiating and concluding an agreement, as a result of which Geralt, following the voice – not of some kind of attraction or predilection, but a genuine vocation – finally joined the ranks of mages. This brings to an end his erstwhile and not particularly sensible existence, which has no future whatsoever.'

'Just think,' said the Witcher after a lengthy silence, 'that not so long ago I believed that nothing more could astonish me. Believe me, Vilgefortz, I'll remember this banquet and this pageant of incredible events for a long time. Worthy of a painting, indeed. The title would be: *Geralt Leaving the Isle of Thanedd, Shaking with Laughter.*'

'I don't understand,' said the sorcerer, leaning forward a little. 'You lost me with the floweriness of your discourse, so liberally sprinkled with sophisticated words.'

'The causes of the misunderstanding are clear to me. We differ too much to understand each other. You are a mighty sorcerer from the Chapter, who has achieved oneness with nature. I'm a wanderer, a witcher, a mutant, who travels the world and slays monsters for money –'

'That floweriness,' interrupted the sorcerer, 'has been supplanted by banality.'

'– We differ too greatly,' said Geralt, not allowing himself to be interrupted, 'and the minor fact that my mother was, by accident, a sorceress, is unable to erase that difference. But just out of curiosity: who was *your* mother?'

'I have no idea,' said Vilgefortz calmly. The Witcher immediately fell silent.

'Druids from the Kovir Circle,' said the sorcerer a moment later, 'found me in a gutter in Lan Exeter. They took me in and raised me. To be a druid, of course. Do you know what a druid is? It's a kind of mutant, a wanderer, who travels the world and bows to sacred oaks.'

The Witcher said nothing.

'And later,' continued Vilgefortz, 'my gifts revealed themselves during certain druidical rituals. Gifts which clearly and undeniably pointed to my origins. I was begat by two people, evidently unplanned, and at least one of them was a sorcerer.'

Geralt said nothing.

'The person who discovered my modest abilities was, of course, a sorcerer, whom I met by accident,' continued Vilgefortz calmly. 'He offered me a tremendous gift: the chance of an education and of self-improvement, with a view to joining the Brotherhood of Sorcerers.'

'And you,' said the Witcher softly, 'accepted the offer.'

'No,' said Vilgefortz, his voice becoming increasingly cold and unpleasant. 'I rejected it in a rude – even boorish – way. I unloaded all my anger on the old fool. I wanted him to feel guilty; he and his entire magical fraternity. Guilty, naturally, for the gutter in Lan Exeter; guilty that one or two detestable conjurers – bastards without hearts or human feelings – had thrown me into that gutter at birth, and not before, when I wouldn't have survived. The sorcerer, it goes without saying, didn't understand; wasn't concerned by what I told him. He shrugged and went on his way, by doing so branding himself and his fellows with the stigma of insensitive, arrogant, whoresons, worthy of the greatest contempt.'

Geralt said nothing.

'I'd had a gutful of druids,' said Vilgefortz. 'So I gave up my sacred oak groves and set off into the world. I did a variety of things. I'm still ashamed of some of them. I finally became a mercenary. My life after that unfolded, as you might imagine, predictably. Victorious soldier, defeated soldier, marauder, robber, rapist, murderer, and finally a fugitive fleeing the noose. I fled to the ends of the world. And there, at the end of the world, I met a woman. A sorceress.'

'Be careful,' whispered the Witcher, and his eyes narrowed. 'Be careful, Vilgefortz, that the similarities you're desperately searching for don't lead you too far.'

'The similarities are over,' said the sorcerer without lowering his gaze, 'since I couldn't cope with the feelings I felt for that woman. I couldn't understand her feelings, and she didn't try to help me with them. I left her. Because she was promiscuous, arrogant, spiteful, unfeeling and cold. Because it was impossible to dominate her, and her domination of me was humiliating. I left her because I knew she was only interested in me because my intelligence, personality and fascinating mystery obscured the fact that I wasn't a sorcerer, and it was usually only sorcerers she would honour with more than one night. I left her because... because she was like my mother. I suddenly understood that what I felt for her was not love at all, but a feeling which was considerably more complicated, more powerful but more difficult to classify: a mixture of fear, regret, fury, pangs of conscience and the need for expiation, a sense of guilt, loss, and hurt. A perverse need for suffering and atonement. What I felt for that woman was hate.'

Geralt remained silent. Vilgefortz was looking to one side.

'I left her,' he said after a while. 'And then I couldn't live with the emptiness which engulfed me. And I suddenly understood it wasn't the absence of a woman that causes that emptiness, but the lack of everything I had been feeling. It's a paradox, isn't it? I imagine I don't need to finish; you can guess what happened next. I became a sorcerer. Out of hatred. And only then did I understand how stupid I was. I mistook stars reflected in a pond at night for those in the sky.'

'As you rightly observed, the parallels between us aren't completely parallel,' murmured Geralt. 'In spite of appearances, we have little in common, Vilgefortz. What did you want to prove by telling me your story? That the road to wizardly excellence, although winding and difficult, is available to anyone? Even – excuse my parallel – to bastards or foundlings, wanderers or witchers—'

'No,' the sorcerer interrupted. 'I didn't mean to prove this road is open to all, because that's obvious and was proved long ago. Neither was there a need to prove that certain people simply have no other path.'

'And so,' smiled the Witcher, 'I have no choice? I have to enter

into a pact with you, a pact which should someday become the subject of a painting, and become a sorcerer? On account of genetics
alone? Give me a break. I know a little about the theory of heredity.
My father, as I discovered with no little difficulty, was a wanderer,
a churl, a troublemaker and a swashbuckler. My genes on the spear
side may be dominant over the genes on the distaff side. The fact
that I can swash a buckler pretty well seems to confirm that.'

'Indeed,' the sorcerer derisively smiled. 'The hourglass has almost
run its course, and I, Vilgefortz of Roggeveen, master of magic,
member of the Chapter, am still discoursing – not unpleasantly –
with a churl and swashbuckler, the son of a churl, a swashbuckler
and a wanderer. We are talking of matters which, as everyone knows,
are typical fireside debate subjects beloved of churlish swashbuck-
lers. Subjects like genetics, for example. How do you even know
that word, my swashbuckling friend? From the temple school in
Ellander, where they teach the pupils to read and write just twenty-
four runes? Whatever induced you to read books in which words
like that and other, similar ones can be found? Where did you perfect your rhetoric and eloquence? And why did you do it? To con-
verse with vampires? Oh, my genetic wanderer, upon whom Tissaia
de Vries deigned to smile. Oh, my Witcher, my swashbuckler, who
fascinates Philippa Eilhart so much her hands tremble. At the rec-
ollection of whom Triss Merigold blushes crimson. Not to mention
the effect you have on Yennefer of Vengerberg.'

'Perhaps it's as well you aren't going to mention her. Indeed, so
little sand remains in the hourglass I can almost count the grains.
Don't paint any more pictures, Vilgefortz. Tell me what this is all
about. Tell me using simple words. Imagine we're sitting by the
fire, two wanderers, roasting a piglet which we just stole, trying and
failing to get drunk on birch juice. Just a simple question. Answer it.
As one wanderer to another.'

'What is the simple question?'

'What kind of pact are you proposing? What agreement are we
to conclude? Why do you want me in your pot? In this cauldron,
which, it seems to me, is starting to boil? What else is hanging in the
air here – apart from candelabras?'

'Hmm,' the sorcerer pondered, or pretended to. 'The question is not simple, but I'll try to answer it. But not as a wanderer to a wanderer. I'll answer … as one hired swashbuckler to another, similar, swashbuckler.'

'Suits me.'

'Then listen, comrade swashbuckler. Quite a nasty scrap is brewing. A bloody fight for life or death, with no mercy shown. One side will triumph, and the other will be pecked apart by ravens. I put it to you, comrade: join the side with the better chance. Join us. Forget the others, spit on them with utter contempt, because they don't stand a chance. What's the point of perishing with them? No, no, comrade, don't scowl at me. I know what you want to say. You want to say you're neutral. That you don't give a shit about any of them, that you'll simply sit out the slaughter, hunkered down in Kaer Morhen, hidden in the mountains. That's a bad idea, comrade. Everything you love will be with us. If you don't join us, you'll lose everything. And then you'll be consumed by emptiness, nothingness and hatred. You'll be destroyed by the approaching time of contempt. So be sensible and join the right side when the time comes to choose. And it will come. Trust me.'

'It's incredible,' the Witcher smiled hideously, 'how much my neutrality outrages everybody. How it makes me subject to offers of pacts and agreements, offers of collaboration, lectures about the necessity to make choices and join the right side. Let's put an end to this conversation, Vilgefortz. You're wasting your time. I'm not an equal partner for you in this game. I can't see any chance of the two of us ending up in a painting in the Gallery of Glory. Particularly not in a battle scene.'

The sorcerer said nothing.

'Set out on your chessboard,' said Geralt, 'the kings, queens, elephants and rooks, and don't worry about me, because I mean as much on your chessboard as the dust on it. It's not my game. You say I'll have to choose? I say you're wrong. I won't choose. I'll respond to events. I'll adapt to what others choose. That's what I've always done.'

'You're a fatalist.'

146

'That's right. Although that's yet another word I ought not to know. I repeat: it's not my game.'

'Really?' said Vilgefortz, leaning across the table. 'In this game, Witcher, on the chessboard, stands a black horse. It's tied to you by bonds of destiny. For good or ill. You know who I'm talking about, don't you? And I'm sure you don't want to lose her, do you? Just know there's only one way not to lose her.'

The Witcher's eyes narrowed.

'What do you want from that child?'

'There's only one way for you to find out.'

'I'm warning you. I won't let anyone harm her—'

'There's only one way you could prevent that. I offered you that option, Geralt of Rivia. Think over my offer. You have the entire night. Think, as you look up at the sky. At the stars. And don't mistake them with their reflection in a pond. The sand has run out.'

'I'm afraid for Ciri, Yen.'

'There's no need.'

'But ...'

'Trust me,' she said, hugging him. 'Trust me, please. Don't worry about Vilgefortz. He's a wily old fox. He wanted to trick you, to provoke you. And he was partly successful. But it's not important. Ciri is in my care, and she'll be safe in Aretuza. She'll be able to develop her abilities here, and no one will interfere with that. No one. But forget about her becoming a witcher. She has other talents. And she's destined for other work. You can trust me.'

'I trust you.'

'That's significant progress. And don't worry about Vilgefortz. Tomorrow will explain many matters and solve many problems.'

Tomorrow, he thought. *She's hiding something from me. And I'm afraid to ask what. Codringher was right. I've got mixed up in a dreadful mess, but now there's no way out. I have to wait and see what tomorrow – which is supposed to explain everything – will bring. I have to trust her. I know something's going to happen. I'll wait. And adapt to the situation.*

He looked at the writing desk.

'Yen?'

147

'I'm here.'

'When you were a pupil at Aretuza ... When you slept in a chamber like this ... Did you have a doll you couldn't sleep without? Which you put on the writing desk during the day?'

'No,' said Yennefer, moving suddenly. 'I didn't have a doll of any kind. Don't ask me about that, Geralt. Please, don't ask me.'

'Aretuza,' he whispered, looking around. 'Aretuza on the Isle of Thanedd. It'll become her home. For so many years ... When she leaves here she'll be a mature woman ...'

'Stop that. Don't think about it and don't talk about it. Instead ...'

'What, Yen?'

'Love me.'

He embraced her. And touched her. And found her. Yennefer, in some astonishing way hard and soft at the same time, sighed loudly. The words they had uttered broke off, perished among the sighs and quickened breaths, ceased to have any meaning and were dissipated. So they remained silent, and focused on the search for one another, on the search for the truth. They searched for a long time, lovingly and very thoroughly, fearful of needless haste, recklessness and nonchalance. They searched vigorously, intensively and passionately, fearful of needless self-doubt and indecision. They searched cautiously, fearful of needless tactlessness.

They found one another, conquered their fear and, a moment later, found the truth, which exploded under their eyelids with a terrible, blinding clarity, tore apart the lips pursed in determination with a moan. Then time shuddered spasmodically and froze, everything vanished, and touch became the only functioning sense.

An eternity passed, reality returned and time shuddered once more and set off again, slowly, ponderously, like a great, fully laden cart. Geralt looked through the window. The moon was still hanging in the sky, although what had just happened ought in principle to have struck it down from the sky.

'Oh heavens, oh heavens,' said Yennefer much later, slowly wiping a tear from her cheek.

They lay still among the dishevelled sheets, among thrills, among steaming warmth and waning happiness and among silence, and all around whirled vague darkness, permeated by the scent of the night and the voices of cicadas. Geralt knew that, in moments like this, the enchantress's telepathic abilities were sharpened and very powerful, so he thought about beautiful matters and beautiful things. About things which would give her joy. About the exploding brightness of the sunrise. About fog suspended over a mountain lake at dawn. About crystal waterfalls, with salmon leaping up them, gleaming as though made of solid silver. About warm drops of rain hitting burdock leaves, heavy with dew.

He thought for her and Yennefer smiled, listening to his thoughts. The smile quivered on her cheek along with the crescent shadows of her eyelashes.

'A home?' asked Yennefer suddenly. 'What home? Do you have a home? You want to build a home? Oh ... I'm sorry. I shouldn't ...'

He was quiet. He was angry with himself. As he had been thinking for her, he had accidentally allowed her to read a thought about herself.

'A pretty dream,' said Yennefer, stroking him lightly on the shoulder. 'A home. A house built with your own hands, and you and I in that house. You would keep horses and sheep, and I would have a little garden, cook food and card wool, which we would take to market. With the pennies earned from selling the wool and various crops we would buy what we needed; let's say some copper cauldrons and an iron rake. Every now and then, Ciri would visit us with her husband and three children, and Triss Merigold would occasionally look in, to stay for a few days. We'd grow old together, beautifully and with dignity. And should I ever get bored, you would play for me in the evening on your homemade bagpipes. Playing the bagpipes – as everyone knows – is the best remedy for depression.'

The Witcher said nothing. The enchantress cleared her throat softly.

'I'm sorry,' she said, a moment later. He got up on an elbow, leaned across and kissed her. She moved suddenly, and hugged him. Wordlessly.

'Say something.'

'I wouldn't like to lose you, Yen.'

'But you have me.'

'The night will end.'

'Everything ends.'

No, he thought. *I don't want it to be like that. I'm tired. Too tired to accept the perspective of endings which are beginnings, and starting everything over again. I'd like ...*

'Don't talk,' she said, quickly placing her fingers on his lips. 'Don't tell me what you'd like and what you desire. Because it might turn out I won't be able to fulfil your desires, and that causes me pain.'

'What do you desire, Yen? What do you dream about?'

'Only about achievable things.'

'And about me?'

'I already have you.'

He remained quiet for a long time, waiting until she broke the silence.

'Geralt?'

'Mm?'

'Love me, please.'

At first, satiated with each other, they were both full of fantasy and invention, creative, imaginative and craving for the new. As usual, it quickly turned out it was at once too much and too little. They understood it simultaneously and once more made love to one another.

When Geralt had recovered his senses, the moon was still in its place. The cicadas were playing wildly, as though they also wanted to conquer anxiety and fear with madness and abandon. From a nearby window in the left wing of Aretuza, someone craving sleep yelled out, fulminating sternly and demanding quiet. From a window on the other side someone else, clearly with a more artistic soul, applauded enthusiastically and congratulated them.

'Oh, Yen ...' whispered the Witcher reproachfully.

'I had a reason ...' She kissed him and then buried her cheek in the pillow. 'I had a reason to scream. So I screamed. It shouldn't be suppressed. It would be unhealthy and unnatural. Hold me, please.'

The Lara Portal, also known as **Benavent's Portal**, after its dis-
coverer. *Located on the Isle of Thanedd, on the uppermost floor of
the Tower of Gulls. A fixed portal, periodically active. Principles
of functioning: unknown. Destination: unknown, but probably
skewed, owing to damage. Numerous forks or dispersions possible.*

*Important information: a chaotic and lethally dangerous portal.
All experimentation categorically forbidden. Magic may not be
used in the Tower of Gulls or in close proximity to it, particularly
not teleportational magic. In exceptional cases, the Chapter will
examine applications for permission to enter Tor Lara and for
inspections of the portal. Applications should be supported by evidence of research work already in progress and of specialisation in
the subject area.*

Bibliography: Geoffrey Monck, The Magic of the Elder Folk;
Immanuel Benavent, The Portal of Tor Lara; *Nina Fioravanti,*
The Theory and Practice of Teleportation; *Ransant Alvaro,*
The Gates of Mystery.

Prohibita (list of banned artefacts),
Ars Magica, Edition LVIII

CHAPTER FOUR

In the beginning there was only pulsating, shimmering chaos, a cascade of images and a whirling abyss of sounds and voices. Ciri saw a tower reaching up to the sky with thunderbolts dancing across the roof. She heard the cry of a raptor and suddenly *became* it. She was flying with enormous speed and beneath her was a stormy sea. She saw a small button-eyed doll and suddenly *was* that doll, and all around her teemed the darkness, pulsing with the sounds of cicadas. She saw a large black and white tomcat and suddenly *was* that cat, surrounded by a sombre house, darkened wood panelling and the smell of candles and old books. Several times, she heard someone call her name; summon her. She saw silver salmon leaping up waterfalls, heard the sound of rain drumming against leaves. And then she heard Yennefer's strange, long-drawn-out scream. And it was that scream that woke her, pulled her out of the chasm of timelessness and chaos.

Now, vainly trying to recall the dream, she could only hear the soft sounds of lute and flute, the jingling of a tambourine, singing and laughter. Dandelion and the group of minstrels he had chanced upon continued to have the time of their lives in the chamber at the end of the corridor.

A shaft of moonlight shone through the window, somewhat lightening the gloom and making the chamber in Loxia resemble a dream world. Ciri threw off the sheet. She was bathed in sweat and her hair was stuck to her forehead. It had taken her a long time to fall asleep the night before; it had been stuffy, even though the window had been wide open. She knew what had caused it. Before leaving with Geralt, Yennefer had encircled the chamber with protective charms. Ostensibly it was in order to prevent anyone from entering, though Ciri suspected their true purpose was to stop her leaving.

153

She was, quite simply, a prisoner. Yennefer, although clearly happy to be back with Geralt, had neither forgiven nor forgotten Ciri's wilful and reckless flight to Hirundum, even though it had led to her reunion with Geralt.

The meeting with Geralt itself had filled Ciri with sadness and disappointment. The Witcher had been taciturn, tense, restless and demonstrably insincere. Their conversation had faltered and limped along, losing its way in sentences and questions which suddenly broke off. The Witcher's eyes and thoughts kept running away from her and fleeing into the distance. Ciri knew where they were running to.

Dandelion's soft, mournful singing and the music he raised from the lute's strings, murmuring like a stream flowing over pebbles, drifted to her from the chamber at the end of the corridor. She recognised it as the melody the bard had started composing some days before. The ballad – as Dandelion had boasted several times – bore the title *Elusive* and was intended to earn the poet first place at the annual bard's tournament due to take place in the later autumn at Vartburg Castle. Ciri listened carefully to the words.

O'er glistening roofs you float
Through lily-strewn rivers you dive
Yet one day I will know your truths
If only I am still alive . . .

Hooves thundered, riders galloped in the night, and on the horizon the sky bloomed with the glow of many fires. A bird of prey screeched and spread its wings, taking flight. Ciri plunged into sleep once more, hearing people calling her name over and over. Once it was Geralt, once Yennefer, once Triss Merigold, finally – several times – a sad, slim, fair-haired girl she didn't recognise, who looked out at her from a miniature, framed in horn and brass.

Then she saw a black and white cat, and a moment later, she again *was* that cat, and seeing with its eyes. She was in a strange, dark house. She saw great shelves of books, and a lectern lit by several candlesticks, with two men sitting at it, poring over scrolls. One of the men was coughing and wiping his lips with a handkerchief. The second, a midget with a huge head, sat on a chair on wheels. He had no legs.

'Extraordinary ...' sighed Fenn, running his eyes over the decaying parchment. 'It's hard to believe ... Where did you get these documents?'

'You wouldn't believe me if I told you,' Codringher coughed. 'Have you only now realised who Cirilla, Princess of Cintra, really is? The Child of the Elder Blood; the last offshoot of that bloody tree of hatred! The last branch and, on it, the last poisoned apple ...'

'The Elder Blood ... So far back in time ... Pavetta, Calanthe, Adalia, Elen, Fiona ...'

'And Falka.'

'By the gods, but that's impossible. Firstly, Falka had no children! Secondly, Fiona was the legitimate daughter of —'

'Firstly, we know nothing about Falka's youth. Secondly, Fenn, don't make me laugh. You know, of course, that I'm overcome with spasms of mirth at the sound of the word "legitimate". I believe that document, because in my opinion it's authentic and speaks the truth. Fiona, Pavetta's great-great-grandmother, was the daughter of Falka, that monster in human form. Damn it, I don't believe in all those insane predictions, prophecies and other poppycock, but when I now recall the Ithlinne forecasts ...'

'Tainted blood?'

'Tainted, contaminated, accursed; it can be understood in various ways. And according to legend, if you recall, it was Falka who was accursed – because Lara Dorren aep Shiadhal had put a curse on her mother—'

'Those are just stories, Codringher.'

'You're right: stories. But do you know when stories stop being stories? The moment someone begins to believe in them. And someone believes in the story of the Elder Blood. In particular, in the part that says *from Falka's blood will be born an avenger who will destroy the old world and build a new one on its ruins.*'

'And Cirilla is supposed to be that avenger?'

'No. Not Cirilla. Her son.'

'And Cirilla is being hunted by –'

'– Emhyr var Emreis, Emperor of Nilfgaard,' finished Codringher coldly. 'Now do you understand? Cirilla, irrespective of her will, is to become the mother of the heir to the throne. Mother to an arch-prince; the Arch-Prince of Darkness, the descendant and avenger of that she-devil Falka. The destruction and the subsequent rebuilding of the world is meant – it seems to me – to proceed in a guided and controlled way.'

The cripple said nothing for a long time.

'Don't you think,' he finally asked, 'we should tell Geralt about this?'

'Geralt?' sneered Codringher. 'Who? You mean that simpleton who, not so long ago, tried to persuade me he doesn't work for gain? Oh, I believe that; he doesn't work for his own gain. But for someone else's. And unwittingly, as a matter of fact. Geralt is hunting Rience; Rience may be on a leash but Geralt doesn't even know there's a collar around his neck. Should I inform him? And so help the people planning to capture this golden-egg laying hen, in order to blackmail Emhyr or ingratiate themselves with him? No, Fenn. I'm not that stupid.'

'The Witcher's on a leash? But who's holding it?'

'Think.'

'Bitch!'

'You said it. The only person who can influence him. Whom he trusts. But I don't trust her and never have. So I'm going to join the game myself.'

'It's a dangerous one, Codringher.'

'There aren't any safe games. Games are either worth a candle or they aren't. Fenn, old man, don't you understand what has fallen into our hands? A golden hen, which will lay for us – and no one else – and it'll be huge egg, with a rich, yellow yolk …'

Codringher coughed violently. When he removed the handkerchief from his mouth there were flecks of blood on it.

'Gold won't cure that,' said Fenn, looking at the handkerchief in his partner's hand. 'Nor give me back my legs …'

'Who knows?'

Somebody knocked at the door. Fenn fidgeted nervously in his wheeled chair.

'Are you expecting anyone, Codringher?'

'I am. The men I'm sending to Thanedd. To fetch our golden hen.'

'Don't open it,' Ciri screamed. 'Don't open the door! Death stands behind it! Don't open the door!'

'All right, all right, I'm just coming,' called Codringher, pulling back the bolts, then turning to his meowing cat. 'And you'll sit quietly, you accursed little beast ...'

He broke off. The men in the doorway were not the ones he had been expecting. Instead, three characters he did not know were standing there.

'The Honourable Mr Codringher?'

'The master's away on business,' said the lawyer, assuming the expression of a halfwit and speaking with a slightly squeaky voice. 'I am the master's butler. The name is Dullord, Mikael Dullord. How may I serve your honourable selves?'

'You cannot,' said one of the individuals, a tall half-elf. 'Since your master is not here, we'll just leave a letter and a message. Here is the letter.'

'I will pass it on without fail,' said Codringher, playing the role of a simple lackey perfectly; bowing subserviently and holding out a hand to take a scroll of parchment tied up with a red cord. 'And the message?'

The cord binding the scroll unwound like a striking snake, lashing and curling itself tightly around his wrist. The tall man jerked hard. Codringher lost his balance and lurched forward, instinctively thrusting his left hand towards the half-elf's chest to stop himself from falling against him. As he fell he was unable to avoid the dagger which was rammed into his belly. He cried out breathlessly and jerked backwards, but the magic cord around his wrist held fast. The half-elf pulled Codringher towards him and stabbed again.

This time the whole of Codringher's weight bore down on the blade.

'That's the message and greetings from Rience,' hissed the tall half-elf, pulling the dagger upwards powerfully and gutting the lawyer like a fish. 'Go to hell, Codringher. Straight to hell.'

Codringher's breath rasped. He felt the dagger blade grate and crunch against his ribs and sternum. He slumped onto the floor, curling up into a ball. He wanted to shout, to warn Fenn, but was only able to screech, and the screech was immediately drowned in a gush of blood.

The tall half-elf stepped over the body and was followed inside by the other two. They were humans.

Fenn was ready for them.

The bowstring thwacked, and one of the thugs crashed onto his back, struck directly in the forehead by a steel ball. Fenn shoved himself backwards in his chair, trying desperately to reload the arbalest with his shaking hands.

The tall man leapt towards him, knocking over the chair with a powerful kick. The midget rolled among the papers strewn over the floor. Waving his small hands and the stumps of his legs helplessly, he resembled a mutilated spider.

The half-elf kicked the arbalest out of Fenn's reach. Paying no attention to the cripple's attempts to struggle away, he hurriedly looked through the documents lying on the lectern. His attention was caught by a miniature in a horn and brass frame, showing a fair-haired girl. He picked it up with the scrap of paper attached to it.

The second thug ignored the one who had been hit by the arbalest ball and came closer. The half-elf raised his eyebrows questioningly. The thug shook his head.

The half-elf picked up several documents from the lectern, tucking them away in his coat, along with the miniature. He then took a handful of quills from the inkwell and set light to them with one of the candlesticks. He turned them around slowly, allowing the fire take good hold and then threw them onto the lectern among the scrolls of parchment, which immediately burst into flames.

Fenn screamed.

158

The tall half-elf took a bottle of ink remover from the burning table, stood over the midget thrashing around on the floor and emptied the contents over him. Fenn gave a tormented howl. The other thug swept an armful of scrolls from a bookshelf and threw them over the cripple.

The fire on the lectern had just reached the ceiling. A second, smaller bottle of solvent exploded with a roar, the flames licking the bookshelves. The scrolls, rolls and files began to blacken, curl up and catch fire. Fenn wailed. The tall half-elf stepped back from the burning pulpit, twisted up a second piece of paper and lit it. The second thug threw another armful of vellum scrolls on the cripple.

Fenn screamed.

The half-elf stood over him, holding the burning brand.

Codringher's black and white cat alighted on a nearby wall. In its yellow eyes danced the reflection of the fire, which had transformed the pleasant night into this horrific parody of day. People were screaming. *Fire! Fire! Water!* People ran towards the building. The cat froze, watching them with astonishment and contempt. Those idiots were clearly heading towards the fiery abyss, from which it had only just managed to extricate itself.

Turning away, unconcerned, Codringher's cat went back to licking its bloodstained paws.

Ciri awoke covered in sweat, with her hands painfully gripping the sheets. Everything was quiet, and the soft darkness was pierced by a dagger-like shaft of moonlight.

A fire. An inferno. Blood. A nightmare ... I don't remember, I don't remember anything ...

She took a deep breath of the crisp night air. The sense of stuffiness had vanished. She knew why.

The protective charms had stopped working.

Something's happened, thought Ciri. She jumped out of bed and quickly dressed. She belted on her dagger. She didn't have a sword any more; Yennefer had taken it from her, giving it to Dandelion for safekeeping. The poet must have gone to sleep, and it was silent in Loxia. Ciri was already wondering whether to go and wake him when she felt a strong pulse and a rush of blood in her ears.

The shaft of moonlight coming through the window became a road. At the end of the road, far away, was a door. The door opened and Yennefer stood there.

'Come with me.'

Other doors opened behind the sorceress's back. One after the other. An endless succession. The black shapes of columns crystallised from the darkness. *Not columns – perhaps they're statues ... I'm dreaming,* thought Ciri, *I don't believe my eyes. I'm dreaming. That isn't a road. It's light, a shaft of light. I can't go along that ...*

'Come with me.'

She obeyed.

Had it not been for the foolish scruples of the Witcher, and his impractical principles, many subsequent events would have run their course quite differently. Many events would probably have not taken place at all. And the history of the world would have unfolded in an alternative way.

But the history of the world unfolded as it unfolded, the sole cause of which was that the Witcher had scruples. When he awoke in the morning with the need to relieve himself, he didn't do what any other man would have done; he didn't go out onto the balcony and piss into a flowerpot of nasturtiums. He had scruples. He dressed quietly without waking Yennefer, who was sleeping deeply, motionless and barely breathing. He left the chamber and went out to the garden.

The banquet was still in progress but, as the sounds indicated, only in a fragmentary form. The lights were still burning in the ballroom windows, illuminating the atrium and beds of peonies. The Witcher went a little further in, among some dense bushes, where he stared at the lightening sky. The horizon was already burning with the purple streaks of dawn.

As he slowly returned, pondering important matters, his medallion vibrated powerfully. He held it in his hand, feeling the vibrations penetrate his entire body. There was no doubt; someone in

Aretuza had cast a spell. Geralt listened carefully and heard some muffled shouts, and a clattering and pounding coming from the cloister in the palace's left wing.

Anyone else would have turned on their heels at once and walked briskly back to where they'd come from, pretending they hadn't heard anything. And then perhaps the history of the world would have unfolded differently. But the Witcher had scruples and was accustomed to acting according to foolish, impractical principles.

When he ran into the cloister and the corridor, he saw that a fight was in progress. Several tough-looking men in grey jerkins were in the act of overpowering a short sorcerer who had been thrown to the ground. The fight was being directed by Dijkstra, chief of Vizimir, King of Redania's intelligence service. Before Geralt was able to take any action he was overpowered himself; two other heavies in grey pinned him to a wall, and a third held the three-pronged blade of a partisan against his chest.

All the heavies had breastplates emblazoned with the Redanian eagle.

'That's called "being in the shit",' explained Dijkstra quietly, approaching him. 'And you, Witcher, seem to have an inborn talent for falling into it. Stand there nice and peacefully and try not to attract anyone's attention.'

The Redanians finally overpowered the short sorcerer and lifted him up, holding him by his arms. It was Artaud Terranova, a member of the Chapter.

The light which made the details visible emanated from an orb suspended above Keira Metz's head – a sorceress with whom Geralt had been chatting at the banquet the previous evening. He barely recognised her; she had exchanged her flowing tulle for severe male clothing, and she had a dagger at her side.

'Handcuff him,' she ordered curtly. A set of handcuffs made of a bluish metal clinked in her hand.

'Don't you dare put those on me!' yelled Terranova. 'Don't you dare, Metz! I am a member of the Chapter!'

'You were. Now you're a common traitor. And you will be treated as such.'

161

'And you're a lousy whore, who—'

Keira took a step back, swayed her hips and punched him in the face with all her strength. The sorcerer's head jerked backwards so hard that for a moment Geralt thought it would be torn from his trunk. Terranova lolled in the arms of the men holding him, blood streaming from his nose and mouth. The sorceress didn't strike him a second time, though her fist was raised. The Witcher saw the flash of brass knuckles on her fingers. He wasn't surprised. Keira was very lightly built, and a blow like that couldn't have been dealt with a bare fist.

He didn't move. The thugs were holding him tightly, and the point of the partisan was pressing against his chest. Geralt wasn't sure if he would have moved, had he been free, or whether he would have known what to do.

The Redanians snapped the handcuffs around the sorcerer's wrists, which were twisted behind his back. Terranova cried out, struggled, bent over and retched and Geralt realised what the handcuffs were made of. It was an alloy of iron and dimeritium, a rare metal characterised by its inhibition of magical powers. The inhibition was accompanied by a set of rather unpleasant side effects for sorcerers.

Keira Metz raised her head, pulling her hair back from her forehead. And then she saw him.

'What the bloody hell is he doing here? How did he get here?'

'He just stepped in,' answered Dijkstra unemotionally. 'He's got a talent for putting his foot in it. What shall I do with him?'

Keira's face darkened and she stamped several times with the high heel of her boot.

'Guard him. I don't have time now.'

She walked quickly away, followed by the Redanians who were dragging Terranova behind them. The shining orb floated behind the sorceress, although it was already dawn and quickly becoming light. On a signal from Dijkstra, the thugs released Geralt. The spy came closer and looked the Witcher in the eyes.

'Don't try anything.'

'What's happening here? What—?'

162

'And don't utter a word.'

Keira Metz returned a short time later; but not alone. She was accompanied by a flaxen-haired sorcerer, introduced to Geralt on the previous day as Detmold of Ban Ard. At the sight of the Witcher, he cursed and smacked his fist into his palm.

'Shit! Is he the one Yennefer's taken a liking to?'

'Yes, that's him,' said Keira. 'Geralt of Rivia. The problem is, I don't know about Yennefer ...'

'I don't know either,' said Detmold, shrugging his shoulders. 'In any case, he's mixed up in this now. He's seen too much. Take him to Philippa; she'll decide. Put him in handcuffs.'

'There's no need,' said Dijkstra with a languid air. 'I'll answer for him. I'll take him to where he ought to be.'

'Excellent,' nodded Detmold, 'because we have no time for him. Come on, Keira, it's a mess up there ...'

'Oh, but aren't they anxious?' muttered the Redanian spy, watching them walk away. 'It's lack of experience, nothing more. And coups d'état and putsches are like green beet soup. They're best served cold. Let's go, Geralt. And remember: peacefully and with dignity. Don't make a scene. And don't make me regret not having you handcuffed or tied up.'

'What's happening, Dijkstra?'

'Haven't you guessed yet?' said the spy, walking beside him, with the three Redanian heavies bringing up the rear. 'Tell me straight, Witcher. How did you wind up here?'

'I was worried about the nasturtiums wilting.'

'Geralt,' said Dijkstra, frowning at him. 'You've fallen head first into the shit. You've swum upwards, and you're holding your head above the surface, but your feet still aren't touching the bottom. Someone's offering you a helping hand, at the risk of falling in and getting covered in it himself. So drop the foolish jokes. Yennefer made you come here, did she?'

'No. Yennefer's still asleep in a warm bed. Does that reassure you?'

The huge spy turned suddenly, seized the Witcher by the arms and shoved him against the wall of the corridor.

'No, it doesn't reassure me, you bloody fool,' he hissed. 'Haven't you got it yet, you idiot, that decent sorcerers who are faithful to kings aren't asleep tonight? That they didn't go to bed at all? Only traitors who have sold out to Nilfgaard are asleep in their warm beds. Traitors, who were preparing a putsch of their own, but for a later date. They didn't know their plans had been rumbled and their intentions second-guessed. And as you can see, they're being dragged out of those warm beds, getting smacked in the teeth with knuckledusters, and having dimeritium bracelets wrapped around their wrists. The traitors are finished. Get it? If you don't want to go down with them, stop playing the fool! Did Vilgefortz manage to recruit you yesterday evening? Or perhaps Yennefer already did. Talk! And fast, before your mouth is flooded with shit!'

'Green beet soup, Dijkstra,' reminded Geralt. 'Take me to Philippa. Peacefully and with dignity. And without causing a scene.'

The spy released him and took a step back.

'Let's go,' he said coldly. 'Up these stairs. But this conversation isn't over yet. I promise you.'

It was bright from the light of lanterns and magical orbs floating beneath the column which supported the vaulting, at the point where four corridors joined. The place was heaving with Redanians and sorcerers. Among the latter were two members of the Council: Radcliffe and Sabrina Glevissig. Sabrina, like Keira Metz, was dressed in grey men's apparel. Geralt realised it was possible to identify the different factions within the putsch by their uniforms.

Triss Merigold crouched on the floor, hunched over a body which was lying in a pool of blood. Geralt recognised the body as that of Lydia van Bredevoort. He knew her by her hair and silk dress. He couldn't have recognised her by her face because it was no longer a face. It was a horrifying, macabre skull, with shining teeth exposed halfway up the cheeks, and a distorted, sunken jaw, the bones badly knitted together.*

---

* The lower part of Lydia van Bredevoort's face, as seen in society and her portraits, was actually an illusion. Experiments on a mysterious artefact had left her with burns, and throat and larynx mutations.

'Cover her up,' said Sabrina Glevissig softly. 'When she died, the illusion vanished ... I said bloody cover her up with something!'

'How did it happen, Radcliffe?' asked Triss, withdrawing her hand from the gilded haft of the dagger which was embedded beneath Lydia's sternum. 'How could it have happened? This was supposed to be bloodless!'

'She attacked us,' muttered the sorcerer and lowered his head. 'She attacked us as Vilgefortz was being escorted out. There was a scuffle ... I have no idea ... It's her own dagger.'

'Cover her face!' said Sabrina, suddenly turning away. She saw Geralt, and her predatory eyes shone like anthracite.

'How did he get here?'

Triss leapt to her feet and sprang towards the Witcher. Geralt saw her hand right in front of his face. Then he saw a flash, and everything faded into darkness. He couldn't see. He felt a hand on his collar and a sharp tug.

'Hold him up or he'll fall,' said Triss, her voice unnatural, feigning anger. She jerked him again, pulling him towards her for a moment.

'Forgive me,' she whispered hurriedly. 'I had to do that.'

Dijkstra's men held him fast.

He moved his head around, activating his other senses. There were movements in the corridors and the air rippled, carrying scents with it. And voices. Sabrina Glevissig swore; Triss mollified her. The Redanians, reeking of an army barracks, dragged the limp body across the floor, rustling the silk of the dress. Blood. The smell of blood. And the smell of ozone; the scent of magic. Raised voices. Footsteps. The nervous clattering of heels.

'Hurry up! It's all taking too long! We ought to be in Garstang by now!'

That was Philippa Eilhart. Sounding anxious.

'Sabrina, find Marti Södergren quickly. Drag her out of bed, if necessary. Gedymdeith's in a bad way. I think it's a heart attack. Have Marti see to him but don't say anything to her or to whoever she's sleeping with. Triss, find Dorregaray, Drithelm and Carduin and bring them to Garstang.'

'What for?'

'They represent the kings. Ethain and Esterad are to be informed about our operation and its consequences. You'll be taking them . . . Triss, you have blood on your hand! Whose is it?'

'Lydia's.'

'Damn it. When? How?'

'Is it important how?' said a cold, calm voice. The voice of Tissaia de Vries. The rustle of a dress. Tissaia was in a ball gown, not a rebel uniform. Geralt listened carefully but could not hear the jingling of dimeritium handcuffs.

'Are you pretending to be worried?' repeated Tissaia. 'Concerned? When revolts are organised, when armed thugs are deployed at night, you have to expect casualties. Lydia is dead. Hen Gedymdeith is dying. A moment ago I saw Artaud with his face carved up. How many more casualties will there be, Philippa Eilhart?'

'I don't know,' answered Philippa resolutely. 'But I'm not backing down.'

'Of course not. You don't back down from anything.'

The air vibrated, and heels thudded on the floor in a familiar rhythm. Philippa walked towards him. He remembered the nervous rhythm of her footsteps when they were walking through the hall at Aretuza together, to feast on caviar. He recalled the scent of cinnamon and muskroot. Now, that scent was mixed with the smell of baking soda. Geralt had no intention of participating in any kind of coup or putsch, but wondered whether – had he decided to – he would have thought about cleaning his teeth beforehand.

'He can't see you, Phil,' said Dijkstra nonchalantly. 'He can't see anything and didn't see anything. The one with the beautiful hair blinded him.'

He heard Philippa's breath and sensed every one of her movements but moved his head around awkwardly, simulating helplessness. The enchantress was not to be fooled.

'Don't bother pretending, Geralt. Triss may have darkened your eyes but she didn't take away your mind. How the hell did you end up here?'

'I dropped in. Where's Yennefer?'

'Blessed are they who do not know,' said Philippa, in a voice devoid of mockery. 'For they will live longer. Be grateful to Triss. It was a soft spell; the blindness will soon pass. And you didn't see anything you weren't meant to. Guard him, Dijkstra. I'll be right back.'

There was a disturbance again. And voices. Keira Metz's resonant soprano, Radcliffe's nasal bass. The clatter of heavy Redanian boots. And Tissaia de Vries's raised voice.

'Let her go! How could you? How could you do that to her?'

'She's a traitress!' responded Radcliffe's nasal voice.

'I will never believe that!'

'Blood's thicker than water,' said Philippa Eilhart, coldly. 'And Emperor Emhyr has promised the elves freedom. As well as their own, independent state. Here, in these lands. After the humans have been slaughtered, naturally. And that was sufficient for her to betray us without a second thought.'

'Answer!' said Tissaia de Vries forcefully. 'Answer her, Enid!'

'Answer, Francesca.'

The clinking of dimeritium handcuffs. The singsong, elven lilt of Francesca Findabair, the Daisy of the Valleys, the most beautiful woman in the world.

'Va vort a me, Dh'oine. N'aen te a dice'n.'

'Will that suffice, Tissaia?' barked Philippa. 'Will you believe me now? You, me, all of us, are – and always were – Dh'oine, humans, to her. And she, Aen Seidhe, has nothing to say to humans. And you, Fercart? What did Vilgefortz and Emhyr promise you, that made you choose treachery?'

'Go to hell, you debauched slut.'

Geralt held his breath, but this time didn't hear the sound of brass knuckles hitting bone. Philippa was more composed than Keira. Or she didn't have any brass knuckles.

'Radcliffe, take the traitors to Garstang! Detmold, give your arm to Arch-Mistress de Vries. Go. I'll join you soon.'

Footsteps. The scent of cinnamon and muskroot.

'Dijkstra.'

'I'm here, Phil.'

'Your men are no longer needed here. They may return to Loxia.'

'Are you absolutely sure—'

'To Loxia, Dijkstra!'

'Yes, Your Grace.' There was scorn in the spy's voice. 'The lackeys can leave. They've done their bidding. Now it is a private matter for the mages. And thus I, without further ado, will leave Your Grace's beautiful presence. I didn't expect gratitude for my help or my contribution to your putsch, but I am certain that Your Grace will keep me in her gracious memory.'

'Forgive me, Sigismund. Thank you for your help.'

'Not at all. It was my pleasure. Hey, Voymir, get your men. I want five to stay with me. Take the others downstairs and board *The Spada*. But do it quietly, on tiptoe, without any fuss, commotion or fireworks. Use side corridors. Don't breathe a word of this in Loxia or in the harbour. That's an order!'

'You didn't see anything, Geralt,' said Philippa Eilhart in a whisper, wafting cinnamon, muskroot and baking soda onto the Witcher. 'You didn't hear anything. You never spoke to Vilgefortz. Dijkstra will take you to Loxia now. I'll try to find you when ... when it's all over. I promised you as much yesterday and I'll keep my word.'

'What about Yennefer?'

'I'd say he's obsessed,' said Dijkstra, returning and shuffling his feet. 'Yennefer, Yennefer ... It's getting tedious. Don't bother yourself with him, Phil. There are more important things to do. Was the expected item found on Vilgefortz?'

'Indeed. Here, this is for you.'

'Oh!' The rustle of paper being unwrapped. 'Oh my, oh my! Excellent! Duke Nitert. Splendid! Baron—'

'Discreetly; no names. And please don't start the executions immediately after your return to Tretogor. Don't incite a premature scandal.'

'Don't worry. The lads on this list – so greedy for Nilfgaardian gold – are safe. At least for the moment. They'll become my sweet little puppets. I'll be able to pull their strings, and later we'll put those strings around their sweet little necks ... Just out of curiosity, were there any other lists? Any traitors from Kaedwen, from Temeria, from Aedirn? I'd be delighted to take a look. Just a glimpse ...'

'I know you would. But it's not your business. Radcliffe and Sabrina Glevissig were given those lists, and they'll know what to do with them. And now I must go. I'm in a hurry.'

'Phil?'

'Yes.'

'Restore the Witcher's sight so he doesn't trip on the stairs.'

The banquet in the Aretuza ballroom was still in progress, but it had become more traditional and relaxed. The tables had been pushed aside, and the sorcerers and enchantresses had brought in armchairs, chairs and stools they'd found in other rooms and were lounging in them and amusing themselves in various ways. Most of their amusements were vulgar. A large group, crowded around a bulky cask of rotgut, were carousing, talking and erupting into laughter from time to time. Those who not long before had been delicately spearing exquisite morsels with little silver forks were now unceremoniously chewing mutton ribs held in both hands. Several of them were playing cards, ignoring the rest. Others were asleep. A couple were kissing passionately in the corner, and the ardour they were displaying indicated it wouldn't stop there.

'Just look at them, Witcher,' said Dijkstra, leaning over the banisters of the cloister and looking down at the sorcerers. 'How merrily they play. Just like children. And meanwhile, their Council has just nicked almost their entire Chapter and are trying them for treason, for cuddling up to Nilfgaard. Look at that couple. They'll be soon looking for a secluded corner, and before they've finish bonking, Vilgefortz will have hanged. Oh, what a strange world it is ...'

'Be quiet, Dijkstra.'

The path leading to Loxia was cut into the slopes of the mountain in a zigzag of steps. The steps connected terraces, which were decorated with neglected hedges, flowerbeds and yellowing agaves in flowerpots. Dijkstra stopped at one of the terraces they passed and walked over to a wall with a row of stone chimeras' heads. Water

169

was trickling from their jaws. The spy leaned over and took a long drink.

The Witcher approached the balustrade. The sea glimmered gold, and the sky was even more kitsch in colour than it was in the paintings filling the Gallery of Glory. Below, he could see the squad of Redanians who had been ordered to leave Aretuza. They were heading for the harbour in well-ordered formation, just crossing a bridge linking the two sides of a rocky cleft.

His attention was suddenly caught by a colourful, lone figure, conspicuous because it was moving quickly. And moving in the opposite direction to the Redanians. Uphill, towards Aretuza.

'Right,' said Dijkstra, urging him on with a cough. 'It's time we were going.'

'Go yourself, if you're in such a hurry.'

'Yeah, right,' scowled the spy. 'And you'll go back up there to rescue your beloved Yennefer. And stir up trouble like a tipsy gnome. We're heading for Loxia, Witcher. Are you kidding yourself or something? Do you think I got you out of Aretuza because of some long-hidden love for you? Well I didn't. I got you out of there because I need you.'

'For what?'

'Are you having me on? Twelve young ladies from Redania's finest families are pupils at Aretuza. I can't risk a conflict with the honourable rectoress, Margarita Laux-Antille. But the rectoress won't give me Cirilla, the Princess of Cintra, the girl Yennefer brought to Thanedd. She'll give her to *you*, however. When you ask her.'

'What gave you the ridiculous idea that I'll ask for her?'

'The ridiculous assumption that you want to make sure Cirilla will be safe. She'll be safe in my care, in King Vizimir's care. In Tretogor. She isn't safe on Thanedd. Refrain from making any sarcastic comments. Yes, I know the kings didn't have the most wonderful plans for her at the beginning. But that has changed. Now it's become clear that Cirilla – alive, safe and in good health – may be worth more in the coming war than ten regiments of heavy horse. Dead, she's not worth a brass farthing.'

'Does Philippa Eilhart know what you're planning?'

170

'No, she doesn't. She doesn't even know I know the girl's in Loxia. My erstwhile beloved Phil may put on airs and graces, but Vizimir is still the King of Redania. I carry out his orders, and I don't give a shit what the sorcerers are plotting. Cirilla will board *The Spada* and sail to Novigrad, from where she'll travel to Tretogor. And she'll be safe. Do you believe me?'

The Witcher leaned over towards one of the chimera heads and drank some of the water trickling from its monstrous maw.

'Do you believe me?' repeated Dijkstra, standing over him.

Geralt stood up, wiped his mouth, and punched him in the jaw with all his strength. The spy staggered but didn't go down. The nearest Redanian leapt forward, intending to seize the Witcher, but grabbed thin air, and immediately sat down, spitting blood and one of his teeth. Then all the others jumped him. There was a chaotic confusion and crush, which was exactly what the Witcher had been hoping for.

One of the Redanians slammed head first into the gargoyle, and the water trickling from its jaws turned red. Another caught the heel of the Witcher's fist in the windpipe and doubled up as though his genitals had been ripped out. A third, smacked in the eye, fell back with a groan. Dijkstra seized the Witcher in a bearlike grip, and Geralt kicked him hard in the ankle with his heel. The spy howled and cavorted hilariously on one leg.

Another heavy tried to strike the Witcher with his short sword but slashed only the air. Geralt caught hold of his elbow in one hand and his wrist in the other. He spun him around, knocking over two others who were trying to get up. The thug he was holding was strong and had no intention of releasing his sword. So Geralt tightened his grip and the man's arm broke with a crack.

Dijkstra, still hopping on one leg, seized a partisan from the ground, hoping to pin the Witcher to the wall with its three-pronged blade. Geralt dodged, seized the shaft in both hands and used the principle – well known to scholars – of the lever. The spy, seeing the bricks and mortar of the wall looming, dropped the partisan but was too late to prevent his crotch slamming into the chimera's head.

Geralt used the partisan to knock another thug off his feet and then held the shaft against the ground and broke it with a kick, shortening it to the length of a sword. He tried out the makeshift club, first by hitting Dijkstra – who was sitting astride the chimera – and then by quietening the moans of the bruiser with the broken arm. The seams of his doublet had burst under both arms some time before, and the Witcher was feeling considerably better.

The last brute on his feet also attacked with a partisan, expecting its length to offer him an advantage. Geralt hit him between the eyebrows, and the bruiser sat down hard on the pot holding the agave. Another of the Redanians – who was unusually stubborn – clung to the Witcher's thigh and bit him painfully. This angered the Witcher, who deprived the rodent of his ability to bite with a powerful kick.

Dandelion arrived on the steps out of breath, saw what was happening and went as white as a ghost.

'Geralt!' he yelled a moment later. 'Ciri's disappeared! She isn't here!'

'I expected as much,' answered the Witcher, bashing the next Redanian, who was refusing to lie down quietly, with his club. 'But you really make a body wait, Dandelion. I told you yesterday that you were to leg it to Aretuza if anything happened! Have you brought my sword?'

'Both of them!'

'The other one is Ciri's, you idiot.' Geralt whacked the heavy trying to get up from the agave pot.

'I don't know much about swords,' panted the poet. 'Stop hitting them, by the gods! Can't you see the Redanian eagle? They're King Vizimir's men! This is treachery and rebellion. You could end up in a dungeon for that ...'

'On the scaffold,' mumbled Dijkstra, drawing a dagger and staggering closer. 'You'll both be for the scaffold ...'

He wasn't able to say anything else because he collapsed on all fours, struck on the side of the head with the stump of the partisan's shaft.

'Broken on the wheel,' pictured Dandelion gloomily. 'After being rent with red-hot pincers ...'

The Witcher kicked the spy in the ribs. Dijkstra flopped over on one side like a felled elk.

'. . . then our bodies quartered,' continued the poet.

'Stop that, Dandelion. Give me both swords and get away from here as quickly as possible. Flee from the island. As far away as you can!'

'What about you?'

'I'm going back up. I have to save Ciri . . . And Yennefer. Dijkstra, lie there nicely and get your hands off that dagger!'

'You won't get away with this,' panted the spy. 'I'll send my men after you . . . I'll get you . . .'

'No you won't.'

'Oh, I will. I've got fifty men on *The Spada* . . .'

'And is there a barber surgeon among them?'

'Eh?'

Geralt came up behind the spy, bent down, seized him by the foot and jerked it, twisting the foot quickly and very powerfully. There was a cracking sound. Dijkstra howled and fainted. Dandelion screamed as if it had been his own ankle.

'I don't much care what they do to me after I've been quartered,' muttered the Witcher.

It was quiet in Aretuza. Only a few diehards remained in the ball-room, but now they had too little energy to make a racket. Geralt avoided it, not wanting to be noticed.

He had some difficulty finding the chamber where he'd spent the night with Yennefer. The palace corridors were a veritable labyrinth and all looked alike.

The ragdoll looked at him with its button eyes.

He sat down on the bed, clutching his head. There was no blood on the chamber floor. But a black dress was draped over the back of a chair. Yennefer had changed. Into men's clothes, the uniform of the conspirators?

Or they'd dragged her out in her underwear. In dimeritium handcuffs.

*

173

Marti Södergren, the healer, was sitting in the window alcove. Hearing his footsteps, she raised her head. Her cheeks were wet with tears.

'Hen Gedymdeith is dead,' she said in a faltering voice. 'It was his heart. I couldn't do a thing ... Why did they call me so late? Sabrina hit me. She hit me in the face. Why? What has happened?'

'Have you seen Yennefer?'

'No, I haven't. Leave me. I want to be alone.'

'Show me the shortest way to Garstang. Please.'

Above Aretuza were three terraces covered with shrubs. Beyond them, the mountain slopes became sheer and inaccessible. Garstang loomed up above the precipice. At its foot the palace was a dark, uniformly smooth block of stone growing out of the rocks. Only the marble and stained-glass windows of its upper storey sparkled and the metal roofs of its domes shone like gold in the sun.

The paved road leading to Garstang and on to the summit wound around the mountain like a snake. There was another, shorter, route: a stairway linking the terraces, which vanished into the black maw of a tunnel just beneath Garstang. It was this stairway that Marti Södergren pointed out to the Witcher.

Immediately beyond the tunnel was a bridge joining the two sides of the precipice. Beyond the bridge, the stairway climbed steeply upwards and curved, vanishing around a bend. The Witcher quickened his pace.

The balustrade was decorated with small statues of fauns and nymphs which gave the impression of being alive. They were moving. The Witcher's medallion began to vibrate intensively.

He rubbed his eyes. The statues were not in fact moving but metamorphosing, transforming from smooth-surfaced carvings to porous, shapeless masses of stone, eroded by strong winds and salt. And an instant later they renewed themselves once more.

He knew what that meant. The illusion disguising Thanedd was becoming unstable and weakening. The bridge was also partly illusory. A chasm with a waterfall roaring at its foot was visible through the hole-riddled camouflage.

There were no dark slabs to indicate a safe way across. He crossed the bridge tentatively, careful of every step, cursing to himself at the time he was wasting. When he reached the far side of the chasm, he heard running footsteps.

He knew who it was at once. Running down the steps towards him was Dorregaray, the sorcerer in the service of King Ethain of Cidaris. He recalled the words of Philippa Eilhart. The sorcerers who represented neutral kings had been invited to Garstang as observers. But Dorregaray was hurtling down the steps at such a speed that it appeared his invitation had suddenly been revoked.

'Dorregaray!'

'Geralt?' panted the sorcerer. 'What are you doing here? Don't stay here. Run away! Get down to Aretuza quickly!'

'What has happened?'

'Treachery!'

'What?'

Dorregaray suddenly shuddered and coughed strangely, then toppled forwards and fell onto the Witcher. Before Geralt could catch hold of him he spotted the grey fletching of an arrow sticking out of his back. He and the sorcerer swayed in an embrace. That movement saved the Witcher's life as a second, identical, arrow, rather than piercing his throat, slammed into the grotesquely grinning face of a stone faun, knocking off its nose and part of its cheek. The Witcher released Dorregaray and ducked down behind the balustrade. The sorcerer collapsed onto him.

There were two archers, and both had squirrels' tails in their hats. One remained at the top of the staircase, pulling his bowstring back, while the other drew his sword and hurtled down the stairway, several steps at a time. Geralt pushed Dorregaray aside and leapt to his feet, drawing his sword. An arrow sang, but the Witcher interrupted the song, deflecting the arrowhead with a quick blow of his sword. The other elf, already close, hesitated for a moment on seeing the arrow deflected. But only for a moment. He came at the Witcher, swinging his blade and ready to strike. Geralt made a short parry, obliquely, so that the elf's sword slid across his. The elf lost his balance, the Witcher spun around smoothly and slashed him across the side of the neck below his ear. Just once. Once was enough.

The archer at the top of the stairway bent his bow again but did not have time to release the string. Geralt saw a flash. The elf screamed, spread out his arms and fell forwards, tumbling down the steps. The back of his jerkin was on fire.

Another sorcerer ran down the steps. On seeing the Witcher, he stopped and raised a hand. Geralt didn't waste time with explanations but flattened himself on the ground as a fiery lightning bolt flew over him with a hiss, pulverising a statue of a faun.

'Stop!' he yelled. 'It's me, the Witcher!'

'Damn it,' the sorcerer panted, running over to Geralt, who could not remember him from the banquet. 'I took you for one of those elven thugs ... How is Dorregaray? Is he still alive?'

'I think so ...'

'Quickly, to the other side of the bridge!'

They dragged Dorregaray across. And luck was on their side, because in their haste they paid no attention to the wavering and vanishing illusion. No one was pursuing them, but the sorcerer nonetheless extended a hand, chanting a spell, and sent a lightning bolt to destroy the bridge. The stones crashed down the walls of the abyss.

'That ought to hold them back,' he said.

The Witcher wiped away the blood pouring from Dorregaray's mouth.

'He has a punctured lung. Can you help him?'

'*I* can,' said Marti Södergren, hauling herself up the steps from the tunnel leading from Aretuza. 'What's happening, Carduin? Who shot him?'

'Scoia'tael,' said the sorcerer, wiping his forehead with a sleeve. 'There's a battle raging in Garstang. Bloody rabble. They're all as bad as each other! Philippa handcuffed Vilgefortz during the night, and Vilgefortz and Francesca Findabair brought Squirrels to the island! And Tissaia de Vries ... She's stirred everything up!'

'Be clearer, Carduin!'

'I'm not hanging around here talking! I'm fleeing to Loxia, and from there I'm going to teleport to Kovir. Everyone in Garstang can go ahead and slaughter each other! It's all meaningless now! It's war! This mayhem was concocted by Philippa to allow the kings to start a war with Nilfgaard! Meanwhile Meve of Lyria and Demavend of Aedirn have provoked Nilfgaard! Do you understand that?'

'No,' said Geralt. 'And we don't want to understand it. Where's Yennefer?'

'Stop it, you two!' screamed Marti Södergren, attending to Dorregaray. 'Help me! Hold him! I can't pull the arrow out!'

They helped her. Dorregaray groaned and trembled, and then the steps shook. At first Geralt thought it was the magic of Marti's healing spells. But it was Garstang. The stained-glass windows suddenly exploded and flames could be seen flickering inside the palace. Smoke was billowing out.

'They're still fighting,' said Carduin, grinding his teeth. 'It's hot down there, one spell after another . . .'

'Spells? In Garstang? But there's an anti-magic aura there!'

'It was Tissaia's doing. She suddenly decided whose side she was on. She took down the blockade, removed the aura and neutralised the dimeritium. Then everyone went for each other! Vilgefortz and Terranova on one side, Philippa and Sabrina on the other . . . The columns cracked and the vaulting collapsed . . . And then Francesca opened the entrance to the cellars, and those elven devils suddenly leapt out . . . We told them that we were neutral, but Vilgefortz only laughed. Before we had time to build a shield, Drithelm had been shot in the eye, and Rejean had been spitted like a hedgehog . . . I didn't wait to see what happened after that. Marti, are you going to be much longer? We have to get out of here!'

'Dorregaray won't be able to walk,' said the healer, wiping her bloody hands on her white ball gown. 'Teleport us, Carduin.'

'From here? You must be insane. It's too close to Tor Lara. The Lara portal gives out emanations which warp any attempts at teleportation. You can't teleport from here!'

'He can't walk! I have to stay with him—'

'Well stay, then!' Carduin stood up. 'And enjoy yourself! Life is dear to me! I'm going back to Kovir! Kovir is neutral!'

'Splendid,' said the Witcher, spitting and watching the sorcerer disappear into the tunnel. 'Friendship and solidarity! But I can't stay with you either, Marti. I have to go to Garstang. Your neutral comrade smashed up the bridge. Is there another way?'

Marti Södergren sniffed. Then she raised her head and nodded.

He was at the foot of the wall in Garstang when Keira Metz landed on his head.

The way he'd been shown by the healer led through some hanging gardens linked by winding steps. The steps were covered in dense ivy and vines and the vegetation made climbing difficult but it also gave cover. He managed to get to the foot of the palace wall undetected and had been looking for a way in when Keira had fallen on him, and the two of them tumbled into some blackthorn bushes.

'I've lost a tooth,' said the sorceress, gloomily, lisping slightly. She was dishevelled, dirty and covered in plaster and soot. There was a large bruise on her cheek.

'And I think I've broken my leg,' she added, spitting blood. 'Is that you, Witcher? Did I land on you? How come?'

'I was wondering the same thing myself.'

'Terranova threw me out of a window.'

'Can you stand?'

'No, I can't.'

'I want to get inside. Unnoticed. Which way is it?'

'Are all witchers,' said Keira, spitting blood again, groaning, and trying to prop herself up on an elbow, 'insane? There's a battle going on in Garstang! It's kicking off so badly the plaster's falling off the ceiling! Are you looking for trouble?'

'No. I'm looking for Yennefer.'

'Oh!' said Keira, giving up her struggles and lying on her back. 'I wish someone would love me like that. Carry me.'

'Another time, perhaps. I'm in a bit of a hurry.'

'Carry me, I said! I'll show you the way into Garstang. I have to get that son of a bitch Terranova. Well, what are you waiting for? You won't find the way yourself, and even if you did, those fucking elves would finish you off ... I can't walk, but I'm still capable of casting a few spells. If anyone gets in our way they'll regret it.'

She cried out when he picked her up.

'Sorry.'

'Don't worry,' she said, wrapping her arms around his neck. 'It's that leg. Did you know you still smell of her perfume? No, not that way. Turn back and go uphill. It's the second entrance on the Tor Lara side. There may not be any elves there ... Ouch! Gently, damn it!'

'Sorry. How did the Scoia'tael get here?'

'They were hidden in the cellars. Thanedd is as hollow as a nut-shell and there's a huge cavern under it; you could sail a ship in if you knew how. Someone must have told them the way— Ouuuch! Be careful! Stop jolting me!'

'Sorry. So the Squirrels came here by sea? When?'

'God knows when. It might have been yesterday, or a week ago. We were preparing to strike at Vilgefortz, and Vilgefortz at us. Vilgefortz, Francesca, Terranova and Fercart ... They conned us good and proper. Philippa thought they were planning a slow seizure of power in the Chapter, and to put pressure on the kings ... But they were planning to finish us off during the Conclave ... Geralt, it's too painful ... It's my leg ... Put me down for a second. Ouuuch!'

'Keira, it's an open fracture. The blood's seeping through your trousers.'

'Shut up and listen. Because it's about your Yennefer. We entered Garstang and went into the debating chamber. There's an anti-magic blockade there, but it doesn't affect dimeritium, so we felt safe. There was an argument. Tissaia and the neutrals yelled at us and we yelled at them. And Vilgefortz just said nothing and smiled ...'

'I repeat: Vilgefortz is a traitor! He's in cahoots with Emhyr of Nilfgaard, and he's inveigled others into the plot! He broke the Law, he betrayed us and the kings ...'

'Slow down, Philippa. I know the grace and favour Vizimir surrounds you with mean more to you than the solidarity of the

179

Brotherhood. The same applies to you, Sabrina, for you play an identical role in Kaedwen. Keira Metz and Triss Merigold represent the interests of Foltest of Temeria, and Radcliffe is a tool of Demavend of Aedirn—'

'What does that have to do with it, Tissaia?'

'The kings' interests don't have to correspond to ours. I know perfectly well what it's all about. The kings have begun the extermination of elves and other non-humans. Perhaps you, Philippa, regard that as legitimate. Perhaps you, Radcliffe, think it appropriate to help Demavend's forces in their hunt for the Scoia'tael. But I am opposed to it. And it doesn't surprise me that Enid Findabair is also against it. But that is not sufficient to call it treachery. Let me finish! I know perfectly well what your kings were planning. I know they want to unleash a war. The measures which were meant to prevent that war may be seen as treachery by Vizimir, but not by me. If you wish to judge Vilgefortz and Francesca; do the same to me!'

'What war do you speak of? My king, Esterad of Kovir, will not support any acts of aggression against the Nilfgaardian Empire! Kovir is, and will remain, neutral!'

'You are a member of the Council, Carduin! Not Kovir's ambassador!'

'Look who's talking, Sabrina.'

'Enough!' Philippa slammed her fist down on the table. 'I shall satisfy your curiosity, Carduin. You ask who is preparing a war? Nilfgaard. They intend to attack and destroy us. But Emhyr var Emreis remembers Sodden Hill and has decided to protect himself by removing the mages from the game first. With this in mind, he made contact with Vilgefortz of Roggeveen. He bought him with promises of power and honour. Yes, Tissaia. Vilgefortz, hero of Sodden, sold us out to become the governor and ruler of all the conquered territories of the north. Vilgefortz, helped by Terranova and Fercart, shall rule the provinces which will be established in place of the conquered kingdoms. It is he who will wield the Nilfgaardian scourge over the people who inhabit those lands and will begin toiling as the Empire's slaves. And Francesca Findabair, Enid an Gleanna, will become queen of the land of the free elves. It will, of course, be a Nilfgaardian protectorate, but it will suffice for the elves so long as Emperor Emhyr will give them a free hand to murder humans. The elves desire nothing so much as to murder Dh'oine.'

'That is a serious accusation. Which means the proof will also have to be as weighty. But before you throw your proof onto the scale, Philippa Eilhart, be aware of my stance. Proof may be fabricated. Actions and their motives may be misinterpreted. But nothing can change existing facts. You have broken the unity and solidarity of the Brotherhood, Philippa Eilhart. You have handcuffed members of the Chapter like criminals. So do not dare to offer me a position in the new Chapter which your gang of traitors – who have sold out to the kings, rather than to Nilfgaaard – intend to create. We are separated by death and blood. The death of Hen Gedymdeith. And the blood of Lydia van Bredevoort. You spilled that blood with contempt. You were my best pupil, Philippa Eilhart. I was always proud of you. But now I have nothing but contempt for you.'

Keira Metz was as pale as parchment.

'It's been quieter in Garstang for some time now,' she whispered. 'It's coming to an end ... They are chasing each other through the palace. There are five floors and seventy-six chambers and halls. That's plenty of room for a chase ...'

'You were going to tell me about Yennefer. Be quick. I'm worried you'll faint.'

'Yennefer? Oh, yes ... Everything was going according to plan until Yennefer suddenly appeared. And brought that medium into the hall ...'

'Who?'

'A girl, aged perhaps fourteen. Very fair hair and huge, green eyes ... She began to prophesy before we'd had time to look at her properly. She talked of the events in Dol Angra. No one had any doubt she was speaking the truth. She was in a trance, and in a trance no one lies.'

'Last night,' said the medium, 'armed forces in Lyrian livery and carrying Aedirnian standards committed acts of aggression against the Empire of Nilfgaard. Glevitzingen, a border outpost in Dol Angra, was attacked. King Demavend's heralds informed the people of the surrounding villages that Aedirn is taking control of the entire country from today. The entire population was incited to rise up against Nilfgaard—'

'That is impossible! It's nothing but vile provocation!'

'You utter that word easily, Philippa Eilhart,' said Tissaia de Vries calmly. 'But do not deceive yourself; your cries will not break her trance. Speak on, child.'

'Emperor Emhyr var Emreis has given the order to answer blows with blows. Nilfgaardian forces entered Lyria and Aedirn at dawn today.'

'And thus,' laughed Tissaia, 'our kings have shown what judicious, enlightened and peace-loving rulers they are. And some of our mages have proved which cause they really serve. Those who might have prevented this imperialist war have been prudently clamped in dimeritium handcuffs and are facing trumped-up charges—'

'That is nothing but a pack of lies!'

'Fuck the lot of you!' roared Sabrina Glevissig suddenly. 'Philippa! What is this all about? What was the purpose of that brawl in Dol Angra? Hadn't we agreed not to begin too soon? Why couldn't that fucking Demavend restrain himself? Why did that slut Meve ...'

'Silence, Sabrina!'

'No, no. Let her speak,' said Tissaia de Vries, raising her head. 'Let her speak of Henselt of Kaedwen's army, which is concentrated on the border. Let her speak of Foltest of Temeria's forces, which no doubt are already launching the boats which have been hidden in undergrowth by the Jaruga. Let her speak of the expeditionary force under the command of Vizimir of Redania, standing ready on the Pontar. Philippa, did you think we were both blind and deaf?'

'It's nothing but an enormous bloody provocation! King Vizimir—'

'King Vizimir,' interrupted the fair-haired medium in an unemotional voice, 'was murdered yesterday evening. Stabbed by an assassin. Redania no longer has a king.'

'Redania has not had a king for a very long time,' said Tissaia de

Vries, rising to her feet. 'The Most Honourable Philippa Eilhart, the worthy successor of Raffard the White, ruled in Redania. A person prepared to sacrifice tens of thousands of beings in order to gain absolute power.'

'Do not listen to her!' yelled Philippa. 'Do not listen to that medium! She's a tool, an unthinking tool ... Who do you serve, Yennefer? Who instructed you to bring that monster here?'

'I did,' said Tissaia de Vries.

'What happened next? What happened to the girl? To Yennefer?'

'I don't know,' said Keira, closing her eyes. 'Tissaia suddenly lifted the blockade. With one spell. I'd never seen anything like it in my life. She stunned and blocked us, then freed Vilgefortz and the others ... And then Francesca opened the entrance to the cellars and suddenly Garstang was swarming with Scoia'tael. They were being led by a freak in armour wearing a winged, Nilfgaardian helmet. Helped by that character with the mark on his face. He knew how to cast spells. And shield himself with magic ...'

'Rience.'

'Perhaps. I don't know. It was hot ... The ceiling caved in. Spells and arrows were flying everywhere; it was a massacre ... Fercart was among their dead, Drithelm and Radcliffe among ours. Marquard, Rejean and Bianca d'Este were killed ... Triss Merigold was hurt. Sabrina was wounded ... When Tissaia saw their bodies she understood her mistake, tried to protect us, tried to calm Vilgefortz and Terranova ... But Vilgefortz ridiculed and laughed at her. Then she lost her head and fled. Oh, Tissaia ... So many dead ...'

'What happened to the girl and to Yennefer?'

'I don't know,' said the sorceress, coughing and spitting blood. She was breathing very shallowly and with obvious difficulty. 'I passed out after one of the explosions. The one with the scar and his elves overpowered me. Terranova beat me black and blue and then threw me out of a window.'

'It isn't just your leg, Keira. You've got some broken ribs.'

'Don't leave me.'

'I have to. I'll come back for you.'

'Yeah, right.'

At first, there was only shimmering chaos, the pulsing of shadows, a confusion of dark and light, and a choir of incoherent voices emerging from the abyss. Suddenly the voices became stronger and, from all around, the screaming and the roaring exploded. The brightness amongst the darkness became a fire consuming the tapestries, seeming to shoot streams of sparks from the walls, the balustrades and the columns supporting the ceiling.

Ciri choked on the smoke and realised it was no longer a dream.

She tried to stand, propping herself up on her arms. Her hand came to rest on something wet, and she looked down. She was kneeling in a pool of blood. Beside her lay a motionless body. The body of an elf. She knew at once.

'Get up.'

Yennefer was standing beside her. She was holding a dagger.

'Mistress Yennefer ... Where are we? I don't remember ...'

The enchantress seized her by the hand.

'I'm with you, Ciri.'

'Where are we? Why is everything on fire? Who's that ... lying there?'

'I told you once, a long time ago, that chaos is reaching out to seize you. Do you remember? No, you probably don't. That elf reached out to get you. I had to kill him using a knife, as his paymasters are just waiting for one of us to reveal ourselves by using magic. And it will happen, but not yet ... Are you totally conscious?'

'Those sorcerers ...' whispered Ciri. 'The ones in the great hall ... What did I say to them? And why did I say it? I didn't want to at all ... But I couldn't stop myself! Why? Why, Mistress Yennefer?'

'Be quiet, my ugly little duckling. I made a mistake. No one's perfect.'

A roar and a terrifying scream resounded from below.

'Come on. Quickly. There's no time.'

They ran along the corridor. The smoke became thicker and thicker. It choked them, blinded them. The walls shook from the explosion.

184

'Ciri.' Yennefer stopped at a junction in the corridors and squeezed the girl's hand tightly. 'Listen to me now. Listen carefully. I have to stay here. Do you see those stairs? Go down them ...'

'No! Don't leave me all alone!'

'I have to. I repeat: go down those stairs. To the very bottom. There'll be a door and, beyond it a long corridor. At the end of the corridor is a stable and a single, saddled horse. Only one. Lead it out and mount it. It's a trained horse; it serves messengers riding to Loxia. It knows the way; just spur it on. When you get to Loxia find Margarita. She will look after you. Don't let her out of your sight—'

'Mistress Yennefer! No! I don't want to be alone!'

'Ciri,' said the enchantress softly. 'I once told you that everything I do is for your own good. Trust me. Trust me, I beg you. Now run for it.'

Ciri was already on the steps when she heard Yennefer's voice one more. The enchantress was standing beside a column, resting her forehead against it.

'I love you, my daughter,' she said indistinctly. 'Run.'

They trapped her halfway down the stairs. At the bottom there were two elves with squirrels' tails in their hats and, at the top, a man dressed in black. Without thinking, Ciri jumped over the banisters and fled down a side corridor. They ran after her. She was quicker and would have escaped them with ease had the corridor not ended in a window.

She looked through the window. A stone ledge – about two spans wide – ran along the wall. Ciri swung a leg over the windowsill and climbed out. She moved away from the window and pressed her back to the wall. The sea glistened in the distance.

One of the elves leaned out through the window. He had very fair hair and green eyes and wore a silk kerchief around his neck. Ciri moved quickly along the ledge towards the next window. But the man dressed in black was looking out of it. His eyes were dark and intense, and he had a reddish mark on his cheek.

'We've got you, wench!'

185

She looked down. She could see a courtyard far below her. There was a narrow bridge linking two cloisters above the courtyard, about ten feet below the ledge she was standing on. Except it was not a bridge. It was the remains of a bridge. A narrow, stone footbridge with the remains of a shattered balustrade.

'What are you waiting for?' shouted the one with the scar. 'Get out there and grab her!'

The fair-haired elf stepped gingerly out onto the ledge, pressing his back against the wall. He reached out to grab her. He was getting closer.

Ciri swallowed. The stone footbridge – the remains of the footbridge – was no narrower than the seesaw at Kaer Morhen, and she had landed on that dozens of times. She knew how to cushion her fall and keep her balance. The witchers' seesaw was only four feet off the ground, however, while the stone footbridge spanned such a long drop that the slabs of the courtyard looked smaller than the palm of her hand.

She jumped, landed, tottered and kept her balance by catching hold of the shattered balustrade. With sure steps, she reached the cloister. She couldn't resist it; she turned around and showed her pursuers her middle finger, a gesture she had been taught by the dwarf Yarpen Zigrin. The man with the scar swore loudly.

'Jump!' he shouted at the fair-haired elf standing on the ledge. 'After her!'

'You're insane, Rience,' said the elf coldly. 'Jump yourself.'

As usual, her luck didn't last. She was caught as she ran down from the cloister and slipped behind a wall into a blackthorn bush. She was caught and held fast in an extremely strong grip by a short, podgy man with a swollen nose and a scarred lip.

'Got you,' he hissed. 'Got you, poppet!'

Ciri struggled and howled because the hands gripping her shoulders transfixed her with a sudden paroxysm of overwhelming pain. The man chuckled.

'Don't flap your wings, little bird, or I'll singe your feathers. Let's have a good look at you. Let's have a look at this chick that's worth so much to Emhyr var Emreis, Imperator of Nilfgaard. And to Vilgefortz.'

Ciri stopped trying to escape. The short man licked his scarred lip.

'Interesting,' he hissed again, leaning over towards her. 'They say you're so precious, but I wouldn't even give a brass farthing for you. How appearances deceive. Ha! My treasure! What if, not Vilgefortz, not Rience, not that gallant in the feathered helmet, but old Terranova gave you to Emhyr as a present? Would Emhyr look kindly on old Terranova? What do you say to that, little clairvoyant? You can see the future, after all!'

His breath stank unbearably. Ciri turned her head away, grimacing. He misread the movement.

'Don't snap your beak at me, little bird! I'm not afraid of little birds. But should I be, perhaps? Well, false soothsayer? Bogus oracle? Should I be afraid of little birds?'

'You ought to be,' whispered Ciri, feeling giddy, a sudden cold sensation overcoming her.

Terranova laughed, throwing his head back. His laugh became a howl of pain. A huge, grey owl had swooped down noiselessly and sunk its talons into his eyes. The sorcerer released Ciri, tore the owl off with a desperate movement and then fell to his knees, clutching his face. Blood poured between his fingers. Ciri screamed and stepped back. Terranova removed his bloodied, mucus-covered fingers from his face and began to chant a spell in a wild, cracked voice. He was not quick enough. A vague shape appeared behind his back, and a witcher's blade whistled in the air and severed his neck at the base of his skull.

'Geralt!'

'Ciri.'

'This isn't the time for tenderness,' said the owl from the top of the wall, transforming into a dark-haired woman. 'Flee! The squirrels will be here soon!'

Ciri freed herself from Geralt's arms and looked up in astonishment. The owl-woman sitting on top of the wall looked ghastly. She was blackened, ragged and smeared in ash and blood.

'You little monster,' said the owl-woman, looking down at her. 'For your inopportune augury I ought to ... But I made your Witcher a promise, and I always keep my promises. I couldn't give you Rience, Geralt. In exchange I'm giving you her. Alive. Flee, both of you!'

Cahir Mawr Dyffryn aep Ceallach was furious. He had seen the girl he had been ordered to capture, but only for a moment. Then, before he had been able to act, the insane sorcerers unleashed such an inferno in Garstang that no action was possible. Cahir lost his bearings among the smoke and flames, blindly stumbling along corridors, running up and down stairs and through cloisters, and cursing Vilgefortz, Rience, himself and the entire world.

He happened upon an elf who told him the girl had been seen outside the palace, fleeing along the road to Aretuza. And then fortune smiled upon Cahir. The Scoia'tael found a saddled horse in the stable.

'Run, Ciri, run. They're close. I'll stop them, you run. Fast as you can! Just like you used to on the assault course!'

'Are you abandoning me too?'

'I'll be right behind you. But don't look back!'

'Give me my sword, Geralt.'

He looked at her. Ciri stepped back involuntarily. She had never seen him with an expression like that before.

'If you had a sword, you might have to kill with it. Can you do it?'

'I don't know. Give me my sword.'

'Run. And don't look back.'

Horses' hooves thudded on the road. Ciri looked back. And she froze, paralysed with fear.

She was being pursued by a black knight in a helmet decorated with raptor wings. The wings whooshed, and the black cloak streamed behind him. Horseshoes sent up sparks from the cobblestones.

She was unable to move.

The black horse burst through the roadside bushes, and the knight shouted loudly. Cintra was in that cry. The night, slaughter, blood and conflagration were in that cry. Ciri overcame her overwhelming fear and darted away. She leapt over a hedge and plunged into a small courtyard with a fountain. There was no way out; it was encircled by smooth, high walls. She could hear the horse snorting behind her. She turned, stumbled backwards and shuddered as she felt a hard, unyielding wall behind her. She was trapped.

The bird of prey flapped its wings, taking flight. The black knight urged his horse on and jumped the hedge separating him from the courtyard. Hooves thudded on the slabs, and the horse slipped, skidded and sat back on its haunches. The knight swayed in the saddle and toppled over. The horse regained its footing but the knight fell off, his armour clattering on the stones. He was on his feet immediately, though, and quickly trapped Ciri, who was pinned into a corner.

'You will not touch me!' she screamed, drawing her sword. 'You will never touch me again!'

The knight moved slowly towards her, rising up like a huge, black tower. The wings on his helmet moved to and fro and whispered.

'You will not escape me now, o Lion Cub of Cintra,' he said, and his cruel eyes burned in the slit of his helmet. 'Not this time. This time you have nowhere to run, o reckless maiden.'

'You will not touch me,' she repeated in a voice of stifled horror, her back pressed against the stone wall.

'I have to. I am carrying out orders.'

As he held out his hand to seize her, Ciri's fear subsided, to be replaced by savage fury. Her tense muscles, previously frozen in terror, began to work like springs. All the moves she had learned in Kaer Morhen performed themselves, smoothly and fluidly. Ciri jumped; the knight lunged towards her but was unprepared for the pirouette which spun her effortlessly out of reach of his hands. Her sword whined and stung, striking unerringly between the plates of his armour. The knight staggered and dropped to one knee as a stream of scarlet blood spurted from beneath his spaulder. Screaming fiercely, Ciri whirled around him with another pirouette and struck the knight again, this time directly on the bell of his helmet, knocking him down onto his other knee. Fury and madness had utterly blinded her, and she saw nothing except the loathsome wings. The black feathers were strewn in all directions. One wing fell off, and the other was resting on the bloodied spaulder. The knight, still vainly trying to get up from his knees, tried to seize her sword in his armoured glove and grunted painfully as the witcher blade slashed through the chainmail sleeve into his hand. The next blow knocked off his helmet, and Ciri jumped back to gather momentum for the last, mortal blow.

She did not strike.

There was no black helmet, no raptor's wings, whose whistling had tormented her in her nightmares. There was no black knight of Cintra. There was a pale, dark-haired young man with stupefyingly blue eyes and a mouth distorted in a grimace of fear, kneeling in a pool of blood. The black knight of Cintra had fallen beneath the blows of her sword, had ceased to exist. Only hacked-up feathers remained of the forbidding wings. The terrified, cowering young man bleeding profusely was no one. She did not know him; she had never seen him before. He meant nothing to her. She wasn't afraid of him, nor did she hate him. And neither did she want to kill him.

She threw her sword onto the ground.

She turned around, hearing the cries of the Scoia'tael approaching fast from Garstang. She knew that in a moment they would trap her in the courtyard. She knew they would catch up with her on the road. She had to be quicker than them. She ran over to the black horse, which was clattering its horseshoes on the paved ground, and urged it into a gallop with a cry, leaping into the saddle in full flight.

'Leave me ...' groaned Cahir Mawr Dyffryn aep Ceallach, pushing away the elves who were trying to lift him up with his good hand. 'I'm fine. It's just a scratch ... After her. Get the girl ...'

One of the elves screamed, and blood spurted into Cahir's face. Another Scoia'tael reeled and fell to his knees, his fingers clutching his mutilated belly. The remaining elves leapt back and scattered all around the courtyard, swords flashing.

190

They had been attacked by a white-haired fiend, who had fallen on them from a wall, from a height that would have broken a normal man's legs. It ought to have been impossible to land gently, whirl in an impossibly fast pirouette, and a split second later begin killing. But the white-haired fiend had done it. And the killing had begun.

The Scoia'tael fought fiercely. They had the advantage, but they had no chance. A massacre was played out before Cahir's eyes, wide with terror. The fair-haired girl, who had wounded him a moment earlier, had been fast, had been unbelievably lithe, had been like a mother cat defending her kittens. But the white-haired fiend who had fallen amongst the Scoia'tael was like a Zerrikan tiger. The fair-haired maid of Cintra, who for some unknown reason had not killed him, seemed insane. The white-haired fiend was not insane. He was calm and cold. And killed calmly and coldly.

The Scoia'tael had no chance. Their corpses piled up on the slabs of the courtyard. But they did not yield. Even when only two of them remained, they did not run away, but attacked the white-haired fiend once more. The fiend hacked off the arm of one of them above the elbow as Cahir watched. He hit the other elf with an apparently light, casual blow, which nonetheless threw him backwards. It tipped him over the lip of the fountain and hurled him into the water. The water brimmed over the edge of the basin in ripples of crimson.

The elf with the severed arm knelt by the fountain, staring vacantly at the blood gushing from the stump. The white-haired fiend seized him by the hair and cut his throat with a rapid slash of his sword.

When Cahir opened his eyes the fiend was standing over him.

'Don't kill me ...' he whispered, giving up his efforts to rise from the ground, now slippery with blood. His hand, slashed by the fair-haired girl, had gone numb and did not hurt.

'I know who you are, Nilfgaardian,' said the white-haired fiend, kicking the helmet with the hacked-up wings. 'You have been pursuing her doggedly and long. But now you will harm her no more.'

'Don't kill me ...'

'Give me one reason. Just one. Make haste.'

'It was I ...' whispered Cahir. 'It was I who got her out of Cintra. From the fire ... I rescued her. I saved her life ...'

When he opened his eyes, the fiend was no longer there. Cahir was alone in the courtyard with the bodies of the elves. The water in the fountain soughed, spilling over the edge of the basin, washing away the blood on the ground. Cahir fainted.

At the foot of the tower stood a building which seemed to be a single, large hall, or perhaps some kind of peristyle. The roof over the peristyle, probably illusory, was full of holes. It was supported by columns and pilasters carved in the shape of scantily clad caryatids with generous breasts. The same kinds of caryatids supported the arch of the entrance through which Ciri had vanished. Beyond the doorway, Geralt noticed some steps leading upwards. Towards the tower.

The Witcher cursed under his breath. He did not understand why she had fled there. He had seen her horse fall as he rushed after her along the tops of the walls. He saw her leap nimbly to her feet, but instead of running along the winding road encircling the peak, she had suddenly rushed uphill, towards the solitary tower. Only later did he notice the elves on the road. Those elves – busy shooting arrows at some men running uphill – saw neither Ciri nor himself. Reinforcements were arriving from Aretuza.

He intended to follow Ciri up the steps when he heard a sound. From above. He quickly turned around. It was not a bird.

Vilgefortz flew down through a hole in the roof, his wide sleeves swishing, and slowly alighted on the floor.

Geralt stood in front of the entrance to the tower, drew his sword and heaved a sigh. He had sincerely hoped that the dramatic, concluding fight would be played out between Vilgefortz and Philippa Eilhart. He didn't have the least bit of interest in this kind of drama.

Vilgefortz brushed down his jerkin, straightened his cuffs, looked at the Witcher and read his mind.

'Infernal drama,' he sighed. Geralt made no comment.

'Did she go into the tower?'

He made no answer. The sorcerer nodded his head.

'So we have an epilogue then,' he said coldly. 'The denouement that draws the play to a close. Or is it perhaps fate? Do you know where those steps lead? To Tor Lara. To the Tower of Gulls. There is no way out of there. It's all over.'

Geralt stepped back between two of the caryatids holding up the doorway, in order to protect his flanks.

'Yes indeed,' he drawled, keeping his eyes on the sorcerer's hands. 'It's all over. Half of your accomplices are dead. The bodies of the elves who were brought to Thanedd are piled up all the way to Garstang. The others ran away. Sorcerers and Dijkstra's men are arriving from Aretuza. The Nilfgaardian who was supposed to take Ciri has probably bled to death already. And Ciri is up there in the tower. No way out of there? I'm glad to hear it. That means there's only one way in. The one I'm blocking.'

Vilgefortz bridled.

'You're incorrigible. You are still incapable of assessing the situation correctly. The Chapter and Council have ceased to exist. The forces of Emperor Emhyr are marching north. Deprived of the mages' assistance and advice, the kings are as helpless as children. In the face of Nilfgaard, their kingdoms are tumbling like sandcastles. I proposed this to you yesterday and repeat it today: join the victors. Spit on the losers.'

'It is you who's lost. You were only a tool to Emhyr. He wanted Ciri, which is why he sent that character with the wings on his helmet. I wonder what Emhyr will do to you when you report this fiasco.'

'You're shooting wildly, Witcher. And you're wide of the mark, naturally. What if I told you that Emhyr is my tool?'

'I wouldn't believe you.'

'Geralt, be sensible. Do you really want to play at theatrics, play out the banal final battle between good and evil? I repeat my proposition of yesterday. It is by no means too late. You can still make a choice. You can join the right side—'

'Join the side I thinned out a little today?'

'Don't grin. Your demonic smiles make no impression on me. Those few elves you hacked down? Artaud Terranova? Trifles,

193

meaningless details. They can be waved aside.'

'But of course. I know your philosophy. Death has no meaning, right? Particularly other people's?'

'Don't be trite. It's a pity about Artaud but, well, too bad. Let's call it . . . settling old scores. After all, I tried to kill you twice. Emhyr grew impatient, so I sent some assassins after you. Each time I did it with genuine reluctance. You see, I still hope they'll paint a picture of us one day.'

'Abandon that hope, Vilgefortz.'

'Put away your sword. Let's go up into Tor Lara together. We'll reassure the Child of the Elder Blood, who is sure to be dying of fright up there somewhere. And then let's leave. Together. You'll be by her side. You will see her destiny fulfilled. And Emperor Emhyr? Emperor Emhyr will get what he wanted. Because I forgot to tell you that although Codringher and Fenn are dead, their work and ideas are still alive and doing very well, thank you.'

'You are lying. Leave this place before I spit on *you*.'

'I really have no desire to kill you. I kill with reluctance.'

'Indeed? What about Lydia van Bredevoort?'

The sorcerer sneered.

'Speak not that name, Witcher.'

Geralt gripped the hilt of his sword tightly and smiled scornfully.

'Why did Lydia have to die, Vilgefortz? Why did you order her death? She was meant to distract attention from you, wasn't she? She was meant to give you time to become resistant to dimeritium, to send a telepathic signal to Rience, wasn't she? Poor Lydia, the artist with the damaged face. Everyone knew she was expendable. Everyone knew that except her.'

'Be silent.'

'You murdered Lydia, wizard. You used her. And now you want to use Ciri? With my help? No. You will not enter Tor Lara.'

The sorcerer took a step back. Geralt tensed up, ready to jump and strike. Vilgefortz did not raise his hand, however, but simply held it out to one side. A stout, two-yard staff suddenly materialised in his hand.

'I know,' he said, 'what hinders you from making a sensible

194

assessment of the situation. I know what complicates and obstructs your attempts at making a correct prediction of the future. Your arrogance, Geralt. I will disabuse you of arrogance. And I will do so with the help of this magic staff here.'

The Witcher squinted and raised his blade a little.

'I'm trembling with impatience.'

A few weeks later, having been healed by the dryads and the waters of Brokilon, Geralt wondered what mistakes he had made during the fight. And came to the conclusion he hadn't made any. His only mistake was made before the fight. He ought to have fled before it even began.

The sorcerer was fast, his staff flickering in his hands like lightning. Geralt's astonishment was even greater when, during a parry, the staff and sword clanged metallically. But there was no time for astonishment. Vilgefortz attacked, and the Witcher had to contort himself using body-swerves and pirouettes. He was afraid to parry. The bloody staff was made of iron; and magical to boot.

Four times, he found himself in a position from which he was able to counterattack and deliver a blow. Four times, he struck. To the temple, to the neck, under the arm, to the thigh. Each blow ought to have been fatal. But each one was parried.

No human could have parried blows like that. Geralt slowly began to understand. But it was already too late.

He didn't see the blow that finally caught him. The impact drove him against the wall. He rebounded from it but was unable to jump aside or dodge. The blow had knocked the breath out of him. He was caught by a second blow, this time on the shoulder, and once again flew backwards, smashing his head against a protruding caryatid's breast on one of the pilasters. Vilgefortz leapt closer, swung the staff and thumped him in the belly, below the ribs. Very hard. Geralt doubled up and was then hit on the side of the head. His knees suddenly went weak and crumpled beneath him. And the fight was over. In principle.

He feebly tried to protect himself with his sword. The blade, caught between the wall and the pilaster, broke under a blow with a shrill, vibrating whine. He tried to protect his head with his left hand, but the staff fell with enough force to break his forearm. The pain utterly blinded him.

'I could smash your brain out through your ears,' said Vilgefortz from far away. 'But this was supposed to be a lesson. You were mistaken, Witcher. You mistook the stars reflected in a pond at night for the sky. Oh, are you vomiting? Good. Concussion. Bleeding from the nose? Excellent. Well, I shall see you later. One day. Perhaps.'

Now Geralt could see nothing and hear nothing. He was sinking, submerging into something warm. He thought Vilgefortz had gone. He was astonished, then, when a fierce blow from the iron staff struck his thigh, smashing the shaft of his femur.

If anything occurred after that, he did not remember it.

'Hang in there, Geralt. Don't give up,' repeated Triss Merigold endlessly. 'Hang in there. Don't die ... Please don't die ...'

'Ciri ...'

'Don't talk. I'll soon get you out of here. Hold on ... Damn I'm too weak, by the gods ...'

'Yennefer ... I have to—'

'You don't have to do anything! You can't do anything! Hang in there. Don't give up ... Don't faint ... Don't die, please ...'

She dragged him across the floor, which was littered with bodies. He saw his chest and belly covered in blood, which was streaming from his nose. He saw his leg. It was twisted at a strange angle and seemed much shorter than the intact one. He didn't feel any pain. He felt cold. His entire body was cold, numb and foreign. He wanted to puke.

'Hold on, Geralt. Help is coming from Aretuza. It'll soon be here ...'

'Dijkstra ... If Dijkstra gets his hands on me ... I'm finished ...'

Triss swore. Desperately.

She dragged him down the steps, his broken leg and arm bouncing down them. The pain returned. It bored into his guts and his temples, and it radiated all the way to his eyes, to his ears, to the top of his head. He didn't scream. He knew screaming would bring him relief, but he didn't scream. He just opened his mouth, which also brought him relief.

He heard a roar.

At the top of the stair stood Tissaia de Vries. Her hair was dishevelled, her face covered in dust. She raised both her hands, and her palms flamed. She screamed a spell and the flames dancing on her fingers hurtled downwards in the form of a blinding sphere, roaring with fire. The Witcher heard the clatter of walls crashing down below and the dreadful cries of people being burnt.

'No, Tissaia!' screamed Triss in desperation. 'Don't do it!'

'They will not enter here,' said the arch-mistress, without turning her head. 'This is Garstang, on the Isle of Thanedd. No one invited those royalist lackeys, who carry out the orders of their short-sighted kings!'

'You're killing them!'

'Be silent, Triss Merigold! The attack on the unity of the Brotherhood has failed. The island is still ruled by the Chapter! The kings should keep their hands off the Chapter's business! This is our conflict and we shall resolve it ourselves! We will resolve our business and then put an end to this senseless war, for it is we, sorcerers, who bear the responsibility for the fate of the world!'

A ball of lightning shot from her hands, and the redoubled echo of the explosion roared among the columns and stone walls.

'Begone!' she screamed again. 'You will not enter this place! Begone!'

The screaming from below subsided. Geralt understood that the attackers had withdrawn from the stairway, had beaten a retreat. Tissaia's outline blurred in front of his eyes. It wasn't magic. He was losing consciousness.

'Run, Triss Merigold,' the enchantress's words came from far away, as if from behind a wall. 'Philippa Eilhart has already fled; she flew away on owl's wings. You were her accomplice in this wicked conspiracy and I ought to punish you. But there has been enough blood, death and misfortune! Begone! Go to Aretuza and join your allies! Teleport away. The portal in the Tower of Gulls no longer exists. It was destroyed along with the tower. You can teleport without fear. Wherever you wish. To your King Foltest, for instance, for whom you betrayed the Brotherhood!'

'I will not leave Geralt ...' groaned Triss. 'He cannot fall into the hands of the Redanians ... He's gravely injured ... He has internal bleeding, and I have no more strength! I don't have the strength to open the portal! Tissaia! Help me please!'

Darkness. Bitter cold. From far away, from behind a stone wall, the voice of Tissaia de Vries:

'I shall help you.'

Evertsen Peter, b. 1234, confidant of Emperor Emhyr Deithwen and one of the true authors of the Empire's might. The chief chamberlain of the army during the time of the Northern Wars (q.v.), from 1290 imperial treasurer of the crown. In the final period of Emhyr's rule, he was raised to the rank of coadjutor of the Empire. During the rule of Emperor Morvran Voor he was falsely accused of misappropriation of funds, found guilty, imprisoned and died in 1301 in Winneburg Castle. Posthumously rehabilitated by Emperor Jan Calveit in 1328.

Effenberg and Talbot, *Encyclopaedia Maxima Mundi,*
Volume V

May Ye All Wail, for the Destroyer of Nations is upon us. Your lands shall they trample and divide with rope. Your cities razed shall be, their dwellers expelled. The bat, owl and raven your homes shall infest, and the serpent will therein make its nest ...

Aen Ithlinnespeath

CHAPTER FIVE

The captain of the squad reined back his mount, removed his helmet and used his fingers to comb his thinning hair, which was matted with sweat.

'Journey's over,' he repeated, seeing the troubadour's questioning gaze.

'What? How d'you mean?' said Dandelion, astonished. 'Why?'

'We aren't going any further. Do you see? The river you see glinting down there is the Ribbon. We were only told to escort you to the Ribbon. That means it's time we were off.'

The rest of the troops stopped behind them, but none of the soldiers dismounted. They were all looking around nervously. Dandelion shielded his eyes with a hand and stood up in the stirrups.

'Where can you see that river?'

'I said it's down there. Ride down the ravine and you'll be there in no time.'

'You could at least escort me to the bank,' protested Dandelion, 'and show me the ford ...'

'There's nothing much to show. Since May the weather's been baking hot, so the water level's dropped. There isn't much water in the Ribbon. Your horse won't have any problem crossing it ...'

'I showed your commander the letter from King Venzlav,' said the troubadour, puffing up. 'He read the contents and I heard him order you to escort me to the very edge of Brokilon. And you're going to abandon me here in this thicket? What'll happen if I get lost?'

'You won't get lost,' muttered another soldier gloomily, who had come closer but had not so far spoken. 'You won't have time to get lost. A dryad's arrow will find you first.'

'What cowardly simpletons,' Dandelion sneered. 'I see you're afraid of the dryads. But Brokilon only begins on the far bank of the

201

Ribbon. The river is the border. We haven't crossed it yet.'

'Their border,' explained the leader, looking around, 'extends as far as their arrows do. A powerful bow shot from that bank will send an arrow right to the edge of the forest and still have enough impetus to pierce a hauberk. You insisted on going there. That's your business, it's your hide. But life is dear to me. I'm not going any further. I'd rather shove my head in a hornets' nest!'

'I've explained to you,' said Dandelion, pushing his hat back and sitting up in the saddle, 'that I'm riding to Brokilon on a mission. I am, it may be said, an ambassador. I do not fear dryads. But I would like you to escort me to the bank of the Ribbon. What'll happen if brigands rob me in that thicket?'

The gloomy soldier laughed affectedly.

'Brigands? Here? In daylight? You won't meet a soul here during the day. Latterly, the dryads have been letting arrows fly at anyone who appears on the bank of the Ribbon, and they're not above venturing deeper into our territory either. No, no need to be afraid of brigands.'

'That's true,' agreed the captain. 'A brigand would have to be pretty stupid to be riding along the Ribbon during the day. And we're not idiots. You're riding alone, without armour or weapons, and you don't look, forgive me, anything like a fighting man. You can see that a mile off. That may favour you. But if those dryads see us, on horseback and armed, you won't be able to see the sun for arrows.'

'Ah, well. There's nothing else for it.' Dandelion patted his horse's neck and looked down towards the ravine. 'I shall have to ride alone. Farewell, soldiers. Thank you for the escort.'

'Don't be in such a rush,' said the gloomy soldier, looking up at the sky. 'It'll be evening soon. Set off when the haze starts rising from the water. Because, you know ...'

'What?'

'An arrow's not so sure in the fog. If fate smiles on you, the dryads might miss. But they seldom miss ...'

'I told you—'

'All right, all right. I've got it. You're going to them on some kind of mission. But I'll tell you something else. They don't care whether it's a mission or a church procession. They'll let fly at you, and that's that.'

'You insist on frightening me, do you?' said the poet snootily. 'What do you take me for, a court scribbler? I, my good men, have seen more battlegrounds than the lot of you. And I know more about dryads than you. If only that they never fire without warning.'

'It once was thus, you're right,' said the leader quietly. 'Once they gave warnings. They shot an arrow into a tree trunk or into the road, and that marked the border that you couldn't cross. If a fellow turned back right then, he could get out in one piece. But now it's different. Now they shoot to kill at once.'

'Why such cruelty?'

'Well,' muttered the soldier, 'it's like this. When the kings made a truce with Nilfgaard, they went after the elven gangs with a will. You can tell they're putting the screws on, for there isn't a night that survivors don't flee through Brugge, seeking shelter in Brokilon. And when our boys hunt the elves, they sometimes mix it with the dryads too, those who come to the elves' aid from the far side of the Ribbon. And our army has also been known to go too far . . . Get my drift?'

'Yes,' said Dandelion, looking at the soldier intently and shaking his head. 'When you were hunting the Scoia'tael you crossed the Ribbon. And you killed some dryads. And now the dryads are taking their revenge in the same way. It's war.'

'That it is. You took the words right out of my mouth. War. It was always a fight to kill – never to let live – but now it's worse than ever. There's a fierce hatred between them and us. I'll say it one more time: if you don't have to, don't go there.'

Dandelion swallowed.

'The whole point,' he said, sitting tall in the saddle and working hard to assume a resolute expression and strike a dashing pose, 'is that I *do* have to. And I'm going. Right now. Evening or no evening, fog or no fog. Duty calls.'

The years of practice paid off. The troubadour's voice sounded beautiful and menacing, austere and cold. It rang with iron and valour. The soldiers looked at him in unfeigned admiration.

'Before you set off,' said the leader, unfastening a flat, wooden canteen from his saddle, 'neck down some vodka, minstrel, sir. Have a good old swig ...'

'It'll make the dying easier,' added the gloomy one, morosely.

The poet sipped from the canteen.

'A coward,' he declared with dignity, when he'd stopped coughing and had got his breath back, 'dies a hundred times. A brave man dies but once. But Dame Fortune favours the brave and holds cowards in contempt.'

The soldiers looked at him in even greater admiration. They didn't know and couldn't have known that Dandelion was quoting from a heroic epic poem. Moreover, from one written by someone else.

'I shall repay you for the escort with this,' said the poet, removing a jingling, leather pouch from his bosom. 'Before you return to the fort, before you're once again embraced by strict mother-duty, stop by at a tavern and drink my health.'

'Thank you, sir,' said the leader, blushing somewhat. 'You are generous, although we— Forgive us for leaving you alone, but ...'

'It's nothing. Farewell.'

The bard adjusted his hat to a jaunty angle over his left ear, prodded his horse with his heels and headed into the ravine, whistling 'The Wedding Party at Bullerlyn', a well-known and extremely indecent cavalry song.

'The cornet in the fort said he was a freeloader, a coward and a knobhead. But he's a valiant, military gentleman, even if he is a poetaster.' The voice of the gloomy soldier was carried to Dandelion's ears.

'Truly spoken,' responded the captain. 'He isn't faint-hearted, you couldn't say that. He didn't even bat an eyelid, I noticed. And on top of that, he's whistling, can you hear? Ho, ho ... Heard what he said? That he's an embarrassador. You can be sure they don't make any old bugger an embarrassador. You've got to have your head screwed on to be made an embarrassador ...'

Dandelion quickened his pace in order to get away as quickly as possible. He didn't want to sabotage the reputation he'd just earned himself. And he knew, with his mouth drying up in terror, that he wouldn't be able to whistle for much longer.

The ravine was sombre and damp, and the wet clay and carpet of rotten leaves lying on it muffled the thudding of his dark bay gelding's hooves. He'd called the horse 'Pegasus'. Pegasus walked slowly, head hanging down. He was one of those rare specimens of horse who could never care less.

The forest had come to an end, but a wide, reedy meadow still separated Dandelion from the banks of the river, which was marked by a belt of alders. The poet reined Pegasus in. He looked around carefully but didn't see anything. He listened out intently but only heard the singing of frogs.

'Well, boy,' he croaked. 'It's do or die. Gee up.'

Pegasus lifted his head a little and stuck up his ears, which normally hung down, questioningly.

'You heard right. Off you go.'

The gelding set off reluctantly, the boggy ground squelching beneath his hooves. Frogs fled with long hops. A duck took flight a few paces in front of them, fluttering and quacking, briefly stopping the troubadour's heart, after which it began pounding very hard and very rapidly. Pegasus showed no interest in the duck whatsoever.

'The hero rode ...' mumbled Dandelion, wiping the cold sweat from the nape of his neck with a handkerchief taken from inside his jerkin, 'rode fearlessly through the wilderness, heedless of the leaping lizards and flying dragons ... He rode and rode ... Until he reached a vast expanse of water ...'

Pegasus snorted and stopped. They were by the river, among reeds and bulrushes, which stood taller than his stirrups. Dandelion wiped his sweaty forehead and tied the handkerchief around his neck. He had been staring at the alder thicket on the far bank until his eyes watered. He saw nothing and no one. The surface of the water rippled from waterweed being swayed by the current, while overhead turquoise and orange kingfishers flitted past. The air twinkled with swarming insects. Fish gulped down mayflies, leaving huge rings on the surface of the water.

Everywhere, as far as the eye could see, there were beaver lodges

– piles of cut branches, and felled and gnawed tree trunks – being washed by the lazy current.

There's an astonishing abundance of beavers here, thought the poet. *And no small wonder. No one bothers those bloody tree-chewers. Neither robbers, hunters nor forest beekeepers venture into this region; not even those interfering fur trappers would dare set their snares here. The ones who tried would have got an arrow through the throat, and the crayfish would have nibbled on them in the ooze by the riverbank. And I, the idiot, am forcing my way out here of my own free will; here, by the Ribbon, over which hangs a cadaverous stench, a stench which even the scent of sweet flag and mint cannot mask . . .*

He sighed heavily.

Pegasus slowly planted his forelegs into the water, lowered his muzzle towards the surface, drank long, and then turned his head and looked at Dandelion. The water dripped from his muzzle and nostrils. The poet nodded, sighed once more and sniffed loudly.

'The hero gazed on the maelstrom,' he quietly declaimed, trying not to let his teeth chatter. 'He gazed on it and travelled on, for his heart knew not trepidation.'

Pegasus lowered his head and ears.

'*Knew not trepidation*, I said.'

Pegasus shook his head, jingling the rings on his reins and bit. Dandelion dug a heel into his side. The gelding entered the water with pompous resignation.

The Ribbon was shallow but very overgrown. Before they had reached the centre of the current, Pegasus was dragging long plaits of waterweed. The horse walked slowly and with effort, trying to shake the annoying pondweed off with every step.

The rushes and alders of the far bank were close. So close that Dandelion felt his stomach sinking low, very low, right down to the saddle itself. He knew that in the centre of the river, entangled in the waterweed, he was an excellent target; a sitting duck. In his mind's eye he could already see bows bending, bowstrings being pulled back and sharp arrowheads being aimed at him.

He squeezed the horse's sides with his calves, but Pegasus was having none of it. Instead of picking up speed, he stopped and lifted

206

his tail. Balls of dung splashed into the water. Dandelion gave a long groan.

'The hero,' he muttered, closing his eyes, 'was unable to cross the raging rapids. He fell in action, pierced by many missiles. He was hidden for ages long in the azure depths, rocked by jade-green algae. All traces of him vanished. Only horse shit remained, borne by the current to the distant sea ...'

Pegasus, clearly relieved, headed jauntily towards the bank without any encouragement, and when he reached the bank, and was finally free of waterweed, even took the liberty of breaking into a canter, utterly soaking Dandelion's trousers and boots. The poet didn't notice it, though, since the vision of arrows aimed at his belly hadn't left him for a moment, and dread crept down his neck and back like a huge, cold, slimy leech. For beyond the alders, less than a hundred paces away, beyond the vivid green band of riverside grass, rose up a vertical, black, menacing wall of trees.

It was Brokilon.

On the bank, a few steps downstream, lay the white skeleton of a horse. Nettles and bulrushes had grown through its ribcage. Some other – smaller – bones, which didn't come from a horse, were also lying there. Dandelion shuddered and looked away.

Squelching and splashing, the gelding, urged on by Dandelion, hauled himself out of the riverside swamp, the mud smelling unpleasantly. The frogs stopped croaking for a moment. It all went very quiet. Dandelion closed his eyes. He stopped declaiming and improvising. His inspiration and daring had evaporated. Only cold, revolting fear remained; an intense sensation, but one utterly bereft of creative impulses.

Pegasus perked up his floppy ears and dispassionately shambled towards the Forest of the Dryads. Called by many the Forest of Death.

I've crossed the border, thought the poet. *Now it will all be settled. While I was by the river and in the water, they could be magnanimous. But not now. Now I'm an intruder. Just like that one ... I might end up a skeleton, too; a warning for people to heed ... If there are dryads here at all. If they're watching me ...*

He recalled watching shooting tournaments, competitions and archery displays at country markets. Straw targets and mannequins, studded or torn apart by arrowheads. *What does a man feel when he's hit by an arrow? The impact? Pain? Or perhaps ... nothing?*

There were either no dryads nearby, or they hadn't made up their minds what to do with this lone rider, because the poet rode up to the forest petrified with fear but in one piece. Entry to the trees was barred by a dense tangle of scrub and fallen trunks, bristling with roots and branches, but in any case Dandelion didn't have the slightest intention of riding up to the very edge, much less of heading deeper into the forest. He was capable of making himself take risks – but not of committing suicide.

He dismounted very slowly and fastened the reins to a protruding root. He didn't usually do that; Pegasus wasn't inclined to wander away from his master. Dandelion was not certain, however, how the horse would react to the whistle and whir of arrows. Up until now he had tried not to expose either Pegasus or himself to sounds of that kind.

He removed a lute from the saddle's pommel. It was a unique, magnificent instrument with a slender neck. *This was a present from a she-elf*, he recalled, stroking the inlaid wood. *It might end up returning to the Elder Folk ... Unless the dryads leave it by my dead body ...*

Close by lay an old tree, blown down in a gale. The poet sat down on the trunk, rested the lute on his knee, licked his lips and wiped his sweaty hands on his trousers.

The day was drawing to a close. A haze rose from the Ribbon, forming a grey-white shroud enveloping the meadows. It was cooler now. The honking of cranes sounded and died away, leaving only the croaking of frogs.

Dandelion plucked the strings. Once, then twice, then a third time. He twisted the pegs, tuned the lute and began to play. And a moment later, to sing.

Yviss, m'evelienn vente cáelm en tell
Elaine Ettariel Aep cór me lode deith ess'viell
Yn blath que me darienn

208

Aen minne vain tegen a me
Yn toin av muirednn que dis eveigh e aep llea ...

The sun vanished behind the trees. It immediately became dark in
the shade of Brokilon's mighty trees.

Ueassan Lamm feainne renn, ess'ell,
Elaine Ettariel,
Aep cor ...

He didn't hear – but he felt – somebody's presence.
'N'te mirę daetre. Sh'aente vort.'
'Don't shoot ...' he whispered, obediently not looking around.
'N'aen aespar a me ... I come in peace ...'
'N'ess a tearth. Sh'aente.'
He obeyed, although his fingers had turned cold and numb on the
strings, and he had difficulty making any sound whatsoever emerge
from his throat. But there was no hostility in the dryad's voice and
he was a professional, dammit.

Ueassan Lamm feainne renn, ess'ell,
Elaine Ettariel,
Aep cor aen tedd teviel e gwen
Yn blath que me darienn
Ess yn e evellien a me
Que shaent te cáelm a'vean minne me striscea ...

This time he took the liberty of glancing over his shoulder.
Whatever was crouching by the tree trunk, very near, resembled a
bush entwined in ivy. But it wasn't a bush. Bushes didn't have such
large, shining eyes.

Pegasus snorted softly, and Dandelion knew that behind him in
the darkness someone was stroking his horse's muzzle.

'Sh'aente vort,' requested the dryad squatting behind him once
again. Her voice was like the pattering of rain on leaves.

'I ...' he began. 'I am ... The comrade of the witcher Geralt ... I know that Geralt— That Gwynbleidd is among you in Brokilon. I have come ...'

'N'te dice'en. Sh'aente, va.'

'Sh'aent,' gently asked a second dryad from behind him, virtually in unison with a third. And maybe a fourth. He couldn't be certain.

'Yea, sh'aente, taedh,' said the thing that a moment earlier the poet had taken to be a birch sapling standing a few paces in front of him, in a silvery, girlish voice. 'Ess'laine ... Taedh ... Sing ... Sing some more about Ettariel ... Yes?'

He did as she asked.

To adore you, is all my life
Fair Ettariel
Let me keep, then, the treasure of memories
And the magical flower;
A pledge and sign of your love.
Silvered by drops of dew as if by tears ...

This time he heard steps approaching.

'Dandelion.'

'Geralt!'

'Yes, it's me. You can stop that racket now.'

'How did you find me? How did you know I was in Brokilon?'

'Triss Merigold ... Bloody hell ...' said Dandelion. He tripped again and would have fallen, had a passing dryad not seized him in a dextrous and astonishingly powerful grip for one so slight.

'Gar'ean, táedh,' she warned in silver tones. 'Va cáelm.'

'Thank you. It's awfully dark here ... Geralt? Where are you?'

'Here. Don't lag behind.'

Dandelion quickened his pace, stumbled once more and almost fell on the Witcher, who had stopped in the dark in front of him. The dryads passed by them silently.

'It's hellishly dark ... Is it much further?'

'No. We'll soon be at the camp. Who, apart from Triss, knows I'm hiding here? Did you let it slip to anyone?'

'I had to tell King Venzlav. I needed safe conduct through Brugge. You wouldn't believe the times we live in ... I also had to have permission for the expedition to Brokilon. But anyway, Venzlav knows you and likes you ... He appointed me an envoy. Just imagine. I'm sure he'll keep it secret, I asked him to. Don't get annoyed now, Geralt ...'

The Witcher came closer. Dandelion couldn't see the expression on his face, only the white hair and bristles of several days' beard growth, which was visible even in the dark.

'I'm not annoyed,' said the Witcher, placing his hand on Dandelion's shoulder. It seemed as though his voice, which up until then had been cold, was somewhat changed. 'I'm glad you're here, you whoreson.'

'It's so cold here,' said Dandelion, shuddering and making the branches they were sitting on creak under him. 'We could get a fire going—'

'Don't even think about it,' muttered the Witcher. 'Have you forgotten where you are?'

'Are you serious ... ?' The troubadour glanced around timidly. 'Oh. No fire, right?'

'Trees hate fire. And they do too.'

'Dammit. Are we going to sit here and freeze? And in the bloody dark? I can't see my hand in front of my face ...'

'Keep it by your side then.'

Dandelion sighed, hunched forward and rubbed his arms. He heard the Witcher beside him breaking some thin twigs in his fingers.

A small green light suddenly flared up in the dark, first of all dim and faint, then quickly becoming brighter. After the first one, many others began to glimmer around them, moving and dancing like fireflies or will-o'-the-wisps above a marsh. The forest suddenly came to life with a shimmering of shadows, and Dandelion began to see the silhouettes of the dryads surrounding them. One of them approached and put something on the ground near them, which looked like a hot, glowing tangle of plants. The poet reached a hand out carefully and took hold of it. The green glow was totally cold.

'What is it, Geralt?'

'Rotten wood and a special kind of moss. It only grows here in Brokilon. And only they know how to weave it all together to make it give off light. Thank you, Fauve.'

The dryad did not answer, but neither did she go away, remaining squatting alongside the pair. She had a garland on her brow, and her long hair fell to her shoulders. Her hair looked green in the light and may actually have been green. Dandelion knew that dryads' hair could be of the weirdest colours.

'Taedh,' she said melodically, raising her flashing eyes to the troubadour. Her fine-featured face was crossed diagonally by two parallel dark stripes of painted camouflage. 'Ess've vort shaente aen Ettariel? Shaente a'vean vort?'

'No ... Later perhaps,' he answered politely, carefully searching for words in the Elder Speech. The dryad sighed and leaned over, gently stroking the neck of the lute, which was lying nearby. She rose nimbly to her feet. Dandelion watched her as she disappeared into the forest towards the others, whose shadows showed faintly in the dim light of the small green lanterns.

'I trust I didn't offend her, did I?' he asked softly. 'They have their own dialect, and I don't know polite expressions ...'

'Check whether you've got a knife in your guts,' said the Witcher, with neither mockery nor humour in his voice. 'Dryads react to insults by sticking a knife in your belly. Don't worry, Dandelion. I'd say they're willing to forgive you a good deal more than slips of the tongue. The concert you gave at the edge of the forest was clearly to their liking. Now you're ard táedh, "the great bard". They're waiting for the next part of 'The Flower of Ettariel'. Do you know the rest? It's not your ballad, after all.'

'It's my translation. I also embellished it somewhat with elven music. Didn't you notice?'

'No.'

'As I thought. Fortunately, dryads are more receptive to art. I read somewhere that they're exceptionally musical. Which is why I came up with my cunning plan. For which, incidentally, you haven't yet praised me.'

'My congratulations,' said the Witcher after a moment's silence. 'It was indeed cunning. And fortune smiled on you, as usual. They shoot accurately at two hundred paces. They don't usually wait until someone crosses onto their bank of the river and begins to sing. They are very sensitive to unpleasant smells. So when the corpse falls into the Ribbon and gets carried away by the current, they don't have to put up with the stench.'

'Oh, whatever,' said the poet, clearing his throat and swallowing. 'The most important thing is I pulled it off and found you. Geralt, how did you ...'

'Do you have a razor?'

'Eh? Of course I do.'

'Lend it to me tomorrow morning. This beard of mine is driving me insane.'

'Didn't the dryads have any? Hmm ... I guess not, they don't have much need for them, do they? Of course, I'll lend it to you. Geralt?'

'What?'

'I don't have any grub with me. Should ard táedh, the great bard, hold out any hopes of supper when visiting dryads?'

'They don't eat supper. Never. And the guards on Brokilon's border don't eat breakfast either. You'll have to survive until noon. I've already got used to it.'

'But when we get to their capital, the famous, Duen Canell, concealed in the very heart of the forest ...'

'We'll never get there, Dandelion.'

'What? I thought ... But you— I mean they've given you sanctuary. After all ... they tolerate ...'

'You've chosen the right word.'

They both said nothing for a long time.

'War,' said the poet finally. 'War, hatred and contempt. Everywhere. In everyone's hearts.'

'You're being poetic.'

'But that's what it's like.'

'Precisely. Right, tell me your news. Tell me what's been happening in the world while they've been tending to me here.'

'First,' said Dandelion, coughing softly, 'tell me what really happened in Garstang.'

'Didn't Triss tell you?'

'Yes, she did. But I'd like to hear your version.'

'If you know Triss's version, you know a more complete and probably more faithful version already. Tell me what's happened since I've been here.'

'Geralt,' whispered Dandelion. 'I don't know what happened to Yennefer and Ciri ... No one does. Triss doesn't either ...'

The Witcher shifted suddenly, making the branches creak.

'Did I ask you about Ciri or Yennefer?' he said in a different voice. 'Tell me about the war.'

'Don't you know anything? Hasn't any news reached you here?'

'Yes, it has. But I want to hear everything from you. Speak, please.'

'The Nilfgaardians,' began the bard after a moment's silence, 'attacked Lyria and Aedirn. Without declaring war. The reason was supposedly an attack by Demavend's forces on some border fort in Dol Angra, which happened during the mages' conclave on Thanedd. Some people say it was a setup. That they were Nilfgaardians disguised as Demavend's soldiers. We'll probably never find out what really happened. In any case, Nilfgaard's retaliation was swift and overwhelming; the border was crossed by a powerful army, which must have been concentrated in Dol Angra for weeks, if not months. Spalla and Scala, the two Lyrian border strongholds, were captured right away, in just three days. Rivia was prepared for a siege lasting months but capitulated after two days under the pressure of the guilds and the merchants who were promised that, should the town open its gates and pay a ransom, it wouldn't be sacked ...'

'Was the promise kept?'

'Yes.'

'Interesting.' The Witcher's voice changed again a little. 'Promises being kept in these times? I won't mention that, in the past, no one would have dreamed of making promises like that, because no one would have expected them. Craftsmen and merchants never opened the gates of strongholds, they defended them; each guild had its own tower or machicolations.'

214

'Money has no fatherland, Geralt. The merchants don't care whose rule they make their money under. And the Nilfgaardian palatine doesn't care who he levies taxes on. Dead merchants don't make money or pay taxes.'

'Go on.'

'After the capitulation of Rivia the Nilfgaardian Army headed northwards at great speed, almost without encountering any resistance. The armies of Demavend and Meve withdrew, unable to form a front in the deciding battle. The Nilfgaardians reached Aldersberg. In order to prevent the stronghold being blockaded, Demavend and Meve decided to join battle. The positions of their armies could have been better ... Bugger it, if there were more light here I'd draw you—'

'Don't draw anything. And keep it brief. Who won?'

'Have you heard, sir?' said a reeve, out of breath and sweating, pushing through the group gathered around the table. 'A messenger has arrived from the field! We have triumphed! The battle is won! Victory! It is our day, our day! We have vanquished our foe, we have beaten him into the ground!'

'Silence,' scowled Evertsen. 'My head is splitting from your cries. Yes, I've heard, I've heard. We've vanquished the foe. It is our day, it is our field and it is also our victory. What a sensation.'

The bailiffs and reeves fell silent and looked at their superior in astonishment.

'Do you not rejoice, Chamberlain, sir?'

'That I do. But I'm able to do it quietly.'

The reeves were silent and looked at one another. *Young pups,* thought Evertsen. *Overexcited young whippersnappers. Actually, I'm not surprised at them. But for heaven's sake, there, on the hill, even Menno Coehoorn and Elan Trahe, forsooth, even the grizzly bearded General Braibant, are yelling, jumping for joy and slapping each other's backs in congratulation. Victory! It is our day! But who else's day could it have been? The kingdoms of Aedirn and Lyria only managed to mobilise three thousand horse and ten thousand foot, of which one-fifth had already been blockaded in the first days of the invasion, cut off in its forts and strongholds. Part of the remaining army had to withdraw to protect its flanks, threatened by far-reaching raids by light horse and diversionary strikes by units of Scoia'tael. The remaining five or six thousand – including no more than twelve hundred knights – joined battle on the fields outside Aldersberg. Coehoorn sent an army of thirteen thousand to attack them, including ten armoured companies, the flower of the Nilfgaard knighthood. And now he's overjoyed, he's yelling, he's thwacking his mace against his thigh and calling for beer ... Victory! What a sensation.*

With a sudden movement, he gathered together the maps and papers lying on the table, lifted his head and looked around.

'Listen carefully,' he said brusquely to the reeves. 'I shall be issuing instructions.'

His subordinates froze in anticipation.

'Each one of you,' he began, 'heard Field Marshal Coehoorn's speech yesterday, to his officers. I would like to point out, gentlemen, that what the marshal said to his men does not apply to you. You are to execute other assignments and orders. My orders.'

Evertsen pondered for a moment and wiped his forehead.

'"War to the castles, peace to the villages," Coehoorn said to his commanders yesterday. You know that principle,' he added at once. 'You learned it in officer training. That principle applied until today; from tomorrow you're to forget it. From tomorrow a different principle applies, which will now be the battle cry of the war we are waging. The battle cry and my orders run: War on everything alive. War on everything that can burn. You are to leave scorched earth behind you. From tomorrow, we take war beyond the line we will withdraw behind after signing the treaty. We are withdrawing, but there is to be nothing but scorched earth beyond that line. The kingdoms of Rivia and Aedirn are to be reduced to ashes! Remember Sodden! The time of revenge is with us!'

Evertsen cleared his throat loudly.

'Before the soldiers leave the earth scorched behind them,' he said to the listening reeves, 'your task will be to remove from that earth and that land everything you can, anything that may increase the riches of our fatherland. You, Audegast, will be responsible for

216

loading and transporting all harvested and stored crops. Whatever is still in the fields and what Coehoorn's gallant knights don't destroy is to be taken.'

'I have too few men, Chamberlain, sir—'

'There will be enough slaves. Put them to work. Marder and you ... I've forgotten your name ... ?'

'Helvet. Evan Helvet, Chamberlain, sir.'

'You'll be responsible for livestock. Gather it into herds and drive it to the designated points for quarantine. Beware of rot-foot and other diseases. Slaughter any sick or suspect specimens and burn the carcasses. Drive the rest south along the designated routes.'

'Yes, sir.'

And now a special task, thought Evertsen, scrutinising his subordinates. *To whom shall I entrust it? They're all striplings, milk still wet on their cheeks, they've seen little, they've experienced nothing ... Oh, I miss those old, hardened bailiffs of mine. Wars, wars, always wars ... Soldiers are always falling, and in great numbers, but the losses among bailiffs, even though much fewer in number, are more telling. You don't see the deficit among the active troops, because fresh recruits always keep replacing them, for every man wants to be a soldier. But who wants to be a bailiff or a reeve? Who, when asked by their sons on returning home what they did during the war, wants to say he measured bushels of grain, counted stinking pelts and weighed wax as he led a convoy of carts laden with spoils along rutted roads, covered in ox shit, and drove herds of lowing and bleating beasts, swallowing dust and flies and breathing in the stench ... ?*

A special mission. The foundry in Gulet, with its huge furnaces. The puddling furnaces, the zinc ore foundry and the huge ironworks in Eysenlaan, annual production of five hundred hundredweight. The foundries and wool manufactories in Aldersberg. The maltings, distilleries, weaving mills and dyeworks in Vengerberg ...

Dismantle and remove. Thus ordered Emperor Emhyr, the White Flame Dancing on the Barrows of his Enemies. As simple as that. Dismantle and remove, Evertsen.

An order's an order. It must be carried out.

That leaves the most important things. The ore mines and their yield.

Coinage. Valuables. Works of art. But I'll take care of that myself. In person.

Alongside the black columns of smoke which were visible on the horizon rose other plumes. And yet others. The army was implementing Coehoorn's orders. The Kingdom of Aedirn had become a land of fires.

A long column of siege engines trundled along the road, rumbling and throwing up clouds of dust. Towards Aldersberg, which was still holding out. And towards Vengerberg, King Demavend's capital.

Peter Evertsen looked and counted and calculated. And added up the money. Peter Evertsen was the grand chamberlain of the Empire; during the war the army's chief bailiff. He had held that position for twenty-five years. Figures and calculations; they were his life.

A mangonel costs five hundred florins, a trebuchet two hundred, an onager at least a hundred and fifty, the simplest ballista eighty. A trained crew requires nine and a half florins of monthly pay. The column heading for Vengerberg, including horses, oxen and minor tackle, is worth at least three hundred marks. Sixty florins can be struck from a mark of pure ore weighing half a pound. The annual yield of a mine is five or six thousand marks …

The siege column was overtaken by some light cavalry. Evertsen recognised them as the Duke of Winneburg's tactical company, one of those redeployed from Cintra, by the designs on its pennants. *Yes,* he thought, *they have something to be pleased about. The battle won, the army from Aedirn routed. Reserves will not be deployed in a heavy battle against the regular army. They will be pursuing forces in retreat, wiping out scattered, leaderless groups. They will murder, pillage and burn. They're pleased because it promises to be a pleasant, jolly little war. A little war that isn't exhausting. And doesn't leave you dead.*

Evertsen was calculating.

The tactical company combines ten ordinary companies and numbers two thousand horse. Although the Winneburgians will probably not take part in any large battles now, no fewer than a sixth of their number will fall in skirmishes. Then there will be camps and bivouacs, rotten victuals, filth, lice, mosquitoes, contaminated water. Then the inevitable

will come: typhus, dysentery and malaria, which will kill no fewer than
a quarter. To that you should include an estimate for unpredictable
occurrences, usually around one-fifth of the total. Eight hundred will
return home. No more. And probably far fewer.

Cavalry companies continued to pass along the road; and infantry
corps followed the cavalry. These, in turn, were followed by marching longbowmen in yellow jerkins and round helmets, crossbowmen
in flat kettle hats, pavisiers and pikemen. Beyond them marched
shield bearers, veterans from Vicovaro and Etolia armoured like
crabs, then a colourful hodgepodge: hirelings from Metinna, mercenaries from Thurn, Maecht, Gheso and Ebbing ...

The troops marched briskly in spite of the intense heat, and the
dust stirred up by their heavy boots billowed above the road. Drums
pounded, pennants fluttered, and the blades of pikes, lances, hal-
berds and guisarmes swayed and glittered. The soldiers marched
jauntily and cheerfully. This was a victorious army. An undefeated
army. *Onward, lads, forward, into battle! On Vengerberg! Destroy our*
foe! Avenge Sodden! Enjoy this merry little war, stuff our money bags
with loot and then home. And then home!

Evertsen watched. And calculated.

'Vengerberg fell after a week-long siege,' finished Dandelion. 'It
may surprise you, but the guilds courageously defended their towers
and the sections of wall assigned to them until the very end. So the
entire garrison and all the townspeople were slaughtered; it must
have been around six thousand people. When news of it got out, a
great flight began. Defeated regiments and civilians began to flee to
Temeria and Redania en masse. Crowds of fugitives headed along
the Pontar Valley and the passes of Mahakam. But not all of them
managed to escape. Mounted Nilfgaardian troops followed them
and cut off their escape ... You know what I'm driving at?'

'No, I don't. I don't know much about ... I don't know much
about war, Dandelion.'

'I'm talking about captives. About slaves. They wanted to take
as many prisoners as possible. It's the cheapest form of labour for
Nilfgaard. That's why they pursued the fugitives so doggedly. It

was a huge manhunt, Geralt. Easy pickings. Because the army had run away, and no one was left to defend the fleeing civilians.'

'No one?'

'Almost no one.'

'We won't make it in time ...' Villis wheezed, looking around. 'We won't get away ... Damn it, the border is so close ... So close ...'

Rayla stood up in her stirrups, and looked at the road winding among the forested hills. The road, as far as the eye could see, was strewn with people's abandoned belongings, dead horses, and with wagons and handcarts pushed to the side of the road. Behind them, beyond the forests, black columns of smoke rose into the sky. Screams and the intensifying sounds of battle could be heard ever closer.

'They're wiping out the rearguard ...' Villis wiped the soot and sweat from his face. 'Can you hear it, Rayla? They've caught up with the rearguard, and they're putting them to the sword! We'll never make it!'

'We're the rearguard now,' said the mercenary drily. 'Now it's our turn.'

Villis blenched, and one of the soldiers standing close by gave a loud sigh. Rayla tugged at the reins, and turned around her mount, which was snorting loudly and barely able to lift its head.

'There's no chance of our getting away,' she said calmly. 'The horses are ready to drop. They'll catch up with us and slaughter us before we make it to the pass.'

'Let's dump everything and hide among the trees,' said Villis, not looking at her. 'Individually, every man for himself. Maybe some of us will manage to ... survive.'

Rayla didn't answer, but indicated the mountain pass with a glance and a wave of her head, then the road and the rearmost ranks of the long column of refugees trudging towards the border. Villis understood. He cursed bitterly, leapt from his saddle, staggered and leaned on his sword.

'Dismount!' he yelled to the soldiers hoarsely. 'Block the road with anything you can! What are you staring at? Your mother bore you once and you only die once! We're the army! We're the rear-guard! We have to hold back our pursuers, delay them ...'

He fell silent.

'Should we delay the pursuers, the people will manage to cross into Temeria, to cross the mountains,' ended Rayla, also dismounting. 'There are women and children among them. What are you gawping at? It's our trade. This is what we're paid for, remember?'

The soldiers looked at one another. For a moment Rayla thought they would actually run away, that they would rouse their wet and exhausted horses for a last, desperate effort, that they would race past the column of fugitives, towards the pass – and safety. She was wrong. She had misjudged them.

They upset a cart on the road. They quickly built a barricade. A makeshift barricade. Not very high. And absolutely ineffectual.

They didn't have to wait long. Two horses, snorting and stumbling, lurched into the ravine, strewing flecks of froth around. Only one of them bore a rider.

'Blaise!'

'Ready yourselves ...' The mercenary slid from the saddle into a soldier's arms. 'Ready yourselves, dammit ... They're right behind me ...'

The horse snorted, skittered a few paces sideways, fell back on its haunches, collapsed heavily on its side, kicked, stretched its neck out, and uttered a long neigh.

'Rayla ...' wheezed Blaise, looking away. 'Give me ... Give me something. I've lost my sword ...'

Rayla, looking at the smoke from fires rising into the sky, gestured with her head to an axe leaning against the overturned cart. Blaise seized the weapon and staggered. The left leg of his trousers was soaked in blood.

'What about the others, Blaise?'

'They were slaughtered,' the mercenary groaned. 'Every last man. The entire troop ... Rayla, it's not Nilfgaard ... It's the Squirrels ... It was the elves who overhauled us. The Scoia'tael are in front, ahead of the Nilfgaardians.'

221

One of the soldiers wailed piercingly, and another sat down heavily on the ground, burying his face in his hands. Villis cursed, tightening the strap of his cuirass.

'To your positions!' yelled Rayla. 'Behind the barricade! They won't take us alive! I swear to you!'

Villis spat, then tore the three-coloured, black, gold and red rosette of King Demavend's special forces from his spaulder, throwing it into the bushes. Rayla, cleaning and polishing her own badge, smiled wryly.

'I don't know if that'll help, Villis. I don't know.'

'You promised, Rayla.'

'I did. And I'll keep my promise. To your positions, boys! Grab your crossbows and longbows!'

They didn't have to wait long.

After they had repelled the first wave, there were only six of them left alive. The battle was short but fierce. The soldiers mobilised from Vengerberg fought like devils and were every bit as savage as the mercenaries. Not one of them fell into the hands of the Scoia'tael alive. They chose to die fighting. And they died shot through by arrows; died from the blows of lance and sword. Blaise died lying down, stabbed by the daggers of two elves who pounced on him, dragging him from the barricade. Neither of the elves got up again. Blaise had a dagger too.

The Scoia'tael gave them no respite. A second group charged. Villis, stabbed with a lance for the third time, fell to the ground.

'Rayla!' he screamed indistinctly. 'You promised!'

The mercenary, dispatching another elf, swung around.

'Farewell, Villis,' she said, placing the point of her sword beneath his sternum and pushing hard. 'See you in hell!'

A moment later, she stood alone. The Scoia'tael encircled her from all sides. The soldier, smeared with blood from head to foot, raised her sword, whirled around and shook her black plait. She stood among the elves, terrible and hunched like a demon. The elves retreated.

'Come on!' she screamed savagely. 'What are you waiting for? You will not take me alive! I am Black Rayla!'

'Glaeddyv vort, beanna,' responded a beautiful, fair-haired elf in a calm voice. He had the face of a cherub and the large, cornflower-blue eyes of a child. He had emerged from the surrounding group of Scoia'tael, who were still hanging back hesitantly. His snow-white horse snorted, tossed its head powerfully up and down and energetically pawed at the bloodstained sand of the road.

'Glaeddyv vort, beanna,' repeated the rider. 'Throw down your sword, woman.'

The mercenary laughed horribly and wiped her face with her cuff, smearing sweat mixed with dust and blood.

'My sword cost too much to be thrown away, elf!' she cried. 'If you want to take it you will have to break my fingers! I am Black Rayla! What are you waiting for?'

She did not have to wait long.

'Did no one come to relieve Aedirn?' asked the Witcher after a long pause. 'I understood there were alliances. Agreements about mutual aid ... Treaties ...'

'Redania,' said Dandelion, clearing his throat, 'is in disarray after Vizimir's death. Did you know King Vizimir was murdered?'

'Yes, I did.'

'Queen Hedwig has assumed power, but bedlam has broken out across the land. And terror. Scoia'tael and Nilfgaardian spies are being hunted. Dijkstra raged through the entire country; the scaffolds were running with blood. Dijkstra is still unable to walk so he's being carried in a sedan chair.'

'I can imagine it. Did he come after you?'

'No. He could have, but he didn't. Oh, but never mind. In any case, Redania – plunged into chaos itself – was incapable of raising an army to support Aedirn.'

'And Temeria? Why didn't King Foltest of Temeria help Demavend?'

'When the fighting began in Dol Angra,' said Dandelion softly, 'Emhyr var Emreis sent an envoy to Vizima ...'

*

'Blast!' hissed Bronibor, staring at the closed doors. 'What are they spending so long debating? Why did Foltest abase himself so, to enter negotiations? Why did he give an audience to that Nilfgaardian dog at all? He ought to have been executed and his head sent back to Emhyr! In a sack!'

'By the gods, voivode,' choked the priest Willemer. 'He is an envoy, don't forget! An envoy's person is sacrosanct and inviolable! It is unfitting—'

'Unfitting? I'll tell you what's unfitting! It is unfitting to stand idly by and watch as the invader wreaks havoc in countries we are allied to! Lyria has already fallen and Aedirn is falling! Demavend will not hold Nilfgaard off by himself! We ought to dispatch an expeditionary force to Aedirn immediately. We ought to relieve Demavend with an assault on the Jaruga's left bank! There are few forces there. Most of the regiments have been redeployed to Dol Angra! And we're standing here debating! We're yapping instead of fighting! And on top of that we are playing host to a Nilfgaardian envoy!'

'Quite, voivode,' said Duke Hereward of Ellander, giving the old warrior a scolding look. 'This is politics. You have to be able to look a little further than a horse's muzzle and a lance. The envoy must be heard. Emperor Emhyr had reason to send him here.'

'Of course he had reason,' snarled Bronibor. 'Right now, Emhyr is crushing Aedirn and knows that if we cross the border, bringing Redania and Kaedwen with us, we'll defeat him and throw him back beyond Dol Angra, to Ebbing. He knows that were we to attack Cintra, we'd strike him in his soft underbelly and force him to fight on two fronts! That is what he fears! So he's trying to intimidate us, to stop us from intervening. That is the mission the Nilfgaardian envoy came here with. And no other!'

'Then we ought to hear out the envoy,' repeated the duke, 'and take a decision in keeping with the interests of our kingdom. Demavend unwisely provoked Nilfgaard and has suffered the consequences. And I'm in no hurry to die for Vengerberg. What is happening in Aedirn is no concern of ours.'

'Not our concern? What, by a hundred devils, are you drivelling on about? You consider it other people's business that the Nilfgaardians are in Aedirn and Lyria, on the right bank of the Jaruga, when only Mahakam separates us from them? You don't have an ounce of common sense ...'

'Enough of this feuding,' warned Willemer. 'Not another word. The king is coming out.'

The chamber doors opened. The members of the Royal Council rose, scraping their chairs. Many of the seats were vacant. The crown hetman and most of the commanders were with their regiments: in the Pontar Valley, in Mahakam and by the Jaruga. The chairs which were usually occupied by sorcerers were also vacant. Sorcerers ... *Yes*, thought Willemer, the priest, *the places occupied by sorcerers here, at the royal court in Vizima, will remain vacant for a long time. Who knows, perhaps for ever?*

King Foltest crossed the hall quickly and stood by his throne but did not sit down. He simply leaned over, resting his fists on the table. He was very pale.

'Vengerberg is under siege,' said the King of Temeria softly, 'and will fall any day now. Nilfgaard is pushing northwards relentlessly. The surrounded troops continue to fight, but that will change nothing. Aedirn is lost. King Demavend has fled to Redania. The fate of Queen Meve is unknown.'

The Council was silent.

'In a few days, the Nilfgaardians will take our eastern border, by which I mean the mouth of the Pontar Valley,' Foltest went on, still very softly. 'Hagge, Aedirn's last fortress, will not withstand them for long, and Hagge is on our eastern border. And on our southern border ... something very unfortunate has occurred. King Ervyll of Verden has sworn fealty to Emperor Emhyr. He has surrendered and opened the strongholds at the mouth of the Jaruga. Nilfgaardian garrisons are already installed in Nastrog, Rozrog and Bodrog, which were supposed to have protected our flank.'

The Council was silent.

'Owing to that,' continued Foltest, 'Ervyll has retained his royal title, but Emhyr is his sovereign. Verden remains a kingdom but, de facto, is now a Nilfgaardian province. Do you understand what

225

that means? The situation has turned about face. The Verdenian strongholds and the mouth of the Jaruga are in Nilfgaard's hands. I cannot attempt to cross the river. And I cannot weaken the army stationed there by forming a corps which could enter Aedirn and support Demavend's forces. I cannot do that. Responsibility for my country and my subjects rests on me.'

The Council was silent.

'Emperor Emhyr var Emreis, the imperator of Nilfgaard,' said the king, 'has offered me a proposition ... an agreement. I have accepted that proposition. I shall now present this proposition to you. And you, when you have heard me out, will understand ... Will agree that— Will say ...'

The Council was silent.

'You will say ...' concluded Foltest. 'You will say I am bringing you peace.'

'So Foltest crumbled,' muttered the Witcher, breaking another twig in his fingers. 'He struck a deal with Nilfgaard. He left Aedirn to its fate ...'

'Yes,' agreed the poet. 'However, he sent his army to the Pontar Valley and occupied and manned the stronghold at Hagge. And the Nilfgaardians didn't march into the Mahakam pass or cross the Jaruga in Sodden. They didn't attack Brugge, which, after its capitulation and Ervyll's fealty, they have in their clutches. That was without doubt the price of Temeria's neutrality.'

'Ciri was right,' whispered the Witcher. 'Neutrality ... Neutrality is always contemptible.'

'What?'

'Nothing. But what about Kaedwen, Dandelion? Why didn't Henselt of Kaedwen come to Demavend and Meve's aid? They had a pact, after all; they were bound by an alliance. But even if Henselt, following Foltest's example, pisses on the signatures and seals on documents, and the royal word means nothing to him, he cannot be stupid, can he? Doesn't he understand that after the fall of Aedirn and the deal with Temeria, it will be his turn; that he's next on the Nilfgaardian list? Kaedwen ought to support Demavend out of good sense. There may no longer be faith nor truth in the world, but surely good sense still exists. What say you, Dandelion? Is there still good sense in the world? Or do only contemptibility and contempt remain?'

Dandelion turned his head away. The green lanterns were close. They were surrounding them in a tight ring. He hadn't noticed it earlier, but now he understood. All the dryads had been listening in to his story.

'You say nothing,' said Geralt, 'which means that Ciri was right. That Codringher was right. You were all right. Only I, the naive, anachronistic and stupid witcher, was wrong.'

Centurion Digod, known by the nickname Half-Gallon, opened the tent flap and entered, panting heavily and snarling angrily. The decurions jumped to their feet, assuming military poses and expressions. Zyvik dextrously threw a sheepskin over the small barrel of vodka standing among the saddles, before the eyes of the centurion had time to adjust to the gloom. Not to save themselves from punishment, because Digod wasn't actually a fervent opponent of drinking on duty or in the camp, but more in order to save the barrel. The centurion's nickname had not come about by accident; the story went that, in favourable conditions, he was capable of knocking back half a gallon of hooch, vigorously and with impressive speed. The centurion could polish off a standard soldier's quart mug as if it were a gill, in one draught, and seldom got his ears wet doing it.

'Well, Centurion, sir?' asked Bode, the bowmen's decurion. 'What have the top brass decided? What are our orders? Are we crossing the border? Tell us!'

'Just a moment,' grunted Half-Gallon. 'What bloody heat ... I'll tell you everything in a moment. But first, give me something to drink because my throat's bone dry. And don't tell me you haven't got any; I can smell the vodka in this tent a mile off. And I know where it's coming from. From under that there sheepskin.'

Zyvik, muttering an oath, took out the barrel. The decurions crowded together in a tight group and clinked cups and tin mugs.

'Aaaah,' said the centurion, wiping his whiskers and eyes. 'Ooooh, that's foul stuff. Keep pouring, Zyvik.'

'Come on, tell us quickly,' said Bode, becoming impatient. 'What orders? Are we marching on the Nilfgaardians or are we going to hang around on the border like a bunch of spare pricks at a wedding?'

'Itching for a scrap?' Half-Gallon wheezed lengthily, spat, and sat down hard on a saddle. 'In a hurry to get over the border, towards Aedirn? You can't wait, eh? What fierce wolf cubs you are, doing nothing but standing there growling, baring your fangs.'

'That's right,' said old Stahler coldly, shuffling from one foot to the other. His legs were as crooked as a spider's, which befitted an old cavalryman. 'That's right, Centurion, sir. This is the fifth night we've slept in our boots, at the ready. And we want to know what's happening. Is it a scrap or back to the fort?'

'We're crossing the border,' announced Half-Gallon brusquely. 'Tomorrow at dawn. Five brigades, with the Dun Banner leading the way. And now pay attention, because I'm going to tell you what was told to us centurions and warrant officers by the voivode and the Honourable Margrave Mansfeld of Ard Carraigh, who'd come straight from the king. Prick up your ears, because I won't tell you twice. And they're unusual orders.'

The tent fell silent.

'The Nilfgaardians have passed through Dol Angra,' said the centurion. 'They crushed Lyria, and reached Aldersberg in four days, where they routed Demavend's army in a decisive battle. Right away, after only six days' siege, they took Vengerberg by means of treachery. Now they're heading swiftly northwards, driving the armies back from Aedirn towards the Pontar Valley and Dol Blathanna. They're heading towards us, towards Kaedwen. So the orders for the Dun Banner are as follows: cross the border and march hard south, straight for the Valley of the Flowers. We have three days to get to the River Dyfne. I repeat, three days, which means we'll be marching at a trot. And, when we get there, not a step across the Dyfne. Not a single step. Shortly after, the Nilfgaardians will show up on the far bank. We do not, heed my words well, engage them. In no way, understood? Even if they try to cross the river, we're only

228

to show them ... show them our colours. That it's us, the Kaedwen Army.'

Although it seemed impossible, the silence in the tent grew even more palpable.

'What?' mumbled Bode finally. 'We aren't to fight the Nilfgaardians? Are we going to war or not? What's this all about, Centurion, sir?'

'That's our orders. We aren't going to war, but ...' Half-Gallon scratched his neck ' ... but to give fraternal help. We're crossing the border to give protection to the people of Upper Aedirn ... Wait, what am I saying ... Not from Aedirn, but from Lormark. That's what the Honourable Margrave Mansfeld said. Yes, and he said that Demavend has suffered a defeat. He's tripped up and is lying flat on his face, because he governed poorly and his politics were crap. So that's the end of him and the end of the whole of Aedirn with him. Our king lent Demavend a pretty penny because he gave him help. One cannot allow wealth like that to be lost, so now it's time to get that money back with interest. Neither can we let our compatriots and brothers from Lormark be taken prisoner by Nilfgaard. We have to, you know, liberate them. For those are our ancient lands: Lormark. They were once under Kaedwen rule and now they shall return to its rule. All the way to the River Dyfne. That's the agreement Our Grace, King Henselt, has concluded with Emhyr of Nilfgaard. Agreements or no agreements, the Dun Banner is to station itself by the river. Do you understand?'

No one answered. Half-Gallon grimaced and waved a hand.

'Ah, sod the lot of you. You don't understood shit, I see. But don't worry yourselves, because I didn't either. For His Majesty the King, the margraves, the voivodes and nobles are there to think. And we're the army! We have to follow orders: get to the River Dyfne in three days, stop there and stand like a wall. And that's it. Pour, Zyvik.'

'Centurion, sir ...' stammered Zyvik. 'And what will happen ... What will happen if the army of Aedirn resists? Or bars the road? After all, we're passing through their country armed. What then?'

229

'Should our compatriots and brothers,' continued Stahler spitefully, 'the ones we're supposedly liberating ... Should they begin to shoot arrows at us or throw stones? Eh?'

'We are to be on the banks of the Dyfne in three days,' said Half-Gallon forcefully. 'And no later. Whoever tries to delay or stop us is clearly an enemy. And our enemies can be cut to ribbons. But heed my words well! Listen to the orders! Burn no villages, nor cottages. Take no goods from anyone. Do not plunder. Rape no women! Make sure you and your men remember this, for should anyone break this order, they will hang. The voivode must have repeated this ten times: we aren't fucking invading, we're coming to give a helping hand! Why are you grinning, Stahler? It's a bloody order! And now get to your units on the double. Get 'em all on their feet. The horses and tack are to shine like the full moon! In the afternoon, all companies are to fall in for inspection; the voivode himself will be drilling them. If I have to be ashamed of one of the platoons, the decurion will remember me. Oh yes, he'll remember! You have your orders!'

Zyvik was the last to leave the tent. Squinting in the bright sunlight, he watched the commotion which had taken over the camp. Decurions were rushing to their units, centurions were running about and cursing, and noblemen, cornets and pages were getting under each other's feet. The heavy cavalry from Ban Ard was trotting around the field, stirring up clouds of dust. The heat was horrendous.

Zyvik quickened his pace. He passed four bards from Ard Carraigh who had arrived the previous day and were sitting in the shadow cast by the margrave's richly decorated tent. The bards were just composing a ballad about the victorious military operation, about the prowess of the king, the prudence of the commanders and the bravery of the humble foot soldier. As usual, to save time, they were doing it before the operation.

'*Our brothers greeted us, they greeted us with breaaad and salt ...*' sang one of the bards, trying out his lyrics. '*They greeted their saviours and liberators, they greeted them with breaaad and salt ...* Hey, Hrafhir, think up a clever rhyme for "salt".'

The second bard suggested a rhyme. Zyvik did not hear what it was.

The platoon, camped among some willows by a pond, leapt up on seeing him.

'Make ready!' roared Zyvik, standing a good way back, so that the smell of his breath would not influence the morale of his subordinates. 'Before the sun rises another four fingers there'll be a full inspection! Everything's to be shining like the sun. Arms, tack, trappings and your mounts. There will be an inspection, and if I have to be ashamed of one of you before the centurion, I'll tear that soldier's legs off. Look lively!'

'We're going into battle,' guessed cavalryman Kraska, tucking his shirt quickly into his trousers. 'Are we going into battle, Decurion, sir?'

'What do you think? Or maybe we're off to a dance, to a Lammas party? We're crossing the frontier. The entire Dun Banner sets off tomorrow at dawn. The centurion didn't say in what array, but we know our platoon will be leading as usual. Now look lively, move your arses! Hold on, come back. I'll say this right now, because there'll be no time later. It won't be a typical little war, lads. The honourable gentlemen have thought up some modern idiocy. Some kind of liberation, or some such. We aren't going to fight the enemy, but we're heading towards our, what was it, eternal lands, to bring, you know, fraternal help. Now pay attention to what I say: you're not to touch the folk of Aedirn, not to loot—'

'What?' said Kraska, mouth agape. 'What do you mean, don't loot? And what are we going to feed our horses on, Decurion, sir?'

'You can loot fodder for the horses, but nothing else. Don't cut anyone up, don't burn any cottages down, don't destroy any crops ... Shut your trap, Kraska! This isn't a village gathering. It's the fucking army! Carry out the orders or you hang! I said: don't kill, don't murder, and don't—'

Zyvik broke off and pondered.

'And if you rape any women, do it on the quiet. Out of sight,' he finished a moment later.

*

231

'They shook hands,' finished Dandelion, 'on the bridge on the River Dyfne. Margrave Mansfeld of Ard Carraigh and Menno Coehoorn, the commander-in-chief of the Nilfgaardian armies from Dol Angra. They shook hands over the bleeding, dying Kingdom of Aedirn, sealing a criminal division of the spoils. The most despicable gesture history has ever known.'

Geralt remained silent.

'On the subject of despicableness,' he said, surprisingly calmly, a moment later, 'what about the sorcerers, Dandelion? The ones from the Chapter and the Council.'

'Not one of them remained with Demavend,' began the poet, soon after, 'while Foltest drove all those who had served him out of Temeria. Philippa is in Tretogor, helping Queen Hedwig to bring the chaos reigning in Redania under control. With her is Triss and three others, whose names I can't recall. Several of them are in Kaedwen. Many of them escaped to Kovir and Hengfors. They chose neutrality, because Esterad Thyssen and Niedamir, as you know, were, and are, neutral.'

'I know. What about Vilgefortz? And the people who stuck by him?'

'Vilgefortz has disappeared. It was expected he would surface in Aedirn after its capture, as Emhyr's viceroy ... But there's no trace of him. Neither of him nor any of his accomplices. Apart from ...'

'Go on, Dandelion.'

'Apart from one sorceress, who has become a queen.'

Filavandrel aep Fidhail waited for the answer in silence. The queen, who was staring out of the window, was also silent. The window looked out onto the gardens which, not so long ago, had been the pride and delight of the previous ruler of Dol Blathanna, the governor of the despot from Vengerberg. Fleeing before the arrival of the Free Elves, who were coming in the vanguard of Emperor Emhyr's army, the human governor had managed to take most of the valuables from the ancient elven palace, and even some of the furniture. But he could not take the gardens. So he destroyed them.

'No, Filavandrel,' said the queen finally. 'It is too early for that, much too early. Let us not think about extending our borders, for at present we are not even certain of their exact positions. Henselt of Kaedwen has no intention of abiding by the agreement and withdrawing from the Dyfne. Our spies inform us he has by no means abandoned his thoughts of aggression. He may attack us any day.'

'So we have achieved nothing.'

The queen slowly held out a hand. An Apollo butterfly, which had flown in through the window, alighted on her lace cuff, folding and unfolding its pointed wings.

'We've achieved more,' said the queen softly, in order not to frighten away the butterfly, 'than we could have hoped for. We have finally recovered our Valley of the Flowers after a hundred years—'

'I would not name it thus.' Filavandrel smiled sadly. 'Now, after the armies have passed through, it should be called the Valley of the Ashes.'

'We have our own country once more,' finished the queen, looking at the butterfly. 'We are a people again, no longer outcasts. And the ash will nourish the soil. In spring the valley will blossom anew.'

'That is too little, Daisy. It is ever too little. We've come down a station or two. Not long ago we boasted we would push the humans back to the sea, whence they came. And now we have narrowed our borders and ambitions to Dol Blathann ...'

'Emhyr Deithwen gave us Dol Blathanna as a gift. What do you expect from me, Filavandrel? Am I to demand more? Do not forget that even in receiving gifts there should be moderation. Particularly when it concerns gifts from Emhyr, because he gives nothing for nothing. We must keep the lands he gave us. And the powers at our disposal are barely sufficient to retain Dol Blathanna.'

'Let us then withdraw our commandos from Temeria, Redania and Kaedwen,' suggested the white-haired elf. 'Let us withdraw all Scoia'tael forces who are fighting the humans. You are now queen, Enid, and they will obey your orders. Now that we have our own small scrap of land, there is no sense in their continuing to fight. Their duty is to return and defend the Valley of the Flowers. Let them fight as a free people in defence of their own borders. Right now they are falling like bandits in the forests!'

The elf bowed her head.

'Emhyr has not permitted that,' she whispered. 'The commandos are to fight on.'

'Why? To what end?' said Filavandrel aep Fidhail, sitting up abruptly.

'I will say more. We are not to support nor to help the Scoia'tael. This was the condition set by Foltest and Henselt. Temeria and Kaedwen will respect our rule in Dol Blathanna, but only if we officially condemn the Squirrels' aggression and distance ourselves from them.'

'Those children are dying, Daisy. They are dying every day, perishing in an unequal contest. As a direct result of these secret pacts with Emhyr, humans will attack the commandos and crush them. They are our children, our future! Our blood! And you tell me we should dissociate ourselves from them? Que'ss aen me dicette, Enid? Vorsaeke'llan? Aen vaine?'

The butterfly took flight, flapping its wings, and flew towards the window, then spun around, caught by currents of hot summer air. Francesca Findabair, known as Enid an Gleanna, once a sorceress and presently the Queen of Aen Seidhe, the Free Elves, raised her head. Tears glistened in her beautiful blue eyes.

'The commandos,' she repeated softly, 'must continue to fight. They must disrupt the human kingdoms and hinder their preparations for war. That is the order of Emhyr and I may not oppose Emhyr. Forgive me, Filavandrel.'

Filavandrel aep Fidhail looked at her and bowed low.

'I forgive you, Enid. But I do not know if they will.'

'Did not one sorcerer think the matter over a second time? Even when Nilfgaard was slaughtering and burning in Aedirn, did none of them abandon Vilgefortz or join Philippa?'

'Not one.'

Geralt was silent for a long time.

'I can't believe,' he said finally, very softly, 'I can't believe none of them left Vilgefortz when the real causes and effects of his treachery came to light. I am – as is generally known – a naive, stupid and

234

anachronistic witcher. But I still cannot believe that the conscience of not one sorcerer was pricked.'

Tissaia de Vries penned her practised, decorative signature beneath the final sentence of the letter. After lengthy reflection, she also added an ideogram signifying her true name alongside. A name no one knew. A name she had not used for a very long time. Not since she became an enchantress.

Skylark.

She put her pen down, very carefully, very precisely, across the sheet of parchment. For a long while she sat motionless, staring at the red orb of the setting sun. Then she stood up and walked over to the window. For some time she looked at the roofs of houses. Houses in which ordinary people were at that moment going to bed, tired by their ordinary, human lives and hardship; full of ordinary human anxiety about their fates, about tomorrow. The enchantress glanced at the letter lying on the table. At the letter addressed to ordinary people. The fact that most ordinary people couldn't read was of no significance.

She stood in front of the looking glass. She straightened her hair. She smoothed her dress. She brushed a non-existent speck from her puffed sleeve. She straightened the ruby necklace on her breast.

The candlesticks beneath the looking glass stood unevenly. Her servant must have moved them while she was cleaning.

Her servant. An ordinary woman. An ordinary human with eyes full of fear about what was happening. An ordinary human, adrift in these times of contempt. An ordinary human, searching in her – in an enchantress – for hope and certainty about tomorrow . . .

An ordinary human whose trust she had betrayed.

The sound of steps, the pounding of heavy soldiers' boots, drifted up from the street. Tissaia de Vries did not even twitch, did not even turn to face the window. It was unimportant to her whose steps they were. Royal soldiers? A provost with orders to arrest the traitress? Hired assassins? Vilgefortz's hit men? She could not care less.

The steps faded into the distance.

The candlesticks beneath the looking glass stood out of kilter.

The enchantress straightened them and corrected the position of a tablecloth, so that its corner was exactly in the centre, symmetrically aligned with the candlesticks' quadrangular bases. She unfastened the gold bracelets from her wrists and placed them perfectly evenly on the smoothed cloth. She examined the tablecloth critically but could not find the tiniest fault. Everything was lying evenly and neatly. As it should have lain before.

She opened the drawer in the dresser and took out a short knife with a bone handle.

Her face was proud and fixed. Expressionless.

It was quiet in the house. So quiet, the sound of a wilted petal falling on the tabletop could be heard.

The sun, as red as blood, slowly sank below the roofs of the houses.

Tissaia de Vries sat down on the chair by the table, blew out a candle, straightened the quill lying across the letter one more time and severed the arteries in both wrists.

The fatigue caused by the daylong journey had made itself felt. Dandelion awoke and realised he had probably fallen asleep during the story, dropping off in mid-sentence. He shifted and almost rolled off the pile of branches. Geralt was no longer lying alongside him to balance the makeshift bed.

'Where did I ...' he said, coughing. He sat up. 'Where did I get to? Ah, the sorcerers ... Geralt? Where are you?'

'Here,' said the Witcher, barely visible in the gloom. 'Go on, please. You were just going to tell me about Yennefer.'

'Listen,' said the poet, knowing perfectly well he'd had absolutely no intention of even mentioning the person in question. 'I really know nothing ...'

'Don't lie. I know you.'

'If you know me so well,' said the troubadour, beginning to bristle, 'why the bloody hell are you making me speak? Since you know me through and through, you ought to know why I'm keeping my counsel, why I'm not repeating the gossip I've heard! You also ought to be able to guess what the gossip is and why I want to spare you it!'

'Que suecc's?' said one of the dryads sleeping nearby, on being woken by his raised voice.

'I beg your pardon,' said the Witcher softly.

Almost all of the green lanterns of Brokilon were out; only a few of them still glimmered gently.

'Geralt,' said Dandelion, interrupting the silence. 'You've always maintained that you don't get involved, that nothing matters to you ... She may have believed that. She believed that when she began this game with Vilgefortz—'

'Enough,' said Geralt. 'Not another word. When I hear the word "game" I feel like killing someone. Oh, give me that razor. I want to have that shave at last.'

'Now? It's still dark ...'

'It's never too dark for me. I'm a freak.'

After the Witcher had snatched the pouch of toiletries from him and headed off towards the stream, Dandelion realised he had shaken off all drowsiness. The sky was already lightening with the promise of dawn. He got up and walked into the forest, carefully stepping over the dryads, who were sleeping cuddled together.

'Are you one of those who had a hand in this?'

He turned around suddenly. The dryad leaning against a pine tree had hair the colour of silver, visible even in the half-light of the dawn.

'A most deplorable sight,' she said, folding her arms across her chest. 'Someone who has lost everything. You know, minstrel, it is interesting. Once, I thought it was impossible to lose everything, that something always remains. Always. Even in times of contempt, when naivety is capable of backfiring in the cruellest way, one cannot lose everything. But he ... he lost several pints of blood, the ability to walk properly, the partial use of his left hand, his witcher's sword, the woman he loves, the daughter he had gained by a miracle, his faith ... Well, I thought, he must have been left with something. But I was wrong. He has nothing now. Not even a razor.'

Dandelion remained silent. The dryad did not move.

'I asked if you had a hand in this,' she began a moment later. 'But I think there was no need. It's obvious you had a hand in it. It's obvious you are his friend. And if someone has friends, and he loses everything in spite of that, it's obvious the friends are to blame. For what they did, or for what they didn't do.'

'What could I have done?' he whispered. 'What could I have done?'

'I don't know,' answered the dryad.

'I didn't tell him everything ...'

'I know.'

'I'm not guilty of anything.'

'Yes, you are.'

'No! I am not ...'

He jumped to his feet, making the branches of his makeshift bed creak. Geralt sat beside him, rubbing his face. He smelled of soap.

'Aren't you?' he asked coolly. 'I wonder what else you dreamed about. That you're a frog? Calm down. You aren't. Did you dream that you're a chump? Well, that dream might have been prophetic.'

Dandelion looked all around. They were completely alone in the clearing.

'Where is she? Where are they?'

'On the edge of the forest. Get ready, it's time you left.'

'Geralt, I spoke with a dryad a moment ago. She was talking in the Common Speech without an accent and told me ...'

'None of the dryads in that group spoke the Common Speech without an accent. You dreamed it, Dandelion. This is Brokilon. Many things can be dreamed here.'

A lone dryad was waiting for them at the edge of the forest. Dandelion recognised her at once – it was the one with the greenish hair who had brought them light during the night and encouraged him to continue singing. The dryad raised a hand, instructing them to stop. In her other hand she was holding a bow with an arrow nocked. The Witcher put his hand on the troubadour's shoulder and squeezed it hard.

'Is something going on?' whispered Dandelion.

'Indeed. Be quiet and don't move.'

The dense fog hanging over the Ribbon valley stifled voices and sounds, but not so much that Dandelion was unable to hear the splash of water and the snorting of horses. Riders were crossing the river.

'Elves,' he guessed. 'Scoia'tael? They're fleeing to Brokilon, aren't they? An entire commando unit . . .'

'No,' muttered Geralt, staring into the fog. The poet knew the Witcher's eyesight and hearing were incredibly acute and sensitive, but he was unable to guess if his assessment was based on vision or hearing. 'It isn't a commando unit. It's what's left of one. Five or six riders, three riderless horses. Stay here, Dandelion. I'm going over there.'

'Gar'ean,' said the green-haired dryad in warning, raising her bow. 'Nfe va, Gwynbleidd! Ki'rin!'

'Thaess aep, Fauve,' replied the Witcher unexpectedly brusquely. 'M'aespar que va'en, ell'ea? Go ahead and shoot. If not, lock me up and don't try to frighten me, because there's nothing you can frighten me with. I must talk to Milva Barring, and I will do so whether you like it or not. Stay there, Dandelion.'

The dryad lowered her head. Her bow too.

Nine horses emerged from the fog, and Dandelion saw that indeed only six of them were bearing riders. He saw the shapes of dryads emerging from the undergrowth and heading to meet them. He noticed that three riders had to be helped to dismount and had to be supported in order to walk towards the trees of Brokilon and safety. The other dryads stole like wraiths across the hillside, which was covered with wind-fallen trees, and vanished into the fog hanging above the Ribbon. A shout, the neighing of horses and the splash of water came from the opposite bank. It also seemed to the poet that he could hear the whistle of arrows. But he was not certain.

'They were being pursued . . .' he muttered. Fauve turned around, gripping her bow.

'You sing a song, taedh,' she snapped. 'N'te shaent a'minne, not about Ettariel. No, my darling. The time is not right. Now is time to kill, yes. Such a song, yes!'

'I,' he stammered, 'am not to blame for what is happening . . .'

The dryad was silent for a moment and looked to one side.

'Also not I,' she said and quickly disappeared into the undergrowth.

The Witcher was back before an hour had passed. He was leading two saddled horses: Pegasus and a bay mare. The mare's saddlecloth bore traces of blood.

'She's one of the elves' horses, isn't she? One of those who crossed the river?'

'Yes,' replied Geralt. His face and voice were changed and unfamiliar. 'The mare belongs to the elves. But she will be serving me for the moment. And when I have the chance, I'll exchange her for a horse that knows how to carry a wounded rider and, when its rider falls, remains by him. It's clear this mare wasn't taught to do that.'

'Are we leaving?'

'You're leaving,' said the Witcher, throwing the poet Pegasus's reins. 'Farewell, Dandelion. The dryads will escort you a couple of miles upstream so you won't fall into the hands of the soldiers from Brugge, who are probably still hanging around on the far bank.'

'What about you? Are you staying here?'

'No. I'm not.'

'You've learned something. From the Squirrels. You know something about Ciri, don't you?'

'Farewell, Dandelion.'

'Geralt ... Listen to me—'

'Listen to what?' shouted the Witcher, before his voice suddenly faltered. 'I can't leave— I can't just leave her to her fate. She's completely alone ... She cannot be left alone, Dandelion. You'll never understand that. No one will ever understand that, but I know. If she remains alone, the same thing will happen to her as once happened to me ... You'll never understand that ...'

'I do understand. Which is why I'm coming with you.'

'You're insane. Do you know where I'm headed?'

'Yes, I do. Geralt, I— I haven't told you everything. I'm ... I feel guilty. I didn't do anything; I didn't know what to do. But now I know. I want to go with you. I want to be by your side. I never told you ... about Ciri and the rumours that are circulating. I met some acquaintances from Kovir, and they in turn had heard the reports of some envoys who had returned from Nilfgaard ... I imagine those rumours may even have reached the Squirrels' ears. That you've already heard everything from those elves who crossed the Ribbon. But let ... let me tell you ...'

The Witcher stood thinking for a long time, his arms hanging limply at his sides.

'Get on your horse,' he finally said, his voice sounding different. 'You can tell me on the way.'

That morning there was an unusual commotion in Loc Grim Palace, the imperator's summer residence. All the more unusual since commotions, emotions or excitement were not at all customary for the Nilfgaardian nobility and demonstrating anxiety or excitement was regarded as a sign of immaturity. Behaviour of that kind was treated by the Nilfgaardian noblemen as highly reprehensible and contemptible, to such an extent that even callow youths, from whom few would have demanded greater maturity, were expected to refrain from any displays of animation.

That morning, though, there were no young men in Loc Grim. Young men wouldn't have had any reason to be in Loc Grim. Stern, austere aristocrats, knights and courtiers were filling the palace's enormous throne room, every one of them dressed in ceremonial courtly black, enlivened only by white ruffs and cuffs. The men were accompanied by a small number of equally stern, austere ladies, whom custom permitted to brighten the black of their costume with a little modest jewellery. They all pretended to be dignified, stern and austere. But they were all extremely excited.

'They say she's ugly. Skinny and ugly.'

'But she allegedly has royal blood.'

'Illegitimate?'

'Not a bit of it. Legitimate.'

'Will she ascend to the throne?'

'Should the imperator so decide ...'

'By thunder, just look at Ardal aep Dahy and Count de Wett ... Look at their faces; as though they'd drunk vinegar ...'

'Be quiet, Your Excellency ... Do their expressions surprise you?

241

If the rumours are true, Emhyr will be giving the ancient houses a slap in the face. He will humiliate them—'

'The rumours won't be true. The imperator won't wed that found-ling! He couldn't possibly ...'

'Emhyr will do whatever he wants. Heed your words, Your Excellency. Be careful of what you say. There have been people who said Emhyr couldn't do this or that. And they all ended up on the scaffold.'

'They say he has already signed a decree concerning an endow-ment for her. Three hundred marks annually, can you imagine?'

'And the title of princess. Have any of you seen her yet?'

'She was placed under the care of Countess Liddertal on her arrival and her house was cordoned off by the guard.'

'They have entrusted her to the countess, in order that she may instil some idea of manners in the little chit. They say your princess behaves like a farm girl ...'

'What's so strange about that? She comes from the north, from barbaric Cintra—'

'Which makes the rumours about a marriage to Emhyr all the more unlikely. No, no, it's utterly beyond the pale. The imperator is to marry de Wett's youngest daughter, as planned. He will not marry that usurper!'

'It is high time he finally married somebody. For the sake of the dynasty ... It is high time we had a little archduke ...'

'Then let him be wed, but not to that stray!'

'Quiet, don't gush. I give you my word, noble lords, that that marriage will not happen. What purpose could such a match serve?'

'It's politics, Countess. We are waging a war. That bond would have political and strategic significance ... The dynasty of which the princess is a member has legal titles and confirmed feudatory rights to the lands on the Lower Yarra. Were she to become the imper-ator's spouse ... Ha, it would be an excellent move. Just look over there, at King Esterad's envoys; how they whisper ...'

'So you support this outlandish relationship, Duke? Or you've simply been counselling Emhyr, is that it?'

'It's my business, Margrave, what I do or don't support. And I would advise you not to question the imperator's decisions.'

'Has he already made his decision then?'

'I doubt it.'

'You are in error then, to doubt it.'

'What do you mean by that, madam?'

'Emhyr has sent Baroness Tarnhann away from the court. He has ordered her to return to her husband.'

'He's broken off with Dervla Tryffin Broinne? It cannot be! Dervla has been his favourite for three years ...'

'Now she has been expelled from the court.'

'It's true. They say the golden-haired Dervla kicked up an awful fuss. Four royal guardsmen had to manhandle her into the carriage ...'

'Her husband will be overjoyed ...'

'I doubt that.'

'By the Great Sun! Emhyr has broken off with Dervla? He's broken off with her for that foundling? For that savage from the North?'

'Quiet ... Quiet, for heaven's sake!'

'Who supports this? Which faction supports this?'

'Be quiet, I said. They're looking at us—'

'That wench – I mean princess – is said to be ugly ... When the imperator sees her ...'

'Are you trying to say he hasn't seen her yet?'

'He hasn't had time. He only returned from Darn Ruach an hour ago.'

'Emhyr never had a liking for ugly women. Aine Dermott, Clara aep Gwydolyn Gor ... And Dervla Tryffin Broinne was a true beauty.'

'Perhaps the foundling will grow pretty with time ...'

'After she's been given a good scrubbing? They say princesses from the north seldom wash—'

'Heed your words. You may be speaking about the imperator's spouse!'

'She is still a child. She is no more than fourteen.'

'I say again, it would be a political union ... Purely formal ...'

243

'Were that the case, the golden-haired Dervla would remain at court. The foundling from Cintra would politically and formally ascend the throne beside Emhyr ... But in the evening Emhyr would give her a tiara and the crown jewels to play with and would visit Dervla's bedchamber ... At least until the chit attained an age when she could safely bear him a child.'

'Hmm ... Yes, you may have something there. What is the name of the ... princess?'

'Xerella, or something of the kind.'

'Not a bit of it. She is called ... Zirilla. Yes, I think it's Zirilla.'

'A barbarous name.'

'Be quiet, damn it ...'

'And show a little dignity. You're squabbling like unruly children!'

'Heed your words! Be careful that I do not treat them as an affront!'

'If you're demanding satisfaction, you know where to find me, Margrave!'

'Silence! Be quiet! The imperator ...'

The herald did not have to make a special effort. One blow of his staff on the floor was sufficient for the black-bereted heads of the aristocrats and knights to bow down like ears of corn blown in the wind. The silence in the throne room was so complete that the herald did not have to raise his voice especially, either.

'Emhyr var Emreis, Deithwen Addan yn Carn aep Monrudd!'

The White Flame Dancing on the Barrows of his Foes. He marched down the double file of noblemen with his usual brisk step, vigorously waving his right hand. His black costume was identical to that of the courtiers, aside from the lack of a ruff. The imperator's dark hair – largely unkempt as usual – was kept reasonably neat by a narrow gold band, and the imperial chain of office glistened on his neck.

The Emhyr sat down on the throne quite carelessly, placing an elbow on the armrest and his chin in his hand. He did not throw a leg over the other armrest, signifying that etiquette still applied. None of the bowed heads rose by even an inch.

The imperator cleared his throat loudly without changing his position. The courtiers breathed again and straightened up. The herald struck his staff on the floor once again.

'Cirilla Fiona Elen Riannon, the Queen of Cintra, the Princess of Brugge and Duchess of Sodden, heiress of Inis Ard Skellig and Inis An Skellig, and suzerain of Attre and Abb Yarra!'

All eyes turned towards the doors, where the tall and dignified Stella Congreve, Countess of Liddertal, was standing. Alongside the countess walked the holder of all those impressive titles. Skinny, fair-haired, extremely pale, somewhat stooped, in a long, blue dress. A dress in which she very clearly felt awkward and uncomfortable.

Emhyr Deithwen sat up on his throne, and the courtiers immediately bowed low again. Stella Congreve nudged the fair-haired girl very gently, and the two of them filed between the double row of bowing aristocrats, all members of the leading houses of Nilfgaard. The girl walked stiffly and hesitantly. *She'll stumble*, thought the countess.

Cirilla Fiona Elen Riannon stumbled.

Ugly, scrawny little thing, thought the countess, as she neared the throne. *Clumsy and, what's more, rather bovine. But I shall make her a beauty. I shall make her a queen, Emhyr, just as you ordered.*

The White Flame of Nilfgaard watched them from his position on the throne. As usual, his eyes were somewhat narrowed and the hint of a sneer played on his lips.

The Queen of Cintra stumbled a second time. The imperator placed an elbow on the armrest of the throne and touched his cheek with his hand. He was smiling. Stella Congreve was close enough to recognise that smile. She froze in horror. *Something is not right,* she thought, *something is not right. Heads will fall. By the Great Sun, heads will fall . . .*

She regained her presence of mind and curtseyed, making the girl follow suit.

Emhyr var Emreis did not rise from the throne. But he bowed his head slightly. The courtiers held their breath.

'Your Majesty,' said Emhyr. The girl cowered. The imperator was not looking at her. He was looking at the noblemen gathered in the hall.

'Your Majesty,' he repeated. 'I'm glad to be able to welcome you to my palace and my country. I give you my imperial word that the day is close when all the titles belonging to you will return to you, along with the lands which are your legal inheritance, which legally and incontrovertibly belong to you. The usurpers, who lord it over your estates, have declared war on me. They attacked me, stating that they were defending your just rights. May the entire world know that you are turning to me – not to them – for help. May the entire world know that here, in my land, you enjoy the reverence and royal name deserving of a queen, while among my enemies you were merely an outcast. May the entire world know that in my country you are safe, while my enemies not only denied you your crown, but even made attempts on your life.'

The Emperor of Nilfgaard fixed his gaze on the envoys of Esterad Thyssen, the King of Kovir, and on the ambassador of Niedamir, the King of the Hengfors League.

'May the entire world know the truth, and among them also the kings who pretended not to know where rightness and justice lay. And may the entire world know that help will be given to you. Your enemies and mine will be defeated. Peace will reign once again in Cintra, in Sodden and Brugge, in Attre, on the Isles of Skellige and at the mouth of the Yarra Delta, and you will ascend the throne to the joy of your countrymen and every one to whom justice is dear.'

The girl in the blue dress lowered her head even further.

'Before that happens,' said Emhyr, 'you will be treated with the respect due to you, by me and by all of my subjects. And since the flame of war still blazes in your kingdom, as evidence of the honour, respect and friendship of Nilfgaard, I endow you with the title of Duchess of Rowan and Ymlac, lady of the castle of Darn Rowan, where you will now travel, in order to await the arrival of more peaceful, happier times.'

Stella Congreve struggled to control herself, not allowing even a trace of astonishment to appear on her face. *He's not going to keep her with him,* she thought, *but is sending her to Darn Rowan, to the end of the world; somewhere he never goes. He has no intention of courting this girl. He isn't considering a quick marriage. He doesn't even want to see*

246

her. Why, then, has he got rid of Dervla? What is this all about?

She recovered and quickly took the princess by the hand. The audience was over. The emperor didn't look at them as they were leaving the hall. The courtiers bowed.

Once they had left Emhyr var Emreis slung a leg over the armrest of his throne.

'Ceallach,' he said. 'To me.'

The seneschal stopped in front of the emperor at the distance decreed by etiquette and bowed.

'Closer,' said Emhyr. 'Come closer, Ceallach. I shall speak quietly. And what I say is meant for your ears only.'

'Your Highness.'

'What else is planned for today?'

'Receiving accrediting letters and granting a formal exequatur to the envoy of King Esterad of Kovir,' recited the seneschal rapidly. 'Appointing viceroys, prefects and palatines in the new provinces and palatinates. Ratifying the title of Count and appanage of—'

'We shall grant the envoy his exequatur and receive him in a private audience. Postpone the other matters until tomorrow.'

'Yes, Your Royal Highness.'

'Inform the Viscount of Eiddon and Skellen that immediately after the audience with the ambassador they are to report to the library. In secret. You are also to be there. And bring that celebrated mage of yours, that soothsayer ... What was his name?'

'Xarthisius, Your Highness. He lives in a tower outside the city—'

'Where he lives is of no interest to me. Send for him. He is to be brought to my apartments. Quietly, with a minimum of fuss, clandestinely.'

'Your Highness ... Is it wise, for that astrologer—'

'That is an order, Ceallach.'

'Yes, sir.'

Before three hours had passed, all of those summoned were present in the imperial library. The summons didn't surprise Vattier de Rideaux, the Viscount of Eiddon. Vattier was the chief of military intelligence. Vattier was often summoned by Emhyr; they were at war, after all. Neither did the summons surprise Stefan Skellen

– also known as Tawny Owl – who served the imperator as coroner
and as the authority on special services and operations. Nothing ever
surprised Tawny Owl.

The third person summoned, however, was astonished to be
asked to attend. Particularly since the emperor addressed him first.

'Master Xarthisius.'

'Your Imperial Highness.'

'I must establish the whereabouts of a certain individual. An individual who has either gone missing or is being hidden. Or is perhaps
imprisoned. The sorcerers I previously gave this task to failed me.
Will you undertake it?'

'At what distance is this individual – may this individual be
– residing?'

'If I knew that, I wouldn't need your witchcraft.'

'I beg your forgiveness, Your Imperial Highness ...' stammered
the astrologer. 'The point is that great distances hinder astromancy,
they practically preclude it ... Hum, hum ... And should this individual be under magical protection ... I can try, but—'

'Keep it brief, master.'

'I need time ... And ingredients for the spells ... If the align-
ment of stars is auspicious, then ... Hum, hum ... Your Imperial
Highness, what you request is an exacting task ... I need time—'

Much more of this and Emhyr will order him to be stuck on a spike,
thought Tawny Owl. *If the wizard doesn't stop jabbering ...*

'Master Xarthisius,' interrupted the imperator surprisingly
politely, even gently. 'You will have everything you need at your
disposal. Including time. Within reason.'

'I shall do everything in my power,' declared the astrologer. 'But
I shall only be able to determine the approximate location ... I mean
the region or radius—'

'I beg your pardon?'

'Astromancy ...' stammered Xarthisius. 'At great distances astromancy only permits approximate localisations ... Very approximate,
with considerable tolerance ... With very considerable tolerance. I
truly know not whether I will be able—'

'You will be able, master,' drawled the imperator and his dark eyes flashed balefully. 'I am utterly confident in your abilities. And as far as tolerance is concerned, the less is yours, the greater will be mine.'

Xarthisius cowered.

'I must know the precise birth date of this individual,' he mumbled. 'To the hour; if possible ... An object which belonged to the individual would also be invaluable ...'

'Hair,' said Emhyr quietly. 'Would hair suffice?'

'Oooh!' said the astrologer, brightening up. 'Hair! That would expedite things considerably ... Ah, and if I could also have faeces or urine ...'

Emhyr's eyes narrowed menacingly and the wizard cowered and made a low bow.

'I humbly apologise, Your Imperial Highness ...' he grunted. 'Please forgive me ... Of course ... Indeed, hair will suffice ... Will absolutely suffice ... When might I be given it?'

'It will be supplied to you today, along with the date and hour of birth. I won't keep you any longer, master. Return to your tower and start examining the constellations.'

'May the Great Sun keep you ever in its care, Your Imperial—'

'Yes, yes. You may withdraw.'

Now for us, thought Tawny Owl. *I wonder what's in store for us.*

'Should anyone,' said the imperator slowly, 'breathe a word of what is about to be said, they will be quartered. Vattier!'

'Yes, Your Highness.'

'How did that ... *princess* ... end up here? Who was involved?'

'She came from the stronghold in Nastrog,' said the chief of intelligence. 'She was escorted here by guardsmen commanded by ...'

'That's not what I bloody mean! How did that girl end up in Nastrog, in Verden? Who had her brought to the stronghold? Who is currently the commandant there? Is it the man who sent the report? Godyvron something?'

'Godyvron Pitcairn,' said Vattier de Rideaux quickly, 'was of course informed about Rience and Count Cahir aep Ceallach's mission. Three days after the events on the Isle of Thanedd, two people showed up in Nastrog. To be precise: one human and the other a half-blood elf. It was they who, citing the names Rience and Count Cahir, handed the princess over to Godyvron.'

'Aha,' said the imperator, smiling, and Tawny Owl felt a shiver running down his back. 'Vilgefortz vouched he would capture Cirilla on Thanedd. Rience assured me of the same. Cahir Mawr Dyffryn aep Ceallach received clear orders in this matter. And so, three days after the scandal on the island, Cirilla is brought to Nastrog on the River Yarra; not by Vilgefortz, nor Rience, nor Cahir, but by a human and a half-elf. Did it not occur to Godyvron to arrest them?'

'No. Shall he be punished for it, Your Highness?'

'No.'

Tawny Owl swallowed. Emhyr was silent, rubbing his forehead, and the huge diamond in his ring shone like a star. A moment later, the imperator looked up.

'Vattier.'

'Your Highness?'

'Mobilise all your subordinates. Order them to arrest Rience and Count Cahir. I presume the two of them are residing in territories as yet unoccupied by our forces. You will use Scoia'tael or Queen Enid's elves to achieve that end. Take the two captives to Darn Ruach and subject them to torture.'

'What information is required, Your Highness?' said Vattier de Rideaux, narrowing his eyes and pretending not notice the paleness on the face of Seneschal Ceallach.

'None. Later, when they're softened up a little, I shall ask them personally. Skellen!'

'Yes, sire.'

'That old fool Xarthisius; if that jabbering copromancer manages to determine what I've ordered him to, then you will organise a search for a certain individual in the area he indicates. You will receive a description. It's possible that the astrologer will indicate a region under our control, and then you will mobilise everyone responsible for that region. The entire civilian and military apparatus. It is a matter of the highest priority. Is that understood?'

'Yes, sire. May I ... ?'

'No, you may not. Sit down and listen, Tawny Owl. Xarthisius will probably not come up with anything. The individual I have ordered him to search for is probably in foreign territory and under magical protection. I'd give my head that the individual I'm looking for is in the same place as our good friend, the sorcerer Vilgefortz of Roggeveen, who has mysteriously vanished. That is also why, Skellen, you will assemble and prepare a special unit, which you will personally command. Use the best men you have. They are to be ready for everything ... and not superstitious. I mean not afraid of magic.'

Tawny Owl raised his eyebrows.

'Your unit,' concluded Emhyr, 'will be charged with attacking and capturing the hideout of Vilgefortz, former good friend and ally that he was, the whereabouts of which is currently unknown to me, and which is probably quite well camouflaged and defended.'

'Yes, sire,' said Tawny Owl emotionlessly. 'I presume that the individual being sought, whom they will probably find there, is not to be harmed.'

'You presume correctly.'

'What about Vilgefortz?'

'He can be ...' The emperor smiled cruelly. 'In his case he *ought* to be harmed, once and for all. Terminally harmed. This also applies to any other sorcerers you happen to find in his hideout. Without exception.'

'Yes, sire. Who is responsible for finding Vilgefortz's hideout?'

'You are, Tawny Owl.'

Stefan Skellen and Vattier de Rideaux exchanged glances. Emhyr leaned back in his chair.

'Is everything clear? If so ... What is it, Ceallach?'

'Your Highness ...' whined the seneschal, to whom no one had paid any attention up until that moment. 'I beg you for mercy ...'

'There is no mercy for traitors. There is no mercy for those who oppose my will.'

'Cahir ... My son ...'

'Your son ...' said Emhyr, narrowing his eyes. 'I don't yet know what your son is guilty of. I would like to hope that he is only guilty

251

of stupidity and ineptitude and not of treachery. If that is the case he will only be beheaded and not broken on the wheel.'

'Your Highness! Cahir is not a traitor ... Cahir could not have—'

'Enough, Ceallach, not another word. The guilty will be punished. They attempted to deceive me and I will not forgive them for that. Vattier, Skellen, in one hour, report for your signed instructions, orders and authorisations. You will then set about executing your tasks at once. And one more thing: I trust I do not have to add that the poor girl you saw in the throne room a short while ago is to remain to everyone Cirilla, Queen of Cintra and Duchess of Rowan. To everyone. I order you to treat it as a state secret and a matter of the gravest national importance.'

All those present looked at the imperator in astonishment. Deithwen Addan yn Carn aep Morvudd smiled faintly.

'Have you not understood? Instead of the real Cirilla of Cintra I've been sent some kind of dolt. Those traitors probably told themselves that I would not recognise her. But I will know the real Ciri. I would know her at the end of the world and in the darkness of hell.'

*The behaviour of the unicorn is greatly mystifying. Although excep-
tionally timid and fearful of people, if it should chance upon a
maiden who has not had carnal relations with a man it will at once
run to her, kneel before her and, without any fear whatsoever, lay
its head in her lap. It is said that in the dim and distant past there
were maidens who made a veritable practice of this. They remained
unmarried and in abstinence for many years in order to be employed
by hunters as a lure for unicorns. It soon transpired, however, that
the unicorn only approached youthful maidens, paying absolutely
no attention to older ones. Being a wise creature, the unicorn indub-
itably knows that remaining too long in the state of maidenhood is
suspicious and counter to the natural order.*

Physiologus

CHAPTER SIX

The heat woke her. It burnt her skin like a torturer's glowing irons.

She could barely move her head, for something held it fast. She pulled away and howled in pain, feeling the skin over her temple tear and split. She opened her eyes. The boulder on which she had been resting her head was dark brown from dry, congealed blood. She touched her temple and felt the remains of a hard, cracked scab under her fingers. The scab, which had been stuck to the boulder and then torn from it when she moved her head, now dripped blood and plasma. Ciri cleared her throat, hawked and spat out sand mixed with thick, sticky saliva. She raised herself on her elbows and then sat up, looking around.

She was completely surrounded by a greyish-red, stony plain, scored by ravines and faults, with mounds of stones and huge, strangely shaped rocks. High above the plain hung an enormous, golden, burning sun, turning the entire sky yellow, distorting visibility with its blinding glare and making the air shimmer.

Where am I?

She gingerly touched her gashed, swollen forehead. It hurt. It hurt intensely. *I must have taken quite a tumble*, she thought. *I must have slid a fair way along the ground.* Her attention turned to her torn clothing and she discovered other sources of pain: in her back, in her shoulder and in her hips. When she hit the ground she had become covered in dust, sharp sand and grit. It was in her hair, ears, mouth and even her eyes, which were smarting and watering. Her hands and elbows, grazed to the raw flesh, were also stinging.

She slowly and cautiously straightened her legs and groaned once more, for her left knee reacted to movement with an intense, dull ache. She examined it through her undamaged trousers but did not find any swelling. When she breathed in, she felt a worrying stabbing in her side, and her attempts to bend her trunk almost made her scream, shooting her through with a sharp spasm which she felt in her lower back. *I'm good and bruised*, she thought. *But I don't think I've broken anything. If I'd broken a bone, it would hurt much more. I'm in one piece, just a bit knocked about. I'll be able to get up. So I'll get up.*

Crouching forward awkwardly, making deliberate movements, she very slowly manoeuvred herself into a position which would protect her injured knee. Then she went onto all fours, groaning and hissing. Finally, after what seemed an eternity, she stood up. Only to fall heavily onto the rock, as the dizziness which blurred her vision instantly took her legs from under her. Sensing a sudden wave of nausea, she lay down on one side. The searing rock stung like red-hot coals.

'I'll never get up ...' she sobbed. 'I can't ... I'll burn up in this sun ...'

A growing, loathsome, intractable pain throbbed in her head. Each movement made the pain more intense, so Ciri stopped moving for a moment. She covered her head with an arm, but the heat soon became unbearable. She knew she would have to hide from it. Fighting the overpowering resistance of her aching body. Screwing her eyes up against the shooting pain in her temples, she crawled on all fours towards a large boulder, sculpted by the wind to resemble a strange mushroom, whose shapeless cap gave a little shade at its foot. She curled up in a ball, coughing and sniffing.

She lay there for a long time, until the sun assaulted her once again with its scorching heat as it wandered across the sky. She moved around to the other side of the boulder, only to find it made no difference. The sun was at its zenith and the stone mushroom gave practically no shade. She pressed her hands to her temples, which were exploding with pain.

She was woken by a shivering which gripped her entire body. The sun's fiery ball had lost its blinding golden glow. Now, hanging lower in the sky above the serrated, jagged rocks, it was orange. The heat had eased off.

Ciri sat up with difficulty and looked around. Her headache was less intense and was no longer blinding her. She touched her head and discovered that the heat had dried the blood on her temple, turning it into a hard, smooth crust. Her entire body still hurt, though, and it seemed to her there was not a single place free of pain. She hawked, sand grating between her teeth, and tried to spit. Unsuccessfully. She leaned back against the mushroom-shaped boulder, which was still hot from the sun. *At last the heat has broken,* she thought. *Now, with the sun sinking in the west, it's bearable, and soon . . .*

Soon, night will fall.

She shuddered. *Where the hell am I? How do I get out of here? And which way? Which way should I go? Or perhaps I should stay in one place and wait until they find me. They must be looking for me. Geralt. Yennefer. They won't just leave me here . . .*

She tried to spit again, and again she could not. And then she understood.

Thirst.

She remembered. Back then, during her escape, she had been tortured by thirst. There had been a wooden canteen tied to the saddle of the black horse she had been riding when she was escaping towards the Tower of Gulls; she remembered it distinctly. But she had been unable to unfasten it or take it with her; she'd had no time. And now it was gone. Now everything was gone. There was nothing save sharp, scalding stones, save a scab on her temple that pulled her skin tight, save the pain in her body and her parched throat, which she couldn't even give relief to by swallowing.

I can't stay here. I have to go and find water. If I don't find water I'll die.

She tried to stand, cutting her fingers on the stone mushroom. She got up. She took a step. And with a howl she toppled over onto her hands and knees, her back arching as spasms of nausea gripped her. Cramps and dizziness seized her so intensively she had to lie down.

I'm helpless. And alone. Again. Everyone has betrayed me, abandoned me, left me all alone. Just like before . . .

Ciri felt invisible pincers squeezing her throat, felt the muscles in her jaw tensing to the point of pain, felt her cracked lips begin to quiver. *There is no more dreadful sight than a weeping enchantress,* rang Yennefer's words in her head.

257

But wait ... No one will see me here ... No one at all ...

Curled up in a ball beneath the stone mushroom, Ciri sobbed uncontrollably in a dry, dreadful lament. Without tears.

When she opened her swollen, gummed-up eyelids, she realised the heat had diminished even more, and the sky – which a short time before had still been yellow – had taken on its characteristic cobalt colour and was astonishingly clear, shot with thin, white strips of cloud. The sun's disc had reddened and sunk lower but was still pouring its undulating, pulsating heat down on the desert. Or perhaps the heat was radiating upwards from the hot stones?

She sat up to find that the pain inside her skull and bruised body had stopped tormenting her. That right now it was nothing in comparison to the terrible suffering growing in her stomach and the cruel itch in her dry throat, which forced her to cough.

Don't give up, she thought. *I can't give up. Just like in Kaer Morhen, I have to get up, defeat the enemy, fight, suppress the pain and weakness inside me. I have to get up and walk. At least I know the direction now. The sun is setting in the west. I have to walk, I have to find water and something to eat. I have to. Or I'll die. This is a desert. I landed in a desert. The thing I entered in the Tower of Gulls was a magical portal, a magical device, which can transport people great distances ...*

The portal in Tor Lara was a strange one. When she ran up to the top floor there was nothing, not even any windows, only bare, mould-covered walls. And on one of the walls burnt an irregular oval filled with an iridescent gleam. She hesitated, but the portal drew her on, summoned her; literally invited her. And there was no other way out; only that shining oval. She'd closed her eyes and stepped inside.

Afterwards, there was a blinding light and a furious vortex, a blast which took her breath away and squeezed her ribs. She remembered the flight through silence, cold and emptiness, then a bright light and she was choking on air. Above her had been blue and down below a vague greyness ...

The vortex spat her out in mid-flight, as a young eagle drops a fish which is too heavy for it. When she smashed against the rock, she lost consciousness. She didn't know for how long.

I read about portals in the temple, she recalled, shaking the sand from her hair. *Some books mentioned teleportation portals, which were either distorted or chaotic. They transported people towards random destinations and threw them out in random places. The portal in the Tower of Gulls must have been one of those. It threw me out somewhere at the end of the world. I have no idea where. No one is going to look for me here and no one will find me. If I stay here I'll die.*

She stood up. Summoning up all her strength and bracing herself against the boulder, she took the first step. Then a second. Then a third.

The first steps made her aware that the buckles of her right shoe had been torn off, and the flapping upper made walking impossible. She sat down, this time intentionally and deliberately, and carried out an inspection of her clothes and equipment. While she concentrated on this task, she forgot about her exhaustion and pain.

The first thing she discovered was the dagger. She had forgotten about it, and the sheath had slid around to her back. Next to the dagger, as usual, was a small pouch on a strap. It had been a present from Yennefer. It contained 'things a lady always ought to have'. Ciri untied it. Unfortunately, a lady's standard equipment had not foreseen the situation she was now in. The pouch contained a tortoiseshell comb, a knife and a combination knife and nail file, a packed, sterilised tampon made from linen fabric and a small jade casket containing hand ointment.

Ciri rubbed the ointment into her cracked face and lips at once, then greedily licked the ointment from her lips. Without much thought, she went on to lick out the entire box, revelling in its greasiness and the tiny amount of soothing moisture. The chamomile, ambergris and camphor used to perfume the ointment made it taste disgusting, but they acted as stimulants.

She strapped the shoe to her ankle with a strip she had ripped from her sleeve, stood up and stamped several times to test it. She unpacked and unfurled the tampon, making a wide headband from it to protect her injured temple and sunburnt forehead.

She stood, adjusted her belt, shifted the dagger nearer to her left hip and instinctively drew it from its sheath, checking the blade with her thumb. It was sharp. She knew it would be.

I'm armed, she thought. *I'm a witcher. No, I won't die here. Hunger? I can endure it. In the Temple of Melitele, it was occasionally necessary to fast for up to two days. But water ... I have to find water. I'll keep walking until I find some. This accursed desert must finish eventually. If it were a very large desert, I would know something about it. I would have noticed it on the maps I used to look at with Jarre. Jarre ... I wonder what he's doing now ...*

I'll set off, she decided. *I'll walk towards the west. I can see where the sun sets. It's the only certain direction. After all, I never lose my way. I always know which way to go. I'll walk all night if I have to. I'm a witcher. When I get my strength back, I'll run like I used to on the Trail at Kaer Morhen. That way I'll get to the edge of the desert quicker. I'll hold out. I have to hold out ... Ha, I bet Geralt's often been in deserts like this one, if not in even worse ones ...*

Off I go.

After the first hour of walking, nothing in the landscape had changed. There was still nothing at all around her apart from stones; greyish-red, sharp, shifting underfoot, forcing her to be cautious. There were scrawny bushes, dry and thorny, reaching out to her from clefts in the rocks with their contorted branches. Ciri stopped at the first bush she encountered, expecting to find leaves or young shoots which she would be able to suck and chew. But the bush only had sharp thorns which cut her fingers. It didn't even have any branches suitable to break off and use as a stick. The second and third bushes were no different and she ignored all the rest, passing by them without stopping.

Dusk fell quickly. The sun sank over the jagged horizon, and the sky lit up red and purple. As darkness fell, it became cold. At first, she greeted it with gladness, for the coolness soothed her sunburnt skin. Soon after, however, it became even colder and Ciri's teeth began to chatter. She walked quicker, hoping that a vigorous pace would warm her up, but the effort revived the pain in her side and knee. She began to limp. On top of that, the sun had completely sunk below the horizon and it was rapidly becoming dark. The moon was new, and the stars twinkling in the sky were no help. Ciri was soon unable to see the ground in front of her. She fell down several times, painfully grazing the skin on her wrists. Twice she caught her feet in clefts in the rocks, and only her well-drilled reactions as she was falling saved her from twisting or breaking an ankle. She realised it was no good. Walking in the dark was impossible.

She sat down on a flat basalt slab, feeling overwhelming despair She had no idea if she was heading in the right direction and had long since lost sight of the point where the sun had disappeared over the horizon. There was now no sign whatsoever of the glow which had guided her during the first hours after nightfall. Around her was nothing but velvety, impenetrable blackness. And bitter cold. Cold which paralysed, which bit at the joints, forcing her to stoop and tuck her head down into her painfully hunched shoulders. Ciri began to miss the sun, even though she knew its return would mean another onslaught of unbearable heat descending upon the rocks. Heat which would prevent her from continuing her journey. Once again, she felt the urge to cry rising in her throat and a wave of desperation and hopelessness overcoming her. But this time the desperation and hopelessness transformed into fury.

'I will not cry!' she screamed in the darkness. 'I am a witcher! I am ...'

An enchantress.

Ciri lifted her hands and pressed her palms against her temples. *The Power is everywhere. It's in the water, in the air, in the earth ...*

She quickly stood up, held her hands in front of her, and then slowly and hesitantly took a few steps, feverishly searching for an underground spring. She was fortunate. Almost immediately, she felt a familiar rushing sound, a throbbing in her ears and the energy emanating from a water vein hidden deep within the earth. She imbibed the Power with cautious inhalations, which she gradually released, knowing she was weak and that, in her state, a sudden shortage of oxygen to the brain might render her unconscious and thwart all her efforts. The energy slowly filled her up, giving her a familiar, momentary euphoria. Her lungs began to work more strongly and more quickly. Ciri brought her accelerated breathing under control; too much oxygen to the brain too rapidly could also have fatal consequences.

She'd done it.

First the aching, she thought. *First the paralysing pain in my shoulders and thighs. Then the cold. I have to raise my body temperature . . .*

She gradually recalled the gestures and spells. She performed and uttered some of them too hurriedly and was instantly seized by cramps and convulsions. A sudden spasm and dizziness made her weak at the knees. She sat down on a basalt slab, stilled her shaking hands and brought her fractured, irregular breathing back under control.

She repeated the formulas, forcing herself to be calm and exact, to concentrate and totally focus her will. And this time the result was immediate. She rubbed the warmth sweeping through her into her thighs and neck. She stood up, feeling the exhaustion vanish and her aching muscles relax.

'I'm an enchantress!' she cried in triumph, holding her arms up high. 'Come, immortal light! I summon you! Aen'drean va, eveigh Aine!'

A small, warm sphere of light floated from her hands like a butterfly, casting shifting mosaics of shadow on the stones. Moving her hand slowly, she stabilised the sphere, guiding it so that it was hanging in front of her. It was not the best idea; the light blinded her. She tried to move the sphere behind her back but again with a disappointing result. It cast her own shadow in front of her, making visibility worse. Ciri slowly moved the shining sphere to the side and suspended it just above her right shoulder. Although the sphere was nowhere as good as the real, magical Aine, the girl was extremely proud of her achievement.

'Ha!' she said proudly. 'It's a pity Yennefer can't see this!'

She began to march jauntily and vigorously, striding quickly and confidently, choosing where to step in the flickering and indistinct chiaroscuro cast by the sphere. As she walked, she tried to recall other spells, but none of them seemed suitable or useful in this situation. Furthermore, some of them were very draining, and she was a little afraid of them, not wanting to use them without an obvious need. Unfortunately, she did not know any which would have been able to create water or food. She knew spells like that existed, but didn't know how to cast any of them.

The hitherto lifeless desert came to life in the light of her magical sphere. Ungainly, glossy beetles and hairy spiders scuttled away to avoid being stepped on. A small reddish-yellow scorpion, pulling its segmented tail behind it, scurried swiftly across her path, disappearing into a crack in the rocks. A long-tailed, green lizard, rustling over the stones, vanished into the gloom. Rodents resembling large mice ran nimbly away from her, leaping high on their hind legs. Several times she saw eyes reflected in the dark, and once she heard a blood-curdling hiss issuing from a pile of rocks. If she'd had thoughts of catching something edible, the hissing completely discouraged her from groping around among the rocks. She began to watch her step more cautiously, and in her mind's eye she saw the illustrations she had studied in Kaer Morhen. Giant scorpions. Scarletias. Frighteners. Wights. Lamias. Crab spiders. Desert-dwelling monsters. She walked on, looking around more timidly and listening out intently, gripping the hilt of her dagger in her sweaty palm.

After several hours, the shining sphere grew faint and the circle of light it was casting shrank and became vague. Ciri, beginning to find it hard to concentrate, uttered the spell again. For a few seconds, the ball pulsated more brightly but soon after darkened and faded once more. The effort made her dizzy. Then she staggered and black and red spots danced in front of her eyes. She sat down hard, crunching the grit and loose stones beneath her.

The sphere finally went out completely. Ciri did not try any more spells; the exhaustion, emptiness and lack of energy she felt inside precluded any chance of success.

A vague glow arose on the horizon, far ahead of her. *I've gone the wrong way*, she realised in horror. *I've muddled everything ... I was heading towards the west at first, and now the sun's going to rise directly in front of me, which means ...*

She felt overwhelming fatigue and sleepiness, which not even the bitter cold could frighten away. *I won't fall asleep*, she decided. *I can't fall asleep ... I just cannot ...*

She was woken by fierce cold and growing brightness, and brought back to her senses by the gut-wrenching pain in her belly and the dry, nagging, burning sensation in her throat. She tried to stand up. She couldn't. Her stiff, painful limbs failed her. Groping around her with her hands, she felt moisture under her fingers.

'Water ...' she croaked. 'Water!'

Shaking all over, she got up onto her hands and knees and then lowered her mouth to the basalt slabs, frantically using her tongue to collect the drops which had gathered on the smooth rock and sucking up the moisture from hollows in the boulder's uneven surface. There was almost half a handful of dew in one of them, which she lapped up with sand and grit, not daring to spit. She looked around.

Carefully, so as not to waste even the tiniest quantity, she used her tongue to gather the glistening drops hanging on the thorns of a stunted shrub, which had mysteriously managed to grow between the rocks. Her dagger was lying on the ground. She could not remember drawing it. The blade was lustreless from a thin layer of dew. She scrupulously and precisely licked the cold metal.

Overcoming the pain which made her whole body stiffen, she crawled on, searching out the moisture on other rocks. But the golden disc of the sun had already burst above the rocky horizon, flooding the desert with blinding, yellow light and instantly drying them. Ciri joyfully greeted the burgeoning warmth, although she was aware that soon she would be mercilessly scorched and longing for the cool of the night again.

She turned away from the glaring orb. The sun was shining in the east. But she had to head towards the west. She had to.

The rapidly intensifying heat soon became unbearable. By noon, it had exhausted her so much that, whether she liked it or not, she had to change her route in order to look for shade. She finally found some protection: a large boulder, shaped like a mushroom. She crawled under it.

And then she saw something lying among the rocks. It was the jade casket which had contained hand ointment but was now licked clean.

She couldn't find the strength inside to cry.

Hunger and thirst overcame her exhaustion and resignation. Staggering, she set off once more. The sun still beat down.

Far away on the horizon, beyond the shimmering veil of heat, she saw something which might have been a mountain range. An extremely distant mountain range.

After night fell, she expended immense effort on generating the Power, but only managed to conjure up the magical sphere after several attempts, and those tired her out to such a degree she was unable to go on. She had consumed all her energy and failed to cast the warming and relaxing spells in spite of repeated attempts. Conjuring up the light gave her courage and raised her spirit, but the cold weakened her. The piercing, bitter cold kept her shivering until dawn, as she waited impatiently for the sunrise. She removed her dagger from its sheath and placed it carefully on a rock so that the dew would condense on the metal. She was absolutely exhausted, but the hunger and thirst drove sleep away. She held out until dawn. It was still dark when she began greedily to lick the dew from the blade. When it grew light, she immediately got on all fours in order to search for more moisture in hollows and crevices.

She heard a hiss.

A large colourful lizard sitting on a nearby rocky ledge opened its toothless jaws at her, ruffled its impressive crest, puffed itself up and lashed the rock with its tail. In front of the lizard she saw a tiny, water-filled crevice.

At first Ciri retreated in horror, but she was quickly seized by desperation and savage fury. Groping around with her trembling hands, she grabbed an angular piece of rock.

'It's my water!' she howled. 'It's mine!'

She hurled the rock. And missed. The lizard jumped on its long-clawed feet and disappeared nimbly into a rocky labyrinth. Ciri flattened herself against the abandoned rock and sucked the rest of the water from the cleft. And then she saw it.

Beyond the rock, in a circular depression, lay seven eggs, all partly protruding from the reddish sand. The girl wasted no time. She fell onto the nest on her knees, seized one of the eggs and sank her teeth into it. The leathery shell burst and collapsed in her hand, the sticky gunk running into her sleeve. Ciri sucked the egg empty and licked her arm. She had difficulty swallowing and couldn't taste anything at all.

She ate every egg and remained on her hands and knees, sticky, dirty, covered in sand, with yolk stuck in her teeth, feverishly digging around in the sand and emitting inhuman, sobbing noises. She froze.

Sit up straight, princess! Don't rest your elbows on the table! Be careful how you serve yourself from the dish! You're dirtying the lace on your sleeves! Wipe your mouth with a napkin and stop slurping! By the gods, has no one ever taught that girl any table manners? Cirilla!

Ciri burst into tears, her head resting on her knees.

She endured the march until noon, when the heat defeated her and forced her to rest. She dozed for a long time, hidden in the shade beneath a rocky shelf. It wasn't cool in the shade, but it was better than the scorching sun. Eventually her thirst and hunger frightened sleep away again.

The distant range of mountains seemed to be on fire and sparkling in the sun's rays. *There might be snow lying on those mountain peaks,* she thought. *There might be ice. There might be streams. I have to get there. I have to get there fast.*

She walked for almost the entire night. She decided to navigate using the night sky. The whole sky was bedecked in stars and Ciri regretted not paying attention during lessons; not wanting to study the atlases of the constellations in the temple library. Naturally enough, she knew the most important of them: the Seven Goats, the Jug, the Sickle, the Dragon and the Winter Maiden, but those were hanging high in the sky, and would have been difficult to navigate by. She finally managed to select one bright star from the twinkling throng, which she thought was indicating the right direction. She didn't know what it was called, so she christened it herself. She named it the Eye.

*

She walked. The mountain range she was heading towards did not get the slightest bit closer; it was still as far away as it had been the previous day. But it pointed the way.

As she walked, she looked around intently. She found another lizard's nest, containing four eggs. She spotted a green plant, no longer than her little finger, which had miraculously managed to grow between the rocks. She tracked down a large brown beetle. And a thin-legged spider.

She ate everything.

At noon, she vomited up everything she had eaten and then fainted. When she came to, she found a patch of shade and lay, curled up in a ball, her hands clutching her painful belly.

She began to march again at sunset. She moved painfully stiffly. She fell down again and again but got up each time and continued walking.

She kept walking. She had to keep walking.

Evening. Rest. Night. The Eye showed her the way. Marching until she reached the point of utter exhaustion, which came well before sunrise. Rest. Fitful sleep. Hunger. Cold. The absence of magical energy; a disaster when she tried to conjure up light and warmth. Her thirst only intensified by licking the dew from the dagger's blade and the rocks in the early hours.

When the sun rose she fell asleep in the growing warmth. She was woken by the searing heat. She stood up and continued on her way.

She fainted after less than an hour's march. When she came to the sun was at its zenith, and the heat was unbearable. She didn't have the strength to look for shade. She didn't have the strength to get to her feet. But she did.

She walked on. She didn't give in. She walked for almost the entire following day, and part of the night.

Once again, she slept through the worst of the heat, curled up in a ball beneath a sloping boulder which was partly buried in the sand. Her sleep had been fitful and exhausting; she had dreamed of water.

Water which could be drunk. Huge, white waterfalls framed in haze and rainbows. Gurgling streams. Small forest springs shaded by ferns with their roots in the water. Palace fountains smelling of wet marble. Mossy wells and full buckets spilling over ... drops of water falling from melting icicles ... Water. Cold, refreshing water, cold enough to make your teeth sting, but with such a wonderful, incomparable taste ...

She awoke, leapt to her feet and began to walk back the way she had come. She turned around, staggering and falling. She had to go back! She had passed water on the way! She had passed a stream, gushing amongst the rocks! How could she be so foolish!

She came to her senses.

The heat subsided; evening was approaching. The setting sun indicated the way west. The mountains. The sun could not be – could not possibly be – at her back. Ciri chased away the visions and choked back her sobs. She turned around and began to march.

She walked the entire night, but very slowly. She did not get far. She was dropping off to sleep as she walked, dreaming of water. The rising sun found her sitting on a rock, staring at the dagger's blade and her naked forearm.

Blood is a liquid, after all. It can be drunk.

She drove away the hallucinations and nightmares. She licked the dew-covered dagger and began to walk.

She fainted. She came around, seared by the sun and the baking stones.

Before her, beyond a shimmering heat haze, she saw the jagged, serrated mountain range.

Closer. Significantly closer.

But she had no more strength. She sat up.

The dagger in her hand reflected the sunlight and burnt hot. It was sharp. She knew that.

Why do you torture yourself? said the calm, pedantic voice of the enchantress, Tissaia de Vries. *Why do you condemn yourself to suffering? It's time you put an end to it!*

No. I won't give in.

You will not endure this. Do you know how you die from thirst? Any moment now you will lose your mind, and then it will be too late. Then you won't be able to end it all.

No. I won't give in. I will endure it.

She sheathed the dagger. She stood up, staggered and fell down. She stood up again, staggered and began to march.

Above her, high in the yellow sky, she saw a vulture.

When she came to again, she couldn't remember having fallen. She couldn't remember how long she had been lying there. She looked up at the sky. Two more vultures had joined the first one wheeling above her. She didn't have enough strength to get up.

She realised this was the end. She accepted it calmly. Almost with relief.

Something touched her.

It nudged her gently and cautiously on the shoulder. After such a long period of solitude, after so long surrounded by lifeless, motionless rocks, the touch made her jerk up, in spite of her exhaustion. It made her attempt to jump to her feet. Whatever had touched her snorted and sprang back, stamping its feet noisily.

Ciri sat up with difficulty, rubbing the encrusted corners of her eyes with her knuckles.

I've gone mad, she thought.

Several paces in front of her stood a horse. She blinked. It wasn't an illusion. It really was a horse. A young horse, not much more than a foal.

She was now fully awake. She licked her cracked lips and cleared her throat involuntarily. The horse jumped and ran some distance away, its hooves grating over the loose stones. It moved very strangely, and its coat was also unusual – neither dun nor grey. Perhaps the effect was just an illusion, created by the sunlight shining behind it.

The horse snorted and took a few steps towards her. Now she could see it better. Well enough to notice, in addition to its uncharacteristic coat colour, the strange peculiarities in its build: the small head, the extremely slender neck, the very thin pasterns and the long, thick tail. The horse stood and looked at her, holding its muzzle in profile. Ciri let out a quiet sigh.

A horn, at least two spans long, protruded from the horse's domed forehead.

An impossible impossibility, thought Ciri, coming to her senses and gathering her thoughts. *There are no unicorns in the world; they've died out. There wasn't even a unicorn in the witcher's tome in Kaer Morhen! I've only read about them in* The Book of Myths *in the temple ... Oh, and there was an illustration of a unicorn in that* Physiologus *I looked through in Mr Giancardi's bank ... But the unicorn in that illustration was more like a goat than a horse. It had shaggy fetlocks and a goat's beard, and its horn must have been two ells long ...*

She was astonished that she could remember everything so well; incidents that seemed to have happened hundreds of years before. Suddenly her head spun and pain twisted her insides. She groaned and curled up in a ball. The unicorn snorted and took a step towards her, then stopped and raised its head high. Ciri suddenly recalled what the books had said about unicorns.

'Please come closer ...' she croaked, trying to sit up. 'You may, because I am ...'

The unicorn snorted, leapt backwards and galloped away, waving its tail vigorously. But after a moment it stopped, tossed its head, pawed the ground with a hoof and whinnied loudly.

'That's not true!' she whined in despair. 'Jarre only kissed me once and that doesn't count! Come back!'

The effort of speaking blurred her vision and she slumped down onto the rock. When she finally managed to raise her head, the unicorn was once more close by. Looking at her inquisitively, it lowered its head and snorted softly.

'Don't be afraid of me ...' she whispered. 'You don't have to ... You can see I'm dying ...'

The unicorn neighed, shaking its head. Ciri fainted.

When she awoke again she was alone. Aching, stiff, thirsty, hungry, and all alone. The unicorn had been a mirage, an illusion, a dream.

And had vanished like a dream. She understood that, accepted it, but still felt regret and despair as though the creature really had existed, had been with her and had abandoned her. Just like everyone had abandoned her.

She tried to stand but could not. She rested her face on the rocks. Very slowly, she reached to one side and felt the hilt of her dagger.

Blood is a liquid. I have to drink.

She heard the clatter of hooves and a snorting.

'You've come back ...' she whispered, raising her head. 'Have you really come back?'

The unicorn snorted loudly. She saw its hooves, close by. Right beside her. They were wet. They were literally dripping with water.

Hope gave her strength, filled her with euphoria. The unicorn led and Ciri followed him, still not certain if she was in a dream. When exhaustion overcame her she fell to all fours. And then crawled.

The unicorn led her among some rocks to a shallow ravine with a sandy bottom. Ciri used the last of her strength to crawl, but she kept going. Because the sand was wet.

The unicorn stopped above a hollow which was visible in the sand, whinnied and pawed powerfully with his hoof; once, twice, three times. She understood. She crawled closer, helping him. She burrowed, breaking her fingernails, digging, pushing the sand aside. She may have sobbed as she did so, but she wasn't certain. When a muddy liquid appeared at the bottom of the hollow, she pressed her mouth to it at once, lapping up the water muddy with sand, so voraciously that the liquid disappeared. It took immense effort for Ciri to control herself. She used the dagger to dig deeper, then sat up and waited. She felt the sand crunching between her teeth and trembled with impatience, but waited until the hollow filled with water again. And then she drank. She drank long.

The third time, she let the water settle somewhat and then drank about four sand-free, sludgy mouthfuls. And then she remembered the unicorn.

'You must be thirsty too, little horse,' she said. 'But you can't drink mud. No horse ever drank mud.'

The unicorn neighed.

Ciri deepened the hollow, reinforcing the sides with stones.

'Wait, little horse. Let it settle a little ...'

'Little Horse' snorted, stamped his hooves and turned his head away.

'Don't be cross. Drink.'

The unicorn cautiously brought its muzzle towards the water.

'Drink, Little Horse. It isn't a dream. It's real water.'

At first Ciri tarried, not wanting to move away from the spring. She had just invented a new way of drinking by pressing a handkerchief she had soaked in the deepened hollow to her mouth, which allowed her to filter out most of the sand and mud. But the unicorn kept insisting; neighing, stamping, running away and returning again. He was calling her to start walking and was indicating the way. After long consideration, Ciri did as he suggested. The animal was right. It was time to go, to go towards the mountains, to get out of the desert. She set off after the unicorn, looking around and making a precise mental note of the spring's location. She didn't want to lose her way, should she ever have to return there.

They travelled together throughout the day. The unicorn, who now answered to Little Horse, led the way. He was a strange little horse. He bit and chewed dry stalks which no normal horse or even a starving goat would have touched. And when he caught a column of large ants wandering among the rocks, he began to eat them too. At first Ciri looked on in astonishment, but then joined in the feast herself. She was hungry.

The ants were dreadfully sour, but possibly because of that they didn't make her nauseous. Aside from that, the ants were in plentiful supply and she was able to get her stiff jaws moving again. The unicorn ate the ants whole while she contented herself with their abdomens, spitting out hard pieces of their chitinous carapaces.

They went on. The unicorn discovered several clumps of yellowed thistles and ate them with relish. This time Ciri did not join him. But when Little Horse found some lizard's eggs in the sand, she ate and he watched her. They continued on their way. Ciri noticed a clump of thistles and pointed them out to Little Horse. After a while, Little Horse drew her attention to a huge, black scorpion with a long tail, which must have measured a span and a half. Ciri trampled the hideous creature. Seeing that she was not interested in eating the scorpion, the unicorn ate it himself, and soon after pointed out another lizard's nest.

It was, it turned out, quite an effective collaboration.

They walked on.

The mountain range was getting closer and closer.

When it was very dark, the unicorn stopped. He slept standing up. Ciri, who was familiar with horses, initially tried to persuade him to lie down; she would have been able to sleep lying on him and benefit from his warmth. But it came to nothing. Little Horse grew cross and walked away, remaining aloof. He refused to behave in the classical way, as described in the learned books; he clearly did not have the slightest intention of resting his head in her lap. Ciri was full of doubts. She even wondered if the books were lying about unicorns and virgins, but there was also another possibility. The unicorn was clearly a foal and, as a young animal, may not have known anything about virgins. She rejected the possibility of Little Horse being able to sense, or take seriously, those few strange dreams she had once had. Who would ever take dreams seriously?

He was somewhat of a disappointment to her. They had been wandering for two days and nights, but he had not found any more water, even though he had been searching for it. Several times he stopped, twisted his head, moved his horn around, and then trotted off, rummaging in rocky clefts or rooting about in the sand with his hooves. He found ants and he found ants' eggs and larvae. He found a lizard's nest. He found a colourful snake, which he deftly trampled to death. But he did not find any water.

Ciri noticed that the unicorn roamed around; he didn't keep to a straight course. She came to the reasonable conclusion that the creature did not live in the desert at all. He had strayed there. Just as she had.

273

The ants, which they were beginning to find in abundance, contained some sour juice, but Ciri began to think more and more seriously about returning to the spring. Should they go even further and not find any water, her strength might not hold out. The heat was still terrible and the march exhausting.

She was just about to explain as much to Little Horse when he suddenly gave a long-drawn-out neigh, waved his tail and galloped off between some jagged rocks. Ciri followed him, eating ants' bodies as she walked.

The considerable expanse between the rocks was occupied by a wide sandy hollow. There was a distinct dip in the centre.

'Ha!' said Ciri, pleased. 'You're a clever pony, Little Horse. You've found another spring. There's got to be water in there!'

The unicorn gave a long snort, circling the hollow at a gentle trot. Ciri came closer. The hollow was large; at least twenty feet wide. It described a precise, regular circle resembling a funnel, as regular as if someone had pressed a gigantic egg into the sand. Ciri suddenly realised that such a regular shape could not have come about by accident. But by then it was too late.

Something moved at the bottom of the crater and Ciri was hit in the face by a sudden shower of sand and small stones. She leapt back, lost her balance and realised she was sliding downwards. The fountains of stones that were shooting out weren't only hitting her – they were also striking the edges of the pit, and the edges were crumbling in waves and sliding towards the bottom. She screamed and floundered like a drowning swimmer, vainly trying to find a foothold. She realised immediately that sudden movements only worsened her situation, making the sand subside more quickly. She turned over on her back, dug in with her heels, and spread her arms out wide. The sand at the bottom shifted and undulated, and she saw some brown, hooked pincers, at least a yard long, emerging from it. She screamed again, this time much louder.

The hail of stones suddenly stopped raining down on her, flying instead towards the opposite edge of the pit. The unicorn reared, neighing frenziedly, and the edge collapsed beneath him. He tried to struggle free from the shifting sand, but in vain; he was getting more and more bogged down and slipping more and more quickly towards the bottom. The dreadful pincers snapped violently. The unicorn neighed in despair, and thrashed around, helplessly striking the slipping sand with his forehooves. His back legs were completely stuck. When he had slid to the very bottom of the pit, he was caught by the horrible pincers of the creature which was concealed in the centre.

Hearing a frenzied wail of agony, Ciri screamed and charged downwards, wresting her dagger from its sheath. When she reached the bottom, she realised her mistake. The monster was hidden deep, and the dagger thrusts didn't even touch it through the layers of sand. On top of that the unicorn, held fast in the monstrous pincers and being dragged into the sandy trap, was frantic with pain and squealing, blindly pounding away with its forehooves and risking fracturing its limbs.

Witcher dances and tricks were useless here. But there was one quite simple spell. Ciri summoned the Power and struck using telekinesis.

A cloud of sand flew up into the air, uncovering the hidden monster, which had latched itself onto the squealing unicorn's thigh. Ciri yelled in horror. She had never seen anything so revolting in her entire life; not in illustrations, nor in any witcher books. She would have been incapable of imagining anything so hideous.

The monster was a dirty grey colour, plump and pot-bellied like a blood-gorged louse, and the narrow segments of its barrel-shaped torso were covered with sparse bristles. It appeared not to have any legs, but its pincers were almost the same length as its entire body.

Deprived of its sandy refuge the creature immediately released the unicorn and began to bury itself with a rapid, urgent wriggling of its bloated body. It performed this manoeuvre extremely ably, and the unicorn, struggling to escape from the trap, helped it by pushing mounds of sand downwards. Ciri was seized by fury and the lust for revenge. She threw herself at the monstrosity, now barely visible beneath the sand, and thrust her dagger into its domed back.

275

She attacked it from behind, prudently keeping away from the snapping pincers, which, it transpired, the monster was able to extend quite far backwards. She stabbed again, and the creature continued to bury itself at astonishing speed. But it was not burying itself in the sand to escape. It was doing so to attack. It only had to wriggle twice more in order to cover itself completely. Once hidden, it violently propelled out waves of stones, burying Ciri up to mid-thigh. She struggled to free herself and lunged backwards, but there was nowhere to escape; she was still in a crater of loose sand, where each movement pulled her downwards. The sand at the bottom bulged in a wave, which glided towards her, and from the wave emerged the clashing, cruelly hooked pincers.

She was rescued by Little Horse. Slipping down to the bottom of the crater, he used his hooves to strike the bulge of sand which betrayed the presence of the monster hidden just beneath the surface. The savage kicks uncovered the grey back and the unicorn lowered its head and stabbed the monster with its horn, striking at the precise point where the head, with its flailing pincers, was attached to the pot-bellied thorax. Seeing that the pincers of the monster, now pinned against the ground, were helplessly raking the sand, Ciri leapt forward and thrust the dagger deep into its wriggling body. She jerked the blade out and struck again. And again. The unicorn shook its horn free and drove its forehooves down powerfully onto the barrel-shaped body.

The trampled monster was no longer trying to bury itself. It had stopped moving entirely. A greenish liquid darkened the sand around it.

They climbed out of the crater with great difficulty. Ciri ran a few paces away and collapsed on the sand, breathing heavily and shaking under the waves of adrenaline which were assaulting her larynx and temples. The unicorn walked in circles around her. He was moving awkwardly. Blood dripped from the wound on his thigh, and ran down his leg onto his fetlock, leaving a red trail as he walked. Ciri got up onto her hands and knees and was violently sick. After a moment she stood up, swayed, and then staggered over to the unicorn, but Little Horse wouldn't let her touch him. He ran away, lay down and rolled on the ground. Then he cleaned his horn, stabbing it into the sand several times.

Ciri also cleaned and wiped the blade of her dagger, still glancing anxiously at the nearby crater. The unicorn stood up, whinnied and then walked over to her.

'I'd like to look at your wound, Little Horse.'

Little Horse neighed and shook his horned head.

'It's up to you. If you can walk, we'll set off. We'd better not stay here.'

Soon after, another vast sandbar appeared in their way, dotted all over with pits, which were hollowed out in the sand almost to the edge of the surrounding rocks. Ciri looked at them in horror; some of the craters were at least twice as big as the one in which they had fought for their lives.

They weren't brave enough to cross the sandbar by weaving their way between the craters. Ciri was convinced they were traps for careless creatures, and the monsters with the pincers lurking in them were only dangerous to the victims that fell in. By being cautious and staying away from the hollows, one could conceivably cut across the sandy ground without fear that one of the monsters would emerge and pursue them. She was sure there was no risk, but she preferred not to find out. The unicorn was clearly of the same opinion; he snorted and ran off, drawing her away from the sandbar. They made their journey longer by giving the dangerous terrain a wide berth, sticking close to the rocks and the hard, stony ground, through which none of the beasts would have been capable of digging.

As she walked, Ciri never took her eyes off the pits. Several times, she saw fountains of sand shooting up from the deadly traps; the monsters were deepening and repairing their lairs. Some of the craters were so close to each other that the stones flung out by one monster ended up in other craters, disturbing the creatures hidden at the bottom, and then a terrible cannonade would begin, with sand whizzing and blasting around like hail.

Ciri wondered what the sand monsters ate in this arid, desolate wilderness. She didn't have to wait long to find out; a dark object flew out of one of the nearby pits in a wide arc, falling close to them with a thump. After a moment's hesitation, she ran down onto the sand from the rocks. The object that had flown out of the crater was a rodent, resembling a rabbit. At least it looked like rabbit fur. For the body was shrunken; as hard and dry as a bone and as light and hollow as a pea pod. There wasn't a drop of blood in it. Ciri shuddered; now she knew what the monsters preyed on.

The unicorn neighed a warning. Ciri looked up. There was no crater in the near vicinity, and the sand was flat and smooth. And then, before her eyes, the smooth, flat sand suddenly bulged and the bulge began to glide quickly towards her. She threw the shrivelled carcass down and hurried back to the rocks.

The decision to steer clear of the sandbar turned out to have been very sensible.

They went on, skirting around even the smallest patches of sand, treading only on rocky ground.

The unicorn walked slowly, limping. The cuts on his thigh continued to bleed. But he still refused to allow her to approach him and examine the wound.

The sandbar narrowed considerably and began to meander. The fine, loose sand was replaced by coarse grit and then larger stones. They had not seen any pits for a long time now, so they decided to follow the path marked out by the remains of the sandbar. Ciri, although once again wearied by thirst and hunger, began to walk faster. There was hope. The rocky shoal was not what it seemed. It was actually the bed of a river with its source in the mountains. There was no water in the river, but it led to some springs which, although they were too small and produced too little water to fill the watercourse, were large enough to drink from.

She walked more quickly but then had to slow down because the unicorn could not keep pace with her. He was walking with visible difficulty, limping, dragging his leg, and planting his hoof awkwardly. When evening came, he lay down. He didn't get up when she approached him. This time he let her examine the wound.

278

There were two cuts, one on each side of his extremely swollen, angrily red thigh. Both cuts were inflamed, both were still bleeding and a sticky, foul-smelling pus was dripping along with the blood.

The monster had been venomous.

The next day it was even worse. The unicorn could barely walk. In the evening, he lay down on the rocks and refused to get up. When she knelt down beside him, he swung his head and horn towards the wounded thigh and neighed. There was suffering in the neighing.

The pus oozed more and more intensively and the smell was repulsive. Ciri took out her dagger. The unicorn whinnied shrilly, tried to stand and then collapsed rump first on the stone.

'I don't know what to do ...' she sobbed, looking at the blade. 'I really don't know ... I'm sure I should cut open the wound and squeeze out the pus and the venom ... But I don't know how. I might harm you even more.'

The unicorn tried to lift its head. It neighed. Ciri sat down on the rocks, clutching her head in her hands.

'They didn't teach me how to tend wounds,' she said bitterly. 'They taught me how to kill, telling me that's how I could save people. It was one big lie, Little Horse. They deceived me.'

Night was falling and it was quickly becoming dark. The unicorn was lying down, and Ciri was thinking frantically. She had collected some thistles and dry stalks, which grew in abundance on the banks of the dried-up riverbed, but Little Horse didn't want to eat them. He laid his head lifelessly on the rocks, no longer trying to lift it. All he could do was blink. Froth appeared on his muzzle.

'I can't help you, Little Horse,' she said in a stifled voice. 'I don't have anything ...'

Except magic.

I'm an enchantress.

She stood up and held out a hand. Nothing happened. She needed a great deal of magical energy, but there wasn't a trace of any here. She hadn't expected that. It astonished her.

But wait, there are water veins everywhere!

She took a few paces, first in one direction and then in the other.

She began to walk around in a circle. She stepped backwards.

Nothing.

'You damned desert!' she shouted, shaking her fists. 'There's nothing in you! No water and no magic! And magic was supposed to be everywhere! That was a lie too! Everybody deceived me, everybody!'

The unicorn neighed.

Magic is everywhere. It's in water, in the earth, in the air ...

And in fire.

Ciri slammed her fist angrily against her forehead. It hadn't occurred to her earlier perhaps because, among the bare rocks, there hadn't even been anything to burn. But now she had a supply of dry thistles and stalks, and in order to create a tiny spark she ought only to need the tiny amount of energy she could still feel inside ...

She gathered more sticks, arranged them in a heap and piled dry thistles around them. She cautiously put her hand in.

'Aenye!'

The pile of sticks glowed brightly, a flame flickered, then flared up, set the leaves on fire, consumed them and shot upwards. Ciri threw on more dry stalks.

What now? she thought, looking at the flame coming back to life. *Now to gather the energy. But how? Yennefer has forbidden me from touching fire energy ... But I don't have a choice! Or any time! I have to act now; the sticks and leaves are burning fast ... the fire will go out ... Fire ... how beautiful it is, how warm ...*

She didn't know when or how it happened. As she stared at the flames she suddenly felt a pounding in her temples. She clutched her breast, feeling as though her ribcage would burst. A pain throbbed in her belly, her crotch and her nipples, which instantly transformed into horrifying pleasure. She stood up. No, she didn't stand up. She floated up.

The Power filled her like molten lead. The stars in the sky danced like stars reflected on the surface of a pond. The Eye, burning in the west, exploded with light. She took that light and with it the Force.

'Hael, Aenye!'

The unicorn neighed in a frenzy and tried to spring up, pushing with its forehooves. Ciri's arm rose automatically, her hand formed a gesture involuntarily, and her mouth shouted out the spell of its own accord. Bright, undulating light streamed from her fingers. The fire roared with great flames.

The waves of light streaming from her hand touched the unicorn's injured thigh, converging and penetrating.

'I wish you to be healed! That is my wish! Vess'hael, Aenye!'

The Power exploded inside her and she was filled with a wild euphoria. The fire shot upwards, and everything became bright around her. The unicorn raised his head, neighed and then suddenly leapt up from the ground, taking a few awkward paces. He bent his neck, swung his head towards his thigh, quivered his nostrils and snorted as if in disbelief. He neighed loud and long, kicked his hooves, swished his tail and galloped around the fire.

'I've healed you!' cried Ciri proudly. 'I've healed you! I'm a sorceress! I managed to draw the power from the fire! And I have that power! I can do anything I want!'

She turned away. The blazing fire roared, shooting sparks.

'We don't have to look for any more springs! We don't have to drink scooped-up mud any longer! I have the power now! I feel the power that's in this fire! I'll make rain fall on this accursed desert! I'll make it gush from the rocks! I'll make flowers grow here! Grass! Cabbages! I can do anything now! Anything!'

She lifted both arms, screaming out spells and chanting invocations. She didn't understand them, didn't remember when she had learnt them – or even if she'd *ever* learnt them. That was unimportant. She felt power, felt strength, was burning with fire. She was the fire. She trembled with the power that had pervaded her.

The night sky was suddenly riven by a slash of lightning. A wind whipped up among the rocks and thistles. The unicorn gave a long neigh and reared up. The fire roared upwards, exploding. The sticks and stems had charred long before; now the rock itself was afire. But Ciri paid no attention to it. She felt power. She saw only the fire. She heard only the fire.

You can do anything, whispered the flames. *You are in possession*

of our power. You can do anything. The world is at your feet. You are
great. You are mighty.

There was a figure among the flames. A tall, young woman with
long, straight, coal-black hair. The woman smiled, wildly, cruelly,
and the fire writhed and danced around her.

You are mighty! Those that harmed you did not know who they had
challenged! Avenge yourself! Make them pay! Make them all pay! Let
them tremble with fear at your feet, teeth chattering, not daring to look
you in the face! Let them beg for mercy but do not grant it to them! Make
them pay! Make them pay for everything! Revenge!

Behind the black-haired woman there was fire and smoke and,
in the smoke, rows of gallows, rows of sharpened stakes, scaffolds,
mountains of corpses. They were the corpses of Nilfgaardians,
of those who had captured and plundered Cintra and killed King
Eist and her grandmother Calanthe, of those who had murdered
people in the streets of the city. A knight in black armour swung
on a gibbet. The noose creaked and crows fought each other to
peck at his eyes through his winged helmet's visor. Other gibbets
stretched away towards the horizon, and on them hung Scoia'tael,
those who killed Paulie Dahlberg in Kaedwen, and those who'd
pursued Ciri on the Isle of Thanedd. The sorcerer Vilgefortz
danced on a towering stake, his beautiful, fraudulently noble
face contorted and blue-black with suffering. The sharpened,
bloodstained point of the stake protruded from his collarbone ...
Other sorcerers from Thanedd were kneeling on the ground,
their hands tied behind their backs and sharpened stakes awaiting
them ...

Stakes piled high with bundles of firewood rose up all the way
to the burning horizon, marked by ribbons of smoke. Chained
to the nearest stake was ... Triss Merigold. Beyond her was
Margarita Laux-Antille ... Mother Nenneke ... Jarre ... Fabio
Sachs ...

No. No. No.

Yes, screamed the black-haired woman. *Death to them all! Take*
your revenge on all of them. Despise them! They all harmed you or wanted
to harm you! Or perhaps they will want to harm you in the future! Hold

them in contempt, for at last the time of contempt is here! Contempt, revenge and death! Death to the entire world! Death, destruction and blood!

There is blood on your hand, blood on your dress . . .

They betrayed you! Tricked you! Harmed you! Now you have the power, so take revenge!

Yennefer's mouth was cut and torn, pouring blood; her hands and feet were shackled, fastened to the wet, dirty walls of a dungeon by heavy chains. The mob around the scaffold shrieked, the poet Dandelion laid his head on the block, the blade of the executioner's axe flashed above him. The street urchins crowded beneath the scaffold unfolded a kerchief to be spattered with blood . . . The screaming of the mob drowned out the noise of the blow, so powerful it made the scaffold shudder . . .

They betrayed you! They deceived and tricked you! To them you were a pawn, just a puppet on a stick! They used you! They condemned you to hunger, to the burning sun, to thirst, to misery and to loneliness! The time of contempt and revenge is come! You have the power! You are mighty! Let the whole world cower before thee! Let the whole world cower before the Elder Blood!

Now the witchers were being led onto the scaffold: Yesemir, Eskel, Coen, Lambert. And Geralt . . . Geralt was staggering, covered in blood . . .

'No!'

Fire surrounded her, and beyond the wall of flames was a furious neighing. Unicorns were rearing, shaking their heads and dashing their hooves against the ground. Their manes were like tattered battle flags, their horns were as long and sharp as swords. The unicorns were huge, as huge as warhorses, much bigger than her Little Horse. *Where had they come from? Where had so many of them come from?* The flame shot upwards with a roar. The black-haired woman raised her hands, and they were covered in blood. The heat billowed her hair.

Let it burn, Falka, let it all burn!

'Go away! Be gone! I don't want you! I don't want your power!

Let it burn, Falka, let it burn!

'I don't want to!'

You do! You desire this! Desire and lust seethe in you like a flame! The pleasure is enslaving you! It is might! It is force! It is power! The most delicious of the world's pleasures!

Lightning. Thunder. Wind. The thudding of hooves and the neighing of unicorns galloping with abandon around the fire.

'I don't want that power! I don't want it! I relinquish it!'

She didn't know if the fire had gone out or if her eyes had clouded over as she slumped to the ground, feeling the first drops of rain on her face.

The being should be divested of its beingness. It cannot be allowed to exist. The being is dangerous. Confirmation?

Negative. The being did not summon the Power for itself. It did it to save Ihuarraquax. The being feels sympathy. Thanks to the being, Ihuarraquax is once more among us.

But the being has the Power. Should it wish to make use of it . . .

It will not be able to use it. Never. It relinquished it. It relinquished the Power. Utterly. The Power disappeared. It is most curious . . .

We will never understand these beings.

We do not need to understand them! We will remove existence from the being. Before it is too late. Confirmation?

Negative. Let us leave this place. Let us leave the being. Let us leave it to its fate.

She did not know how long she lay on the rocks, trembling, staring at the changing colours of the sky. It was by turns dark and light, cold and hot, and she lay powerless, dried out like that dead rodent's carcass sucked dry and thrown from the crater.

She did not think about anything. She was alone. She was empty. Now she had nothing and she felt nothing inside. There was no thirst, hunger, fatigue or fear. Everything had vanished, even the will to survive. She was one great, cold, dreadful void. She felt that void with all her being, with every cell of her body.

She felt blood on her inner thighs. She did not care. She was empty. She had lost everything.

The colour of the sky was changing. She did not move. Was there any point in moving in such a void?

She did not move when hooves thudded around her, when horseshoes clanged. She did not react to the loud cries and calls, to the excited voices, to the horses' snorts. She did not move when hard, powerful hands seized her. When she was lifted, she drooped limply. She did not react to the jerking or the shaking, to the harsh, aggressive questions. She did not understand them and did not want to understand.

She was empty and indifferent. She reacted indifferently to water being splashed on her face. When a canteen was put to her mouth, she did not choke. She drank. Indifferently.

Neither did she care later. She was hauled up onto a saddle. Her crotch was tender and painful. She was shivering so she was wrapped in a blanket. She was numb and limp, on the verge of fainting, so she was fastened by a belt to the rider sitting behind her. The rider stank of sweat and urine. She did not care.

There were riders all around. Many riders. Ciri looked at them indifferently. She was empty. She had lost everything. Nothing mattered any longer.

Nothing.

Not even the fact that the knight in command of the riders wore a helmet decorated with the wings of a raptor.

When the fire was lit at the foot of the criminal's pyre and the flames began to engulf her, she began to hurl abuse at the knights, barons, sorcerers and lord councillors gathered in the square; using such words that terror seized them all. Although at first only damp logs were placed on the pyre, in order that the she-devil would not perish quickly and would know the full agony of fire, now came the order to throw on more dry sticks and put an end to the torture as quickly as possible. However, a veritable demon had entered the accursed one; for although she was already sizzling well, she uttered no cries of anguish, but instead began to hurl even more awful abuse. 'An avenger will be born of my blood,' she cried. 'From my tainted Elder Blood will be born the avenger of the nations and of the world! He will avenge my torment! Death, death and vengeance to all of you and your kin!' Only this much was she able to cry out before the flame consumed her. Thus perished Falka; such was her punishment for spilling innocent blood.

Roderick de Novembre, *The History of the World,*
Volume II

CHAPTER SEVEN

'Look at her. Sunburnt and covered in cuts. She's an outcast. She's drinking like a fish and is as ravenous as a wolf. She came out of the east, I tell you. She crossed Korath. She crossed the Frying Pan.'

'Rubbish! No one survives the Frying Pan. She's come out of the west, down from the mountains, along the course of the Suchak. She barely touched the edge of Korath and that was enough for her. We found her lying in a heap on the ground, almost lifeless.'

'The desert also drags on for miles to the west. So where did she walk from?'

'She didn't walk, she'd been riding. Who knows how far? There were hoof prints by her. Her horse must have thrown her in the Suchak valley, and that's why she's battered and bruised.'

'Why is she so important to Nilfgaard, I wonder? When the prefect sent us off on that search party, I thought some important noblewoman had gone missing. But her? An ordinary slummock, a shabby drudge, and dazed and mute to boot. I really don't know, Skomlik, if we've found the one we're after ...'

'That's 'er. But ordinary she is not. Had she been ordinary, we'd have found her dead.'

'It was a close thing. There's no doubt the rain saved her. The oldest grandfathers can't recall rain in the Frying Pan, dammit. Clouds always pass by Korath ... Even when it rains in the valleys, not a single drop falls there!'

'Look at her wolfing down that food. It's as if she'd had nothing in her gob for a week ... Hey, you, slut! Like that pork fat? And that dry bread?'

'Ask her in Elven. Or in Nilfgaardian. She doesn't understand Common Speech. She's some kind of elven spawn ...'

'She's a simpleton, not right in the head. When I lifted her onto the horse this morning, it was like holding a wooden doll.'

'Don't you have eyes?' asked the powerful, balding one they called Skomlik, baring his teeth. 'What kind of Trappers are you, if you haven't rumbled her yet? She's neither stupid, nor simple. She's pretending. She's a strange and cunning little bird.'

'So why's she so important to Nilfgaard? They've promised a reward. There are patrols rushing around all over the place . . . Why?'

'That I don't know. Though it might be an idea to ask her . . . A whip across the back might encourage her . . . Ha! Did you mark how she looked at me? She understands everything, she's listening carefully. Hey, wench! I'm Skomlik, a hunter. Also called a Trapper. And this, look here, is a whip. Also called a knout! Want to keep the skin on your back? Then let's hear it—'

'Enough! Silence!'

A loud, stern order, tolerating no opposition, came from another campfire, where a knight and his squire were sitting.

'Getting bored, Trappers?' asked the knight menacingly. 'Then get down to some work. The horses need grooming. My armour and weapons need cleaning. Go to the forest for wood. And do not touch the girl! Do you understand, you churls?'

'Indeed, noble Sir Sweers,' muttered Skomlik. His comrades looked sheepish.

'To work! Carry out my orders!'

The Trappers made themselves busy.

'Fate has really punished us with that arsehole,' muttered one of them. 'Oh, that the prefect put us under the command of that fucking knight—'

'Full of himself,' muttered another quietly, glancing around stealthily. 'And, after all, it was us Trappers what found the girl . . . We had the hunch to ride into the Suchak valley.'

'Right enough. We deserve the credit, but His Lordship will take the bounty. We'll barely see a groat . . . They'll toss us a florin. "There you go, be grateful for your lord's generosity, Trapper".'

'Shut your traps,' hissed Skomlik. 'He might hear you . . .'

Ciri found herself alone by the fire. The knight and squire looked at her inquisitively, but said nothing.

The knight was a middle-aged but still robust man with a scarred face. When riding, he wore a helmet with birds' wings, but they were not the wings Ciri had first seen in her nightmares and later on the Isle of Thanedd. He was not the Black Knight of Cintra. But he was a Nilfgaardian knight. When he issued orders, he spoke the Common Speech fluently, but with a marked accent, similar to that of the Elves. However, he spoke with his squire (a boy not much older than Ciri) in a language resembling the Elder Speech, but harder and less melodious. It had to be Nilfgaardian. Ciri, who spoke the Elder Speech well, understood most of the words. But she didn't let on that she understood. The Nilfgaardian knight and his squire had peppered her with questions during the first stop, at the edge of the desert known as the Frying Pan or Korath. She hadn't answered then, because she had been indifferent and stupefied. Befuddled. A few days into the ride, when they had left the rocky ravines and rode down into green valleys, Ciri had already fully recovered her faculties. At last she began to notice the world around her and react to it, albeit apathetically. But she continued to ignore questions, so the knight stopped speaking to her at all. He appeared not to pay her any attention. Only the ruffians – the ones calling themselves Trappers – took an interest in her. And they also tried to question her. Aggressively.

But the Nilfgaardian in the winged helmet swiftly took them to task. It was clear who was the master and who was the servant.

Ciri pretended to be a simple mute, but she listened intently. She slowly began to understand her situation. She had fallen into Nilfgaard's hands. Nilfgaard had hunted her and found her, no doubt having located the route the chaotic portal in Tor Lara had transported her along. The winged knight and the Trappers had achieved what neither Yennefer nor Geralt had been able to do.

What had happened to Yennefer and Geralt on Thanedd? Where was she? She feared the worst. The Trappers and their leader, Skomlik, spoke a simple, slovenly version of the Common Speech, but without a Nilfgaardian accent. The Trappers were ordinary men, but were serving the knight from Nilfgaard. They were looking

291

forward to the thought of the bounty the prefect would pay them for finding Ciri. In florins.

The only countries which used florins and where the people served Nilfgaardians were the Provinces in the far south, administered by imperial prefects.

The following day, during a stop by the bank of a stream, Ciri began to consider her chances of escaping. Magic might help her. She cautiously tried the most simple spell, a mild telekinesis. But her fears were confirmed. She didn't have even a trace of magical energy. Having foolishly played with fire, her magical abilities had deserted her utterly.

She became indifferent once more. To everything. She became withdrawn and sank into apathy, where she remained for a long while.

Until the day the Blue Knight blocked their path across the moorland.

'Oh dear, oh dear,' muttered Skomlik, looking at the horsemen barring their way. 'This means trouble. They're Varnhagens from the stronghold in Sarda ...'

The horsemen came closer. At their head, on a powerful grey, rode a giant of a man in a glittering blue, enamelled suit of armour. Close behind him rode a second armoured horseman, while two more in simple, dun costumes – clearly servants – brought up the rear.

The Nilfgaardian in the winged helmet rode out to meet them, reining in his bay in a dancing trot. His squire fingered the hilt of his sword and turned around in the saddle.

'Stay back and guard the girl,' he barked to Skomlik and his Trappers. 'And don't interfere!'

'I ain't that stupid,' said Skomlik softly, as soon as the squire had ridden away. 'I ain't so stupid as to interfere in a feud between the lords of Nilfgaard ...'

'Will there be a fight, Skomlik?'

'Bound to be. There's an ancestral vendetta and blood feud between the Sweers and the Varnhagens. Dismount. Guard the wench, because she's our best asset and our profit. If we're lucky, we'll get the entire bounty that's on her head.'

'The Varnhagens are sure to be hunting the girl too. If they overcome us, they'll take her from us ... And there's only four of us ...'

'Five,' said Skomlik, flashing his teeth. 'One of the camp followers from Sarda is a mucker of mine, if I'm not mistaken. You'll see; the benefits from this ruckus will come to us, not to Their Lordships ...'

The knight in the blue armour reined in his grey. The winged knight came to a halt facing him. The Blue Knight's companion trotted up and stopped behind him. His strange helmet was decorated with two straps of leather hanging from the visor, resembling two long whiskers or walrus tusks. Across his saddle, Two Tusks held a menacing-looking weapon somewhat resembling the spontoons carried by the guardsmen from Cintra, but with a considerably shorter shaft and a longer blade.

The Blue Knight and the Winged Knight exchanged a few words. Ciri could not make out what they were saying, but their tone left her in no doubt. They were not words of friendship. The Blue Knight suddenly sat up straight in the saddle, pointed fiercely at Ciri, and said something loudly and angrily. In answer, the Winged Knight cried out just as angrily and shook his fist in his armoured glove, clearly sending the Blue Knight on his way.

And then it began.

The Blue Knight dug his spurs into his grey and charged forward, yanking his battleaxe from a holder by his saddle. The Winged Knight spurred on his bay, pulling his sword from its scabbard. Before the armoured knights came together in battle, however, Two Tusks attacked, urging his horse into a gallop with the shaft of his spontoon. The Winged Knight's squire leapt on him, drawing his sword, but Two Tusks rose up in the saddle and thrust the spontoon straight into the squire's chest. The long blade penetrated his gorget and hauberk with a crack, the squire groaned loudly and thudded to the ground, grasping the spontoon, which was thrust in as far as the crossguard.

The Blue Knight and the Winged Knight collided with a crash and a thud. The battleaxe was more lethal but the sword was quicker.

The Blue Knight was hit in the shoulder and a piece of his enamelled spaulder flew off to one side, spinning, its strap flapping behind it. The knight shuddered in the saddle and streaks of crimson glistened on the blue armour. The impact pushed the warriors apart. The Winged Nilfgaardian turned his bay back, but then Two Tusks fell upon him, raising his sword to strike two-handed. The Winged Knight tugged at his reins and Two Tusks, steering his horse with his legs, galloped past. The Winged Knight managed to strike him in passing, however. Ciri saw the metal plate of the rerebrace deform and blood spurt out from beneath the metal.

The Blue Knight was already coming back, swinging his battle-axe and screaming. The two knights exchanged thundering blows at full tilt and then drew apart. Two Tusks fell on the Winged Knight once more; their horses collided and their swords clanged. Two Tusks slashed the Winged Knight, destroying his rerebrace and rondel. The Winged Knight straightened up and struck a powerful blow from the right into the side of Two Tusk's breastplate. Two Tusks swayed in the saddle. The Winged Knight stood in his stirrups and struck another mighty blow, between the dented and cloven pauldron and the helmet. The blade of the broad sword cut into the metal with a clang and became caught. Two Tusks tensed up and shuddered. The horses came together, stamping their hooves and gnashing their teeth on their bits. The Winged Knight braced himself against his pommel and pulled his sword out of Two Tusks's body. Two Tusks toppled from his saddle and crashed under the horses' hooves. The sound of horseshoes striking and twisting armour rang out as he was trampled by his own mount.

The Blue Knight turned his grey and attacked, lifting his battle-axe. The wound to his hand impeded his efforts to control his horse. The Winged Knight noticed this and stole up deftly from the right, standing in his stirrups to deliver a terrible blow. The Blue Knight caught the blow on his battleaxe and knocked the sword out of the Winged Knight's hand. The horses crashed together once more. The Blue Knight was immensely strong; the heavy axe in his hand rose and fell like a twig. A blow thudded on the Winged Knight's armour, making the bay sit down on its haunches. The Winged Knight swayed, but remained in the saddle. Before the battleaxe had time to fall again, he released the reins and twisted his left hand, seizing a heavy angular mace hanging from a leather sword knot, and hit the Blue Knight savagely on the helmet. The helmet rang like a bell and now it was the turn of the Blue Knight to sway in his saddle. The horses squealed, trying to bite each other and not wanting to separate.

The Blue Knight, although clearly dazed by the blow from the mace, managed to strike again with his battleaxe, hitting his opponent in the breastplate with a thud. It seemed an absolute miracle that they were both able to stay in the saddle, but it was simply owing to their high pommels and cantles. Blood dripped down the sides of both horses; particularly conspicuous on the grey's light coat. Ciri looked on in horror. She had been taught to fight in Kaer Morhen, but she could not imagine how she could have faced either of those two strongmen. Or parry even one of their powerful blows.

The Blue Knight seized the helve of the battleaxe, which was plunged deeply into the Winged Knight's breastplate, in both hands. He bent forward and heaved, trying to push his opponent out of the saddle. The Winged Knight struck him hard with the mace; once, twice, three times. Blood spurted from the peak of the helmet, splashing onto the blue armour and the grey's neck. The Winged Knight spurred his bay away, the impetus of the horse wrenching the axe's blade from his breastplate. The Blue Knight, swaying in the saddle, released the helve. The Winged Knight transferred the mace to his right hand, rode up, and struck with a vicious blow, shoving the Blue Knight's head against his horse's neck. Taking the reins of the grey in his free hand, the Nilfgaardian struck again with his mace. The blue suit of armour rang like a cast-iron pot and blood gushed from the misshapen helmet. One more blow and the Blue Knight fell head first under the grey's hooves. The grey trotted away, but the Winged Knight's bay, evidently specially trained, trampled the fallen knight with a clatter. The Blue Knight was still alive, evidenced by his desperate cries of pain. The bay continued to trample him with such force that the wounded Winged Knight could not stay in the saddle and fell alongside him with a thud.

'They've finished each other off, dammit,' grunted the Trapper who was holding Ciri.

'Noble knights. The plague and the pox on them all,' spat another.

The Blue Knight's servants were watching from a distance. One of them wheeled his horse around.

'Stop right there, Remiz!' yelled Skomlik. 'Where are you going? To Sarda? In a hurry to get to the gallows?'

The servants came to a halt. One of them looked over, shielding his eyes with his hand.

'Is that you, Skomlik?'

'Yes, it is! Get over here, Remiz, don't worry! Knightly spats aren't our business!'

Ciri had suddenly had enough of inaction. She nimbly tore herself free from the Trapper holding her, set off at a run, caught hold of the Blue Knight's grey, and with one leap was in the saddle with the high pommel.

She might have managed her escape had not the servants from Sarda been mounted and on fresh horses. They caught up with her without difficulty and snatched the reins from her. She jumped off and sprinted towards the forest, but the horsemen caught her once again. One of them seized her by the hair in full flight, then pulled and dragged her behind him. Ciri screamed, hanging from his arm. The horseman threw her down at Skomlik's feet. The knout swished, and Ciri howled and curled up in a ball, protecting her head with her hands. The whip swished again, cutting into the backs of her hands. She rolled away, but Skomlik jumped after her, kicked her, and then pinned her down with his boot.

'Trying to escape, you viper?'

The knout swished. Ciri howled. Skomlik kicked her again and lashed her with the knout.

'Stop hitting me!' she screamed, cowering.

'So you can talk, bitch! Cat let go of your tongue? I'll teach you—'

'Control yourself, Skomlik!' shouted one of the Trappers. 'Do you want to beat the life out of her or what? She's worth too much to waste!'

'Bloody hell,' said Remiz, dismounting. 'Is she the one Nilfgaard's spent a week searching for?'

'That's right.'

'Ha! All the garrisons are hunting for her. She's some kind of important personage to Nilfgaard. They say a mighty sorceror divined that she must be somewhere in the area. That's what they were saying in Sarda, at least. Where did you find her?'

'In the Frying Pan.'

'That's not possible!'

'It is, it is,' said Skomlik angrily, frowning. 'We've got her and the reward's ours. Why are you standing around like statues? Bind the little bird and get her up in the saddle! Let's scram, boys! Look lively!'

'I think the Honourable Sweers,' said one of the Trappers, 'is still breathing ...'

'But not for long. Curse him! We're riding straight to Amarillo, boys. To the prefect. We'll deliver the wench to him and pick up the bounty.'

'To Amarillo?' Remiz scratched the back of his head, and looked at the scene of the recent fight. 'And right into the hangman's hands? What will you tell the prefect? That the knights battered each other to death and you're all in one piece? When the whole story comes out the prefect will have you hanged, and send us back to Sarda under guard ... And then the Varnhagens will take the bounty. You might want to head for Amarillo, but I'd rather disappear into the forest ...'

'You're my brother-in-law, Remiz,' said Skomlik. 'And even though you're a son of a bitch for beating my sister you're still a mate. So I'll save your skin. We're going to Amarillo, I said. The prefect knows there's a feud between the Sweers and the Varnhagens. They met and did each other in. That's normal for them. What could we have done? And we – heed my words – found the wench afterwards. We did, the Trappers. You're a Trapper now, too, Remiz. The

297

prefect hasn't got a bloody clue how many of us set off with Sweers. He won't count us up ...'

'Haven't you forgotten something, Skomlik?' asked Remiz in a slow drawl, looking at the other servant from Sarda.

Skomlik turned around slowly, then as quick as a flash pulled out a knife and thrust it hard into the servant's throat. The servant rasped and then collapsed on the ground.

'I don't forget about anything,' said the Trapper coldly. 'We're all in it together. There are no witnesses, and not too many heads to divide the bounty amongst either. To horse, boys, and on to Amarillo! There's a fair distance between us and the bounty, so let's not hang around!'

After leaving a dark, wet, beech forest, they saw a village at the foot of the mountain: a dozen or so thatched cottages inside the ring of a low stockade enclosing a bend in a small river.

The wind carried the scent of smoke. Ciri wiggled her numb fingers, which were fastened by a leather strap to the pommel. She was numb all over; her buttocks ached unbearably and she was being tormented by a full bladder. She'd been in the saddle since daybreak. She had not rested during the night, since she had been forced to sleep with her hands fastened to the wrists of two Trappers lying on either side of her. Each time she moved, the Trappers reacted with curses and threats to beat her.

'It's a village,' said one of them.

'I can see that,' responded Skomlik.

They rode down the slope, their horses' hooves crunching through the tall, dry grass. They soon found themselves on a bumpy track leading straight to the village, towards a wooden bridge and a gate in the stockade.

Skomlik reined back his horse and stood up in his stirrups.

'What village is this? I've never stopped here. Remiz, do you know these parts?'

'Years ago,' said Remiz, 'this village was called White River. But when the unrest began, some locals joined the rebels. Then the Varnhagens of Sarda put it to the torch, murdered the villagers or took them prisoner. Now only Nilfgaardian settlers live here, all newcomers. And the village has been renamed Glyswen. These settlers are fierce, nasty people. I'm telling you, let's not dally. We should ride on.'

'We have to let the horses rest,' protested one of the Trappers, 'and feed them. And my belly's rumbling like I've swallowed a brass band. Why worry about the settlers? They're just rabble. Scum. We'll wave the prefect's order in front of their noses. I mean, the prefect's a Nilfgaardian like them. You watch, they'll bow down before us.'

'I can just see that,' growled Skomlik. 'Has anyone seen a Nilfgaardian bow? Remiz, is there an inn in this 'ere Glyswen?'

'Yes. The Varnhagens didn't burn it down.'

Skomlik turned around in the saddle and looked at Ciri.

'We'll have to untie her,' he said. 'We can't risk anyone recognising her ... Give her a mantle. And a hood for her head ... Hey there! Where you going, you slummock?'

'I have to go into the bushes—'

'I'll give you bushes, you slut! Squat by the track! And mark: don't breathe a word in the village. Don't start getting clever! One squeak and I'll slit your throat. If I don't get any florins for you, no one's getting any.'

They approached at a walk, the horses' hooves thudding on the bridge. Right away, some settlers armed with lances emerged from behind the stockade.

'They're guarding the gate,' muttered Remiz. 'I wonder why.'

'Me too,' Skomlik muttered back, raising himself in his stirrups. 'They're guarding the gate, and the stockade's down by the mill. You could drive a wagon through there ...'

They rode closer and reined in their horses.

'Greetings, gentlemen!' called out Skomlik jovially, but somewhat unnaturally. 'Good day to you.'

'Who are you?' asked the tallest of the settlers brusquely.

'We, mate, are the army,' lied Skomlik, leaning back in the saddle. 'In the service of His Lordlyship, the prefect of Amarillo.'

The settler slid his hand down the shaft of his lance and scowled at Skomlik. He clearly couldn't recall when he and the Trapper had become mates.

'His Lordship the prefect sent us here,' Skomlik continued to lie, 'to learn how his countrymen, the good people of Glyswen, are faring. His Lordlyship sends his greetings and enquires if the people of Glyswen need any kind of help.'

'We're getting by,' said the settler. Ciri noticed he spoke the Common Speech in a similar way to the Winged Knight, with the same accent, as though he was trying to imitate Skomlik's lazy speech pattern. 'We've got used to looking after ourselves.'

'The prefect will be pleased to hear it. Is the inn open? We're parched ...'

'It's open,' said the settler grimly. 'For the moment.'

'For the moment?'

'For the moment. For we'll soon be pulling it down. The rafters and planks will serve us for a granary. The inn's no use to anyone. We toil in the fields and don't visit the inn. The inn only serves travellers, mostly of a sort that aren't to our liking. Some of that kind are drinking there now.'

'Who's that?' asked Remiz, blanching somewhat. 'Not from the stronghold in Sarda, by any chance? Not the Honourable Varnhagens?'

The settler grimaced and moved his lips around, as though intending to spit.

'Unfortunately not. They're the Lords Barons' militiamen. The Nissirs.'

'The Nissirs?' frowned Skomlik. 'Where did they come from? Under whose command?'

'Their commander is tall and black-haired, with whiskers like a catfish.'

'Eh!' Skomlik turned to his companions. 'We're in luck. We only know one like that, don't we? It's sure to be our old comrade "Trust Me" Vercta. Remember him? And what are the Nissirs doing here, mate?'

'The Lords Nissir,' explained the settler grimly, 'are bound for Tyffi. They honoured us with a visit. They're moving a prisoner. They've caught one of those of Rats.'

'Of course they have,' snorted Remiz. 'And why not the Nilfgaardian emperor?'

The settler frowned and tightened his grip on the shaft of his lance. His companions murmured softly.

'Go to the inn, sirs,' said the settler, the muscles in his jaw working, 'and talk to the Lords Nissir, your comrades. You claim to be in the prefect's service, so ask the Lords Nissirs why they're taking the criminal to Tyffi, rather than impaling him on a stake right here, right now, as the prefect ordered. And remind the Lords Nissirs, your comrades, that the prefect is in command here, not the Baron of Tyffi. We already have the oxen yoked up and the stake sharpened. If the Lords Nissirs don't want to, we'll do the necessary. Tell them that.'

'I'll tell them. Rely on me,' said Skomlik, winking meaningfully at his comrades. 'Farewell, gentlemen.'

They set off at a walk between the cottages. The village appeared deserted; there was not a soul around. An emaciated pig was rooting around by one of the fences and some dirty ducks were splashing around in the mud. A large black tomcat crossed the riders' path.

'Ugh, ugh, bloody cat,' said Remiz, leaning over, spitting and making a sign with his fingers to protect himself from black magic. 'He ran across our path, the son of a bitch!'

'I hope he chokes on a mouse!'

'What was it?' said Skomlik, turning back.

'A cat. As black as pitch. He crossed our path, ugh, ugh.'

'To hell with him,' said Skomlik, looking all around. 'Just look how empty it is. But I saw the people in their cottages, watching. And I saw a lance blade glint in that doorway.'

'They're guarding their womenfolk,' laughed the man who had wished ill on the cat. 'The Nissirs are in the village! Did you hear what that yokel was saying? It's obvious they don't like them.'

'And no wonder. Trust Me and his company never pass up a chance. They'll get what's coming to them one day, those Lords Nissirs. The barons call them "keepers of the peace", and that's what they're paid to do. To keep order and guard the roads. But try

301

whispering "Nissir" near a peasant's ear, and you'll see. He'll shit his pants in fear. But they'll get their comeuppance. They'll slaughter one too many calf, rape one too many wench, and the peasants will tear them apart with their pitchforks. You'll see. Did you notice their fierce expressions by those gates? They're Nilfgaardian settlers. You don't want to mess with them ... Ah, and here's the inn ...'

They urged the horses on.

The inn had a slightly sunken, very mossy thatched roof. It stood some distance from the cottages and farm buildings, although it marked the central point of the entire area encircled by the dilapidated stockade; the place where the two roads passing through the village crossed. In the shadow cast by the only large tree in the vicinity were two enclosures; one for cattle and the other for horses. In the latter stood five or six unsaddled horses. On the steps leading up to the door sat two individuals in leather jerkins and pointed fur hats. They were both nursing earthenware mugs, and between them stood a bowl full of bones picked clean of meat.

'Who are you?' yelled one of them at the sight of Skomlik and his company dismounting. 'What do you want? Be off with you! This inn is occupied by the forces of law and order!'

'Don't holler, Nissir, don't holler,' said Skomlik, pulling Ciri down from the saddle. 'And get that door open, because we want to go inside. Your commander, Vercta, is a friend of ours.'

'I don't know you!'

'Because you're naught but a stripling. Me and Trust Me served together years ago, before Nilfgaard came into power here.'

'Well, if you say so ...' The fellow hesitated, letting go of his sword hilt. 'You'd better come inside. It's all the same to me ...'

Skomlik shoved Ciri and another Trapper grabbed her by the collar. They went inside.

It was gloomy and stuffy, and smelled of smoke and baking. The inn was almost empty – only one of the tables was occupied, standing in a stream of light coming through a small window with some kind of animal skin stretched across it. A small group of men were sitting at the table. The innkeeper was bustling around in the background by the fireplace, clinking beer mugs.

302

'Good cheer to you, Nissirs!' boomed Skomlik.

'We don't shake hands with any old brigands,' growled a member of the company sitting by the window, who then spat on the floor. Another stopped him with a gesture.

'Take it easy,' he said. 'They're mates, don't you recognise them? That's Skomlik and his Trappers. Welcome, welcome!'

Skomlik brightened up and walked towards the table, but stopped on seeing his companions staring at the wooden post holding up the roof timbers. At its base, on a stool, sat a slim, fair-haired youth, strangely erect and stiff. Ciri saw that his unnatural position derived from the fact that his hands were twisted behind him and tied together, and his neck was attached to the post by a leather strap.

'May the pox seize me,' loudly sighed one of the Trappers, the one holding Ciri by the collar, 'Just look, Skomlik. It's Kayleigh!'

'Kayleigh?' Skomlik tilted his head. 'Kayleigh the Rat? Can't be!'

One of the Nissirs sitting at the table, a fat man with hair shorn in an exotic topknot, gave a throaty laugh.

'Might just be,' he said, licking a spoon. 'It is Kayleigh, in all his foulness. It was worth getting up at daybreak. We're certain to get half a mark of florins of good imperial coin for him.'

'You've nabbed Kayleigh. Well, well,' frowned Skomlik. 'So that Nilfgaardian peasant was telling the truth—'

'Thirty florins, dammit,' sighed Remiz. 'Not a bad sum ... Is Baron Lutz of Tyffi paying?'

'That's right,' confirmed the other Nissir, black-haired and black-moustached. 'The Honourable Baron Lutz of Tyffi, our lord and benefactor. The Rats robbed his steward on the highway; he was so enraged he offered a bounty. And we, Skomlik, will get it; trust me. Ha, just look, boys, how his nose is out of joint! He doesn't like it that we nabbed the Rat and not him, even though the prefect ordered the gang to be tracked down!'

'Skomlik the Trapper,' said the fat man with the topknot, pointing his spoon at Ciri, 'has also caught something. Do you see, Vercta? Some girl or other.'

'I see,' said the black-moustached man, flashing his teeth. 'What's this, Skomlik? Are you feeling the pinch so much you kidnap children for the ransom? What scruff is this?'

'Mind your own business!'

'Who's touchy?' laughed the one with the topknot. 'We only want to check she's not your daughter.'

'His daughter?' laughed Vercta, the one with the black moustache. 'Chance would be a fine thing. You need balls to sire a daughter.'

The Nissirs roared with laughter.

'Fuck off, you dolts!' yelled Skomlik, puffed up. 'All I'll tell you is this, Vercta. Before Sunday's past you might be surprised to hear who people will be talking about. You and your Rat, or me and my prize. And we'll see who's the more generous: your baron or the imperial prefect of Amarillo!'

'You can kiss my arse,' declared Vercta contemptuously, and went back to slurping his soup. 'You, your prefect, your emperor and the whole of Nilfgaard, trust me. And don't get crabby. I'm well aware Nilfgaard's been hunting some girl for a week, so hard you can't see the road for dust. I know there's a bounty on her. But I don't give a monkey's. I have no intention of serving the Nilfgaardians and I curse them. I serve Baron Lutz now. I answer to him; no one else.'

'Unlike you,' rasped Skomlik, 'your baron kisses the Nilfgaardian hand and licks Nilfgaardian boots. Which means you don't have to. So it's easy for you to talk.'

'Easy, now,' said the Nissir in a placatory manner. 'That wasn't against you; trust me. It's fine that you found the wench Nilfgaard's searching for, and I'm glad you'll get the reward and not those bloody Nilfgaardians. And you serve the prefect? No one chooses his own master; it's them that chooses, ain't it? Come on, sit down with us, we'll have a drink since we're all here together.'

'Aye, why not,' agreed Skomlik. 'But first give us a bit of twine. I'll tie the wench to the post next to your Rat, all right?'

The Nissirs roared with laughter.

'Look at 'im, the terror of the borderland!' cackled the fat one with the topknot. 'The armed forces of Nilfgaard! Bind 'er up, Skomlik, bind 'er up good and tight. But use an iron chain, because your important captive is likely to break her bonds and smash your face in before she escapes. She looks so dangerous, I'm trembling!'

Even Skomlik's companions snorted with suppressed laughter. The Trapper flushed, twisted his belt, and walked over to the table.

'Just to be sure she won't make a run for it—'

'Do as you bloody want,' interrupted Vercta, breaking bread. 'If you want to talk, sit down and get a round in. And hang the wench up by her feet from the ceiling, if you wish. I couldn't give a shit. It's just bloody funny, Skomlik. Perhaps she *is* an important prisoner to you and your prefect, but to me she's a skinny, frightened kid. Want to tie her up? She can barely stand, never mind escape; trust me. What are you afraid of?'

'I'll tell you what I'm afraid of,' said Skomlik, pursing his lips. 'This is a Nilfgaardian settlement. The settlers didn't exactly greet us with bread and salt, and they said they've already got a stake sharpened for your Rat. And the law's with them, because the prefect issued an edict that any brigands that are caught should be punished on the spot. If you don't give them their prisoner, they're ready to sharpen a stake for you too.'

'Oh dear, oh dear,' said the fat man with the topknot. 'They're only fit to scare birds, the rascals. They'd better not interfere with us, because blood will be spilt.'

'We won't give them the Rat,' added Vercta. 'He's ours and he's going to Tyffi. And Baron Lutz will put the whole case to rights with the prefect. Let's not waste our breath. Sit you down.'

The Trappers, sliding their sword belts around, were happy to join the Nissirs' table, yelling at the innkeeper and pointing in unison at Skomlik as their sponsor. Skomlik kicked a stool towards the post, yanked Ciri by the arm and pushed her so hard she fell over, banging her shoulder against the knee of the boy who was tied to the post.

'Sit there,' he snarled. 'And don't you dare move, or I'll thrash you like a dog.'

'You louse,' growled the stripling, looking at him through half-closed eyes. 'You fucking ...'

Ciri didn't know most of the words which erupted from the boy's angry, scowling mouth, but from the change coming over Skomlik's

305

face she realised they must have been extremely filthy and offensive. The Trapper blanched with rage, took a swing, hit the boy in the face, then seized him by his long, fair hair and shoved him, banging the back of his head against the post.

'Hey!' called out Vercta, getting up from the table. 'What's going on over there?'

'I'll knock the mangy Rat's teeth out!' roared Skomlik. 'I'll tear his legs from his arse!'

'Come here and stop your screeching,' said the Nissir, sitting down, draining his mug of beer in a single draught and wiping his moustache. 'You can knock your prisoner around all you like, but hands off ours. And you, Kayleigh, don't play the hero. Sit still and ponder over the scaffold that Baron Lutz is having built. The list of punishments the hangman's going to perform on you is already written, trust me, and measures three ells. Half the town's already placing bets about how far down the list you'll make it. So save your strength, Rat. I'm going to put a small sum on that you won't let me down and you'll hold out at least to castration.'

Kayleigh spat and turned his head away, as much as the strap around his neck would allow. Skomlik hauled up his belt, threw Ciri a baleful glance, sitting perched on the stool, then joined the company at the table, cursing, since all that remained in the jug of beer the innkeeper had brought them were streaks of froth.

'How did you catch Kayleigh?' he asked, indicating to the innkeeper that he wanted to extend the order. 'And alive? Because I can't believe you knocked off the other Rats.'

'To tell the truth,' answered Vercta, critically examining what he had just picked from his nose, 'we were lucky. He was all alone. He'd left the gang and nipped over to New Forge for a night with his girlfriend. The village headman knew we weren't far away and sent word. We got there before sun-up and collared him in the hay; he didn't even squeal.'

'And we all had some sport with his wench,' cackled the fat one with the topknot. 'If Kayleigh hadn't satisfied her that night, there was no harm done. We satisfied her so thoroughly in the morning she couldn't move her arms or legs!'

'Well, I tell you, you're incompetent fools,' declared Skomlik loudly and derisively. 'You fucked away a pretty penny, you thickheads. Instead of wasting time on the wench, you ought to have heated up a branding iron and made the Rat tell you where his gang were spending the night. You could've had the lot of 'em. Giselher, Reef and the rest. The Varnhagens of Sarda offered twenty florins for Giselher a year ago. And for that whore, what's her name ... Mistle, wasn't it? The prefect would give even more after what she did to his nephew at Druigh, when the Rats fleeced that convoy.'

'You, Skomlik,' grimaced Vercta, 'were either born stupid, or a hard life has driven all the good sense out of your head. There are six of us. Do you expect me to take on the whole gang with six men, or what? And we won't miss out on the bounty, either. Baron Lutz will warm Kayleigh's heels in the dungeons. He'll take his time, trust me. Kayleigh will sing, he'll betray their hideouts and base, then we'll go there in force and number, we'll surround the gang, and pick them out like crayfish from a sack.'

'Yeah, right. They'll be waiting for you. They'll find out you've got Kayleigh and lie low in their other hideouts and in the rushes. No, Vercta, you have to stare the truth in the face: you fucked up. You traded the reward for a woman. That's you all over ... nothing but fucking on your mind.'

'You're the fucker!' Vercta jumped up from the table. 'If you're in such a hurry, go after the Rats with your heroes yourself! But beware, because taking on the Rats, Your Honourable Nilfgaardian Lackeyship, isn't the same as catching young wenches!'

The Nissirs and Trappers began to trade insults with each other. The innkeeper quickly brought them more beer, snatching the empty jug from the hand of the fat one with the topknot, who was aiming it at Skomlik. The beer quickly took the heat out of the quarrel, cooled their throats and calmed their tempers.

'Bring us victuals!' yelled the fat one to the innkeeper. 'Scrambled egg and sausage. Beans, bread and cheese!'

'And beer!'

'What are you goggling at, Skomlik? We're in the money today! We fleeced Kayleigh of his horse, his pouch, his trinkets, his sword, his saddle and sheepskin, and we sold everything to the dwarves!'

'We sold his wench's red shoes as well. And her beads!'

'Ho, ho, enough to buy a few rounds, indeed! Glad to hear it!'

'Why are you so glad? We've got beer money, not you. All you can do is wipe the snot from your prisoner's nose or pluck lice from her! The size of the purse reflects the class of prisoner, ha, ha!'

'You sons of bitches!'

'Ha, ha, sit down. I was jesting, shut your trap!'

'Let's drink to settle our differences! The drinks are on us!'

'Where's that scrambled egg, innkeeper, a plague on you! Quickly!'

'And bring us that beer!'

Huddled on the stool, Ciri raised her head, meeting Kayleigh's furious green eyes staring at her from under his tousled fringe of fair hair. A shudder passed through her. Kayleigh's face, though not unattractive, was evil, very evil. Ciri could see that this boy, although not much older than her, was capable of anything.

'The gods must have sent you to me,' whispered the Rat, piercing her with his green stare. 'Just think. I don't believe in them, but they sent you. Don't look around, you little fool. You have to help me ... Listen carefully, scumbag ...'

Ciri huddled down even more and lowered her head.

'Listen,' hissed Kayleigh, indeed flashing his teeth like a rat. 'In a moment, when the innkeeper passes, you'll call him ... Listen to me, by the devil ...'

'No,' she whispered. 'They'll beat me ...'

Kayleigh's mouth twisted, and Ciri realised that being beaten by Skomlik was by no means the worst thing she might encounter. Although Skomlik was huge, and Kayleigh thin and bound, she sensed instinctively which of them she ought to fear more.

'If you help me,' whispered the Rat, 'I'll help you. I'm not alone. I've got comrades who don't abandon a friend in need ... Get it? And when my comrades arrive, when it all kicks off, I can't stay tied up to this post. Those scoundrels will carve me up ... Listen carefully, dammit. I'll tell you what you're to do ...'

308

Ciri lowered her head even further. Her lips quivered.

The Trappers and the Nissirs were devouring the scrambled eggs, and smacking their lips like wild boars. The innkeeper stirred something in a cauldron and brought another jug of beer and a loaf of rye bread to the table.

'I'm hungry,' squeaked Ciri obediently, blanching slightly. The innkeeper stopped, looked at her in a friendly way, and then looked around at the revellers.

'Can I give her some food, sir?'

'Bugger off!' yelled Skomlik indistinctly, flushing and spitting scrambled eggs. 'Get away from her, you bloody spit-turner, before I wrench your legs off! None of that! And you sit still, you gadabout, or I'll—'

'Hey, Skomlik, are you sodding crazy, or what?' interrupted Vercta, struggling to swallow a slice of bread piled high with onions. 'Look at him, boys, the skinflint. He stuffs himself on other people's money, but stints on a young girl. Give her a bowl, innkeeper. I'm paying, and I decide who gets it and who doesn't. And if anyone doesn't like it, he may get a smack in his bristly chops.'

Skomlik flushed even more, but said nothing.

'That's reminded me,' added Vercta. 'We must feed the Rat, so he won't collapse on the road, or the baron would flay us alive, trust me. The wench can feed him. Hey, innkeeper! Knock up some grub for them! And you, Skomlik, what are you grumbling about? What's not to your liking?'

'She needs to be watched,' said the Trapper, nodding at Ciri, 'because she's a strange kind of bird. Were she a normal wench, then Nilfgaard wouldn't be chasing after her, nor the prefect offering a reward ...'

'We can soon find out if she's ordinary or not,' chuckled the fat one with the topknot. 'We just need to look between her legs! How about it, boys? Shall we take her to the barn for a while?'

'Don't you dare touch her!' snapped Skomlik. 'I won't allow it!'

'Oh, really? Like we're going to ask you!'

'I'm putting the bounty and my head on the line, to deliver her there in one piece! The prefect of Amarillo—'

'Fuck your prefect. We're paying for your drinks and you're denying us some fun? Hey, Skomlik, don't be a cheapskate! And you won't get into trouble, never fear, nor will you miss out on the reward! You'll deliver her in one piece. A wench isn't a fish bladder, it doesn't pop from being squeezed!'

The Nissirs burst into loud chuckles. Skomlik's companions chimed in. Ciri shuddered, went pale and raised her head. Kayleigh smiled mockingly.

'Understand now?' he hissed from his faintly smiling mouth. 'When they get drunk, they'll start on you. They'll rape you. We're in the same boat. Do what I told you. If I escape, you will too ...'

'Grub up!' called the innkeeper. He didn't have a Nilfgaardian accent. 'Come and get it, miss!'

'A knife,' whispered Ciri, taking the bowl from him.

'What?'

'A knife. And fast.'

'If it's not enough, take more!' said the innkeeper unnaturally, sneaking a glance at the diners and putting more groats into the bowl. 'Be off with you.'

'A knife.'

'Be off or I'll call them ... I can't ... They'll burn down the inn.'

'A knife.'

'No. I feel sorry for you, missy, but I can't. I can't, you have to understand. Go away ...'

'No one,' she said, repeating Kayleigh's words in a trembling voice, 'will get out of here alive. A knife. And fast. And when it all starts, get out of here.'

'Hold the bowl, you clod!' yelled the innkeeper, turning to shield Ciri with his body. He was pale and his jaws were chattering slightly. 'Nearer the frying pan.'

She felt the cold touch of a kitchen knife, which he was sliding into her belt, covering the handle with her jacket.

'Very good,' hissed Kayleigh. 'Sit so that you're covering me. Put the bowl on my lap. Take the spoon in your left hand and the knife in your right. And cut through the twine. Not there, idiot. Under my elbow, near the post. Be careful, they're watching.'

Ciri's throat went dry. She lowered her head almost to the bowl.

'Feed me and eat yourself.' The green eyes staring from half-closed lids hypnotised her. 'And keep cutting. As if you meant it, little one. If I escape, you will too ...'

True, thought Ciri, cutting through the twine. The knife smelled of iron and onion, and the blade was worn down from frequent sharpening. *He's right. Do I know where those scoundrels will take me? Do I know what that Nilfgaardian prefect wants from me? Maybe a torturer's waiting for me in Amarillo, or perhaps the wheel, gimlets and pincers. Red-hot irons ... I won't let them lead me like a lamb to the slaughter. Better to take a chance ...*

A tree stump came crashing in through the window, taking the frame and broken glass with it. It landed on the table, wreaking havoc among the bowls and mugs. The tree stump was followed by a young woman with close-cropped fair hair in a red doublet and high, shiny boots reaching above the knee. Crouching on the table, she whirled a sword around her head. One of the Nissirs, the slowest, who hadn't managed to get up or jump out of the way, toppled over backwards with the bench, blood spurting from his mutilated throat. The girl rolled nimbly off the table, making room for a boy in a short, embroidered sheepskin jacket to jump in through the window.

'It's the Raaats!!' yelled Vercta, struggling with his sword, which was entangled in his belt.

The fat one with the topknot drew his weapon, jumped towards the girl who was kneeling on the floor, and swung. But the girl, even though she was on her knees, deftly parried the blow, spun away, and the boy in the sheepskin jacket who had jumped in after her slashed the Nissir hard across the temple. The fat man fell to the floor, suddenly as limp as a palliasse.

The inn door was kicked open and two more Rats burst inside. The first was tall and dark, dressed in a studded kaftan and a scarlet headband. He sent two Trappers to opposite corners with swift blows of his sword and then squared off with Vercta. The second, broad-shouldered and fair-haired, ripped open Remiz, Skomlik's brother-in-law, with a sweeping blow. The others rushed to escape, heading for the kitchen door. But the Rats were already entering that

311

way too; a dark-haired girl in fabulously coloured clothes suddenly erupted from the kitchen. She stabbed one of the Trappers with a rapid thrust, forced back another with a moulinet, and then hacked the innkeeper down before he had time to identify himself.

The inn was full of uproar and the clanging of swords. Ciri hid behind the post.

'Mistle!' shouted Kayleigh, tearing apart the partially cut twine and struggling with the strap still binding his neck to the post. 'Giselher! Reef! Over here!'

The Rats were busy fighting, though, and only Skomlik heard Kayleigh's cry. The Trapper turned around and prepared to thrust, intending to pin the Rat to the post. Ciri reacted instinctively, like lightning, as she had during the fight with the wyvern in Gors Velen and on Thanedd. All the moves she had learnt in Kaer Morhen happened automatically, almost without her conscious control. She jumped out from behind the post, whirled into a pirouette, fell on Skomlik and struck him powerfully with her hip. She was too small and lightly built to shove the hefty Trapper back, but she was able to disrupt the rhythm of his movement. And draw his attention towards her.

'You bitch!'

Skomlik took a swing, his sword wailing through the air. Once again, Ciri's body instinctively made a graceful evasive manoeuvre and the Trapper almost lost his balance, lunging after his thrusting blade. Swearing foully, he struck again, putting all his strength behind the blow. Ciri dodged nimbly, landing surely on her left foot, and whirled into a pirouette in the other direction. Skomlik slashed again, but again was unable to make contact.

Vercta suddenly fell between them, spattering them both with blood. The Trapper stepped back and looked around. He was surrounded by dead bodies. And by the Rats, who were approaching from all sides with drawn swords.

'Don't move,' said the dark one in the red headband, finally releasing Kayleigh. 'It looks like he really wants to hack that girl to death. I don't know why. Nor why he hasn't managed to yet. But let's give him a chance, seeing as he wants it so much.'

'Let's give her a chance too, Giselher,' said the broad-shouldered one. 'Let it be a fair fight. Give her some hardware, Iskra.'

Ciri felt the hilt of a sword in her hand. It was a little too heavy for her.

Skomlik panted furiously, and lunged at her, brandishing his blade in a flashing moulinet. He was slow. Ciri dodged the blows which began raining down on her using quick feints and half turns, without even attempting to parry them. Her sword merely served her as a counterweight for her evasive manoeuvres.

'Incredible,' laughed the girl with the close-cropped hair. 'She's an acrobat!'

'She's fast,' said the colourful girl who had given Ciri the sword. 'Fast as a she-elf. Hey, you, fatty! Perhaps you'd prefer one of us? You're getting no change out of her!'

Skomlik withdrew, looked around, then suddenly leapt forward, trying to stab Ciri with a thrust like a heron seizing its prey. Ciri avoided the thrust with a short feint and spun away. For a second she saw a swollen, pulsating vein on Skomlik's neck. She knew that in that position he wouldn't be able to avoid the blow or parry it. She knew where and how to strike.

But she did not strike.

'That's enough.'

She felt a hand on her shoulder. The girl in the colourful costume shoved her aside, and at the same time two other Rats – the one in the short sheepskin coat and the close-cropped one – pushed Skomlik into the corner of the inn, blocking him in with their swords.

'Enough of this lark,' repeated the flamboyantly dressed girl, turning Ciri towards herself. 'It's going on too long. And you're to blame, miss. You could've killed him, but you didn't. I don't think you'll live long.'

Ciri shuddered, looking into the huge, dark, almond-shaped eyes, seeing the teeth exposed in a smile. Teeth so small they made the smile seem ghoulish. Neither the eyes nor the teeth were human. The colourful girl was an elf.

'Time to run,' said Giselher, the one in the scarlet headband, sharply. He was clearly the leader. 'It's indeed taking too long! Mistle, finish off the bastard.'

The close-cropped girl approached, raising her sword.

'Mercy!' screamed Skomlik, falling on his knees. 'Spare my life! I have young children ... Very young ...'

The girl struck savagely, twisting at the hips. Blood splashed the whitewashed wall in a wide, irregular arc of crimson flecks.

'I can't stand little children,' said the close-cropped girl, wiping blood off the fuller with a quick movement of her fingers.

'Don't just stand there, Mistle,' urged the one in the scarlet head-band. 'To horse! We must fly! It's a Nilfgaardian settlement; we don't have any friends here!'

The Rats sped out of the inn. Ciri didn't know what to do, but she didn't have time to think. Mistle, the close-cropped one, pushed her towards the door.

Outside the inn, among pieces of broken beer mugs and chewed bones, lay the bodies of the Nissirs who had been guarding the entrance. Settlers armed with lances were running up from the village, but at the sight of the Rats bursting out of the inn they disappeared among the cottages.

'Can you ride?' yelled Mistle at Ciri.

'Yes ...'

'So let's go. Grab a horse and ride! There's a bounty on our heads and this is a Nilfgaardian village! They're all grabbing bows and spears! Jump on and follow Giselher! Keep to the middle of the track and stay away from the cottages!'

Ciri hurdled a low fence, seized the reins of one of the Trappers' horses, jumped into the saddle, and slapped the horse on the rump with the flat of the sword, which had never left her hand. She set off at a swift gallop, overtaking Kayleigh and the flamboyant elf they called Iskra. She raced with the Rats towards the mill. She saw a man with a crossbow emerging from behind one of the cottages, aiming at Giselher's back.

'Cut him down!' she heard from behind her. 'Have him, girl!'

Ciri leaned back in the saddle, forcing the galloping horse to change direction with a tug of the reins and pressure from her heels, and swung her sword. The man with the crossbow turned around at the last moment and she saw his face contorted in terror. Ciri's arm, which was raised to strike, hesitated for a moment, which was enough for the galloping horse to carry her past him. She heard the clang of the bowstring being released. Her horse squealed, its croup twitched and it reared up. Ciri jumped, wrenching her feet from the stirrups and landed nimbly, dropping into a crouch. Iskra, galloping up, leaned out of the saddle to swing powerfully, and slashed the crossbowman across the back of his head. He fell to his knees, toppled forward and fell headlong into a puddle, splashing mud. The wounded horse neighed and thrashed around beside him, finally rushing off between the cottages, kicking vigorously.

'You idiot!' yelled the she-elf, passing Ciri at full pelt. 'You bloody idiot!'

'Jump on!' screamed Kayleigh, riding over to her. Ciri ran up and seized the outstretched hand. The impetus jerked her, her shoulder joint creaking, but she managed to jump onto the horse and cling to the fair-haired Rat. They galloped off, overtaking Iskra. The elf turned back, pursuing one more crossbowman, who had thrown down his weapon and fled towards some barn doors. Iskra caught him with ease. Ciri turned her head away. She heard the mutilated crossbowman howl briefly and savagely, like an animal.

Mistle caught them up, pulling a saddled riderless horse behind her. She shouted something which Ciri didn't hear properly, but understood at once. She let go of Kayleigh, jumped onto the ground at full speed, and ran over to the horse, which was dangerously close to some buildings. Mistle threw her the reins, looked around and shouted a warning. Ciri turned around just in time to avoid the treacherous thrust of a spear, dealt by a stocky settler who had appeared from behind a pigsty, with a nimble half turn.

What happened later haunted her dreams for a long time after. She remembered everything, every movement. The half turn which saved her from the spear blade placed her in an ideal position. The spearman was leaning well forward, unable either to jump away or to protect himself with the spear shaft he was holding in both hands. Ciri thrust flat, spinning the opposite way in a half turn. For a moment, she saw a mouth open to scream in a face with the bristle of several days of beard growth. She saw the forehead lengthened

315

by a bald patch, fair-skinned above the line where a cap or hat had protected it from the sun. And then everything she saw was blotted out by a fountain of blood.

She was still holding the horse by the reins, but the horse shied, howling, and thrashed around, knocking her to her knees. Ciri did not release the reins. The wounded man moaned and wheezed, thrashing about convulsively among the straw and muck, and blood spurted from him as though from a stuck pig. She felt her gorge rising.

Right alongside, Iskra reined back her horse. Seizing the reins of the still stamping, riderless horse, she tugged, pulling Ciri – still clutching the reins – up onto her feet.

'Into the saddle!' she yelled. 'Get out of here!'

Ciri fought back nausea and jumped into the saddle. There was blood on the sword, which she was still holding. She struggled to overcome the desire to throw the weapon as far away as she could.

Mistle rushed out from between some cottages, chasing two men. One of them managed to get away, leaping over a fence, but the second, hit by a short thrust, fell to his knees, clutching his head in both hands.

Mistle and Iskra leapt into a gallop, but a moment later pulled up their horses, bracing themselves in their stirrups, because Giselher and the other Rats were returning from near the mill. Behind them rushed a pack of armed settlers, yelling loudly to summon up their courage.

'After us!' yelled Giselher, riding past at full speed. 'After us, Mistle! To the river!'

Mistle, leaning over to one side, tugged on her reins, turned her horse back and galloped after him, clearing some low wattle fences. Ciri pressed her face against her horse's mane and set off after her. Iskra galloped along beside her. The speed blew her beautiful, dark hair around, revealing a small, pointed ear decorated with a filigree earring.

The man wounded by Mistle was still kneeling in the middle of the road, rocking back and forth and holding his bloody head in both hands. Iskra wheeled her horse around, galloped up to him and struck downwards with her sword, powerfully, with all her strength. The wounded man wailed. Ciri saw his severed fingers fly up like woodchips from a chopping block and fall onto the ground like fat, white grubs.

She barely overcame the urge to vomit.

Mistle and Kayleigh waited for them by a gap in the stockade; the rest of the Rats were already far away. The foursome set off in a hard, fast gallop, and hurtled across the river, splashing water which spurted up above the horses' heads. Leaning forward, pressing their cheeks against the horses' manes, they climbed up a sandy slope and then flew across a meadow, purple with lupines. Iskra, riding the fastest horse, took the lead.

They raced into a forest, into damp shade, between the trunks of beeches. They had caught up with Giselher and the others, but they only slowed for a moment. After crossing the forest and reaching moorland, they once again set off at a gallop. Soon Ciri and Kayleigh had been left behind, the Trappers' horses unable to keep pace with the beautiful, pedigree mounts the Rats were riding. Ciri had an additional difficulty; she could barely reach the big horse's stirrups, and at a gallop was unable to adjust the stirrup leathers. She could ride without stirrups as well as she could with, but knew that in that position she would not be able to endure a gallop for long.

Fortunately, after a few minutes, Giselher slowed the pace and stopped the leading group, letting Ciri and Kayleigh catch up with them. Ciri slowed to a trot. She still couldn't shorten the stirrup leathers, since there were no holes in the straps. Without slowing, she swung her right leg over the pommel and switched to side-saddle.

Mistle, seeing the girl's riding position, burst out laughing.

'Do you see, Giselher? She isn't only an acrobat, she's a circus rider, too! Eh, Kayleigh, where did you happen upon this she-devil?'

Iskra, reining back her beautiful chestnut, skin still dry and raring to gallop on, rode over, pushing against Ciri's dapple grey. The horse neighed and stepped back, tossing its head. Ciri tightened the reins, leaning back in the saddle.

'Do you know the reason you're still alive, you cretin?' snarled the elf, pulling her hair away from her forehead. 'The peasant you

317

so mercifully spared released the trigger too soon, so he hit the horse and not you. Otherwise you'd have a quarrel sticking into your back up to its fletchings! Why do you carry that sword?'

'Leave her alone, Iskra,' said Mistle, stroking the sweaty neck of her mount. 'Giselher, we have to slow down or we'll ride the horses into the ground! I mean, no one's chasing us right now.'

'I want to cross the Velda as quickly as possible,' said Giselher. 'We'll rest on the far bank. Kayleigh, how's your horse?'

'He'll hold out. He's no racehorse, but he's a powerful beast.'

'All right, let's go.'

'Hold on,' said Iskra. 'What about this chit?'

Giselher looked back, straightened his scarlet headband, and rested his gaze on Ciri. His face and its expression somewhat resembled Kayleigh's; the same malevolent grimace, the same narrowed eyes, the thin, protruding lower jaw. He was older than the fair-haired Rat, though, and the bluish shadow on his cheeks was evidence that he was already shaving.

'Yeah, true,' he said brusquely. 'What about you, wench?'

Ciri lowered her head.

'She helped me,' chimed in Kayleigh. 'If it hadn't been for her, that lousy Trapper would have nailed me to the post . . .'

'The villagers saw her escaping with us,' added Mistle. 'She cut one of them down and I doubt he survived. They're settlers from Nilfgaard. If the girl falls into their hands, they'll club her to death. We can't leave her.'

Iskra snorted angrily but Giselher gestured to her to be quiet.

'She can ride with us,' he decided, 'as far as Velda. Then we'll see. Ride your horse normally, maid. If you don't manage to keep up, we won't look back. Understood?'

Ciri nodded eagerly.

'Talk, girl. Who are you? Where are you from? What's your name? Why were you travelling under escort?'

Ciri lowered her head. During the ride she'd had time to try to invent a story. And she had thought up several. But the leader of the Rats didn't look like someone who would believe any of them.

'Right,' pressed Giselher. 'You've been riding with us for a few hours. You're taking breaks with us, but I haven't even heard the sound of your voice. Are you dumb?'

Fire shot upwards in flames amid a shower of sparks, flooding the ruins of the shepherd's cottage in a wave of golden light. As if obedient to Giselher's order, the fire lit up Ciri's face, in order more easily to uncover the lies and insincerity in it. *But I can't tell them the truth*, Ciri thought in desperation. *They're robbers. Brigands. If they find out about the Nilfgaardians, that the Trappers caught me for the bounty, they may want to claim it for themselves. And anyway, the truth is too far-fetched for them to believe.*

'We got you out of the settlement,' continued the gang leader slowly. 'We brought you here, to one of our hideouts. We gave you food. You're sitting at our campfire. So tell us who you are.'

'Leave her be,' said Mistle suddenly. 'When I look at you, Giselher, I see a Nissir, a Trapper or one of those Nilfgaardian sons of bitches. And I feel as if I'm being interrogated, chained to a tor-turer's bench in a dungeon!'

'Mistle's right,' said the fair-haired boy in the short sheepskin jacket. Ciri shuddered to hear his accent. 'The girl clearly doesn't want to say who she is, and it's her right. I didn't say much when I joined you, either. I didn't want you to know I'd been one of those Nilfgaardian bastards—'

'Don't talk rubbish, Reef.' Giselher waved a hand. 'It was differ-ent with you. And you, Mistle, you're wrong. It's not an interroga-tion. I want her to say who she is and where she's from. When I find out, I'll point out the way home, and that's all. How can I do that if I don't know ... ?'

'You don't know anything,' said Mistle, turning to look at him. 'Not even if she has a home. And I'm guessing she doesn't. The Trappers picked her up on the road because she was alone. That's typical of those cowards. If you send her on her way she won't survive in the mountains. She'll be torn apart by wolves or die of hunger.'

'What shall we do with her, then?' asked the broad-shouldered one in an adolescent bass, jabbing a stick at the burning logs. 'Dump her outside some village or other?'

'Excellent idea, Asse,' sneered Mistle. 'Don't you know what peasants are like? They're short of labourers. They'll put her to work grazing cattle, after first injuring one of her legs so she won't be able to run away. At night, she'll be treated as nobody's property; in other words she'll be anybody's. You know how she'll have to pay for her board and lodgings. Then in spring she'll get childbed fever giving birth to somebody's brat in a dirty pigsty.'

'If we leave her a horse and a sword,' drawled Giselher, without taking his eyes off Ciri, 'I wouldn't like to be the peasant who tried to injure her leg. Or tried knocking her up. Did you see the jig she danced in the inn with that Trapper, the one Mistle finished off? He was stabbing at thin air. And she was dancing like it was nothing ... Ha, it's true, I'm more interested in where she learnt tricks like that than in her name or family. I'd love to know—'

'Tricks won't save her,' suddenly chipped in Iskra, who up until then had been busy sharpening her sword. 'She only knows how to dance. To survive, you have to know how to kill, and she doesn't.'

'I think she does,' grinned Kayleigh. 'When she slashed that guy across the neck, the blood shot up six foot in the air ...'

'And she almost fainted at the sight of it,' the elf snorted.

'Because she's still a child,' interjected Mistle. 'I think I can guess who she is and where she learnt those tricks. I've seen girls like her before. She's a dancer or an acrobat from some wandering troupe.'

'Since when have we been interested in dancers and acrobats? Dammit, it's almost midnight and I'm getting sleepy. Enough of this idle chatter. We need a good night's sleep, to be in New Forge by twilight. The village headman there – I don't think you need reminding – shopped Kayleigh to the Nissirs. So the entire village ought to see the night sky glow red. And the girl? She's got a horse, she's got a sword. She earned both of them fairly and squarely. Let's give her a bit of grub and a few pennies. For saving Kayleigh. And then let her go where she wants to. Let her take care of herself ...'

'Fine,' said Ciri, pursing her lips and standing up. A silence fell, only interrupted by the crackling of the fire. The Rats looked at her curiously, in anticipation.

'Fine,' she repeated, astonished at the strange sound of her own voice. 'I don't need you, I didn't ask for anything ... And I don't want to stay with you! I'll leave—'

'So you aren't dumb,' said Giselher sombrely. 'Not only can you speak, you're cocky, with it.'

'Look at her eyes,' snorted Iskra. 'Look how she holds her head. She's a raptor! A young falcon!'

'You want to go,' said Kayleigh. 'Where to, if I may ask?'

'What do you care?' screamed Ciri, and her eyes blazed with a green light. 'Do I ask you where you're going? I couldn't care less! And I don't care about you! You're no use to me! I can cope ... I'll manage! By myself!'

'By yourself?' repeated Mistle, smiling strangely. Ciri fell silent and lowered her head. The Rats also fell silent.

'It's night,' said Giselher finally. 'No one rides at night. And no one rides alone, girl. Anyone who's alone is sure to die. There are blankets and furs over there, by the horses. Take what you need. Nights in the mountains are cold. Why are you goggling your green eyes at me? Prepare yourself a bed and go to sleep. You need to rest.'

After a moment of thought, she did as he said. When she returned, carrying a blanket and a fur wrap, the Rats were no longer sitting around the campfire. They were standing in a semicircle, and the red gleam of the flames was reflected in their eyes.

'We are the Rats of the Marches,' said Giselher proudly. 'We can sniff out booty a mile away. We aren't afraid of traps. And there's nothing we can't bite through. We're the Rats. Come over here, girl.'

She did as she was told.

'You don't have anything,' added Giselher, handing her a belt set with silver. 'Take this at least.'

'You don't have anyone or anything,' said Mistle, smiling, throwing a green, satin tunic over her shoulders and pressing an embroidered blouse into her hands.

'You don't have anything,' said Kayleigh, and the gift from him was a small stiletto in a sheath sparkling with precious stones. 'You are all alone.'

'You don't have anyone,' Asse repeated after him. Ciri was given an ornamental pendant.

'You don't have any family,' said Reef in his Nilfgaardian accent, handing her a pair of soft, leather gloves. 'You don't have any family or ...'

'You will always be a stranger,' completed Iskra seemingly carelessly, placing a beret with pheasant's feathers on Ciri's head with a swift and unceremonious movement. 'Always a stranger and always different. What shall we call you, young falcon?'

Ciri looked her in the eyes.

'Gvalch'ca.'

The elf laughed.

'When you finally start speaking, you speak in many languages, Young Falcon! Let it be then. You shall bear a name of the Elder Folk, a name you have chosen for yourself. You will be Falka.'

Falka.

She couldn't sleep. The horses stamped and snorted in the darkness, and the wind soughed in the crowns of the fir trees. The sky sparkled with stars. The Eye, for so many days her faithful guide in the rocky desert, shone brightly. The Eye pointed west, but Ciri was no longer certain if that was the right way. She wasn't certain of anything any longer.

She couldn't fall asleep, although for the first time in many days she felt safe. She was no longer alone. She had made a makeshift bed of branches out of the way, some distance from the Rats, who were sleeping on the fire-warmed clay floor of the ruined shepherd's hut. She was far from them, but felt their closeness and presence. She was not alone.

She heard some quiet steps.

'Don't be afraid.'

It was Kayleigh.

'I won't tell them Nilfgaard's looking for you,' whispered the fair-haired Rat, kneeling down and leaning over her. 'I won't tell them about the bounty the prefect of Amarillo has promised for you. You saved my life in the inn. I'll repay you for it. With something nice. Right now.'

He lay down beside her, slowly and cautiously. Ciri tried to get up, but Kayleigh pressed her down onto her bed with a strong and firm, though not rough, movement. He placed his fingers gently on her mouth. Although he needn't have. Ciri was paralysed with fear, and she couldn't have uttered a cry from her tight, painfully dry throat even if she had wanted to. But she didn't want to. The silence and darkness were better. Safer. More familiar. She was covered in terror and shame. She groaned.

'Be quite, little one,' whispered Kayleigh, slowly unlacing her shirt. Slowly, with gentle movements, he slid the material from her shoulders, and pulled the edge of the shirt above her hips. 'And don't be afraid. You'll see how nice it is.'

Ciri shuddered beneath the touch of the dry, hard, rough hand. She lay motionless, stiff and tense, full of an overpowering fear which took her will away, and an overwhelming sense of revulsion, which assailed her temples and cheeks with waves of heat. Kayleigh slipped his left arm beneath her head, pulled her closer to him, trying to dislodge the hand which was tightly gripping the lap of her shirt and vainly trying to pull it downwards. Ciri began to shake.

She sensed a sudden commotion in the surrounding darkness, felt a shaking, and heard the sound of a kick.

'Mistle, are you insane?' snarled Kayleigh, lifting himself up a little.

'Leave her alone, you swine.'

'Get lost. Go to bed.'

'Leave her alone, I said.'

'Am I bothering her, or something? Is she screaming or struggling? I just want to cuddle her to sleep. Don't interfere.'

'Get out of here or I'll cut you.'

Ciri heard the grinding of a knife in a metal sheath.

'I'm serious,' repeated Mistle, looming indistinctly in the dark above them. 'Get lost and join the boys. Right now.'

Kayleigh sat up and swore under his breath. He stood up without a word and walked quickly away.

Ciri felt the tears running down her cheeks, quickly, quicker and quicker, creeping like wriggling worms among the hair by her ears. Mistle lay down beside her, and covered her tenderly with the fur.

But she didn't pull the dishevelled shirt down. She left it as it had been. Ciri began to shake again.

'Be still, Falka. It's all right now.'

Mistle was warm, and smelled of resin and smoke. Her hand was smaller than Kayleigh's; more delicate, softer. More pleasant. But its touch stiffened Ciri once more, once more gripped her entire body with fear and revulsion, clenched her jaw and constricted her throat. Mistle lay close to her, cradling her protectively and whispering soothingly, but at the same time, her small hand relentlessly crept like a warm, little snail, calmly, confidently, decisively. Certain of its way and its destination. Ciri felt the iron pincers of revulsion and fear relaxing, releasing their hold; she felt herself slipping from their grip and sinking downwards, downwards, deep, deeper and deeper, into a warm and wet well of resignation and helpless submissiveness. A disgusting and humiliatingly pleasant submissiveness.

She moaned softly, desperately. Mistle's breath scorched her neck. Her moist, velvet lips tickled her shoulder, her collarbone, very slowly sliding lower. Ciri moaned again.

'Quiet, Falcon,' whispered Mistle, gently sliding her arm under her head. 'You won't be alone now. Not any more.'

The next morning, Ciri arose with the dawn. She carefully slipped out from under the fur, without waking Mistle, who was sleeping with parted lips and her forearm covering her eyes. She had goose flesh on her arm. Ciri tenderly covered the girl. After a moment's hesitation, she leaned over and kissed Mistle gently on her close-cropped hair, which stuck up like a brush. She murmured in her sleep. Ciri wiped a tear from her cheek.

She was no longer alone.

The rest of the Rats were also asleep; one of them was snoring, another farted just as loudly. Iskra lay with her arm across Giselher's chest, her luxuriant hair in disarray. The horses snorted and stamped, and a woodpecker drummed the trunk of a pine with a short series of blows.

Ciri ran down to a stream. She spent a long time washing, trembling from the cold. She washed with violent movements of her shaking hands, trying to wash off what was no longer possible to wash off. Tears ran down her cheeks.

Falka.

The water foamed and soughed on the rocks, and flowed away into the distance; into the fog.

Everything was flowing away into the distance. Into the fog.

Everything.

They were outcasts. They were a strange, mixed bag created by war, misfortune and contempt. War, misfortune and contempt had brought them together and thrown them onto the bank, the way a river in flood throws and deposits drifting, black pieces of wood smoothed by stones onto its banks.

Kayleigh had woken up in smoke, fire and blood, in a plundered stronghold, lying among the corpses of his adoptive parents and siblings. Dragging himself across the corpse-strewn courtyard, he came across Reef. Reef was a soldier from a punitive expedition, which Emperor Emhyr var Emreis had sent to crush the rebellion in Ebbing. He was one of the soldiers who had captured and plundered the stronghold after a two-day siege. Having captured it, Reef's comrades abandoned him, although Reef was still alive. Caring for the wounded was not a custom among the killers of the Nilfgaardian special squads.

At first, Kayleigh planned to finish Reef off. But Kayleigh didn't want to be alone. And Reef, like Kayleigh, was only sixteen years old.

They licked their wounds together. Together they killed and robbed a tax collector, together they gorged themselves on beer in a tavern, and later, as they rode through the village on stolen horses, they scattered the rest of the stolen money all around them, laughing their heads off.

Together, they ran from the Nissirs and Nilfgaardian patrols.

Giselher had deserted from the army. It was probably the army of the lord of Gheso who had allied himself with the insurgents from Ebbing. Probably. Giselher didn't actually know where the press gang had dragged him to. He had been dead drunk at the time.

When he sobered up and received his first thrashing from the drill sergeant, he ran away. At first, he wandered around by himself, but after the Nilfgaardians crushed the insurrectionary confederation the forests were awash with other deserters and fugitives. The fugitives quickly formed up into gangs. Giselher joined one of them.

The gang ransacked and burnt down villages, attacking convoys and transports, and then dwindled away in desperate escapes from the Nilfgaardian cavalry troops. During one of those flights, the gang happened upon some forest elves in a dense forest and met with destruction; met with invisible death, hissing down on them in the form of grey arrows flying from all sides. One of the arrows penetrated Giselher's shoulder and pinned him to a tree. The next morning, the one who pulled the arrow and dressed his wound was Aenyeweddien.

Giselher never found out why the elves had condemned Aenyeweddien to banishment, for what misdeed they had condemned her to death; since it was a death sentence for a free elf to be alone in the narrow strip of no-man's-land dividing the free Elder Folk from the humans. The solitary elf was sure to perish should she fail to find a companion.

Aenyeweddien found a companion. Her name, meaning 'Child of the Fire' in loose translation, was too difficult and too poetic for Giselher. He called her Iskra.

Mistle came from a wealthy, noble family from the city of Thurn in North Maecht. Her father, a vassal of Duke Rudiger, joined the insurrectionary army, was defeated and vanished without trace. When the people of Thurn were escaping from the city at the news of an approaching punitive expedition by the notorious Pacifiers of Gemmera, Mistle's family also fled, but Mistle got lost in the panic-stricken crowd. The elegantly dressed and delicate maiden, who had been carried in a sedan chair from early childhood, was unable to keep pace with the fugitives. After three days of solitary wandering, she fell into the hands of the manhunters who were following the Nilfgaardians. Girls younger than seventeen were in demand. As long as they were untouched. The manhunters didn't touch Mistle, not once they'd checked she really was untouched. Mistle spent the entire night following the examination sobbing.

In the valley of the River Velda, the caravan of manhunters was routed and massacred by a gang of Nilfgaardian marauders. All the manhunters and male captives were killed. Only the girls were spared. The girls didn't know why they had been spared. Their ignorance did not last long.

Mistle was the only one to survive. She was pulled out of the ditch where she had been thrown naked, covered in bruises, filth, mud and congealed blood, by Asse, the son of the village blacksmith, who had been hunting the Nilfgaardians for three days, insane with the desire for revenge for what the marauders had done to his father, mother and sisters, which he'd had to watch, hidden in a hemp field.

They all met one day during the celebrations of Lammas, the Festival of the Harvest, in one of the villages in Gheso. At the time, war and misery had not especially afflicted the lands on the upper Velda – the villages were celebrating the beginning of the Month of the Sickle traditionally, with a noisy party and dance.

They didn't take long to find each other in the merry crowd. Too much distinguished them. They had too much in common. They were united by their love of gaudy, colourful, fanciful outfits, of stolen trinkets, beautiful horses, and of swords – which they didn't even unfasten when they danced. They stood out because of their arrogance and conceit, overconfidence, mocking truculence and impetuousness.

And their contempt.

They were children of the time of contempt. And they had nothing but contempt for others. For them, only force mattered. Skill at wielding weapons, which they quickly acquired on the high roads. Resoluteness. Swift horses and sharp swords.

And companions. Comrades. Mates. Because the one who is alone will perish; from hunger, from the sword, from the arrow, from makeshift peasant clubs, from the noose, or in flames. The one who is alone will perish; stabbed, beaten or kicked to death, defiled, like a toy passed from hand to hand.

They met at the Festival of the Harvest. Grim, black-haired, lanky Giselher. Thin, long-haired Kayleigh, with his malevolent eyes and mouth set in a hateful grimace. Reef, who still spoke with a Nilfgaardian accent. Tall, long-legged Mistle, with cropped, straw-coloured hair sticking up like a brush. Big-eyed and colourful Iskra, lithe and ethereal in the dance, quick and lethal in a fight, with her narrow lips and small, elven teeth. Broad-shouldered Asse with fair, curly down on his chin.

Giselher became the leader. And they christened themselves the Rats. Someone had called them that and they took a liking to it.

They plundered and murdered, and their cruelty became legendary.

At first the Nilfgaardian prefects ignored them. They were certain that – following the example of other gangs – they would quickly fall victim to the massed ranks of furious peasantry, or that they would destroy or massacre each other themselves when the quantity of loot they collected would make cupidity triumph over criminal solidarity. The prefects were right with respect to other gangs, but were mistaken when it came to the Rats. Because the Rats, the children of contempt, scorned spoils. They attacked, robbed and killed for entertainment, and they handed out the horses, cattle, grain, forage, salt, wood tar and cloth stolen from military transports in the villages. They paid tailors and craftsmen handfuls of gold and silver for the things they loved most of all: weapons, costumes and ornaments. The recipients fed and watered them, put them up and hid them. Even when whipped raw by the Nilfgaardians and Nissirs, they did not betray the Rats' hideouts or favoured routes.

The prefects offered a generous reward; and at the beginning, there were people who were tempted by Nilfgaardian gold. But at night, the informers' cottages were set on fire, and the people escaping from the inferno died on the glittering blades of the spectral riders circling in the smoke. The Rats attacked like rats. Quietly, treacherously, cruelly. The Rats adored killing.

The prefects used methods which had been tried and tested against other gangs; several times they tried to install a traitor among the Rats. Unsuccessfully. The Rats didn't accept anyone. The close-knit and loyal group of six created by the time of contempt didn't want strangers. They despised them.

Until the day a pale-haired, taciturn girl, as agile as an acrobat, appeared. A girl about whom the Rats knew nothing.

Aside from the fact that she was as they had once been; like each one of them. Lonely and full of bitterness, bitterness for what the time of contempt had taken from her.

And in times of contempt anyone who is alone must perish.

Giselher, Kayleigh, Reef, Iskra, Mistle, Asse and Falka. The prefect of Amarillo was inordinately astonished when he learnt that the Rats were now operating as a gang of seven.

'Seven?' said the prefect of Amarillo in astonishment, looking at the soldier in disbelief. 'There were seven of them, not six? Are you certain?'

'May I live and breathe,' muttered the only soldier to escape the massacre in one piece.

His wish was quite apt; his head and half of his face were swathed in dirty, bloodstained bandages. The prefect, who was no stranger to combat, knew that the sword had struck the soldier from above and from the left – with the very tip of the blade. An accurate blow, precise, demanding expertise and speed, aimed at the right ear and cheek; a place unprotected by either helmet or gorget.

'Speak.'

'We were marching along the bank of the Velda towards Thurn,' the soldier began. 'We had orders to escort one of Chamberlain Evertsen's transports heading south. They attacked us by a ruined bridge, as we were crossing the river. One wagon got bogged down, so we unharnessed the horses from another to haul it out. The rest of the convoy went on and I stayed behind with five men and the bailiff. That's when they jumped us. The bailiff, before they killed him, managed to shout that it was the Rats, and then they were on top of us ... And put paid to every last man. When I saw what was happening ...'

'When you saw what was happening,' scowled the prefect, 'you spurred on your horse. But too late to save your skin.'

'That seventh one caught up with me,' said the soldier, lowering his head. 'That seventh one, who I hadn't seen at the beginning. A young girl. Not much more than a kid. I thought the Rats had left

329

her at the back because she was young and inexperienced . . .'

The prefect's guest slipped out of the shadow from where he had been sitting.

'It was a girl?' he asked. 'What did she look like?'

'Just like all the others. Painted and done up like a she-elf, colourful as a parrot, dressed up in baubles, in velvet and brocade, in a hat with feathers—'

'Fair-haired?'

'I think so, sir. When I saw her, I rode hard, thinking I'd at least bring one down to avenge my companions; that I'd repay blood with blood . . . I stole up on her from the right, to make striking easier . . . How she did it, I don't know. But I missed her. As if I was striking an apparition or a wraith . . . I don't know how that she-devil did it. I had my guard up but she struck through it. Right in the kisser . . . Sire, I was at Sodden, I was at Aldersberg. And now I've got a souvenir for the rest of my life from a tarted-up wench . . .'

'Be thankful you're alive,' grunted the prefect, looking at his guest. 'And be thankful you weren't found carved up by the river crossing. Now you can play the hero. Had you'd legged it without putting up a fight, had you reported the loss of the cargo without that souvenir, you'd soon be hanging from a noose and clicking your heels together! Very well. Dismissed. To the field hospital.'

The soldier left. The prefect turned towards his guest.

'You see for yourself, Honourable Sir Coroner, that military service isn't easy here. There's no rest; our hands are full. You there, in the capital, think all we do in the province is fool around, swill beer, grope wenches and take bribes. No one thinks about sending a few more men or a few more pennies, they just send orders: give us this, do that, find that, get everyone on their feet, dash around from dawn to dusk . . . While my head's splitting from my own troubles. Five or six gangs like the Rats operate around here. True, the Rats are the worst, but not a day goes by—'

'Enough, enough,' said Stefan Skellen, pursing his lips. 'I know what your bellyaching is meant to achieve, Prefect. But you're wasting your time. No one will release you from your orders. Don't count on it. Rats or no Rats, gangs or no gangs, you are to continue with the search. Using all available means, until further notice. That is an imperial order.'

'We've been looking for three weeks,' the prefect said with a grimace. 'Without really knowing who or what we're looking for: an apparition, a ghost or a needle in a haystack. And what's the result? Only that a few men have disappeared without trace, no doubt killed by rebels or brigands. I tell you once more, coroner, if we've not found your girl yet, we'll never find her. Even if someone like her were around here, which I doubt. Unless—'

The prefect broke off and pondered, scowling at the coroner.

'That wench ... That seventh one riding with the Rats ...'

Tawny Owl waved a hand dismissively, trying to make his gesture and facial expression appear convincing.

'No, Prefect. Don't expect easy solutions. A decked out half-elf or some other female bandit in brocade is certainly not the girl we're looking for. It definitely isn't her. Continue the search. That's an order.'

The prefect became sullen and looked through the window.

'And about that gang,' added Stefan Skellen, the Coroner of Imperator Emhyr, sometimes known as Tawny Owl, in a seemingly indifferent voice, 'about those Rats, or whatever they're called ... Take them to task, Prefect. Order must prevail in the Province. Get to work. Catch them and hang them, without ceremony or fuss. All of them.'

'That's easy to say,' muttered the prefect. 'But I shall do everything in my power to, please assure the imperator of that. I think, nonetheless, that it would be worth taking that seventh girl with the Rats alive just to be sure—'

'No,' interrupted Tawny Owl, making sure not to let his voice betray him. 'Without exception, hang them all. All seven of them. We don't want to hear any more about them. Not another word.'

END OF VOLUME TWO